They passed a young woman standing by the trail. "Hi," she said. "I am Aloe Vera. My talent is soothing burns. May I have a ride?"

"Of course not," Umlaut said snootily, and left her behind. She was obviously one of the lowly commoners who didn't deserve any attention, let alone a ride.

Sammy came to a field of pebbles and stopped. This must be the place. The high horse halted, and Umlaut dismounted. The moment he was off the horse, he felt chagrin: why had he treated that woman, Aloe, so shabbily? At least he could have been courteous.

He saw that the pebbles of the field were labeled. Each one said SENT. Someone must have sent it here. So what did that have to do with the price of beans in a beanie?

PIERS ANTHONY

UP IN A
HEAVAL

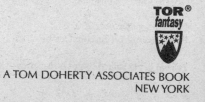

TOR® fantasy

A TOM DOHERTY ASSOCIATES BOOK
NEW YORK

This is a work of fiction. All the characters and events portrayed in this book are either products of the author's imagination or are used fictitiously.

UP IN A HEAVAL

Cover art by Dave Kramer

A Tor Book
Published by Tom Doherty Associates, LLC
175 Fifth Avenue
New York, NY 10010

www.tor.com

Tor® is a registered trademark of Tom Doherty Associates, LLC.

ISBN 0-812-57499-0
EAN 978-0-812-57499-9

First edition: October 2002
First mass market edition: October 2003

Printed in the United States of America

0 9 8 7 6 5 4 3 2

Contents

UP IN A HEAVAL

PROLOG

D emons did not normally assume mortal form or substance, but on rare occasion it was convenient for negotiation. The dialogue between the Demon JU $(P/I)^{TER}$ and the Demoness FO $(R/N)^{AX}$ occurred in neutral territory: the domain of the Demon X $(A/N)^{TH}$. Jupiter, whose magic was the strong force, animated a nondescript male mortal body crafted for the occasion by Xanth, while Fornax borrowed the semblance of a lesser female demon. Xanth himself was in the humanoid form of Nimby, a donkey-headed dragon.

"What do you want?" Jupiter demanded, employing the cumbersome mortal sonic language so as to adhere to the limitations of the mortal form. "We defeated your last ploy and rescued Demon Earth from your clutch; you have no further influence in this region."

"I have spot visitation rights," Fornax replied similarly. "I made a deal with a mortal girl in Demon Earth's domain. But I want more."

"We all want more," Jupiter retorted. "That is why we contest constantly for status at each other's expense."

"Exactly. But in this case I want a lesser thing. Having

become acquainted with several mortal characters of the Land of Xanth, I find the mortal state intriguing. I wish to take this land to my own galaxy and vivisect it and its creatures."

"No you don't!" Xanth protested. "That's my realm. Your challenge for status is with Jupiter; this is merely the setting for your limited dialogue."

"Here is the nature of my offer: The stakes are your Land of Xanth against my empty contraterrene equivalent. If I win, I will transform Xanth to CT matter so that I may safely handle it, then vivisect it to discover what is intriguing about it. If Jupiter wins, I will turn over my contraterrene realm to you, so that your mortal characters can animate it and have a vast new realm to play in."

"Those are fair stakes," Xanth agreed. "But why contest with Jupiter when you could contest directly with me?"

The form of the demoness assumed enormous beauty and sexiness. "You have already committed your interest to a female creature; I can't distract you or your representative by employing mortal opposite-gender allure. Jupiter has not committed, so perhaps can be swayed, providing me a reasonable edge."

"I doubt it," Jupiter said. "I know your nature, Demoness."

"Since when did knowledge have any relevance to a male?"

"Males are rational. Females are emotional."

"Really?" She oriented on Jupiter's form, slowly drawing up the hem of her skirt. The thighs of the form she had assumed were very firm and well fleshed. His eyeballs locked into place and began to sweat. She had made her point.

"Agreed," Jupiter said. He did not say that his interest had been aroused, but of course she knew it.

"If you win, I will also visit you in this fleshly form and do whatever you request, provided it is limited to a mortal nature." She let her décolletage descend slightly.

Jupiter's mortal breath quickened. He nodded.

"Agreed," Xanth said. "Now the rules of engagement."

"The Land of Xanth to be the setting," Fornax said as she let her hem and neckline drift back into place. "We will select Xanth characters to represent our interests. One must accomplish a particular task, or fail to accomplish it. On that will hinge the decision."

"Agreed," Jupiter said, flexing his eyeballs to restore their circulation. "I choose this character I have animated, rendering him apparent for the occasion."

"But you must not animate him yourself," Fornax said. "You must set him up and let him proceed without further direction, so that the outcome is not determined by direct Demon power."

"Agreed. That is standard practice when we employ facsimiles. I will give him the semblance of body, life, and awareness, with a minor talent, and dissolve him when the game is done."

"The semblance?" Fornax asked. "Why not the reality?"

"We terrene Demons do not have established mortal forms and do not live and die as they do," Jupiter explained. "We have no direct experience, so must emulate. The real mortals will not know the difference."

Her form nodded. "Neither do we contraterrene Demons. That is one reason I wish to dissect some mortals, discovering the secret of their living state. I understand they also have souls, which are a deeper mystery."

"Souls greatly complicate their existence," Xanth said. "I have been studying them for some time, without yet approaching a sufficient comprehension. It seems a soul is one thing it is necessary to possess in order to appreciate."

"I would like to borrow and study a soul," Fornax said.

"So would I," Jupiter agreed.

"They can't be taken," Xanth said. "They must be given."

"Remarkable," Fornax said. She reoriented on Jupiter. "Your entity must not know his origin or nature."

"Emulation can go only so far," Jupiter said. "If he operates long among genuine mortals, he will inevitably catch on, because he will discover what they can't: that he is limited in duration."

"Then herein perhaps we have a basis for our game," she said. "Give your character a pretext and a chore to accomplish. If he succeeds before he discovers his nature, the victory is yours. If he fails, or realizes before he succeeds, it is mine."

"Agreed."

Fornax smiled. "Not quite so simple, Jupiter. I am not satisfied to have a simple task simply accomplished. If your golem possesses a Demon's single-mindedness, he will forge through and accomplish his task regardless of the consequences elsewhere."

"Readily fixed," Demon Xanth said. "We can provide him with a soul emulation, giving him a strong conscience, compassion, and sense of fairness. He can be a surpassingly decent person, not given to single-mindedness at the expense of others."

"But if he is highly intelligent or talented, he will still accomplish it readily."

"I will make him of moderate intellect, with a moderate talent," Jupiter said. "With a store of useless incidental information rather than insight."

"One more thing: I will utilize this present character, whose purpose will be to prevent your character from accomplishing his mission."

"But he will never succeed, if a Demon opposes him."

"I will be indirect, motivating the female whose form I have borrowed, and will not allow her to understand the full nature of the contest. Then I will set her loose, as you will do for yours."

"You will employ female wiles to distract him," Jupiter said accusingly.

"Of course. It's the natural female emotional course."

"Then my character should have a general appeal for females, as a natural rational male."

Nobody was fooling anybody, but they liked the sparring. "Granted. Let them be mysteriously drawn to him. The challenge will be fair."

"Yes, it will be fair," Jupiter agreed grimly.

They settled down to detail bargaining, crafting a game that each agreed was fair. Occasionally Fornax allowed some interesting flesh to show, reminding Jupiter of the stakes. This was the essence of Demon interaction.

1

EMULATION

It all started, others agreed later, with Umlaut. Because he wasn't what he seemed to be. His talent was emulation, which was mostly a matter of causing others to see him as he represented himself to be, to a degree. But it might as well have been troublE with a capital *E,* because of the mischief it led to. It was the teenth of the month, and all the teens were out, but that was only the setting.

At the moment Umlaut was pretending to be a seventeen-year-old girl. The age was right, but not the gender. He was doing it to escape the attention of a real girl who had taken an unwholesome fancy to him. In fact she was chasing him. That might have been all right, for Sherry was pretty enough, except for her talent. That was in her kisses: They were sweeter than wine. Which was fine, up to a point. Unfortunately her first kiss made him feel so pleasant that he wanted more, and three made him tipsy, and last time he had awakened next morning with a dreadful hangover and no memory of the date. But Sherry's father had warned him that if he did it again, he'd have to marry her. That might not have been so bad, except that what good was an experience if he couldn't remember it? So he was trying to take it easy, at least until he figured out whether he really wanted to marry a sixteen-year-old girl just yet. She thought he was strong, handsome, and suitable; now he regretted emulating her ideal man quite so thoroughly. It would be impossible to do it continuously, and what would happen when she found out how dully ordinary he really was?

Umlaut rounded a bend and spied a group of teenagers having a party. That seemed ideal; he could merge with them and conceal himself until Sherry gave up the chase. Then he could sneak away, free, and return to his normal, somewhat inadequate self.

He ran up to them, hastily adjusting his emulation to make him seem like one of them. "Sorry I got lost," he said somewhat breathlessly. "What's up?"

"We just got a package of Wetti shirts," the tallest and handsomest boy replied. "We traded a rock hound for them."

"Rock hound?"

"Don't you remember? We found it in the old rock mine last week. Friendly dog made of stone."

"Oh, sure," Umlaut said. Of course he didn't remember, because he hadn't been part of this group. Then, to hide his ignorance, he changed the subject. "What are Wetti shirts?"

"We're not sure, but they say they're a lot of fun for girls to wear and great for contests. So why don't you be the first? Put one on." He shoved the package at Umlaut. Of course he took Umlaut for a girl, because that was what he was emulating.

At that point Sherry rounded the turn and ran up. She was breathing hard with the effort. She was a fairly full-figured girl, and several of the boys were looking with interest. "Have you seen Umlaut?" she panted.

"Who?"

"A strong, handsome, suitable boy, running down this path." She paused for a deeper breath, straining a shirt button or two in the process, along with a male eyeball or two.

"No, only another—"

"Try a Wetti shirt," Umlaut said quickly, shoving the package at her. "They're great fun for girls and contests."

"Now wait," the boy protested. "She's not one of us."

That got Sherry's dander up. The dander immediately flew

off in search of a flock of deese, but that didn't stop Sherry. She grabbed the boy by a lapel and planted a kiss on his face. "You were saying?" she demanded, well knowing her power.

The boy looked pleasantly dazed, as if he had just downed a glass of something intoxicatingly sweet. "She's one of us," he decided.

Sherry took a shirt from the package and put it on over her blouse. Suddenly a wash of water fell on her, making her scream pleasantly. The new shirt turned transparent and clung to her body, which seemed about twice as fully formed as before. "I like it," she said. "Who else is in this contest?"

"Contest?" the boy asked, his eyes locked to her front profile. So were the eyes of the other boys in the group, and some of the girls, though there might have been a difference in the girls' expressions.

"The shirt is for contests," she reminded him. "How can I win, if nobody else competes?"

"This girl, what's her name," the boy said, prying his eyes away and turning to Umlaut.

Oops. Umlaut couldn't put on one of those shirts. Emulation had its limits, and it would be shattered if his top half got transparently wet. Then the teens would all know he was an impostor, and Sherry would nab him. All she had to do was plant one sweet kiss on him, and he'd linger for another and be lost. Next morning he'd wake up with a headache and married. He simply wasn't ready for that, apart from the problem of fooling her. Because Sherry, however sweet her kisses and full her body, was not his idea of the perfect wife. Anyway, he was too young to marry.

He bolted. "Hey!" the boy cried. In a moment all of them were chasing him.

Now he was in twice as much trouble as before. Where could he go to escape?

He came up on a young woman who was walking in the same direction. "Uh, hello," he said somewhat breathlessly.

She turned to face him. She had an explorer's cap and a name tag saying Miss Guide. "May I help you?"

"Yes! Please tell me where I can escape a group of pursuing teens!"

"Take the left fork," she said. "Though you are welcome to dally a bit."

"Thank you!" He ran on ahead of her. Belatedly he wondered why she might want to dally with another girl.

But before he found a fork, he came up on another young woman. From behind she had a remarkable figure, and from before also, when he passed her. Her name tag said Miss In Form. "Is the left fork the one?" he gasped.

"In Dubitably," she agreed.

"Thanks!" He ran on.

He overhauled a third young woman, this one wearing a many-feathered bonnet. Her name tag said Miss Chief.

"Is the—?" he started.

"Oh, yes," she agreed. "You'll make a fine Indian maiden."

"Thanks!" He ran on. But something was nagging one corner of his mind. Those young women—if their name tags were literal, they might not be the best sources of information. Misguide, Misinform, Mischief . . .

Then he spied a fork in the path. The left fork was marked CONTEST BEACH and the right fork CASTLE ZOMBIE. Ordinarily Umlaut would have preferred the left, especially if he could have watched all the girls in the group donning Wetti shirts for the contest. But at the moment the right fork seemed better. Nobody much who wasn't a zombie went there.

Sure enough, the pursuit soon languished. Umlaut knew the teens wouldn't be too disappointed, because Sherry liked to kiss people, especially boys. But just in case any of the girls followed, he kept running. He let his emulation lapse; he'd run by the castle and then go home.

He almost collided with a group of teen zombie girls. He hadn't realized that zombies had teens, but of course they would be out today if they existed.

"Ooooz, ughsh!" one cried. "A live bzoy!"

"Who caresz?" another demanded. "He'z male."

"Say, yesh," a third said. "Letz kisz him!"

For some reason that escaped him at the moment, Umlaut did not want to be kissed by a group of zombie girlz. So he quickly refurbished his emulation. "I'm notz a boy," he protested. "I'm anozer zombie girzl."

"Oh, zo you are," the second girl said, disappointed. "Whatz you got?"

"Wetti shirts," Umlaut said, realizing that he still carried the package. "They're good for girls in contests."

"Letz try them!" the first girl said.

The zombies quickly took the remaining shirts and put them on. In a moment all were thoroughly soaked, their upper bodies showing to disadvantage. What looked great on live girls was somewhat sordid on zombie girls.

"Ooooz, ughsh!" they exclaimed, quickly appreciating that fact. "We look awzful!"

They tried to remove the shirts, but the wet things clung, tangling with the regular clothing underneath, so that the effect became worse. The girls were screaming with frustration as bits of cloth tore and dangled.

"What's going on here?" It was an irate black girl who appeared to be fully alive.

"Wetzi shirs," a zombie girl explained. "Contezt."

"A wet T-shirt contest? Zombies have no business getting into that. Who put you up to this nonsense?"

"Zhee did!" the girls said, pointing to Umlaut.

More mischief! Umlaut tried to shrink away but couldn't think of a suitable emulation on the spur of the moment; the spur merely jabbed him uncomfortably.

The black girl turned on Umlaut, a small black cloud forming over her head. "I'll deal with you later," she said menacingly. "For now, go muck out the dungeon."

Umlaut decided not to argue; he was in enough trouble already. This was evidently a person of authority. He hurried toward the castle.

He had expected something pretty dingy. He had underestimated the case. Castle Zombie up close was a festering ruin of an edifice. The moat was covered with sludge, and there was slime on the worn stones. The drawbridge was rotten and about to collapse. He did not want to try to cross over it.

"Got a problem?" It was a young man, fully alive.

Umlaut decided to stick with his zombie girl emulation. "Who zhou?"

The man smiled. "I am Justin Tree, master of Castle Zombie. You don't recognize me?"

Umlaut thought fast. "Bad eyz."

"Of course; I should have realized. And you can't see the bridge clearly enough to cross."

"Yez. I waz zent to muck the dunzeon."

"Oh, yes, Breanna has been meaning to assign a crew for that. The dragon manure is accumulating. Don't be concerned; that bridge is stronger than it looks. Just walk across and take the first stairway down. You'll find a spading fork at the dungeon entrance."

"Zank youz." Umlaut walked cautiously across, and the bridge did turn out to be solid enough.

So the man was Justin Tree. Umlaut had heard of him. He had married a Black Wave girl a year or so back. That would be the one who had sent him here: Breanna of the Black Wave. They had taken over the castle after the original zombie master had retired. It looked as if they still had a lot of cleaning up to do.

He found the stairway down, as slimy as the rest of it. He made his way below. Now he got nervous: What was this about a dragon? A dungeon was not his idea of fun, and a dungeon and a dragon were definitely worth avoiding. But the only way out was back past the master of the castle. So he went on.

There was the spading fork. He picked it up. If the dragon attacked, maybe he could use the fork to warn it back. That didn't seem very promising, but what else was there? Maybe he could simply duck into a small, dark passage and hide from it. He might emulate an ogre, but that would set back only a medium to small dragon.

He walked on through cobwebbed passages and chambers, his eyes adjusting to the gloom. It wasn't pitch dark so much as intensely dim, with wan weak beams of light seeping through crevices in the walls. This dungeon region was huge; he could get lost in it. So he went back to the foot of the stairway, then advanced again, this time scraping a line with a tine of the fork. That would be his sure trail back. It was easier to make a good mark, one that would show up in the dusky recesses, if he walked backward and held it down behind his progress.

It got more difficult, because a layer of mucky manure was building up, thickening as he progressed. He would have a big job to do, once he had his route marked. Where was he supposed to put all this stuff? The odor was awful.

He bumped into something. Startled, he turned. There was a monstrous snout. "The dragon!" he cried and scrambled to escape. But his feet slipped on the solidified stench, and he fell on his rear and slid into a wall. He was done for.

After a moment he realized two things: His bottom was sore from the fall, and the dragon hadn't eaten him. He climbed to his feet, rubbing his soiled posterior. "Ooo, that smarts," he said.

The dragon moved. The huge nose nudged a shelf Umlaut hadn't seen before, and a bottle fell off and rolled toward him. He stooped to pick it up. The crude label said HEALING.

Could that be true? If so, by what mischance had the monster happened to knock that particular bottle down at this time? Good fortune had never been Umlaut's forte.

He decided to try it. He opened the bottle, poured a drop of goo on his hand, and slid the hand down inside his pants to smear the stuff on his rear. Immediately he felt its benefit; not only did his bottom stop smarting, it suddenly felt great. He had gotten a bit tired from the constant bending and pressing on the fork; now his energy had been restored. It truly was healing elixir.

But the mystery remained: How had what he needed been so providentially presented to him—by the action of a dragon? Umlaut did not have a lot of belief in coincidences, at least not favorable ones. Normally they just got him into deeper trouble.

Could the dragon have done it intentionally? That seemed incredible, but added to the fact that the creature had not attacked when it could have, it was a possibility. "Did you do that on purpose?" he inquired.

The huge head nodded.

Still, that was not absolute proof. "Are you going to gobble me up as soon as I turn my back on you?"

The snout moved sidewise in a ponderous *no* gesture.

This was becoming more interesting. "Do you understand my words?"

The head nodded.

"What is two plus one?"

The head bobbed three times.

"You're intelligent!" Umlaut exclaimed.

The dragon hesitated.

"For an animal," Umlaut amended.

The head nodded.

"So you understand me and mean me no harm?"

Another nod.

"Well, that's fine, because I have come here to muck out your stall. Do you happen to know where I can dump the stuff?"

The dragon turned and slithered away. Umlaut hesitated, then decided that it was best to trust the creature, since he could not get the job done otherwise. He followed.

The dragon led him to a large chamber with a hole in the floor. "An oubliette!" Umlaut said. "Dump it down there?"

The dragon nodded.

"But there's a lot of this stuff. Won't it eventually fill up the oubliette?"

The head shook no.

"Magic? Or fast composting?"

That seemed to be the case. At any rate, the dragon nodded.

"Well, I'd better get started," Umlaut said. "I think I'll need more than a fork, though."

The dragon slithered to another chamber, leading him to a two-wheeled cart. That would help.

Umlaut worked. Soon he forgot how he had come here and just focused on the job. It did need to be done, and no one else was here to do it. He started with the chambers closest to the oubliette and worked slowly outward.

Then the dragon nudged him. Umlaut jumped; he had almost forgotten the creature's presence, though the dragon was obviously the source of all this manure. "Something wrong?" he asked.

The dragon made a sidewise motion with its snout, then slithered away. Umlaut followed. They went to the foot of the stairs. Breanna of the Black Wave stood there, holding a burning torch. "I think there's been a mistake," she said. "We don't have any record of a zombie girl of your description, and the zombies don't know you." She raised the torch. "In fact you don't look like a zombie at all—or a girl."

Oops. Umlaut had let his emulation lapse again. Did it matter? "I'm a living boy named Umlaut," he said. "I got caught up in things."

"Why didn't you protest when I sent you to the dungeon? I thought you were a misbehaving zombie girl."

"It was easier just to go."

She glanced at the dragon. "I see you are getting along well enough with Drivel."

"Drivel Dragon? That's his name?"

"Zombies tend to have descriptive names. He drools."

"I hadn't noticed."

"Well, come on. We'll get you cleaned up and give you supper and a bed for the night, and you can go on your way in the morning with our apology for the misunderstanding."

Umlaut looked at the dragon. "What about Drivel?"

"He won't fit in the castle. He was here when we took over. We feed him and let him be."

"This is not a vicious or stupid creature. Why is he confined?"

"We don't know. The Zombie Master didn't mention him."

Umlaut made what he suspected was a foolish decision. "Thanks, no thanks. I'll stay down here with him. The job's a long way from being done."

"But it's not your job! I mean to get up a cleanup crew, in due course. It's just taking us time to catch up on everything."

"Well, I'll help you catch up. Maybe I can find out why Drivel was locked in here."

"You can't find out! There are no records of him. We just have to accept what is."

Umlaut knew better but just had to make an issue. "I don't know much about you, Breanna of the Black Wave, but from what I heard, you never put up with 'what is' before."

The woman looked stunned. "You're right! I've become part of the status quo. I'm ashamed."

Umlaut was surprised by her change. "I guess we all get caught up in things."

"For sure! You really want to stay down here?"

"Yes. And try to find out what is the case with Drivel. He's certainly not violent."

"I'll bring your food right down." She handed him the torch, turned, and mounted the steps.

Umlaut turned to the dragon. "Am I being foolish?" he asked.

The dragon shrugged. That was a considerable maneuver, a long ripple along its nearer torso, but the meaning seemed clear enough.

"Here's the thing: I don't have much experience with dragons, but it is my understanding that they generally eat people and anything else they catch. Instead you have been friendly to me. That makes me think that you're not an ordinary dragon. You helped me do my job; maybe I can help you in return. If I can just figure out how."

Drivel nodded.

"So maybe if I talk enough, and you agree or disagree, I can figure it out. Then maybe we'll know what's next."

The dragon nodded.

"Is there a place I can put this torch?"

Drivel nosed a section of a wall. Umlaut went there and found a notch in a nook. He set the base of the torch in the notch, and the polished indentation of the nook served to reflect the light outward.

Breanna arrived back with a small cart. She paused at the top of the steps. "I'll toss Drivel's stakes down, but that won't work for your supper; you'll have to come here for it."

Umlaut went up the steps and found a very nice meal on a tray. Then Breanna tossed down one stake after another. They were evidently from a nearby garden, meat-flavored posts. They smelled like fresh flesh.

"See you in the morning," Breanna said as she departed.

They ate together, by the flickering light of the torch. Drivel seemed to like his stakes well enough. Umlaut tried a bite of one: yes, exactly like raw meat.

While they ate, they conversed, in their fashion. Umlaut talked and Drivel nodded or negated, and they zeroed in on the story. Soon it came reasonably clear. There were some surprises.

Drivel was not actually a dragon. In fact he was not even male. He—she—was a female water serpent whose name was Sesame. She had been chased by a persistent male of her species whose favor she did not desire, so she had fled to where he would not follow: Castle Zombie.

"Me too!" Umlaut agreed. "In my fashion."

But the moat had been too unsanitary for her taste, so she had had to make her way into the dungeon. Unfortunately a storm had come, and the zombies had battened down the hatches, or whatever it was they did, and Sesame had gotten closed in. A real dragon might have burned its way out, but she was merely a stranded sea serpent without fire, smoke, or steam, and without legs or claws. So she was trapped.

"But weren't you uncomfortable out of the water?" Umlaut asked.

She certainly was. Fortunately the dungeon was dank, and the slime on the walls was damp, and when it rained some water leaked in. She had found basins to collect it, so that she was able to drink and sometimes even to bathe. She had become acclimatized to existing out of the water; after all, many serpents were able to cope on land, and so could she.

"But weren't you hungry?"

Yes indeed. So she had approached a zombie who was storing something in the dungeon, representing herself as a male dragon, because she didn't know how close her serpent suitor might be lurking and needed to remain concealed. The zombie had told Breanna, who had assumed that the dragon was supposed to be there and had arranged for food. Stakes and chops from the local meat trees were fine.

"You have my talent!" Umlaut exclaimed.

The dragon/serpent looked at him quizzically.

"I mean you can emulate things. You certainly seemed like a male dragon to me. And I would have seemed like a zombie maiden to you, if I had thought to maintain my emulation."

It turned out that she had taken him for a zombie girl, then realized that he wasn't when he had started working and muttering bad words as he got grimed. Girls, of course, didn't know any bad words.

"So we're two of a kind," Umlaut said. "Which is odd, because talents aren't supposed to repeat."

Sesame shook her head. Further dialogue established her position: that talents did repeat, as shown with the curse fiends who all had the same talent of cursing, and the flying centaurs, whose talent was flying or making themselves light enough to fly. Also, similar talents could be implemented different ways, as with the centaurs who might fly by having powerful wings, or by lightening magic. But mainly there was no rule about it; folk had just assumed that talents could not repeat, without any proof. It was folklore.

"You're right," Umlaut said. "You must have thought about this somewhat."

She had. She had always been a cerebral sort, which set her apart from others of her kind. It was a frustration, because no other serpents were interested in philosophical questions. They cared mainly about chomping the next fish or unwary human swimmer, and about breeding. She had nothing against either pursuit but did not care to be limited to them when the universe was such a fascinating mystery. So she had been exploring the fringes of the watery domain, including Castle Zombie, when she was spied by a land serpent interested only in breeding and got caught away from the sea.

"Castle Zombie is well beyond the fringe of the sea," Umlaut protested. "It's landlocked, in fact junglelocked."

So she had discovered. She had reached it by swimming up a river, then portaging to its moat. It was a fine, intriguing castle, if only she weren't locked into it.

"But you don't need to be locked in anymore. I'm sure they'll let you go, once they realize it's a mistake."

But first she had to verify whether the land serpent remained watching. He could slither faster than she could on land, so she had to be sure not to alert him. She did not want to be subjected to involuntary breeding. But perhaps that was something that Umlaut, a male, would not understand.

Umlaut thought about his relationship with Sherry and decided that he did understand. "Breeding is fine, in its place, at the right time, with the right other person," he said. "But if any of those factors are wrong, then it's not fine. I fled a too-ardent girl on my way here."

He did understand! She was thrilled. It was just about the first time she had encountered anyone else who understood anything halfway obscure. Did he have an obscure mind?

He laughed. "No, just a garden variety human mind."

She would like to meet more minds like that. She had not realized that human folk had them. But of course she could not go among humans and converse with them, because they wouldn't trust her not to gobble them, and because she couldn't talk in their language. She couldn't explain to them that she really didn't like to eat human flesh. It smelled bad, no offense, and tasted worse.

Umlaut began to get a glimmer of an inkling of a notion. He pounced on it before it escaped. "Why don't we travel together? I could talk with the people, and you could listen, and I could ask your questions for you. Then you could meet all the obscure minds you want to."

Oh, that sounded scrumptious! She could just kiss him, except that she didn't want to scare him.

"Well, I think I have pretty well come to trust you," Umlaut said. "You can kiss me if you want to. Just don't swallow me."

She would try not to do that. Would he move into deeper shadow with her?

Umlaut began to get nervous. But nothing in their long dialogue indicated that she wished him any harm, so this would be a good test of his trust. If she chomped him, he would know better next time. If there were ever a next time. He followed her away from the torch.

When it was almost quite dark, he stopped moving. "Here I am." What had he let himself in for? A chomping, or a slavering of drool?

A pretty girl kissed him on the mouth. Startled, he put his arms around her. She was cool and lithe, with a dress made of fine scales. Where had she come from?

Then he caught on. "Sesame!"

She nodded. It was indeed her. The scales were not of her dress, but of her neck, and of course she had no arms or hair. She had emulated a girl, using the darkness to hide her real outline. She had known it wouldn't work very well in the light, but with only their lips touching, the emulation was effective. Did he like it?

"Yes, actually," he said. "How did you learn to kiss like a girl?"

Well, she *was* a girl—a girl serpent. Kissing came naturally with the gender.

"I wonder if I could kiss like a serpent?" he asked. "I never thought to try an emulation like that."

There was no time like the present, she intimated. She would emulate herself, and he could try being serpentine. She would let him know how well it worked.

Umlaut focused. He had seldom tried animals before, and never a serpent, but the principle should be similar. He thought of himself as a big, powerful, flexing male serpent, looking for a female to kiss. There just happened to be a nice female in range. He shot his head forward and gave her a toothy smooch.

She jerked back, her coils roiling desperately. In a moment she was gone. What had happened?

Then, embarrassed, she returned. He had felt so much like a male serpent that she had thought for a moment that the land serpent had gotten in and was about to force her to breed. She had spooked. She was apologetic.

Umlaut was rather pleased. "I was that good?"

Yes, he had been that good. She would have enjoyed it, had she not spooked.

"When you kissed me, I thought it was a pretty girl," Umlaut said. "I tried to embrace her, before I realized."

Exactly, Sesame agreed. When they couldn't see each other, they could emulate more effectively, because vision did not belie the effect. She had never had occasion to experiment in such a manner before, perhaps because it would not have been safe with a real male serpent.

"Or with a real human girl," he agreed. "Things could go too far, too fast."

It struck her that different as they were in form and gender, some things about their lives were very similar.

"Yes," he agreed. In truth, he had liked Sesame's kiss better than Sherry's. Then he thought of something else. "Maybe—I don't want to be objectionable, but maybe we should try to find out what the limits of our talents are, before we try going out to travel. Suppose I emulate a serpent, and you emulate a girl, and we kiss again? Could we fool each other simultaneously?"

She agreed it would be worthwhile to find out. So they tried it. And it was a disaster. They both recoiled.

"Girls taste awful!" Umlaut exclaimed, wiping off his mouth.

And serpents were fanged and lipless, she agreed.

"Which is exactly what we would discover if we kissed while neither of us was emulating. We are of different kinds, physically."

Which was of course obvious, she agreed. But didn't he have better things to do than travel with a serpent?

"Actually, no," he said thoughtfully. "My life has been pretty much marking time so far. I always thought I'd like to go out and have big adventures in faraway places, but I never knew how to get started. Maybe this is the way."

They decided to see about it in the morning. Then they settled down to sleep. Sesame coiled into the shape of a mattress, and Umlaut lay down on it. It was very comfortable.

Just as he was drifting off to sleep, the girl kissed him again. He kissed her back, knowing who it was. But he was glad it was dark.

2

LETTERS

In the morning they woke to wan light. The torch had guttered out, but day was squeezing through crevices. Sesame showed him where there were several basins of water she had collected, and Umlaut used one to wash up. He took off his clothing and rinsed it and hung it on snags of stone to dry.

"I'd better finish this mucking job before I dress again," he decided.

Sesame was apologetic. She had not liked soiling the dungeon floor, but no provision had been made for her in that respect. Normally she left her manure in dirt or water. She had just had to make do, with regret. The oubliette was not convenient for her anatomy, or she would have used that, as it was enchanted never to fill up.

"That's all right," Umlaut said. "I just want to finish the job I started, before I go."

He was remarkably decent for his kind, she suggested.

He got to work and made progress. Then, as he was finishing up the chamber where the stairs were, there was suddenly extra light as a door opened. There was Breanna of the Black Wave, with another cartful of food.

And there he stood, with nothing on. He froze, with no idea what to do.

"You've got so much muck on you, I can't even see your clothing," Breanna remarked. "But really, you didn't have to continue that chore. I told you it was a mistake."

He realized that she couldn't tell that he had no clothing on. What a relief! "Not much farther to go," he said. "Then I think we should talk."

"For sure." She gave them their food and departed.

They ate, meanwhile considering their plans. They would leave the castle and travel together, meeting random people. Umlaut would talk with them, evoking their minds, and if there were any danger, Sesame would handle it. She was, after all, a good-sized serpent, similar to the ones that found employment defending moats. She could handle land as long as they spent the nights near water. It promised to be a fair adventure.

Then Umlaut finished the mucking, dumped the last of it into the oubliette, went to another basin of water, washed, and donned his mostly dry clothes. He was ready for the next stage. "I guess I'll have to go up alone to explain things to Breanna and to look around the castle," he said. "You'll have to trust me on that."

She would. He had been trusting her all along, after all. She indicated it was nice to have company with a mind, after a year alone in the dungeon.

It was now about noon, and the light in the dungeon was brighter than it had been. He paused as he was about to mount the stairs. There was something behind them, where he hadn't had to clean. Curious, he looked.

There was a small window in the wall, letting light in. Below it, inside, was a pile of papers. It looked as if someone had pushed the papers through the slot from outside, and no one had collected them inside. Small wonder—probably nobody had known about them. Sesame hadn't; she didn't read and couldn't write. She understood human talk, a private ability a number of animals had developed, but that was the extent of it.

He picked one up. It was a sealed letter addressed to the Demon Jupiter. Who was that? Umlaut knew about demons;

they popped in and out of existence and usually meant mischief to mortal folk. But he hadn't known they received letters.

"Do you know the Demon Jupiter?" he asked Sesame.

She shook her head. Then she reconsidered. It took a while to fathom what she meant, but in time he had it: She didn't know of any local demon by that name but understood there was a major Demon in another realm by that title. Maybe that was the one. If so, this could be important.

"I'd better ask Breanna," he decided. "I'll take it up with me."

He mounted the stairs. He paused at the top. "Oh, is it all right if I tell them your real nature? That you're not a dragon?"

She nodded, trusting him.

He opened the door, which wasn't locked, and stepped into the brighter light of the real world. He saw a zombie standing guard. "Where is Breanna?"

"Thash," the zombie said, pointing with a rotten finger.

"Thank you." Umlaut walked in that direction. When he came to a door, he knocked.

It opened. Breanna stood there. "Oh, yes, I almost forgot. What's on your mind?"

"First, I'm ready to go. So is the dragon."

"The dragon!"

"It's not really a dragon. It's a serpent. It was trapped in the dungeon."

"You mean it doesn't belong there?"

"That's right. I guess it happened to come just about the time you took over the castle, so you didn't know."

"For sure!"

"So we figure to travel together for a while, see the sights, you know? I cleaned out the muck, so it's reasonably clean now. But maybe if you ever have any other creature down there, you should set up some, uh, sanitary facilities, so it doesn't have to mess the floor."

"For sure," she repeated.

"And we found some letters."

"Letters?"

"I picked one up. I thought it might be important." He handed it to her.

Breanna studied it. "The Demon Jupiter! You bet it's important! This is from Mundania. How'd it get down in the dungeon?"

"There seems to be a—a mail slot. There's a pile of letters there. I guess you didn't know about that either."

"There's oodles we didn't know about running this castle," she agreed. "The Zombie Master didn't put much in writing, so maybe he didn't remember everything. At least I can take care of this letter."

"How can you deliver it? I understand he's far away."

"On another planet," she agreed. "I happen to know him. I'll forward this to him on the Internet."

"What kind of net?"

"It's an extension of the Xanth Xone. I've got a Mesh site there. Here, I'll show you. I'll send this as an E-mail attachment." She led the way to another chamber. "Com Pewter set up a station here," she explained, "so we can connect."

Umlaut saw some kind of metallic contraption with a glassy screen. Breanna punched some buttons, and the screen showed a series of little boxes and arrows. She punched more buttons, and words appeared: DEMON JUPITER: LETTER FORWARDED BY ATTACHMENT. She fed the envelope into a slot, and it disappeared. In a moment another message appeared: ATTACHMENT: LETTER TO DEMON JUPITER.

"Now I'll push the Send button and it's done," she said. She did so, and the screen showed a letter sprouting wings and flying away. Then it went blank. "Done."

"That goes to Jupiter?" Umlaut asked dubiously.

"For sure. Now let's see to your serpent."

"First I need to check around outside. There may be another serpent lurking."

"And they don't get along?"

"You might say that. I need to be sure it's not there."

"No problem. I'll have the zombies do a search." She went to the zombie standing guard. "Hey, Sludge! Tell Fay Tall to organize a search around the castle. Are there any serpents there?"

"Yeshum," the zombie agreed and shuffled off.

"Fay Tall is a zombie who appears to be fully alive for half a day at a time," Breanna explained. "Then he reverts to normal. He hates it."

"I guess I'd hate to revert to being a zombie," Umlaut said.

"You got that wrong. It's the fully alive state he hates. It sets him apart from the other zombies."

Umlaut was taken aback. He decided not to argue the case. "Anyway, if the way is clear, can you open the dungeon door so Drivel can slither out?"

"For sure. I wish we'd known he didn't belong. He didn't say anything."

Umlaut decided that the serpent's gender was no business of anyone else's. "Serpents don't talk."

"So how do you know so much about him?"

"He understands human talk. I talked and he agreed or disagreed. In time I got his story."

"I wish I'd thought of that! I just never realized he didn't belong there. There's a lot more to this job than I thought."

The zombie Sludge returned. "All schlear," it reported.

"All clear," Breanna repeated. "Let's go open the dungeon gate."

They walked down outside the castle, between the wall and the moat. There was a large door. "We closed this when there was a storm," Breanna said. "Then never got around to opening it again. Now I feel so stupid; of course that's when we trapped Drivel inside." She put her brown hands on a plank and pushed it up, freeing the door.

Umlaut pulled it open. "Drivel!" he called. "It's all clear. We can leave now."

The serpent emerged, blinking in the bright light.

"I'm—we—we're sorry," Breanna said awkwardly. "I apologize to you for trapping you in there. We just didn't realize."

Sesame nodded. Then she glanced at Umlaut.

"He doesn't care to swim in that moat," Umlaut said. "No offense. He's not a zombie. Is it okay to use the bridge?"

"Sure. Whatever you want." Breanna got out of the way. Sesame slithered smoothly up the bank and to the drawbridge and on across it. Umlaut followed. "Thanks!" he called as they reached the outer bank.

"We'll check those other letters," Breanna said. "Come back in a day or three and we'll let you know."

"Okay." Umlaut walked on, pacing Sesame's slither. But that reminded him of the letters. "Why don't we check where they came from?" he suggested. "You can smell the trail?"

She could. She slithered to the side to parallel the moat and soon picked up the scent.

"What it is? Human?"

Sesame tried but was unable to convey what had delivered the letters, except that it was neither human nor serpent. There had been a number of trips, and the scent trail seemed to have existed for at least six months.

"Why would anyone or anything deliver letters from Mundania to Castle Zombie?" Umlaut asked rhetorically.

The serpent had no idea.

The trail bore west through the deepest jungle. Here dragons and other dangerous creatures lurked, but Sesame smelled none of them by the trail. The trail itself was a bit sticky, as if someone had poured noxious goo on the ground to mark it. Maybe that repelled the other creatures.

Then it crossed a small river. They had no trouble with this; they both swam across. There were leathery-backed tooth-mouthed green allegories in it, but they eyed Sesame and decided not to make an issue.

But there was no trail on the other side. The serpent sniffed and sniffed and could not find it.

"It must go lengthwise under the river," Umlaut said. "It could come out anywhere. We'll have to search the whole length of it."

Sesame sighed. They started in, following the river upstream. It wound around, trying to distract them, but they held firm—and did not find the trail.

"I wish we had some magic help," Umlaut said.

At that point a cat appeared. It was male, reddish, and reasonably plump. It approached them as if it wanted to make their acquaintance.

Umlaut considered, then decided to question the cat in the

same manner he had questioned the serpent. "Do you understand me?" he asked.

The cat nodded.

"Are you looking for us?"

Another nod.

"Do you know where the letter trail resumes?"

Another nod.

Well, now. Umlaut focused, questioning the cat in more
detail. Suddenly he recognized it: "Sammy Cat!" he exclaimed. "The one who came with Jenny Elf, before she got
married and settled down. The one who can find anything."

Except home, it turned out. It seemed that Sammy Cat had
felt a bit out of place among the werewolves—Jenny was now
a princess of werewolves—so had decided to go on his own
mission. He had changed his mind but was unable to return
to the werewolf island and Jenny because that was now home.

"Maybe we can make a deal," Umlaut suggested. "You
help us find the letter trail, and we'll help you find Werewolf
Island." He glanced at Sesame to make sure she agreed.

Sammy agreed to the deal. Then he headed downstream.

"We were going the wrong way!" Umlaut said ruefully.
But of course their choices had been upstream or downstream;
they had been as likely to go wrong as right.

They followed the cat as he plunged through the jungle.
Sesame had no problem, but Umlaut found it hard to squeeze
through cat- or serpent-diameter holes in the thick foliage.
"Um, could you find a path that I can follow?" he called.

Sammy reappeared. He was sorry. When he searched for
something, he just tended to go for it. Jenny Elf had always
been crying, "Wait for me!" but he still tended to do it without thinking. But he would try.

Thereafter, the route was easier to follow. Unfortunately it
soon led to a tangle tree. "This isn't safe!" Umlaut cried.

But it turned out that it *was* safe: The tangle tree had fed
recently and was quiescent. They followed its nice path in,
skirted the deadly trunk, and followed another path out. The
one out was not nearly as nice as the one in. Umlaut appreciated that the tree wanted creatures to come in, not go out,
but wasn't sure how it managed to make the paths that way.

There were many things about the Land of Xanth he didn't properly understand.

Progress downstream was much quicker than it had been upstream, perhaps because it was downhill. Reasonably soon they reached the sea. Sammy stopped.

"You mean the path never does cross the river?" Umlaut asked, dismayed. "It goes straight on into the sea?"

That was the case.

"But we wanted to see who was delivering the letters."

Sammy made a stiff-backed circle. That wasn't what Umlaut had said. He had asked for the trail, not the carrier.

"I guess I wasn't very clear," Umlaut admitted. "You're right. Now we'd better go find Werewolf Island. It must be somewhere along the coast here."

But then Sammy changed his mind. Home could wait. Would it be all right if he stayed with them for a while, sharing their adventure? One reason he had changed his mind before was the danger; it had seemed as if every predator had a taste for fat cat. But with Sesame along, the danger was much less.

Umlaut exchanged another glance with Sesame. They had come to understand each other pretty well, so that a glance could convey a lot. "Sure. We could use your talent to find interesting things."

In that case, Sammy indicated, he would show them the letter carrier.

"You can do that? Why didn't you say so before?"

Sammy gave him a look of patient tolerance. Umlaut hadn't asked, of course.

They crossed the river. First Sesame swam, with Sammy perched on her head, glaring the colored loan sharks away. Then she swam back to accompany Umlaut as he swam. The sharks looked eager to take one of his arms or legs, but Sesame wouldn't let them. They were clearly disgusted. Umlaut had come to think of the big serpent as harmless but realized that that was because she was his friend. She remained a formidable predator, probably equivalent to a dragon, only without fire, smoke, or steam.

They followed the river back upstream to the place they had first come to it. Then Sammy settled down for a catnap.

"I guess it's not time yet," Umlaut said. "Why don't we forage for food while we wait? We're not partial to each other's food, so maybe we should do it separately, then meet here in an hour or so."

Sesame agreed and slithered off. Umlaut spied a very nice looking pie tree and picked a pie. He bit into it and almost choked—it was a sweetie pie, revoltingly sweet. He looked at the others and saw that they were similar; this was a sweetie pie tree. So he suppressed his objection and ate it. He had been taught to eat any food he picked rather than waste it. Next time he would be more careful.

In an hour or so Sesame Serpent returned. She was a little thicker in the middle and looked satisfied; she had found her meal. Umlaut did not inquire.

But she looked askance at him. It seemed that he looked and smelled sickeningly sweet. The pie had had its effect. Umlaut was disgusted.

Sammy woke, looked at Umlaut, and turned his back, evincing annoyance.

"I can't help it!" Umlaut protested. "It was all there was to eat."

But Sammy had a cure. He sniffed out a nearby path that went north and south. It had a paved surface and a dotted line along its center. All Umlaut needed to do was stand there a moment, and he would no longer be too sweet.

He shrugged and tried it. Suddenly there was the blare of a horn and a demon zoomed toward him at impossible speed. "Watch where you're going, jerk!" the demon yelled. Umlaut threw himself to one side, just in time, and the demon swerved the other way—and crashed into the sweetie pie tree. Pies flew up, and one landed on the demon. Rather, *in* the demon, for the thing's mouth was open to yell another imprecation. There was nothing for the demon to do but swallow it.

"What did you think you were doing, speeding like that?" Umlaut demanded angrily. "You could have run me over!"

The demon extricated himself from the tree. "Oh, I'm so sorry," he said with saccharine politeness. "But you know, I *am* a speed demon. It's my nature." Then he got back on the path and *bbbrrrzzzzpp!* he was gone, except for a sweet cloud of smoke.

In a moment another demon zoomed by, stirring up a cloud of dust and leaves. "Those speed demons think they own the forest!" Umlaut griped. Then he saw Sesame and Sammy gazing at him. "What!?"

In third moment it came clear: He was no longer sickeningly sweet. The experience with the speed demons had wiped that right out of him. And the first demon had swallowed a pie and turned sweet. Served him right.

"Okay, you cured me, Sammy," he said grudgingly. "Now how about the letter carrier?"

Sammy shrugged. Not yet. He settled down for another catnap, assuming the aspect of a speed bump on the speed demons' path. Sesame settled down for a snooze or two of her own. She had reptilian patience and a full tummy.

Frustrated, Umlaut walked around the area, just in case there was anything interesting. He discovered a tree he didn't recognize, with small pretzel-twisted fruits. The trunk ascended, then bent down, then rose again, forming a giant letter *N*. He hesitated, then decided that the fruits were unlikely to be poisonous. He picked one and ate it. It was good, neither too sweet nor sour. He should have eaten this instead of the sweetie pies.

Suddenly he was very angry. He spat out the fruit, and the passion faded. The fruit must have caused his mood.

He tried another. This time he suffered a mental picture of the nearby region of Xanth, as if he could envision it without being blocked by the trees or mountains.

A bulb flashed over his head. "N-vision!" he cried. "It's an N-tree and has N-shaped fruits. The first one was N-rage." Then, curious, he tried other fruits and identified N-oble, N-sure, N-trance, N-shroud, and N-joy. Satisfied with that last one, he stopped picking and eating.

Sammy turned to face the river. Its surface was rippling, but it wasn't an allegory; they were staying well clear. An eye broke the surface, then another. These were followed by eyestalks, then by a glistening hump. Finally it slid entirely out of the water: a huge snail. There was a knapsack on its shell and printed words: MUNDANIA SNAILS.

They all stared as the snail slid grandly on toward Castle Zombie. It completely ignored them. It crossed the speed demon path, paying no heed to the speeding demons, who veered crazily to avoid it. It passed within range of a tangle tree, but the tree's tentacles recoiled from it, evidently knowing better than to get stuck on it. It was sublimely untouchable, caring about nothing and nobody. It left behind a fresh trail of slime.

"Let's not inquire further," Umlaut said, and serpent and cat agreed.

They conferred and decided to return to Castle Zombie to report on their discovery, then decide where to go next. They took another route Sammy showed them, and it was surprisingly easy to follow; they fairly flew along it. That made Umlaut suspicious. "Are you sure this goes where we're going?" he asked Sammy.

The cat reconsidered and shook his head.

"Then why are we on it?"

Sammy seemed to be unable to answer. He just kept following it, and Sesame and Umlaut went too. It was the easiest thing to do.

Then they came to an identifying sign: PATH OF LEAST RESISTANCE.

"Oh, no! This isn't right!"

But they seemed to be unable to stop. They had to follow the path, because any alternative was more difficult. Sammy had gotten caught when looking for a path to the castle, and they had followed him unthinkingly. It occurred to Umlaut that following anyone unthinkingly was not the best course.

Umlaut looked desperately around for some way to get off the path, because he was sure it would not be healthy to stay on it too long. Where did it lead?

All too soon, he saw: into a dreadful bog with a sign identifying it as DISASTER. They would never get out of that.

He had to find a way to break the spell of the path. But all he saw by the side was a colony of ants. "Help!" he called.

Surprisingly, one of them responded. It was an ant with a huge head. It held up a small paper sign. ARE YOU ADDRESSING ME?

"Yes!" Umlaut cried. "Who are you?"

The ant held up another placard. I AM INTELLIG ANT.

Ouch! Puns were inferior things at the best of times, but that one was not the best. But what choice did they have? "If you're so smart, tell us how to get off this path."

SEEK THE HELP OF THE RESIST ANTS.

By this time they were past the first ant colony and approaching another, just before the path disappeared into the bubbling bog. That had to be the resist ants. "Help!" he called again.

The ants responded. They charged across the path and linked legs so as to form a living cordon. The three travelers collided with it and bounced back, landing in a pile off the path. They were finally free of its compulsion.

Umlaut picked himself up. "Thanks," he said. "You saved us from disaster. What can we do for you in return?"

The Intellig Ant approached with a placard. THEY WANT A PORPOISE.

This set him back somewhat. "Seafood? To eat? I don't think I want to do that."

LOOK AT THE POOL.

He looked and saw that at the edge of the bog was a section of open water. A creature swam there, restlessly. It was the shape of a loan shark, but different.

THAT IS REASON. HE HAS NO PORPOISE. FIND HIM A PORPOISE.

Oh. Another pun. What else was to be expected along the Path of Least Resistance?

Still, this seemed to be beyond the scope of what they could accomplish. "I'm not sure—"

Sammy Cat took off, bounding across the terrain.

"We'll do it," Umlaut said and followed the cat. "Wait for me!"

Sammy led them to another pond. There was a swimming creature similar to the other. "Are you a porpoise?" Umlaut asked it.

It turned out that this was indeed a lady porpoise. Surely a fit companion for Reason.

"We would like you to meet a creature who needs you," Umlaut said. "We'll try to make a channel for you to swim." Indeed, Sesame was already at work on it, jamming her snout through the dirt and muck of the fringe of the bog, gouging out a shallow channel.

In due course they had cut a channel connecting the two pools. The porpoise wriggled along it and joined Reason, who greeted her with delight. Reason and a porpoise—a perfect couple.

Now they felt free to depart. Sammy scouted out another path, a safe one, and they followed cautiously. There were no further problems, and they reached the castle well ahead of the giant snail, unsurprisingly.

Breanna of the Black Wave saw them coming. "Sammy!" she exclaimed, picking up the cat and stroking him. He purred.

"We saw a snail," Umlaut said. "It's bringing letters from Mundania." He preferred not to mention the misadventure with the Path of Least Resistance.

Breanna nodded. "That explains why they are so old. I collected them from the dungeon, and some of them go back months. We had no idea they were being delivered here."

"I guess a Mundane snail wouldn't know the local Xanth addresses," Umlaut said. "So it brought them to the nearest castle with a mail slot."

"For sure. They are supposed to go to all manner of residents. We'll have the zombies deliver them to the people they are addressed to. It will take a while, but they're already so late it shouldn't make much difference."

"Well, I think we'll be on our way now," Umlaut said. "We want to explore Xanth before Sammy goes home."

"But he can't find home," Breanna said. "I know where it is; I can have a zombie take him there."

Sammy jumped from her arms. He wasn't ready to go home yet.

"For sure," Breanna murmured, seeing the way of it. "I guess all those wolves get tiresome, and Jenny's signaling the stork." She looked pensive half a moment. "So am I."

There was a swirl of smoke in the air before them. It formed into a vaguely human face. "Salubrious," it said.

"What?" Umlaut asked.

"Greeting, welcome, accosting, addressing, heralding—"

"Salutation?"

"Whatever," the face said crossly, as a voluptuous body extended downward from it.

"Oh, hello, Metria," Breanna said. "You know Sammy Cat, and these are Umlaut Human and Drivel Dragon." She turned to the others. "This is the Demoness Metria."

The shape was now fully formed, with a drooping décolletage over a very full bosom and lifting skirt over a similarly full bottom. "You don't look much like a dragon," she said to Sesame.

The serpent quickly emulated the dragon, having allowed that to lapse. The demoness blinked. "But maybe I mislooked."

"Mis what?" Umlaut asked somewhat stupidly. He couldn't manage an intelligent comment at the moment because his own eyes were locked onto Metria's illustriously heaving bosom.

"Misinformed, misbegotten, mistaken, misapprehended—"

"Never mind," Breanna said somewhat curtly. "What brings you here, Metria?"

"Oh, that," the demoness said. "There's a message from Magician Humfrey."

"The Good Magician? What's he want with us?"

"He wants to know what the inferno you said to Demon Jupiter."

"What the what?" Umlaut asked, still locked onto her bosom, heave by heave.

"Hades, purgatory, pandemonium, underworld, perdition—"

"Blazes?" Umlaut asked.

"Whatever," she agreed crossly, taking another heave.

"Cut it out," Breanna snapped. "We didn't say anything to Demon Jupiter. All we did was forward a letter to him."

The demoness started to fade, finally freeing Umlaut's eyes. "Humfrey will be glad to know that."

"Hold up a moment," Breanna said. "What's *with* the Demon Jupiter?"

The fading reversed at the top but continued at the bottom, so that the demoness was visible only from the waist up. Umlaut tried to safeguard his eyes before they fell back into her swelling bosom, but lost. "Him? Oh, just some nonsense about a spot."

"Must be the Red Spot," Breanna said. "He's got one. Why does that concern us?"

"He doesn't seem to want it anymore."

"Doesn't want his Red Spot? Why do you think that?"

"Because it seems he just threw it at the Demon Earth."

"He *what*?"

"Hurled, cast, tossed, flung, pitched—"

"Stop it!" Breanna snapped. "That spot is no tiny ball, it's a huge red storm. And Earth is firmly attached to Xanth. If that thing blots out Earth, it'll blot out Xanth too. This is real mischief! Whatever possessed Jupiter to do that?"

Metria shrugged, yanking Umlaut's eyes upward with her thorax. "I wouldn't know. Must have been something in that letter you so nicely forwarded."

"The letter!" Breanna exclaimed in horror. "It must have insulted him. It's my fault for forwarding that missive. I should abase myself."

"Or go to the attic," Umlaut suggested.

"Attic?"

"The basement is still sort of smelly. So maybe an attic is better than abasement."

She gave him a strange look, and he realized that he had spoken clumsily, again. "Maybe I should. Now we're all in deep bleep."

"Deep what?" the demoness asked.

"Muck, manure, fertilizer, humus, dirt—"

"Poop?"

"Whatever," Breanna said crossly. "Hey, now you've got *me* doing it! I mean we're all in trouble. Because we didn't know what was in that letter."

"Interesting. Well, toodle-doo." This time the demoness faded out too quickly to be stopped.

Breanna shook her head. "What a mess!"

Sesame and Sammy nodded agreement.

3

CHALLENGES

"Maybe I shouldn't have found that letter," Umlaut said, feeling guilty.

"Maybe I shouldn't have forwarded it unopened," Breanna said. "For sure, I'll check the others first. But right now we have a bad problem. I'll have to consult with the Good Magician to find out what to do about it. What a thing to happen when I'm still learning the zombie business."

A moderately dim bulb flashed over Umlaut's head. "We can do that," he said.

Distracted, Breanna didn't understand immediately. "Do what?"

"Consult with the Good Magician. We can go there, so you won't have to. We—we have some responsibility in this matter too."

Breanna considered. "It's nobody's fault; it just happened. But we do need to do something. That Demon Jupiter is nobody to fool around with. Okay, if you want to go, then go ahead. But hurry. That spot won't take long to get here."

"Well, Sammy can surely find the castle, but it may take us several days to get there by foot."

"No time for that. I'll have Roy carry you."

"Who?"

But she was already hurrying away to find Roy.

Umlaut turned to the other two. "I thought you'd like to see the Good Magician's castle. But if you'd rather not, I can leave you here and do it myself. I'll give the answer to Breanna, then we can head out on our own adventure, just as we planned."

Both serpent and cat shook their heads. They wanted to come along.

"I wonder who Roy is?" Umlaut asked. "Maybe a big horse or unicorn or something, who can run very fast."

Sammy looked past him and shuddered. Then Sesame did the same.

"Well, maybe with a wagon, so we can ride in it."

They continued to stare and shudder. Finally Umlaut turned to follow their gazes.

A giant bird was coming to a landing. "A roc!" he exclaimed. "We're going by air!"

So why were they still shuddering?

Then he saw the bird in more detail. It was a zombie roc. "Oh, no!" he breathed. But it was too late to say no.

The three exchanged another glance. They shrugged. How bad could it be?

There was a wicker cage at the roc's feet, large enough for them all. They got into it, Sesame curling around the bottom, Umlaut and Sammy sitting on her coils.

There was a blast of foul air as the roc pumped his monstrous wings and lifted off the ground. Roy's flesh might be a bit rotten, but his flight feathers were evidently sufficient. Umlaut wrinkled his nose, and the two others nodded. None of them were keen on zombie power but had little choice at the moment. Certainly Umlaut was not about to comment openly and perhaps hurt the big bird's feelings and get dropped.

They saw the Land of Xanth spread below them, like a disjointed carpet, with the blue sea on one side and a huge crevice on another. "What's that?" Umlaut asked, surprised.

It turned out that Sammy Cat knew, having been there. They played the yes/no question game and gradually got the answer: That was the Gap Chasm, a huge cut across the center of Xanth that had been forgotten for eight hundred years, thanks to a forget spell, but now was generally known. Its sides were sheer, so that creatures who got into it had trouble getting out, and the dread Gap Dragon cruised the bottom, steaming and gobbling what it caught.

"Steaming?" Umlaut asked.

Yes, steaming. Dragons were of three general types: fire breathers, smokers, and steamers. The one in the Gap Chasm was Stanley Steamer. He could cook a creature with a single jet of steam and was one of the most fearsome dragons extant. Except when Princess Ivy was around; then he was tame.

"You know Princess Ivy?" Umlaut asked, amazed.

It turned out that Sammy knew just about everyone who was anyone. Jenny Elf had made many friends before she got married, so the cat had became acquainted with them too. He could find any of them, when he wanted to.

It occurred to Umlaut that this could be a useful contact if they needed to meet any important people. But why would they need to? They were just doing an errand for Breanna of the Black Wave.

The bird angled downward. There was a castle ahead. "That must be the Good Magician," Umlaut said.

Sammy sent him a superior look: What else could it be?

Roy Roc touched down, bounced, slid, and ground to a spinning halt. It was not a pretty landing, and bits of zombie rot flew out, but they were safely down.

"Thank you so much," Umlaut said, scrambling out of the somewhat dented wicker cage. Sammy and Sesame were hardly slower about it.

The bird nodded. Then he spread his wings, pumped more rot into the air, and squeezed out a takeoff. In a moment only the stench remained.

"Well, he did get us here quickly," Umlaut said. "We are surely duly grateful."

The others agreed. Now they addressed the castle. It looked considerably neater and cleaner than Castle Zombie, which was no surprise. The stone walls were firm, the pennants were bright, the moat was clear, and the drawbridge was down across it and looked firm and healthy. What a change—and what a relief.

But something was wrong. When they approached the castle, it turned out to be made of cardboard. The moat was a painted disk, the walls were interlocked in jigsaw puzzle fashion, and the main gate was painted; it wouldn't open.

"This is the Good Magician's Castle?" Umlaut asked Sammy.

Sammy fidgeted. It turned out that he had not invoked his finding power, trusting the roc to know the way. And the roc had landed at the wrong castle.

Umlaut sighed. Then he stepped across the moat and knocked on the painted door. "Anybody home?" he called.

A much smaller door opened inside the big one. A young man's head popped out. "You like it anyway?"

"It's cardboard!" Umlaut exclaimed.

"Well, maybe I overreached. You see, my talent is to make any drawn thing become real. So this time I drew the Good Magician's Castle. But I guess there are limits, because when it got big, it stopped being solid. It's real, just not quite what I wanted."

"I guess you have to work on that some more," Umlaut said. "We're looking for the real Good Magician's Castle."

"Oh that's just east of here. You can't miss it." The door shut.

They walked around the cardboard castle and went east. And came up against a raging river. It was plainly too violent for them to swim across. Even Sesame shrank back.

Umlaut turned to Sammy. "Can you find help?"

The cat bounded north. "Wait for us!" But Sammy wasn't good at waiting. Fortunately it was not far. They approached two girls who were having a picnic in a glade.

The girls looked up, alarmed. Suddenly a mass of green Stuff appeared and shaped itself into a fence between Umlaut and the girls. He had to stop moving before he crashed into it.

He recognized defensive magic. "We're not attacking you," he called. "We're just looking for help to get across the river. I'm Umlaut, and these are my friends Sesame Serpent and Sammy Cat."

"Sammy!" one girl cried. The fence dissolved back into

Stuff, which then disappeared. Sammy joined the girls and received some heavy petting.

The girls turned out to be Mol and Kel. Mol's talent was creating; Kel's was molding. So Mol had created the mass of Stuff, and Kel had shaped it into the fence. Both were more than willing to do Umlaut a favor, now that they knew he was with Sammy.

"Well, uh, if you can make us a bridge across the river, we'd appreciate that."

"We will," Mol said, kissing him on the left ear.

"Right away," Kel added, kissing his right ear.

"Uh, thanks."

They walked to the river. Mol made a huge mass of blue Stuff, and Kel shaped it into an arch that fell across the river. It was not Xanth's fanciest bridge, but it sufficed. They climbed carefully across it to the other side of the river. The girls followed, bending down to hang on to the arch with their hands, not awfully careful about how much of their legs showed. Umlaut tried not to look, without success.

"Uh, thanks," Umlaut said in his usual awkward fashion.

"We can do more than that," Mol said, kissing his left ear again.

"Much more," Kel agreed, kissing his right ear again.

Umlaut sort of liked it but knew that he couldn't dally here. "We, uh, have to get on to the Good Magician's Castle."

"Too bad," Mol said. "Maybe on the way back?"

"Uh, maybe." He wasn't sure exactly what they had in mind, but was mightily tempted.

They moved on. Sesame glanced at him sidelong, and he knew why: He was awkward and clumsy and nothing special in his natural state, so why did girls like him? It was a mystery.

They made it without further event to the real Good Magician's Castle, which looked exactly like the cardboard replica, except that the moat water was real and so, surely, was the stone in the walls.

"Now all we have to do is enter the castle, ask for the Good Magician, and ask him what to do about that Red Spot," Umlaut said. "How complicated can that be?"

But Sammy Cat stirred restlessly, and Sesame Serpent looked doubtful. What was their problem?

Then he saw that the way across the bridge was blocked by an enormous pile of large jigsaw puzzle pieces. Each piece was painted with black or white squares. Some of the white squares had letters of the alphabet on them, and some had numbers in their corners. "What's this mess?" he asked.

Sammy Cat started to go into a series of motions and gestures indicating a complicated explanation, but Umlaut cut him off. "We don't have time for this. Let's just go around this rubble."

Still they were doubtful. Sammy was contemplating the puzzle pieces, and Sesame was staring at the moat. Now Umlaut looked at the moat too but saw nothing untoward. "We can swim across; there's no slime in that water."

But the moment he stepped toward the water, an array of swimming monsters appeared. He wasn't sure of their exact types, but they all seemed to have gleaming eyes, sharp fins, and big teeth. "Maybe it's too cool to swim."

He decided that he did have time after all to fathom what Sammy had to say. He questioned the cat and soon understood. "You mean this is a challenge? We can't get inside unless we handle three challenges? That's ridiculous!"

Yet it seemed to be so. Sammy knew something about the Good Magician's little eccentricities. He did not like to be bothered by frivolous questions, so he put obstacles in the way of querents (it was a struggle to elicit that obscure term from the cat; it meant people who asked questions) and refused to talk to them unless they got past them. Apparently only a few had the stamina or wit to handle the challenges, so the Good Magician was not bothered too often. So here was a challenge, and they had either to handle it or give up and go away, which might satisfy the magician.

For some reason he couldn't quite identify, that annoyed Umlaut. "Here we come to ask a question that may enable us to save Earth and Xanth from destruction or worse, and we have to go through this nonsense." The others agreed but had no way to bypass the nonsense.

There was something about the pile of puzzle pieces they had to understand or handle, in order to get by them. What could that be? Umlaut was just about annoyed enough to tackle it. If only he could figure out how.

He picked up a white piece with the letter C on it. He turned it over, but it was blank on back. He looked at another, with the letter A. There seemed to be many different letters. What was he supposed to do with them?

He looked at Sammy and Sesame, but they had no better idea than he did.

"Well, maybe if I put them in order," he said. He laid down the A and searched through the pile for a B, then added the C. He continued until he had the whole alphabet and the numbers 0 through 9. But when it was complete, nothing happened. Also, there were many duplicate letters left in the pile, which hardly seemed diminished. So this did not seem to be the answer.

"Maybe if I made a word or two." He collected letters and spelled out GOOD MAGICIAN. Still nothing happened.

He had had enough. "What am I going to do with you?"

There was a stir in the air. A cloud formed. A voice issued from it. "What did you have in intellect?"

"In what?"

"Reason, sense, recall, understanding, memory—"

"Mind?"

"Whatever," the cloud replied crossly.

"Hello, Demoness Metria."

The cloud shaped into a divinely human figure. Fortunately this time it was covered by a reasonably proper dress that extended from neck to ankles, so Umlaut did not lose control of his eyeballs. "How did you know it was me?"

"I made a wild guess and got lucky. What brings you here?"

"You seemed to be eager to do something, so naturally I came to be a part of it."

"Why?"

"Because I get dulled by routine."

"Do you mean bored?"

"That's not the prescribed format."

"I'm tired of that kind. Here I'm supposed to figure out what to do with these bleeping blocks, and I hate it."

"Oooo, what you said!"

"Well, I'm annoyed. Do you have any idea what to do with them?"

She gazed at the pile. "Dump them into the moat?"

Umlaut considered that. He looked at Sammy and Sesame. It was true that they had not yet tried that.

He picked up the *A* block and tossed it at the water. It sailed around in a loop and landed back on the pile. "Why did I have this nasty suspicion that that wouldn't work?"

"I have no idea," the demoness said. "I'm still waiting for you to tell me what you had in mind for me."

"I don't have anything in mind for you! I was talking about this confounded pile of pieces."

"Then it must be time for a diversion." Her dress shrank a size.

"No it isn't!" Umlaut said. He was beginning to appreciate why Breanna had been short with the demoness. It was hard to get things done efficiently while she was distracting people.

"Not even one this size?" The dress shrank another size, but the body didn't; things were getting rather tight.

"No size! Go away!"

"There must be something really interesting going on," Metria said, looking around. Umlaut realized that he should not have demanded that she depart. It had the effect of stiffening her resolve to remain.

So he tried to make the best of it. "We're up against some sort of challenge and can't figure it out. But if we can't, you can't either, so you might as well not bother to try."

"Right. There is no point in trying. Let's consider storks." Her dress shrank another size, revealing a bit too much flesh.

He realized that she must have caught on. She wasn't here to help, anyway. He tried to ignore her, but it was not possible to ignore that exposed flesh. His eyes struggled but soon locked relentlessly into place.

Only his voice remained. "Get your uncovered hide out of here!" he said crossly.

There was a stir by the bridge. The demoness heard it and turned to look. In the process she freed Umlaut's eyes. He quickly shaded them with his hand so as not to get caught again when she turned back.

"Now *that's* interesting," Metria murmured, gazing at the bridge.

Indeed it was. The puzzle pieces were moving by themselves, forming a tall, slick wall with a display of letters across and downward.

"What's going on?" he asked, amazed.

"It's forming a crossword puzzle," Metria replied. "How did you make it do that?"

"I didn't. I was just trying to get rid of you, and suddenly it started."

"No, it had to be you, because you're the querent. What did you say to it?"

"Nothing! I told you to get your uncovered hide out of here."

"So you did," she agreed. "And naturally I was about to respond by uncovering it the rest of the way, like this."

Umlaut clapped his hand completely across his eyes just in time to shut out the eyeball-gluing sight. Some other time he might have liked to have peeked, but he knew better than to yield at this moment. "So I did nothing. Now you can go."

"You have to have done article."

He knew better than this too but couldn't stop himself. "Done what?"

"Deed, item, being, exploit, procedure—"

"Something?"

"Whatever," she agreed crossly.

Then a bulb flashed over his head. "Cross! That's what did it."

"Did what?"

"Solved the challenge! It's a crossword puzzle. I said a cross word."

"But I was cross before you were, and it didn't do anything."

"You're not the one with the challenge."

She considered a moment. "I think he's got it. Curses, foiled again." She was silent.

For a moment Umlaut thought she was still there. Then Sesame nudged him, and he looked. The demoness was gone.

"She was trying to mess me up, and instead she helped me

handle the challenge," he said. "No wonder she was cross."
Then he laughed. It certainly served her right.

They looked at the crossword wall. It had an intricate display of words across and down that interlinked. For example,
the word CROSS went across, and the word WORD crossed
it going down, using the same O. Umlaut had not seen such
a device before and was intrigued. It seemed to be a fairly
efficient way to write words, because the sharing of letters
meant that more words could be made without expanding the
number of letters. Black squares showed where the words
ended, and those squares formed a neat pattern across the
board. There was a certain crude art to it.

However, the wall still blocked off the drawbridge.
(DRAW shared the letter D with BRIDGE.) He was sure he
couldn't go around it. So either there was more to the puzzle
than he had solved so far, or this was another challenge. Either way, he had to figure it out.

Now he saw that not all the white spaces had letters. Some
were blank. Also, there were words on either side of the puzzle squares. On the left it said *Across*, and on the right it said
Down, and of course those did not manage to share their O.
He wondered whether that made them feel unfulfilled.

Sammy nudged his leg. He looked down. The cat walked
up to the left-side words and rubbed against them.

Oh. He needed to pay attention to what they said, instead
of merely admiring the overall form.

The words turned out to be questions. The first was 1
across: WHO ARE YOU?

"I am Umlaut, of course," he said. "Does it matter?" But
of course it was foolish to talk to a board. He had heard of
a king who could talk to inanimate things and make them
answer, but that was not his own talent.

So why was this board asking him his name?

Sesame nudged his right arm. He looked, and she moved
her snout forward to touch the central portion of the board.
There was a series of blanks—one of the missing words.

Once again a bulb flashed. "Maybe my name fits there!"

Now he saw that a few loose blocks remained. He sorted
through them, picking out the letters of his name. U LAUT.

But the *M* was missing. How could he fill it in with a letter missing?

Then he cursed himself for a fool. He put the letters into place. The letter *M* was there, in another word that his name crossed.

The second hint said: 2 down: WHERE ARE YOU GO-ING?

"Into the Good Magician's Castle," he said impatiently. But he saw immediately that that didn't fit. So he tried again. "On a quest." That didn't fit, either.

Sammy nudged him. He looked down. The cat had scratched a bare place on the ground and set a red cherry in the center of it. What was the significance of that?

Then yet another bulb flashed. "Red Spot!" he exclaimed. "I'm on a quest to solve the problem of the Red Spot!"

But that was two words, and there was space for only one word, six letters long. The last letter was *T*, because it intersected the end of his crosswise name.

But if he jammed them together, it would make one word. Quickly he gathered letters and filled in REDSPOT.

The third hint said 3 down: WHAT IS THIS?

"A bleeping nuisance," he said with half a smile. But it took him only a moment, or perhaps an instant and a half, to come up with the missing word, because it overlapped the *A* in his name. He gathered the letters and filled it in. CHAL-LENGE.

The board flashed. He had solved the second challenge, with the help of his friends.

But it still blocked the way across the bridge. What remained to be done?

"The third challenge," he muttered. "It must relate to this in some way. What can it be?"

He had no idea. He gazed at the board, pondering. Was there something wrong with it? He didn't see anything.

He looked at his companions. They had gone to sleep. Sesame had formed a neat coil, with Sammy snoozing on top of it. The serpent's head rested comfortably on a checkered box. On the box was the word SPELL.

Still another bulb flashed. Umlaut had never had so many go off in such a short time; he was lucky his head wasn't burning out. "That has to be a spell checker," he said. "To check the spelling of the puzzle."

He leaned down, carefully moved Sesame's head to the side, and picked up the box. It was featureless, aside from the word and design. How was he supposed to use it?

He shook it. It rattled. "Oh, it's a box," he said. "There's something inside."

Sammy made a *Duh!* expression.

Umlaut turned the box over. Nothing there. He felt around its sides. He found a panel that felt slightly loose. He pushed it to the side, and it slid across to reveal a button. He pushed the button, and the top of the box sprang open. He had figured it out, mostly by chance, mishap, and blind luck, as was his usual mode. Rather than being a box to check spelling, maybe it was a checkered box holding spells.

Inside were several small objects. They didn't look like spells, but of course he had no idea what a solid spell looked like. He picked out a pair of two little horns. They expanded in his hands, becoming the size of feet. He tried blowing into one, but it made no sound. So maybe they weren't horns. In that case, what were they?

He tried putting one on his foot. It fit. It was a shoe! He put the other on, and it fit well enough. But when he tried to walk in them, he tripped. It wasn't him, it was the shoes; they refused to go anywhere. Something was wrong with them.

He set them aside and took out another object. This one resembled a slice of bread, and it too expanded in his hand to normal size. But when he tried to take a bite of it, he couldn't; the thing was rubbery and inedible. Maybe it was supposed to be food, but there was something wrong with it, just as was the case with the shoes.

He tried another object. This looked like a statuette of a woman with rather healthy thighs under her skirt. She wore a hat that looked like a lens on top, almost as if it were meant to shine a light. Maybe this was a decorative flashlight. He pointed the lens and squeezed the body, but nothing happened. So maybe this was another broken spell.

Another object looked like a small piece of cake. It expanded in his hand, and now it looked more like a ramp or path, or perhaps a walk. Cake in the shape of a walk? "Cakewalk!" he said. But nothing happened. He had either misunderstood, or this was another broken spell.

"Everything in this box seems to be broken," he said. "Maybe the challenge is to fix them. But I don't know the first thing about magic, or even the second or third things. How can I fix what I don't understand?"

Sammy Cat looked at him as if he were being stupid. Cats were good at that, he realized. So how was he being stupid?

"Maybe I'm taking too much on myself," he said. "These challenges must be for all three of us. What do you folk think of this?"

Sesame wriggled, so he went into the nineteen-questions routine with her and learned that she thought he should look for another spell: one to check and fix the others. That could be the challenge: to find out how to use the tool he had.

It did seem to make sense. He checked the other objects and spied one that looked like a checker in the game of checkers. That was bound to be it. A single checker did not make a checker game, so it must be another kind of checker. A spell checker.

He held it in his hand and touched it to a shoe horn. The horn honked with a big bass rumble. He touched the other, and it honked with a delicate ladylike titter. The horns were working now.

He put the shoes on his feet again. This time they walked with him, and with each step they honked. *HONK! Honkie. HONK! Honkie.* It was a wild combination. They certainly were a pair of shoe horns, sounding off as they hit the ground. The spell checker had checked and fixed them.

He touched the checker to the inedible slice of bread. The slice heated and turned dark at the edges. It was toasting! It was a piece of toast.

He was about to try a bite when a toothy fish leaped out of the moat, snapped up the toast, and landed back in the water. "Hey!" Umlaut protested. "You stole my toast!"

But the fish did not get to enjoy its stolen morsel. Another fish bit off half of it before the first fish could swallow it. Then both fish looked stricken. They rolled over on their backs and floated there, dead to the world.

Umlaut stared. Just what kind of toast was this? Was the Good Magician trying to poison him?

Then he laughed, catching on. "It's coma toast!" he exclaimed. "It puts folk into a coma."

There was a groan from the moat. Not from the comatose fish but from others around them. They had heard the pun.

Umlaut touched the checker to the statuette light. It abruptly grew into a full-sized woman. "Well, I never!" she said and walked away. Her thighs glowed right through her skirt.

"Cellulight," Umlaut murmured appreciatively. Another spell had been fixed. There was another groan from the moat.

He touched the checker to the cakewalk. It expanded, extending toward the crossword board and through it. The board disappeared, and the walk went on across the bridge, unrolling like a red carpet.

"I believe we have resolved the third challenge," Umlaut said. He glanced at the moat. "What does your kind think of that?" But he got no answer; the moat monsters had disappeared.

They followed the red carpet across the moat and into the castle. A young woman met them at the gate. "Hello, Umlaut, Sesame, Sammy," she said. "I am Wira, the Good Magician's daughter-in-law. Please come this way." She turned and walked into the castle.

There was something odd about her. It wasn't that she knew their names. Humfrey was the Magician of Information, so he knew everything worth knowing; naturally he had their names. It was something about the way she had looked at them.

Sammy nudged him. When he looked at the cat, he put a paw over his face as if he couldn't see, then pointed the paw at Wira.

"She can't see?" Umlaut asked, surprised.

"It is true," Wira said without turning. "I am blind. But I know my way around the castle."

Umlaut was glad she couldn't see him blushing. He had forgotten that it wasn't safe to talk to the animals while a person was listening.

Wira brought them to a pleasant interior chamber. There

was a tall veiled woman. "This is the Gorgon, Humfrey's designated wife this month," she said. "Mother Gorgon, there are Umlaut, Sesame, and Sammy, here with a question."

"Of course," the Gorgon said. "The Good Magician will be with you in a moment." She proffered a plate of cheese. "Have some Gorgonzola."

Umlaut belatedly remembered something. "You—aren't you—?"

"The one who stones those who see my face," she finished for him. "Fortunately I wear a veil, as you may have noticed."

"Uh, yes," Umlaut agreed, embarrassed again. He was not socially precocious, as someone he couldn't remember had informed him some time back. Or to put it into words he had less trouble understanding, he could be sort of stupid around people. Maybe that was why he related so well to animals. He took a piece of cheese and tasted it. It was very good.

The Gorgon offered the plate to Sammy, who pawed off a piece, and then she fed a piece to Sesame. The woman did not seem to find it odd that two of the visitors were animals.

"Do you understand that the Good Magician requires a year's service, or the equivalent, from each querent?" the Gorgon asked.

Oops. Umlaut had forgotten about that. He looked at the other two. They shrugged. "I suppose," he said. It seemed unkind to make them serve when they were only trying to save Xanth from a horrible threat, but the Good Magician had a well-earned reputation for being grumpy and difficult. This was going to interfere with their plan to explore Xanth.

When they finished the cheese, Wira returned. She had faded out without their noticing; she was very quiet. "The Good Magician will see you now."

They followed her up a winding flight of stairs. Umlaut was interested to see how Sesame's torso bent to conform to the stairs, in a series of steps. She had a marvelously limber body.

They came to a tiny, dingy, dusky study surrounded by books. In the center was a gnomelike man on a high stool, poring over a huge tome. That was the famous Book of Answers, the secret of his power of information. "The querents are here, Father," Wira said and faded back.

"We want to know how to save Xanth from the Red Spot," Umlaut said.

The gnome looked up. "Deliver the letters."

"The zombies are doing that," Umlaut said. "What about the Red Spot?"

Humfrey didn't answer. His eyes were back on the tome.

Wira reappeared. "That is the Answer," she murmured.

"The Answer? It sounds more like the Service."

"That, too," Wira agreed. "Now you must go. He gets grumpy when visitors linger too long."

Soon they found themselves back with the Gorgon, who seemed like a far more reasonable figure compared to the magician. "He didn't tell us how to stop the Red Spot," Umlaut complained, "just to deliver the letters. But the zombies are already doing that."

"It has become your task," the Gorgon said. "Humfrey's answers always make sense, once understood. You must do as he says, and it will work out."

Umlaut saw that this made no more sense to Sammy and Sesame than it did to him. But what else could they do? It hadn't occurred to him that the worst of the challenges would be to figure out what the Answer meant.

4

MOONS OF IDA

Back at Castle Zombie, Breanna was surprised. "Humfrey told you to deliver the letters? And that's the Answer as well as the Service? That's even crazier than usual for him."

"For sure," Umlaut said with a grim smile, borrowing her phrase. "But it seems we have to do it."

"It seems you do," she agreed. "We'll help you however we can. We can locate the folk the letters go to, for one thing."

"Sammy Cat can do that."

She nodded. "I forgot about him. Well, I'll turn the letters over to you. But there's one thing—"

"We have to read them first," he said, "so nobody else gets mad enough to hurl anything at us."

"For sure. There was one addressed to me, so I took it. It was perfectly innocent, congratulating me on my wedding to Justin Tree and wishing us well. Nothing to make me want to throw anything at anybody. But we can't trust any of them, after the way Demon Jupiter reacted." She brought him a package of letters. "I guess you can just carry them along with you and make a big circle route, delivering them more efficiently. But this is going to be a big job, regardless, with a whole lot of traveling."

"Well, we did want to travel," he said bravely.

"You will certainly do that! Those letters go all over Xanth. Which one will you start on?"

Umlaut was at a loss. "I haven't thought about that. I don't even know to whom they go."

"Maybe just close your eyes and pick one."

"There should be more design to it than that, I think. Some must be more pressing than others. But which ones?"

Sesame nudged his elbow. He looked at her. "You have an opinion? Let's have it."

They went into nineteen questions, and he got her point: The letters were not necessarily important in themselves but as a mechanism to discover how to stop the Red Spot from obliterating Earth and Xanth. So they should look for that letter, not a random one.

"Good point," Umlaut said. "But I still have no way of judging which the key letter is."

"Ask Sammy," Breanna suggested.

He turned to the cat. "Sammy, where is the letter with the Answer?"

But the cat turned his back and settled down on a zombie pillow for a snooze.

"That's his way of saying he doesn't know," Breanna said. "Cats don't like to admit ignorance. Maybe it's not in a letter but in something that will be discovered when the letter is delivered."

"So we're back to circle one," Umlaut said morosely.

But Sesame had another idea. After about fourteen questions he got it: "The Zombie Master! He must know, because the letters are being delivered to Castle Zombie. It must be something that got set up before and fell in the crevice."

A puff of smoke appeared. "Fell in the what?"

"Cleft, chink, slit, flaw, rift—"

"Crack?" the cloud inquired, forming into a head with a face.

"Whatever," Umlaut agreed crossly. "Hello, Metria."

The rest of the body formed, heaves and all. "So what are you up to now?"

Umlaut had caught on to her nature. If he tried to pretend it was nothing, she would be assured that it was something. Then she would stay around, exercising his helpless eyeballs until they smoked. So he told the truth, hoping it would bore her so that she would depart. "We're delivering letters."

"Why bother?"

"The Good Magician says this will solve the problem of Demon Jupiter's Red Spot."

"Oh, that. Utterly drilling."

"Utterly what?"

"Boring!" Breanna said quickly. "Now if you're not going to help, why don't you seduce him and be done with it."

"Never!" The demoness faded out.

Umlaut stared at her. "You told her to seduce me?"

"You have to know how to handle her. She was trying to do that, so I told her to do it, so she reversed, a victim of her own perversity. But that dodge won't work again. You'll have to figure out some other gimmick. Meanwhile, get on your way to Princess Ida."

"But I thought we had decided to start with the Zombie Master."

"He's now residing at his retirement home, Zombie World. That's the nth Moon of Ida."

"The whath moon?"

"It's so far along the chain that we don't know what number it is in the series. But he set up a shortcut to it, or at least a marked path. Princess Ida will set it up for you. In fact, I think there's a letter to her in the pile; you can drop two stones with one bird." She handed him a knapsack. "I put the letters in here. Remember, read each one before you deliver it, just in case."

"Princess Ida," he agreed, salvaging what he could of this as he donned the knapsack. "Where is she?"

Sammy launched out of his nap and headed for the horizon. "Castle Roogna," Breanna said. "That way." She pointed after the cat.

"Wait for us!" he cried, running after Sammy. But he was already far behind. How had Jenny Elf ever managed to keep up with this feline?

Sesame slithered beside him, traveling far more readily

through the mixed brush. She gave him a look and a nod.

Taking the hint, he emulated a light serpent rider and jumped on her back. His hands clung to her sleek scales, and she formed a niche to hold him in place. Then, sniffing the scent of the disappeared cat, she slithered on at a swift rate.

"Thanks!" he gasped.

They slithered rapidly through glade and forest, o'er hill and dale, and across a river or two. It all went by so rapidly he hardly had time to assimilate it.

Until they came to a third river. There was something swimming in it that Sesame didn't understand, so she stopped at the bank. She could scare back sharks or allegations, but it wasn't smart to swim with an unknown menace.

But it turned out to be a boy. He spied them and waded out. He had gills on his neck and fins on his arms and legs, but these faded as he came ashore. "My name's Kiel," he said. "I have the talent of adaptation. When I want to swim, I grow gills and fins; when I want to fly, I grow wings."

"I'm Umlaut, with the talent of emulation. But I can't take it nearly as far as you can. I just halfway look the part; I'm not real. It is similar with Sesame here."

"Too bad," Kiel said. He dived back into the water, forming gills again as he did.

They concluded that the water must be safe and swam across. Umlaut was a bit jealous of those who had more substantial talents than he did, but he didn't want to say so.

Soon a fancy castle hove into view. This was surely Castle Roogna, famed residence of King Dor and Queen Irene. Umlaut wondered whether there would be three challenges to get into it, but that turned out not to be the case.

Sammy ran right past the snoozing moat monster and into the castle, and Sesame slithered after him. Three little girls appeared, looking to be about six years old. One had a nice green dress, another a brown dress, and the third a red dress, and their hair seemed to match. All three wore cute little crowns.

Sammy tried to run past them, followed closely by Umlaut and Sesame, but one hummed a melody, the second played a harmonica, and the third beat on a little drum. Suddenly a magic web held the three visitors in stasis. This was strong magic.

"Who are you?" the first asked. Then she answered her own question. "Sammy Cat!"

Everybody knew Sammy!

The magic eased, turning them loose. "And I'm Umlaut, and this is Sesame Serpent," Umlaut said, completing the introduction. "We're looking for Princess Ida."

"We're the three princesses, Melody, Harmony, and Rhythm," the second child said.

"You don't want to eat Aunt Ida, do you?" the third asked, looking at Sesame.

"We just want to give her a letter," Umlaut said quickly. "And visit Zombie World."

"Oh, that's all right," the first princess said. Umlaut thought she must be Melody, because they seemed to speak in turns, as she was the first to have spoken and the first one named.

"She's nice," the one who must be Harmony said.

"Next door down," the one who must be Rhythm said. Sammy took off again.

"Thank you, Princesses," Umlaut said, hurrying after the cat.

The princesses faded out, literally. Umlaut was sure they weren't demons, but they evidently had some magic tricks.

The door opened as they reached it. A sensible-seeming adult woman stood there. She wore a conservative crown too. A tiny sphere revolved around her head. "Princess Ida?" Umlaut inquired somewhat breathlessly.

"Indeed," the woman agreed.

"We—"

"The princesses told me," Ida said. "Do come in."

Thus they found themselves in her small chamber. Sesame coiled tightly to fit.

"We have—" Umlaut began again.

"A letter for me? How nice!"

"Only—"

"You have to read it first? Be welcome."

Princess Ida seemed to have a pretty good grasp of the situation. Umlaut took off the knapsack and sorted through it

until he found the letter addressed to PRINCESS IDA, CAS-
TLE ROOGNA, LAND OF XANTH.

This was embarrassing. He should have looked at the letter
before coming here, but somehow there had been no time.
"It's because—"

"There can be severe negative reactions," the princess said.
She handed him a simple letter opener.

"Uh, yes." He slit open the letter and unfolded the single
sheet of paper within. "Uh, maybe if I read it aloud."

"That will be fine," Princess Ida agreed.

Umlaut remained embarrassed, but there was nothing to do
but plow on. He cleared his throat and read:

Dear Princess Ida,

Despite your living in Xanth and me in Mundania, I
believe we have a great deal in common.

Around your head orbits Ptero. On that planet is Pyramid, Torus, Cone, Tangle, and who knows how many
others.

I too have worlds swirling around, only luckily they
are on the inside and not visible. If others were to see
them, I would immediately be institutionalized by med-
ical "experts" and labeled as "mentally challenged" (being encouraged to think deeper is a good thing, but the
term recently has been given negative connotations). If
that didn't happen, the other probability would result in
my being incarcerated in some creepy government sci-
entific laboratory where they would perform numerous
unspeakable "tests" on my brain. Using an understated
summary: Mundania is weird.

My world is concepts, or complex thoughts and ideas.
One of them is called Creative Chaos. Many people live
there; some of the most important are named Character,
Imagination, Mythology, Dreamer, and Designer. Another world is called Hort City, in which resides all the
plant life of this portion of Mundania. One is called Literature. There dwell all the great and mighty words of
past centuries, as well as ones that have come to be today. There are many, many more. Vestiges of everyone
of our realm who ever lived, or ever will exist, are there.

This all requires a great deal of controlled organization. At times worlds are permitted to merge and run amok. Then a new manifestation is created. This one is called Stress—a very common affliction here in Mundania, yet one to be avoided at all costs.

Though my various worlds are populated by an infinite number of beings, I am thankful that there are no actual real visitors. If others intruded, I fear the Stress Sector would become a dictator state. I admire your coping abilities.

Sincerely,
Arjayess

Umlaut looked up. "That's the whole of it. Seems like a nice enough letter. No cause to hurl anything."

"Indeed not," Princess Ida agreed. "Yet I commend your caution, for we certainly don't want any more mischief thrown our way."

"You seem like a nice person," Umlaut said. He realized he was being patronizing. "I mean, for a princess." That was worse. "Uh—"

Princess Ida laughed. "Thank you. I see you encountered the three mischievous little princesses."

"Yes," he said gratefully. She had nicely defused his clumsiness, making it seem as if he had reason to question the niceness of princesses. She *was* a nice person. "Um, if you don't mind my asking, just what is your magic talent?"

"Let's hold that answer in abeyance for the nonce," she said. "Now you must go on to deliver the Zombie Master's letter. That will be a bit more complicated."

"Uh, yes," he agreed. "The letters were found in Castle Zombie, so we thought maybe he would know something about them."

"Surely he will," she agreed. She was a very agreeable person. She glanced at Sammy and Sesame. "With Sammy to locate the Zombie Master or Millie the Ghost once you reach Zombie World, and Sesame to facilitate travel there, you certainly seem to have planned well for this expedition."

Of course he hadn't planned it at all; it had just happened. "Well—"

"I don't wish to bore you, but I need to be certain you understand the refinements of this particular expedition," Princess Ida continued. "You see, you will not be able to visit that realm physically. Only your three souls will travel there. Your bodies will be safe here, of course, and most of your souls."

Umlaut wasn't sure he liked the sound of this. "*Most* of?"

"There is a series of worlds, each rather smaller than the prior, so less of your soul is required. By the time you reach Zombie World, the amount is almost infinitesimally tiny. So the great majority of your souls will remain with your bodies. But do not be concerned—you will be fully aware and real on Zombie World. When it is time to return, merely concentrate on that, and you will very soon awaken here, your mission accomplished."

"But if there are so many worlds, how can we ever find our way?"

"Sammy will lead you. Fortunately the Zombie Master prepared a shortcut route for visitors to follow. He felt that necessary because zombies are not necessarily the most alert folk, and he did not want them to become lost. They go there to retire, not to wander endlessly in foreign worlds."

"Uh, yes." Umlaut found this more confusing than he cared to admit. "I wouldn't want to get lost."

"Wouldn't it be awful if one lost its way in a comic strip! All those dreadful puns. Zombies don't have much of a sense of humor; that portion of their brains is among the first to rot out." She paused reflectively. "I wonder whether that is the problem with those notorious cri-tics? A rotting of their brains. That would account for a lot."

"I guess," Umlaut agreed doubtfully. What was a comic strip? What was a cri-tic? Maybe he was better off not knowing.

"Meanwhile I shall settle down to compose a response to Arjayess in Mundania," Princess Ida said. "She is correct: We do have things in common. It was nice of her to write."

Umlaut wondered how she knew the letter writer was female, but he didn't ask. Maybe it had to do with her magic talent, the one she didn't care to tell him about yet.

Princess Ida had them settle down comfortably, as if for

sleep. Umlaut and Sammy Cat lay on Sesame's resilient coils. Then the princess brought something for them to sniff. First Sammy, whom she cautioned not to race ahead too fast, then Umlaut.

He sniffed and found himself rising out of his sleeping body. It was weird. The body lay there, but he was an ethereal being passing through it, floating in space just above it. It was unconscious, but it had his substance. He was—just his soul.

He looked around and spied a floating blob hovering above the sleeping cat. "Sammy!" he called and had to form a mouth to do it, and a head to support the mouth, and a body to bear the head. He looked down at himself and saw his cloudy substance assuming his natural form; all it took was concentration.

Meanwhile Sammy was forming his own body, converting from blob to cat. He looked at Umlaut and issued a soundless *Mew!* For there did not seem to be sound here, though it seemed they could hear each other.

A third shape rose, issuing from the coils of Sesame Serpent. The shape was twisting around uncertainly, threatening to tie itself into a knot.

"Here, Sesame!" Umlaut called silently. "Form your image!"

The end part of the stretched-out cloud turned to point at him. Then her body took shape. She was learning how to do it.

Umlaut looked around again, this time beyond their little group. And suffered an odd vision. Princess Ida was sitting there, surprisingly large, gazing blankly through them. She couldn't see them but knew they were there. She lifted one hand and pointed to the little moon that orbited her head. Ptero, it was called. Where they were going.

He oriented on that moon, and it seemed to swell in size. So did Princess Ida. She was now a giant, and the room about her was astonishingly huge and getting larger.

Oh—they were getting smaller! "Go for the moon!" Umlaut called to the others.

Sammy came to life and bounded for Ptero. How he bounded Umlaut wasn't sure, as there was nothing to bound on, but the cat was moving well. Umlaut followed, moving his legs in a running motion, and that worked too. Sesame slithered, and that worked as well as the bounding and running did. Umlaut couldn't feel any ground and knew he was floating in air, yet he was moving just as if there was solidity there.

Planet Ptero looked ever larger. Now it seemed that they were falling toward it, and the reason it looked so big was that they were getting closer. One of the magic things about the Land of Xanth was called perspective, in which distant things made themselves look small, and close things looked large. Now Ptero was doing it too.

Then he saw a trail of glowing footprints in the air. They were somewhat sloppy around the edges, as if the shoe leather was rotting. The Zombie Master's marked route to the Zombie World! Sammy was bounding along it, but anybody could have followed it.

The trail led right down to the surface of the planet, which was now enormous. The tracks came to touch the land, showing the way to a distant castle. They followed. Umlaut was hardly aware of the scenery, except that it was pretty, with colored fog shrouding the distances.

"Please help!"

That was real sound: a maiden's voice. Umlaut looked and saw a tangled mess of foliage to the side, and beyond it on a small hill a pretty girl without a lot of clothing on. He paused for a better view. "Who are you? What's wrong?" he called to her.

"I'm Caitlin," she called back. "I can't tell you what's wrong."

This was odd. "Why not?"

"Because I have the talent of knowing when, not what. This is the time, but that's all I know."

"Then how do you know you need help?"

"This is the time of my crisis. Something awful will happen if I don't get help. So please help me. It will take only a moment. I earnestly beseech you, kind traveler."

Umlaut looked at Sammy and Sesame, who had paused when he did. "Can we spare a moment?"

They both looked doubtful. The Zombie Master's track went forward, not to the side. But Caitlin was so earnestly beseeching him for help it was difficult to refuse. He decided to spare a moment.

He left the trail and walked to the tangled foliage. It was in a strip that extended between him and the maiden. He was about to step into it when Sesame slithered before him, shaking her head.

Umlaut hesitated, for he knew Sesame was trying to look out for his welfare. But then Caitlin made a cute pleading gesture, and his resolve returned. "Why not?" he asked. "She needs help, and it's only a moment."

The serpent was insistent, so he played nineteen questions with her and learned that she recognized the area by Princess Ida's description: It was a comic strip. One of the locations where egregious puns abided. A place to be avoided.

"But there's no way around," Umlaut protested. "I have to cross."

Sesame nevertheless felt that this distraction should not be allowed. They should go on to deliver the letter to the Zombie Master and then help the damsel on the return route if she still needed it. That made sense.

Caitlin leaned forward imploringly. The front of her blouse was a bit low and loose. Umlaut decided that the best thing to do was help her now. He stepped over the serpent and into the tangle.

He found himself standing chest deep in a small field of grain. To one side was a sign identifying a red patch as YOUR GRAIN. To the other side was a green patch marked HIS GRAIN. In front was a scintillating silvery-white patch marked MY GRAIN. That was nice to know; he must be going the right way, though he could no longer see the damsel in distress. Fortunately he had not yet encountered any bad puns.

He tried to push on forward, but the standing grain was too thick. Then he saw another little sign: EAT ME. Maybe he had to eat some in order to get through it. So he took a few silvery-white grains and put them in his mouth.

Immediately there was a shining silvery-white bar before his eyes. He reached out to take it, but his hand passed through it—it was illusion. Then his head began to ache. The ache was awful; in fact it felt as if his head was about to explode. What had brought this on? All he had done was take a mouthful of my grain.

A dim bulb flashed. He had heard of that. It gave folk terrible headaches. He hadn't swallowed the grain, so he spat it out.

The pain faded. The grain remained, but it no longer was as thick. He had fallen afoul of a dreadful pun but figured it out in time, so it could no longer hurt him. That was just as well, because he would not care to have another headache like that. Ever.

But now he was mired in the comic strip. He looked back, but the grain had closed in solidly behind him. He had to proceed forward. He saw several paths; which one was best for his purpose? They had labels: G, PG, PG-13, R, and X. He had no idea what the labels meant; maybe they referred to whoever had made the paths. The most open route seemed to be X; it went straight ahead with no artistic diversions. Naturally he took that one. He stepped onto it.

Some cloth appeared, curtaining the path. On it were the words WARNING: POTENTIALLY OBJECTIONABLE MATERIAL FOR PRUDES. P TRAP.

"I don't care what it is," Umlaut muttered, pushing on by. "I just want to get across this comic strip."

Beyond the cloth veil the scene changed. He stood amid a group of attractive young women. "Well, now, what have we here?" one murmured dulcetly. She had a rather eye-catchingly full white blouse.

"I'm just passing through, if you please," Umlaut said. So many pretty girls so close made him a bit nervous, because he was nothing special, and he hadn't thought to emulate anything special.

"This looks like a teenage boy," another woman said. She had an eyeball-locking full posterior.

"Who perhaps has not yet joined the Adult Conspiracy," a third woman said. She had pupil-dilating firm thighs just below a too-short skirt.

"Perhaps we should do him a favor, then," the first said. She drew open her blouse to show a bra overflowing with gently heaving flesh.

"And overcome the Adult Conspiracy by showing him our

P's," the second said. She started to draw down her skirt.

Suddenly Umlaut caught on. This was a path of ill repute! They were about to show him things they knew no boy under age eighteen should see.

He turned and lurched back past the cloth veil. Now he recognized its shape: panties! Had they been occupied, he would have freaked out. The P trap wasn't a prude trap, it was a panty trap. And those women had been about to spring it. What would have happened to him if he had seen panties?

He lunged on back off the path. Now he understood the designations: they were ratings, and X was the forbidden one. He had foolishly blundered right onto it. This was worse than a mere pun; it was dangerous.

He reoriented and this time took the G-rated path. That led him through a pleasant garden and on to a bridge across a ditch. He could see that the ditch was filled with festering puns, beginning with a small offshoot labeled SON OF A DITCH. He did not want to get down into that, so he would cross the bridge. But he was cautious, realizing that everything in this region was a moderate pun, a bad pun, or, worst of all, an egregious pun. He had to be careful where he set his feet, lest he step on a pun and get it all over his shoe. Yuck!

The bridge was labeled CANTILEVER. He had heard of the principle: a vertical post with a horizontal projection, counterbalancing the business end of the bridge. That was all right to use. He could see the damsel in distress on the other side, so he had made progress. Soon he would be with her and able to help.

He set a cautious foot on the bridge. Nothing happened. He took another step. No problem. Still, he didn't quite trust this. He had encountered no pun, and there was bound to be one. Where was it lurking?

He decided to retreat while he considered. He wanted to figure this out before he got caught, rather than after. He didn't want to risk another headache, or another panty trap, or worse.

He turned and tried to take a step back. But his feet wouldn't go that way. He could go forward across the bridge but not back to the side he started on. Had he already fallen into whatever trap it represented?

Then he remembered the name of the bridge. Cantilever. "Can't I leave her!" he exclaimed. That was the trap.

But he hadn't actually joined the woman yet, so maybe it hadn't quite closed on him. He tried another tack: Instead of turning, he simply tried to back off the bridge. And he succeeded! He took two steps backward, and he was off. He had fathomed the pun and avoided mischief.

Or had he? He was still in the comic strip, with no way out of it except the bridge. He certainly wasn't going to try the ditch. And he hadn't helped the damsel in distress. So he hadn't accomplished anything. His seeming victory was hollow.

"Bleep, I'm going to do what I set out to do, and bleep the consequences," he said. He forged back onto the bridge and across it.

But then Caitlin stepped onto the other side, intercepting him before he cleared the bridge. "Oh, thank you, stranger!" she exclaimed. "You have helped me." She flung her arms about him and gave him a kiss that lifted his hair halfway off his scalp.

"But I haven't done anything yet," he gasped when he had a chance to take a breath. Her extreme affection made him nervous, though her kiss was not sweeter than wine, fortunately.

"Yes you have. You came to help me just at the right when, and now I'll never have to suffer the wrong what. You deserve your reward." She kissed him again, with an alarming amount of feeling.

"But—" he gasped, not at all sure what kind of reward she had in mind.

"Let's lie down right here on the bridge and do it," she said, glancing down to where a soft mattress had appeared.

This was coming to resemble the panty trap, and that made him even more nervous. "I have to get back to my friends and explain the delay," he said.

"Can't," she said, drawing him down with her.

He tried to resist, but she was very persuasive. "Can't what?"

"Can't tell ever. Your friends will never know." She was unbuttoning his shirt.

"I don't understand."

"Didn't you see the sign? This is the Can't Tell Ever Bridge. You can never tell what happens here. You don't think I'd do this otherwise, do you?" She drew him down onto the mattress with her.

This had the punnish ring of truth. "What can't I tell?"

"How I inducted you into the Adult Conspiracy, of course." She kissed him again.

Then he heard a rustling. It sounded like the slither of a big serpent. Sesame was coming to rescue him! "Over here!" he called.

"Curses, foiled again," the girl muttered and faded away, along with the mattress.

Umlaut got up and stumbled on across the bridge. There were Sammy and Sesame. "Am I glad to see you!"

Both nodded. They were looking at his shirt.

Oh. He buttoned it. An explanation was needed. "I—" But that was as far as he got. He discovered that he couldn't tell. Ever. The bridge would not allow it.

5

ZOMBIE WORLD

It turned out that Sammy had found a way across the comic
strip that wasn't too arduous and had led Sesame through.
The two had arrived just in time to save Umlaut from a
fate worse than—actually it hadn't seemed worse, or even
bad, just different. But it didn't matter, because it hadn't happened and anyway he couldn't tell.

As they walked along the bank just beyond the comic strip,
Umlaut looked back. He saw Caitlin, standing where he had
first seen her, looking into the ditch as if expecting someone
to emerge from it. Didn't she know that he had already done
so? After all, she had joined him on the bridge. She was
acting as if none of that had happened.

Well, he wasn't going to get involved with her again, even
off the bridge. She obviously was not what she appeared to
be.

Sammy plunged into the comic strip. There was a loud
creak. Umlaut wasn't sure about this, but Sesame followed
the cat without concern, so he did too.

The creaking got louder. What in the worlds could it be?
Then they came to a small river or stream. No, it was a

creek—and it creaked. Oh. Another egregious pun. What had he expected?

Slightly farther along, the creek became a chain. Umlaut paused to verify that, but it was so: The water flowed creakily into interlocking loops, forming the chain. The chain continued over a ridge and turned to water again where the land was low. Oh, that was how the creek got over the ridge, since water generally had a problem flowing upward.

Umlaut touched the chain, curious whether it was solid. The chain drew back with another creak. It evidently did not like to be touched.

Sesame was pausing, looking back at him. "I'm coming," he reassured her. "Just verifying a chain reaction."

The serpent dropped her snout in a groan motion, and Umlaut realized he had just fallen into another pun. "Sorry about that," he muttered.

He ran on. Something stung his ankle. It was an ant. He brushed it off and followed the other two out of the comic strip. They had made it back across, suffering only two awful puns. But somehow he wasn't happy. In fact he was sad. He sat on the ground and moaned.

Sammy and Sesame looked at him, uncertain what his problem was. "I'm dejected," he explained unhappily. "Everything seems pointless and miserable. I don't know why I ever got into this depressing business."

Then a very dull sad bulb blinked. He hadn't escaped another pun after all. "That ant that stung me!" he exclaimed. "It was a depress-ant!"

Both animals did their best to groan. The comic strip had struck again.

However, now that he knew what had happened, he was able reluctantly to push it aside and resume traveling. Soon he had left the depression behind. But he intended never to get near a comic strip again.

They encountered an old man wearing an ornate suit, walking with a low, rounded, armored creature. The man hesitated when he saw Sesame, so Umlaut reassured him. "I'm Umlaut, and these are my friends Sesame Serpent and Sammy Cat. We're not looking for any trouble. We're on our way to Zombie World."

"I am Matt A Door, and this is my friend Arme Dillo," the old man said, looking reassured. "We're looking for the Good Magician."

Umlaut did his best to be diplomatic but bungled it as usual. "Aren't you too old to handle challenges and all that?"

"That's my problem," Matt said. "On this world we are whatever age we want to be, except for me. Mine is a long sad story you will surely want to hear in exquisite detail."

"No, uh, we have to get on to—"

"Magician Humfrey was married to his first wife Dana or Dara Demoness for barely two years, and like many of her kind she was a phenomenally sexy creature when she chose to be. No sooner had the stork delivered his first son, Dafrey, than she gave her soul to the baby and took off, leaving Humfrey a divorcé. So he had to remarry the Maiden Taiwan in order to have help raising Dafrey."

"That's very interesting," Umlaut said insincerely. "But we have to—"

"Then Dara discovered that she hadn't quite succeeded in giving away her whole half soul. She still had a little bit of conscience left, interfering with her demonly freedom. Souls can be awkward for those accustomed to being without them. So she paid another visit to Humfrey by night, pretending to be the Maiden Taiwan, and got him to summon the stork with her again. Then she took off again, and he never knew that the Maiden's surprising ardency was not really hers. Then when the stork delivered her second son, that was me. My talent is making doors into unobtainable areas."

"Uh, fascinating. But—"

"Dara dumped the rest of her soul on me and was finally free. She did not take very good care of me, being now without conscience or love, so I set out to find my father, not knowing it was the Good Magician himself. I wandered off the enchanted path and stumbled into a big bird. She was the Roc of Ages. She had a maternal bent and nestled me under her wing. There I slept and aged until accidentally knocked free by Arme Dillo. At that point I discovered that I was no longer a child of two but a man of one hundred and forty-seven. I had slept more than a lifetime under that wing."

"Horrible," Umlaut said. "But—"

"So I decided to go see the Good Magician, hoping to find a way to recover my lost youth. But I didn't know where to find him. So I made a door to this realm, which is unreachable by regular folk who don't want to leave their bodies behind, and discovered that he's my real father. Actually I ran into Dara, who told me, though I don't think she told me everything. All I need to do is find him, but since he is accessible here, my talent won't help; my magic doors open only on the inaccessible. So I'm searching the old-fashioned way: afoot. Have you seen him?"

"No," Umlaut said, glad that the recitation was finally done. But then he thought of something he would rather not have realized. "Did you take youth elixir or something, to live so long?"

"No."

"Then you must have died of old age in your sleep. You are here in soul form. That's what Dara didn't tell you. It is too late to get your youth back."

"You must be right," Matt said, appalled. "This is awful." He wandered away, accompanied by Arme.

Umlaut realized belatedly that Matt might have preferred not to learn that he was dead. Somehow he had messed up again. He had good intentions but was such a klutz.

They approached the castle, and it looked just like the real Castle Roogna. Actually, maybe it was real, on its own terms.

Three adult princesses came out to greet them. They looked somehow familiar. One wore green, another brown, and the third red. The second carried a harmonica, and the third a little drum.

Umlaut stared impolitely. Could it be?

"Hello, Sammy!" the first said, picking up the cat and hugging him. "You didn't forget Melody."

"Hi, Sesame," the second said. "I haven't seen you since I was six years old. I'm glad you didn't forget Harmony." She hugged the serpent's foresection.

"And Umlaut," the third princess said, giving him a hug. "You seem younger than I remember you. I'm Rhythm."

"But—but you're only six years old!" he protested.

All three princesses laughed. "This is your first visit to Ptero, isn't it," Melody said.

"Time is different here," Harmony added.

"We can be any age we choose to be, just by traveling," Rhythm concluded. "We're twenty-three at the moment."

After some further explanations, Umlaut got it straight: On this world, time was geography. When a person traveled east, or "from," she became younger; west, or "to," she became older. They moved Castle Roogna around so they could live in it at whatever age they cared to be. It was all perfectly ordinary, they assured him. Six was the only age they couldn't be, because that was their current year of full mortal existence in Xanth.

"And this is my fiancé Anomy," Melody said, introducing him to a rather ordinary-seeming man. "He was once a real dastard, but he reformed."

Umlaut couldn't make sense of this, so he didn't comment. Probably he had misheard, as a princess would not use a bad word.

"And what brings you three here?" Harmony inquired.

"We are looking for Zombie World," Umlaut explained. "The Zombie Master's trail led here."

"Of course," Rhythm agreed. "Zombie World is far up the line. We'll take you to Princess Ida." She took his arm.

Umlaut was a bit disconcerted. She was a princess, and six years older than he was, and a lovely young woman. He felt indistinctly out of place. But what could he do? He suffered himself to be drawn on into the castle. Melody was carrying Sammy, and Harmony was chatting sociably with Sesame, seeming to understand the serpent's thoughts more readily than Umlaut did. But of course they had Sorceress-class magic and could do what they chose.

Princess Ida looked seventeen years older but was definitely the same person. Except that her little moon was the shape of a four-sided pyramid. Each triangular side was a different color: red, blue, green, and gray. Umlaut had never heard of a four-colored pyramidal world, but evidently one existed.

"Aunt Ida, these folk are going to Zombie World," Melody said brightly. "They're following the Zombie Master's trail."

"Naturally," Ida agreed, as if this happened every day. "No need to leave your bodies for that destination, just focus on the footsteps."

Now Umlaut saw the Zombie Master's tracks walking up through the air toward the world of Pyramid, growing smaller as they approached it. Sammy was already climbing the air, following them, growing smaller, and Sesame was slithering after him, her head section becoming smaller than her tail section. So Umlaut spoke a brief thank you to Princess Ida and ran after his friends.

Soon they were slanting down toward the expanding world. It was rotating grandly, showing one side full face and then another. The edges seemed to be quite sharp, with no rounding off; even a river he saw went around the corner in a fold rather than a bend, changing color as it did. Apparently the rules of magic differed on this world, just as they did on Ptero. He had never before realized just how versatile magic was. He had assumed that what he knew in Xanth was the way it was everywhere, except for drear Mundania, where there was very little magic. Did Xanth seem dreary to the inhabitants of these other worlds?

The footprints oriented on the blue face and came to land there. Here everything was in shades of blue: mountains, trees, rivers, animals, buildings. Otherwise it was reasonably familiar.

They came to a blue lake. The footsteps crossed it, so they followed. Apparently this trail was enchanted, so that they could walk it without splashing into the lake. There was a blue isle, and on the isle was a blue ridge, and near that was a blue house. The prints went up to its door.

They knocked, and Princess Ida appeared. She was about the age of the one on Ptero, but all blue, from hair to toes. What appeared to be a doughnut orbited her head. "Uh, we're going to Zombie World," Umlaut said awkwardly. "I'm Umlaut, and this is Sesame Serpent, and—"

"Sammy!" she exclaimed, picking him up. The cat had friends everywhere. Then she looked back at Umlaut. "You will want to continue following the tracks. You are fortunate he left the trail, for otherwise your travel would be much complicated."

"Complicated?"

"You would have to eat and drink and sleep and ask directions. That means interacting with the natives. Asking favors."

He still didn't get it. "Favors?"

"On this world, anyone who does a favor gains size. Anyone who receives it loses size. So most prefer to give rather than to receive, for selfish reasons. You are spared that, as the trail conveys you swiftly without the need to pause along the way."

"Oh. Yes. Thank you for clarifying that." Then something slightly disturbing occurred to him. "Is that a favor?"

Ida laughed. "No. I have an arrangement with the Zombie Master, to help travelers along their way. He and I settled accounts separately."

"Accounts?"

"I get to follow the trail myself, when I wish to, and see the other worlds. That's his return favor to me. I delight in such sightseeing."

This seemed odd. After a moment he figured out what was bothering him. "You can go to another world—circling your own head?"

"Yes. Isn't it wonderful? I thought for a long time that I couldn't, but then I learned that I could, since it is merely soul travel. My body remains here, of course."

"Uh, yes," he agreed. Their own bodies remained in Xanth; they were now mere souls, though they seemed much the same. But smaller. He tried to imagine how small, thinking of the sphere of Ptero, then the much smaller Pyramid. And it seemed these were merely the beginning of a long chain. He got dizzy.

"Don't try to make too much sense of it," Princess Ida recommended. "It's one of those things a person must accept on faith, so as to remain sane. Just accept each world on its own terms as you come to it."

The dizziness began to clear. "I will. Thanks."

"Remember that each world is unique to itself in custom as well as form. The next one incurs a burden of emotion for favors rendered, rather than size."

"I don't understand."

"One who does a service for another comes to like that person, or even love him. So it is best to be cautious about doing or receiving favors, unless you can arrange to exchange favors. Then they cancel out."

"We'll be careful," Umlaut promised, shaken. Instead of getting accustomed to these new worlds, he was becoming increasingly nervous about them.

"Now you had better follow the trail to Torus."

"Torus?"

"The doughnut."

He felt stupid again. "Oh. Thanks." He saw the tracks proceeding through the air toward the moon, as before.

Princess Ida released Sammy, and he bounded up the trail, becoming rapidly smaller, until he disappeared onto the doughnut world. "Wait for us!" Umlaut called belatedly and followed with Sesame.

"So nice to meet you, Umlaut and Sesame," Ida called after them. Now she seemed mountainously large.

"Same here," Umlaut called back, afraid his voice wouldn't reach that expanding distance.

They landed on the inner surface of Torus and followed the tracks to what turned out to be the Sarah Sea and across it to the isle of Niffen. There were many wild creatures there, but they remained clear of the trail.

The Ida here was as helpful as the others had been, and soon they were on their way to her moon, which was shaped like a cone filled with water. After that the worlds tended to blur in Umlaut's mind; each was distinct and original in many ways, but there was only so much he could assimilate on one trek. The Ida on Cone lived under its huge sea, inside its pointed end. Somehow they were able to breathe down there. There was a lot going on at the rim of the sea, but Umlaut didn't catch its nature.

They went on to Dumbbell, which was shaped like its name; everyone there was a fitness freak, even a supremely muscular Ida in the center of the bar. Then Pincushion, with huge pins stuck in it. And Spiral, like a grandly whirling galaxy. And Tangle, like knotted spaghetti. And Motes, a swirling collection of blobs of rock. Trapezoid, Shoe, Implosion, Puzzle, Octopus, Tesseract, Fractal—he simply could not hold them all in his mind, though each was surely deserving of plenty of attention, because each had a world full of plants, creatures, and odd people living there.

Then at last one registered: Zombie! They had finally reached Zombie World. It looked like a spoiled tomato from space, but it was real and whole on its own terms. It was so impossibly tiny, in the scheme of derivative worlds, that it pained his mind just to consider the matter, yet it loomed now as one more complete planet. It had sickening slime-covered seas and rotting vegetation and creatures who shed putrid gobs of flesh as they walked, but it was home to refugee zombies, and they surely loved it.

"I hope our business here is done soon," Umlaut muttered. Both Sammy and Sesame nodded.

The tracks ended at the surface of the planet. They were just to lead zombies in, not to bring visitors all the way to the Zombie Master. Umlaut's party would have to locate him on their own.

Fortunately they had Sammy. He bounded ahead, and they followed, hoping soon to come to a replica of Castle Zombie.

Then Sammy halted. There was a swarm of bees ahead, buzzing dangerously. It wouldn't be smart to challenge those. But they blocked off Sammy's route.

"Maybe they're not as dangerous as they look," Umlaut said hopefully.

Then a road hog rushed through. It seemed that such swine were everywhere, even here, and didn't give way to anybody or anything. Umlaut wondered whether they were related to the speed demons. The boarish creature ran right into the swarm of bees.

The swarm pounced. A bee stung the hog on the tail, and it squealed with outrage. But already it was changing. Now it was coming to resemble a zombie hog.

"Those are zom-bees!" Umlaut exclaimed. "Their stings make creatures resemble zombies! Naturally that would be the kind for this world."

That answered his question: These bees were indeed dangerous, more so than the regular kind. They would have to go around the swarm.

They tried, but the jungle was thick. They did not want to touch the slime-coated trees or the sludge-coated ground. Sammy's route had avoided such things, but now they were stuck with the regular zombie terrain.

Umlaut saw the shine of water in the distance. "That looks like a clear lake," he said. "Maybe we can make a raft or boat and cross the worst of it."

The others agreed. They picked their way cautiously to the edge of the lake. There was a black shack with a boat tied nearby. That looked ideal. Maybe they could borrow that boat.

A black man reclined outside the shack. "What can I do for you?" he inquired as they approached.

"We'd like to borrow your boat," Umlaut said.

The man eyed them. "You don't look much like zombies."

"We aren't. We have to deliver a letter to the Zombie Master."

"Is it an emergency?"

Umlaut exchanged a glance with his companions. "I wouldn't call it that, but we think it is necessary."

"In that case, I'll take you there. I'm Preston Black." He held out his hand.

Umlaut took it. "Thanks. You don't look much like a zombie either."

"That's because I wasn't dead long before I was zombied. There's no rot on me. I even kept my talent."

"What's your talent?"

"You'll see."

They went to the boat. It was larger than it had looked from a distance; there was room for them all, including Sesame.

Umlaut looked across the water. "What is the name of this lake?"

"It's not a lake, it's a sea. The Emergen Sea. It is not safe to use it unless there's a real need." Preston lifted a pole and pushed it against the water. The boat moved out.

"You pushed the water!" Umlaut exclaimed, surprised.

"That's my talent. I can move whatever I press on."

"But it was the boat that moved, not the water."

"It was the water that moved," Preston said. "And the whole sea with it, and the rest of the planet. I pushed them away." He pushed again.

Umlaut decided not to argue, since they were getting where they were going. The man could be right.

While they were moving, Umlaut had nothing to do, so he brought out the letter to read. That way he wouldn't have to embarrass himself by reading it in front of its recipient.

It was from HELPMASTER, UNIVERSAL AID, in Mundania, and the date was classified.

Sir:
For an extended period of time I have been monitoring events taking place in your land. How this has been accomplished is of no importance to yourself.

It has been brought to my attention that in the near future you intend to turn over the care of your castle to two living humans. Do you deem this a wise move? Are these humans to be trusted? You must keep in mind your esteemed position. All the zombies look to you for guidance and protection. If they have placed valuable objects with you for safekeeping, will said belongings be concealed from these humans?

I realize you well know your business; you would not have attained your place of authority otherwise. However, from personal experience with "people" I must advise you to exercise extreme caution.

With kind regards,
Zombie.guard.inc

Umlaut considered that. The letter was obviously well out of date; that snail was a terror in that respect. The Zombie Master had turned over the castle to Justin Tree and Breanna of the Black Wave a year ago. So it was way too late for him to exercise caution of any kind.

Well, at least it seemed to be a harmless letter. Umlaut folded it and put it away. He would have no concern about delivering it.

"Uh-oh," the boatman said.

Umlaut didn't like the sound of that. "What's wrong?"

"We're coming to the Dire Straits. That's where everything goes wrong."

Umlaut saw that there was an ominous ripple in the water ahead, where the lake narrowed. "There isn't an alternate route?"

"Not today. Usually the straits are elsewhere, but they must have moved in overnight. We'll have to chance them."

Umlaut wasn't easy about that but saw no alternative. In any event, the craft had already been caught up by the swift current of the straits. Maybe today would be the exception, when things didn't go wrong.

"Oh, no!" Preston Black groaned.

That did not sound unduly promising. "What is it?"

"Scylla and Charybdis are on duty today."

"Silly and Charitable? They don't sound too bad."

Preston glanced at him as if he were the zombie. "I gather you don't know your mythology."

"I guess I don't," Umlaut agreed.

"Scylla was once a pretty nymph, but she annoyed a god, who turned her into a six-headed sea monster with a taste for live meat. She was a terror for passing ships because she would snatch six crewmen off their decks and eat them. So they learned to avoid her. Then she teamed up with Charybdis, who was a whirlpool that liked to swallow ships whole. When a ship tried to avoid Charybdis, it got too close to Scylla, so she still got her meal."

"But couldn't ships simply sail around them both?"

"Not in narrow passages."

Umlaut was beginning to get a glimmer of the problem. "They're here? How did that happen?"

"In the course of time they got old and died. They appealed to the Zombie Master, who zombied them on condition that they not bother regular Xanth folk. So they joined him here on Zombie World."

And now this boat faced zombie monsters. Things were certainly going wrong in the Dire Straits. It was too late to turn back; the current had a firm grip on the boat.

Umlaut gazed ahead. There just to the right was a huge whirling depression in the ooze covering the water. That would be the zombie whirlpool. To the left were six snakelike heads projecting from the water. "Why, she's a serpent!"

Sesame took an interest. She gave Umlaut a *Leave this to me* glance and slithered to the front of the boat, building an emulation as she went. Soon she seemed to have several ugly zombie sea monster heads. She was good!

The boatman steered the boat left, as there was no point in feeding the whirlpool. Scylla's heads loomed close, ready to pounce, each more rotten than the others. But they were met by Sesame's heads. The two monsters held a brief twelve-headed dialogue. Then Scylla backed off and disappeared under the slime.

"I never saw the like," Preston said. "What did she do?"

"I think she invoked professional courtesy," Umlaut said. "One sea monster doesn't intrude on the domain of another."

"I could get to like a monster like that," Preston said as Sesame dissolved the emulation, her heads coming together and merging into one. "She just saved us from a bad chomping and swallowing. Of course a zombie can't be killed, and neither can a resident of the soul worlds, so I would have been back on duty after Scylla finished digesting me, but I wouldn't have enjoyed it much."

It occurred to Umlaut that the three travelers would have enjoyed it even less, since they weren't zombies or residents and could be killed. He gave Sesame's foresection a hug. "Thanks, monster." It was no insult to call her monster, because that was what she was. Most monsters were justly proud of their heritage.

She turned her head and kissed him on the ear, momentarily emulating a human girl. His ear tingled pleasantly.

"Funny thing," Preston said. "Usually trouble comes in threes. We just got past two monsters, but there should have been something else."

They were through the Dire Straits. Umlaut looked around. Where was Sammy?

Then he spied the cat. Sammy had one paw jammed into a knothole in the hull. The boat had sprung a leak, and Sammy had plugged it. "Found it. A leak."

Preston went to the cat. "Right you are. That could have sunk us while we were distracted by the monsters." Sammy pulled out his paw, and a jet of water appeared. The boatman jammed a plug into the hole. It was fixed, except for a little bilge water.

Soon they came to a dock. Beyond it was Castle Zombie, just like the one in Xanth. "Thank you," Umlaut said as they disembarked.

"Thank *you*," Preston replied. "That was a fine little spot adventure. Things get dull around here."

They walked up the path to the castle. The drawbridge was down across the scummy moat, so they walked and slithered across it. Sesame gave Umlaut a *This is eerily familiar* look, and he agreed.

A zombie met them at the front gate. "We have a letter for the Zombie Master," Umlaut told it.

The zombie just stood there, dripping rot. After a moment Umlaut realized that he had not told it to do anything, so it wasn't doing anything. "Please tell the Zombie Master he has visitors."

The zombie shuffled into the castle. Soon an old woman came out to meet them. There was something interesting about her. "I am Millie the Ghost," she said.

"I am Umlaut, and these are Sesame Serpent and Sammy Cat. We are visitors from Xanth with a letter for the Zombie Master."

"From Xanth!" she exclaimed, pleased. "We don't receive many living visitors from there. Jonathan will be pleased. Come this way." She turned to lead them into the castle. There was still something interesting about her. Maybe it was just her clothing; both her blouse and skirt fit very nicely.

When they entered the Zombie Master's private suite, things changed. There was no rot or slime here, and no odor of decay. It was just like Castle Roogna, with carpets on the floor, tapestries on the walls, and clean brightness throughout.

The Zombie Master appeared. He was a dourly handsome old man who reminded Umlaut of a funeral director, though he had never met one of those. After introductions, Millie went to fetch refreshments, and Umlaut gave him the letter. "I read it first. It's not that I want to snoop, but when we forwarded a letter to the Demon Jupiter without knowing what was in it, he hurled the Red Spot at us."

"I understand," Jonathan said. "It is best to be cautious." He glanced at the letter. "This seems to have taken some time to reach me."

"It was delivered by a giant snail."

"Ah, the Mundanian snail mail. No wonder. There were going to be some deliveries from Mundania, but nothing came of that before we left."

"The snail was slow to get it started," Umlaut said. "But why deliver to Castle Zombie?"

"It was convenient to the coast and a river. Apparently they wanted a private route."

"They found one," Umlaut agreed. "There's something else: Did you know that a monster got locked in the dungeon?"

"Why, no. The last time I was down there was just before a storm, to secure the dungeon door. I thought it was empty."

And Breanna had thought the monster belonged there. It had all been an accident of timing.

Millie returned with some pastries. They looked good, but Umlaut hesitated.

"Don't be concerned," Jonathan said. "That is not zombie food. Millie makes only normal food." He patted her on the bottom. "And she's no longer a ghost, despite the name. Her talent is sex appeal. Perhaps you noticed."

"Jonathan!" Millie protested, pleased.

So that explained what was interesting about her. It had never occurred to him that an old person could have such a talent. Umlaut covered the awkwardness by changing the subject. "We almost got swallowed by a six-headed sea monster on the way in. We were relieved not to become food for it."

Jonathan smiled. "Ah, you met Scylla. The consequence would not have been as bad as you might think. This is a derivative world, populated only by tiny fragments of souls, however solid it may appear. You would not have died but merely lost your places here. You would have awakened back on Xanth and had to start the process over. An inconvenience, of course, but not a lethal one."

Oh. "It made us nervous at the time."

"We shall be happy to give you a tour of Zombie World," Jonathan said. "We have many delightfully rotten things and creatures here."

"Thanks, but we have other letters to deliver," Umlaut said quickly.

"That is unfortunate. In that case, you had best be on your way. Merely close your eyes and concentrate on Xanth, and you will soon be back there."

That seemed almost too simple. But Umlaut saw Sammy Cat close his eyes and disappear, followed by Sesame, so he bid farewell, closed his own eyes, and concentrated.

There was a remarkable swirling shifting, as if he had been swallowed by Charybdis the whirlpool. When he opened his eyes, he was back in Princess Ida's chamber, lying on Sesame's coils. They were indeed back.

6

SOUFFLÉ SERPENT

S esame Serpent watched as Umlaut checked the pile of letters. There was one addressed to Queen Irene. She should be right here in Castle Roogna. That was the sensible one to deliver next.

"Unfortunately, she is away today," Princess Ida said. "Queenly duties, you know; a person's time is not necessarily her own. You will have to wait until tomorrow. But I'm sure there is room for you here in the castle for the day and night."

"But we're not royal," Umlaut protested. "We're just—us. Nobody special." He was right about that, Sesame thought, though somewhat klutzy in other ways.

"Every person is special in some way," the princess reassured him. "I will see to it immediately." She departed.

Umlaut checked with Sammy and Sesame. Sammy had been here before and wasn't concerned. Sesame herself did not feel at home in a castle, especially after her long stay in the dungeon, and she indicated that.

"Maybe you could stay in the moat," Umlaut suggested. "You could emulate a moat monster."

She liked that idea. It was an easy emulation, as she was more at home in the water than on land.

The three little princesses appeared, cute enough to eat. Not that Sesame would, of course; that would be a breach of guestly protocol. "Oh, goody!" Princess Melody exclaimed, clapping her little hands.

"You're staying the night," Princess Harmony added, playing half a note on her harmonica.

"We'll have lots of fun with you," Princess Rhythm concluded, bonking a single bonk on her drum.

Sesame saw Umlaut try to exchange a wary glance with his companions, but a princess intercepted it and diverted it to the ceiling. The three were little bundles of mischief. Staying at Castle Roogna no longer seemed like such a good idea, but the princesses were not about to let them get away.

"We were about to go out to the moat," Umlaut said desperately.

Little Melody clapped her hands again. "Goody! You can meet Soufflé!"

Sesame froze: She was wary of male serpents. They had forgotten that the moat was occupied.

"Right this way," little Harmony chimed in.

"He should love you," little Rhythm concluded, glancing at Sesame.

Now what were they to do? Sesame tried to think of something suitably clever to get them out of this, as the trio of princesses hustled them along through the hall, but her mind was numb. She turned a pleading look on Umlaut. He had to say something but probably could think of nothing but the truth. Sure enough, desperately, he tried that.

"Wait! We have a problem with this! Two or three problems, in fact."

"We love problems," Melody said.

"We love double problems better," Harmony agreed.

"We love triple problems best of all," Rhythm finished.

It certainly was difficult to turn them off. "We don't want to meet Soufflé," Umlaut said. "Yet."

"But he's a nice serpent," Melody said.

"The nicest," Harmony agreed.

"He baby-sits us," Rhythm explained.

A moat monster baby-sat children? That was a new one. Sesame managed to exchange a glance with Umlaut, indicating that she remained wary. It might be that Soufflé had a side that children did not see. How could that be explained to children without violating the dread human Adult Conspiracy? Umlaut seemed to be only barely conversant with it himself, being at borderline age, but Sesame knew enough to be assured that the princesses were way too young for any smell of it. Naturally, being human children, they neither understood nor accepted the restrictions.

Umlaut tried, in his sweetly clumsy fashion. "A—another serpent chased Sesame, and she didn't like that."

"We chase each other all the time," Melody said. "It's called tag. It's fun."

"This wasn't exactly a game chase. She had to hide."

"Maybe it was hide-and-seek," Harmony said. "That's fun too."

"This wasn't fun. She was afraid he would—would do something to her." What a struggle! Sesame was glad for the moment that she didn't have to try to handle it.

They looked at him. "Is there something we don't understand?" Melody asked.

"Maybe. She just doesn't want to meet him."

"There's only one thing that makes someone fudge like that," Harmony said grimly.

Sesame did not like the sound of this. "So maybe we'll stay inside after all," Umlaut said hopelessly. He really *wasn't* very good at this.

"And that is the Adult Conspiracy," Rhythm concluded triumphantly.

They had caught on. Now the blubber was in the blaze. "We'd better leave now," Umlaut said.

"Oh, no you don't," Melody said.

"You're going to tell us exactly what—" Harmony added.

"Exactly what?" Princess Ida inquired. She had returned just barely on the edge of the nick of time. Sesame wondered whether that was really coincidence; adult human women seemed to have ways of knowing things.

"Oh, nothing," Rhythm said innocently. Little halos appeared over all three heads.

"That's nice," Princess Ida said, hardly fooled. She turned to the visitors. "Let me show you to your room."

Their room was upstairs, and very nice. There was a huge tub big enough for Sesame to curl up in so she could sleep in water after all, and a lovely sandbox for Sammy. There was a fine soft bed for Umlaut; humans did seem to prefer such things, being sort of bony and angular. But the most remarkable thing was a huge tapestry on the main wall, showing a detailed picture of the Land of Xanth. It was so well done that the scene seemed almost real.

Princess Ida saw them looking. "I hope you don't mind sharing the room with the Magic Tapestry," she said. "It is harmless and can be entertaining if you like to look around or review history."

"History?" Umlaut asked blankly. Sesame shared his blankness.

"The Magic Tapestry shows anything you wish it to, if you are qualified to see it. For example, you could view your own past experiences."

"We could?" He was astonished, as was Sesame.

"I will demonstrate." She glanced at the tapestry, and the picture shifted to show Sesame slithering rapidly o'er hill and dale, carrying Umlaut, following Sammy Cat. When they reached the castle, it showed them meeting the three little princesses, then Princess Ida herself. Sesame was amazed.

"This is amazing," Umlaut said, voicing her thought.

"Merely magic," Princess Ida said. "I will come for you when it is time for supper." She departed, leaving them to the wonders of the tapestry.

"If she thought this would fascinate us, she was right," Umlaut said. "What shall we watch?"

Sammy had a notion. He tried to convey it by gestures, but Umlaut was unable to figure it out. Sesame understood him, of course, but that was because she wasn't human and didn't have the human physical or mental limitations. "Can you make it orient yourself?"

The cat concentrated. The scene shifted. There was a young male serpent slithering contentedly along.

"Who is that?"

Sammy bounded to the window and pointed down toward the moat.

"Soufflé? But this is a young serpent. I haven't met Soufflé, but he must be much older."

But soon Sammy clarified that: This was Soufflé when young, several centuries ago, and he hadn't changed much since. Sesame marveled at that, because serpents did age, though they remained suitably sinuous.

"Centuries ago?" Umlaut asked, dumbfounded. "He can't be *that* old!"

Sesame was of course interested. This was a way she could learn about Soufflé without having to meet him. She might be able to judge whether it was safe.

They settled down and watched. Gradually Sesame seemed to be getting into the scene, like an invisible observer, and she knew the others were also. The tapestry had that effect; maybe it was part of its magic.

Soufflé slithered along without a care in the world other than finding a new puddle to splash in. He was near great Lake Ogre Chobee, where the ogres and chobees coexisted at the fringe of land and water. He was steering clear of both, because a chobee might have a vicious chomp and an ogre could squeeze juice from a stone with just one ham-hand.

He heard a human cry. That interested him, so he slithered toward the sound. Soon he came to a remarkable scene. The ground was sooty and smoldering, with licks of fire interspersed by jets of steam and roiling clouds of smoke. In fact it looked like hell.

A man ran by. He was the one who had screamed. He was naked and barefooted, wincing as he ran over hot coals. But he couldn't pause to avoid them, because a pack of werewolves was chasing him. They were huge and slavering, their teeth gleaming white, their eyes gleaming red. Their paws seemed to have no trouble with the burning ground. They were gaining on the fleeing man, and he knew it; his terrified glances back showed them coming ever closer. Soon they would have him.

Soufflé slithered into a crevice, concealing himself. He wanted to understand what was going on before he got involved. He could handle a werewolf or two, but not a whole pack. He watched as they charged by.

Then it got worse: The ground rose into a ridge, and the

ridge ended in a cliff. Beyond it was a dusky lowland that might offer an escape, but it was too far below to risk. The man sheered away, terrified anew.

The werewolves' teeth snapped at the man's heels. Now they had him cornered. He was caught between them and the cliff.

Teeth nipped his bare butt. The man screamed again and leaped off the cliff, his scream descending with him. The wolves milled about at the brink, frustrated. He had gotten away after all.

The fall was surely enough to kill him, but somehow it didn't. He bounced on a rocky ledge, fell again, bounced again, and finally landed in a heap at the base. Was he dead? No, not quite; a finger stirred, then a toe.

Soufflé slithered down the cliff, bracing against its numerous cracks and crevices, following the more precipitous route of the man. Perhaps he would be able to help.

But this gloomy region was not empty. Shapes loomed horribly. They were zombies! Not nice sanitary ones, but awful rotters with sagging eyeballs and dripping goo. The stench was appalling.

The man dragged himself up and staggered onward. The zombies followed, reaching for him. He tried to run but could not move much faster than they did. He was barely staying ahead of their slimy fingers.

Soufflé followed, staying mostly behind cover, observing. He still wasn't quite sure what was going on.

The zombies were just about to catch the man. But he came across a steep upward rocky slope. He scrambled up it, just managing to elude the grasping hands. The zombies could not mount the slope; their own goo defeated them, causing them to slide down as fast as they climbed up. The man had won freedom again, somehow.

But now a new threat appeared: grotesque shapes in the sky. "There he is!" one screeched. They were harpies—gross half-human birds. "There's Slander! Get him!"

Slander? What kind of a name was that? Soufflé slithered on, watching and listening, trying to keep under cover so that the dreadful harpies would not spy him. How could the poor man escape these dirty birds?

Slander tried. He ducked under the cover of spreading trees so that the harpies could not dive-bomb him. But some of them flew low, under the foliage, and came at him from the sides. "Corner him! Corner him!" they screeched. "We've got him now!"

Almost. Slander spied another drop-off. He lunged for it and hurled himself into a heaving sea. The waves rose up to slap his face and try to drown him, but somehow he bobbled to the surface, surviving.

Soufflé slithered quietly down the slope and into the water, still watching. The end had to be near.

There was a roiling in the water, as of something huge stirring in the depths. Slander saw it and tried to swim for shore, but the current sucked him back toward the roiling. He could not escape. Meanwhile the harpies circled overhead, and both the wolves and zombies were making their way down toward the sea, just in case. The deck was really stacked against the fugitive. (It wasn't clear how the top floor of a ship could be stacked, but the saying had to come from somewhere.)

The only possible escape seemed to be to reach a tiny isle set in the sea, where a lovely maiden with large eyes, small ankles, and flowing hair watched anxiously. She lifted a delicate hand to beckon. The man struggled toward that isle.

A tentacle reached out of the water, followed by three more. It looked like gross seaweed but had more animation. Soon a veritable garden of them sprouted from the waves and oriented on the thrashing man.

Soufflé recognized it now: It was a kraken, one of the most fearsome sea monsters. The floundering man was absolutely done for. There was little or no way he could reach the isle before the monster caught him.

The maiden, seeing this, heaved her fetching bosom and screamed. It was an excellent scream, resounding across the waves and echoing from the rocks and cliffs. Even the wolves, zombies, and harpies paused to savor it with admiration. Only the kraken ignored it, having more important business at hand.

Soufflé slid into the water and swam toward the man. He wasn't all that partial to human folk and didn't even know this one, but something about this scenario bothered him. Maybe it was the evident alarm of the maiden; he had always been intrigued by damsels in distress, even the human variety. He reached the man, then placed himself between him and the oncoming kraken. "Back off!" he hissed in serpentine.

The kraken lifted an eyeball on a stalk and looked at him. "Who the bleep are you?" It spoke in Tentacular, but Soufflé could understand that well enough. After all, the various sea monsters needed to have some means of communication with each other, so that they did not intrude on each other's territories unless they meant to.

"I am Soufflé Serpent."

"And I am Krakatoa Kraken."

"I am sorry to know you," Soufflé hissed politely. "Now go away, or we will tangle."

"We certainly will!" the kraken agreed. "You have no business here."

"I am making it my business to save this wretch from a horrible fate."

"Horrible fate!" the tentacles signaled. "You have no idea what's happening."

"Be that as it may, I am taking him out of here. Now back off or I will chomp you."

"You can't chomp me!" The kraken threw a few dozen tentacles at him.

So Soufflé chomped off a few half dozen of them. "I warned you."

"Ooo, that smarts!" the kraken signaled. It backed off, somewhat to Soufflé's surprise. Normally krakens liked nothing better than a good tangle.

Soufflé returned to the man, who was still thrashing aimlessly. He made a niche in his body under him and bore the man up and along. He swam to the small island in the sea, where the werewolves and zombies could not reach, and deposited the man there.

"Stop your interference!" a harpy screeched, diving at Soufflé. He ducked his head, avoiding her. But then three more dived. He reversed coils and knocked them out of the air with a well-placed tail sweep. They tumbled heads under tails, screeching indignantly. After that they kept their distance.

Now at last he could tend to the oddly named Slander, the man all these monsters were chasing. He was sitting on the shore, looking quizzically at Soufflé. So was the screaming maiden, who was now standing beside him. That was another surprise. Gratitude, despair, curiosity—such emotions were understandable. But quizzical? Something was reasonably odd here.

Then the man spoke. "I see you don't understand, serpent," he said. "So before we curse you, I will try to make you understand. Curses are generally better when their rationales are grasped."

Curse? The oddity was ballooning.

"Here is the situation: We are curse friends (known by the uninitiated as curse fiends—what a difference an omitted letter makes!) and actors in rehearsal for a new play."

A play! Soufflé remembered that the curse fiends did put on plays and set great store by them. No wonder the maiden was so pretty: She was an actress.

"This one is entitled *Just Deserts* and features a human version of a cri-tic named Slander who throughout his life took inordinate delight in tormenting those whose creativity, industry, and talent far exceeded his own. He read books, viewed plays, and absorbed illusion shows with the express purpose of destroying the reputations, artistry, and livelihood of those devising and presenting them. If there were no legitimate criticisms to make, he invented them. After all, in his mind the end justified the means, and the end was to ruin anything remotely artistic or popular.

"As it happened, he had a girlfriend who had been under the delusion that she could change him for the better. Thus she tolerated his unkindnesses without response in kind. But finally his incessant carping and condemnation was too much for her, and she swallowed the expiration label on a jar of log jam and expired.

"Thus Slander's life. What concerns us is his afterlife. When he died he found himself in a hell crafted by all those he had maligned in life. Now the desks were turned, and the oppressor became the victim. He was harried mercilessly from sight to site. When he finally straggled to the isle where his dead beloved was stranded, and begged for her help, she would cruelly shove him back into the sea. Thus she repaid him in kind, laughing hilariously as the monsters tore him apart." He paused while the lady demonstrated with lift of her lovely leg, a push of her tender toes, and a hilarious laugh. "Then the scenario would start again with a fresh cast of monsters. Only when the critic suffered as much as he had made others suffer would he finally be freed to expire in peace. That was bound to take some time."

The man eyed Soufflé directly. "What you blundered into, in your dull reptilian way, was a dress rehearsal. You have ruined it, and we shall have to start over. We take strong exception to such interference. Accordingly, I shall now roundly curse you, covering both your routine and your prospective romantic existence, and we shall then drive you out of our set. You must exist in your own hell, not intruding on ours. Do you understand?"

It seemed pointless to try to argue, even if he could have had a human voice. He had tried to help, and his ignorance had resulted in the opposite. He knew that curse fiends were not the forgiving type. So he nodded his head.

"We hereby curse you to serve an endless life of drudgery and servitude until you find your one true love—who will avoid or reject you." The man made a gesture with his hands, and the woman made a similar gesture, somewhat like throwing. Something invisible but powerful struck Soufflé across the snout. Suddenly he was filled with terror. He knew it was the curse, but that didn't help.

He slithered into the sea and swam as rapidly as he could away from the land. The kraken pursued him in the water, the harpies harried him from the air, and the werewolves and zombies raced along the shore to prevent him from seeking land. Worst of all, he could hear the woman laughing at him, her vibrant voice packed with ridicule and contempt. What an ignominious retreat—exactly as they had intended.

Soufflé dived deep down into the cold darkness beneath. Only the kraken could follow him there, but it couldn't keep up because it had lost some half tentacles. So he escaped.

But he didn't escape the curse. He found himself impelled

to seek the most lowly of employments, which was that of moat monster. Moats were not at all like the open sea. They were shallow and narrow and went around in circles, and often they were dirty, because castle sewage tended to leak into them. No self-respecting monster would perform such onerous duty unless bribed or ensorceled to do so. Bribes were no good for Soufflé, because he had to serve without recompense, and anyway he didn't like the taste of human babies. And he was, of course, ensorceled by the curse. So he sought the job others avoided, and in the course of time served at every castle that was respectable in Xanth, and some that weren't. Castle Roogna was dull during its defunct days, but then Rose of Roogna came, and she was a delight. Good Magician Humfrey and his several serial wives were interesting, and the nameless castle in the sky was fascinating. Later Castle Roogna was occupied again, with the sound of little feet on the floors and little splashes in the moat. They even let him baby-sit princesses on occasion. So though it was technically a curse, this aspect no longer bothered him much. Of course he would like to swim in the deep deep deeps of the sea again sometime, but he couldn't go there until the curse abated.

Which left the romantic aspect. For centuries he had not even seen a lady serpent, and of course which of them would even associate with a lowly moat monster? So his chances of ever finding true love, or even passable acquaintance, were remote. Unless he somehow abridged the curse—and how could he do that? So Soufflé endured and made the best of it. The best was tolerable, on better days.

There was actually one advantage to the curse, which it took him some time to fathom: He wasn't aging. He was in a kind of stasis, unable to grow old, because fading out would release him from his chore. So he seemed like the same young monster he had been at the outset, except for the increasing gravity of demeanor his long experience brought him. If the curse ended, he would resume aging, but it would be worth it, because he would finally be able to return to the seas and to find love. He dreamed of that.

The scene stopped with Soufflé snoozing in the moat. Sesame realized that the Magic Tapestry had brought the sequence up to the present, so there was no more historical animation.

Umlaut looked at Sesame and saw the tear in her eye and a little heart floating just above her snout. She had gotten a bit too much involved with Soufflé's history and now was embarrassingly smitten by him. "You must be the one," he told her. "At least, maybe you can be if you want to be. If there's a way to abate the curse. There seems to be no need to fear Soufflé; he is evidently a very nice serpent, unfairly condemned for doing what he thought was right."

Those were her sentiments exactly.

"Let's go down and meet him," Umlaut said.

They went down and out. But as they approached the moat, Sesame hung back. She didn't want to; it was the curse, making her avoid Soufflé.

"That's confirmation," Umlaut said. "You're the one. You can't approach him. But I can. Shall I tell him?"

Regretfully, she nodded and retreated back to their room. She would watch their encounter on the Magic Tapestry. She slithered quickly there and fixed her gaze on the scene.

Umlaut and Sammy went out on the drawbridge. Soufflé emerged from his snooze and came to sniff noses with Sammy. They had evidently met before.

"Uh, I am Umlaut," Umlaut said. "I have an, er, message for you." She didn't actually hear him but could tell what he was saying from the awkward way his mouth moved. "We have just seen your life history on the Magic Tapestry and know how you were cursed long ago. We think it was too great a punishment for too small an offense; you were only trying to do a decent thing."

Soufflé nodded appreciatively. It was obvious that he understood every word, even if he couldn't speak in human dialect. He was like Sesame in that respect; many animals learned human talk as a second language.

"Traveling with me is a lady serpent named Sesame, with a talent of emulation similar to mine. She has been wary of male serpents, having had a bad experience, but now feels she knows you. She came to meet you, but the curse prevented her." Umlaut paused for the significance of that to sink in. "I think she is the one for you. That's why the curse stops her. But maybe we can find a way to end the curse. Then—"

Soufflé nodded gratefully. He did understand. Then he sank slowly into the water, leaving only a little red heart floating where his head disappeared. Umlaut had done a good job, for a human being, and Sesame really appreciated it.

Umlaut and Sammy returned to their room to rejoin Sesame. "This is a remarkable romance," Umlaut said. "You can't meet each other, but you both understand." Indeed, Sesame was still gazing at the tapestry's image of Soufflé's heart floating on the moat water.

Later Princess Ida came to escort them to dinner. This was a fancy affair, enlivened not only by the three little princesses but also by two eleven-year-old cousins, the princesses Dawn and Eve, and their mother Electra. While the three little princesses were full of fun and mischief, the two older ones were more subtly mischievous. Dawn had flame red hair and green eyes, wore a bright dress, and could tell anything about any living thing, while Eve had black hair and eyes, wore a dark dress, and could tell anything about any inanimate thing. Sesame privately judged that by the time they reached the Adult Conspiracy—maybe even before then—they would be dangerous.

Sammy and Sesame had a table to themselves. It seemed that animals didn't generally eat in the royal dining hall, but as special guests these were allowed. The story about Sesame and Soufflé had gotten around—little princesses had very sharp ears—and there was some sympathy.

As the meal finished, young Princesses Dawn and Eve quietly approached Umlaut. "You're an interesting person," Dawn said. "You're not living."

"I'm not living here," Umlaut said, startled by the statement.

"And you're not dead," Eve said. "So neither of us knows about you."

They were serious. "I don't understand."

"Neither do we," Dawn said as they moved on.

Odd indeed. But then Sammy and Sesame rejoined him, pretending that they hadn't overheard, and the matter evidently escaped his mind.

That evening while the others watched the Magic Tapestry—they were interested in the activities of cats and serpents around Xanth—Umlaut read the letter to Queen Irene. He moved his lips as he read silently, so Sesame picked it up.

Dear Queen Irene,

Happy birthday to you next week on the 15th of Apull.

Irene has always been a special name to me because one of my daughter's names is Irene. She is not a queen; however, in another country across the ocean she would be a princess. In this part of Mundania, she simply is a wife and mother of two beautiful girls, Jordyn and Jenny—like our friend Jenny Elf. Irene is what we call a homemaker. Oh, yes, she is also learning a discipline of self-defense called karate. This is in case she meets any tangle trees or ogres. She thinks being a mother makes her too old to scream prettily or fling her hair about, but she can still deliver a good swift kick where it will do the most good.

Did you know Irene means "peace"? At least it does here.

Having said all that, I had better introduce myself. My name is Arjayess and I was banished to Mundania many years ago. I have written to Breanna of the Black Wave and Jenny Elf. I am hoping to become friends with more Xanthians because I believe that is my original home. My talent is visions of people, places, and events in Xanth. My other talent, like yours, is growing plants. Although there is no actual magic in Mundania except my visions (and rainbows), surrounding myself with growing and flowering things brings much happiness to me.

I wish there were a way for us to meet. Wouldn't it be wonderful if we could exchange seeds from our worlds? I hope to write again before you and Dor must fade away.

Arjayess

Again, this seemed ordinary human business. Sesame did not see anything here that either incited rage or solved the problem of the Red Spot. It was way out of date, of course, and they were not delivering the letters in the order they had been written. But regardless of their order, what was the secret of these letters?

Next morning Queen Irene and King Dor returned from their trip and held an audience for their visitors. Sesame expected a serious occasion, but that was ruined by the voices. It seemed that the king's magic talent was making the inanimate talk, and talk it did, often impertinently.

"Look at this!" a floor tile said. "A little cat and a big snake."

"So the snake brought its meal along," a wallboard retorted.

"If you bits of fuel for the fireplace are quite through," Queen Irene said sternly, "we shall proceed."

The tile and board were silent. Evidently they understood the threat.

Queen Irene glanced imperiously at Umlaut. "I understand you have something for me?"

"Uh, yes, Your Majesty," he said, flustered. This was, after all, human royalty; Sesame would have reacted similarly in the presence of a king snake. He gave her the letter.

She glanced at it, evidently absorbing it in a moment. "She has a daughter named Irene and a granddaughter named Jenny," she remarked to King Dor.

"That's nice," he said amiably.

Queen Irene glanced at Sammy. "And how is the real Jenny Elf doing?" she inquired. "I gather marriage becomes her, as does being a princess."

Sammy nodded.

She looked at Sesame. "And it seems you have a curse to alleviate. Unfortunately we can't help you there. Curses generally have to be abated by those who make them."

Sesame nodded. The queen had a somewhat daunting presence and did not seem to be inviting much of a dialogue.

"I could make the figures in the tapestry talk to you, if that would help," King Dor suggested, "but I doubt that the answer to that curse is there. The tapestry merely shows what, not what might be."

Sesame nodded; that was her conclusion also.

"Probably the Demon Xanth could null the curse, if he

wanted to," Dor continued. "But he seldom has much interest in mortal affairs."

"Except his own affair with a mortal," the throne remarked wickedly. Several tiles snickered.

Irene's gaze returned to Umlaut. "For whom is your next letter?"

He evidently hadn't thought about that. He wasn't much for looking ahead. "Uh, I'm trying to make them close to each other." He fumbled with the packet, exhibiting his typical human awkwardness. It dropped to the floor and the letters spread out. One flopped over so that its name was down.

"Princess Ivy," a floor tile said, reading it.

"Our daughter," Queen Irene said. "How nice. But she is not at Castle Roogna at the moment. That's why we are baby-sitting the three little princesses."

He seemed to be committed. "Uh, where is she?" he asked as he clumsily gathered up the letters.

"Why, she and Grey are visiting his parents at the Isle of Cats. That is, however, not the easiest site to reach."

Sammy took off. If Umlaut was awkward, Sammy was impetuous. That was why it was surely best to have a sensible serpent with their party. "I guess we're going there anyway," Umlaut said as he lurched after the cat. "Thank you, Your Majesty!" His foot skidded on the floor and he almost went down. Fortunately Sesame, anticipating this clumsiness, steadied him with her body.

"Welcome," Queen Irene said. The faintest of smiles hovered near her lips, as if she found something amusing. She would have made a fine serpent.

"Good riddance, oaf!" another tile said.

Then they were on their way from the throne room and on out of the castle. For some reason Sesame felt out of sorts, though this mischief had not been her doing. She would try to see that the awkward human man made it through his mission without hurting himself. He was after all a pretty decent sort, for a human, and he had helped her escape the zombie dungeon.

7

SIDESTEPPING

Sammy ran ahead, as usual. Umlaut emulated a light serpent rider, and Sesame emulated a big black racer snake, and they managed to follow halfway close behind.

The cat was bearing westward. There was surely all manner of folk, monsters, terrain, and magic between them and the Isle of Cats, but Sammy was evidently selecting a route that avoided all that. That was one advantage of having him along. Of course the disadvantage was that he seemed to have no in-between state of motion; he was either a speeder or a speed bump.

Despite their velocity, it took time to reach the coast. Umlaut was getting hungry. "Maybe we should pause to eat!" he called.

Sammy heard him. He veered to one side or the other and led them into a grove of pie trees. There were many ripe pies and a great variety. Umlaut harvested a nice cherry pie, Sammy had catnip pie, and Sesame feasted on liver pies. She passed up the liverworst and liverokay in favor of the liverbest.

But before they finished eating and cleaning up, something loomed in the sky to the north. It was a gray patch of fog, floating just above the forest. It seemed to be drifting slowly east, then west, as if looking for something. In the process it was getting somewhat strung out. "What an ugly cloud," Umlaut remarked.

Sammy looked at him as if he had done something stupid. "Well, it is," he said defensively. "What about it?"

Sammy gave the signal for nineteen-questions mode, so Umlaut cooperated. Actually he had a better way: He emulated feline mode so that he could better relate and came to understand the cat much better. It was almost as if he were speaking Feline, which was a surprisingly comprehensive mode of communication. Soon he learned what he had done: He had insulted the worst of clouds, Cumulo Fracto Nimbus, who was usually out looking for parades or picnics to rain on. Their little group had a passing resemblance to a picnic. Now they were going to get it.

"From that little bit of mist?" Umlaut asked incredulously. "It couldn't even squeeze out ten drops of rain, let alone a storm."

But now Sesame was gazing with alarm at the cloud. Umlaut looked again and saw that the fog had coalesced and grown to small cloud size. Its surface had darkened and resembled a bulbous face. He held his hand out at arm's length to measure it. "It's no bigger than a man's hand," he said.

But both his companions seemed concerned. They wanted to get out of here.

"Oh, all right," Umlaut agreed. "We won't have any trouble leaving it behind, and we have to get on to the Isle of Cats anyway."

Sammy flinched. A spot dialogue got the reason: Fracto could hear him. Now the ornery cloud knew where they were going.

"Who cares?" he demanded. "It's just vapor."

For some reason the others remained doubtful. They got moving again, but now Umlaut was aware of the sky. He watched to see when the stupid cloud fell behind them, but somehow it didn't. It kept growing, and its leading edge seemed actually to be gaining. That was probably just a fluke of air currents. How could a cloud decide where to go?

A chill gust of wind caught them, and the first sheet of rain came down, just missing them behind. Umlaut began to be concerned. Could his friends be right? He had never heard of a conscious, self-directed cloud, but anything was possible, and it seemed that this one had a bad reputation.

They moved on at speed, but then a bolt of lightning struck the ground just ahead with a loud clap of thunder. The bolt bounced on the ground, burning hot, trying to set fire to the dry leaves. This was dangerous! "We'd better find cover!" Umlaut called.

Sammy veered again, and in one and a half moments led them to a snug cave in the side of a minor mountain. They got in it just before the next sheet of rain crashed down. It was clean and roomy and warm. "Thanks, Sammy," Umlaut said. "This is perfect."

But the cat seemed apologetic. Another interview determined why: This was the closest suitable cave, but it wasn't ideal. It was the home of a Ptero-bull who had managed to emigrate from Ida's moon Ptero but affected other folk adversely. If it returned before the storm ended, they would be uncomfortable.

"I'm not worried," Umlaut said. "Certainly I'm not going out in that storm." For now the thunder and lightning were continuous, and the rain so dense it looked like a waterfall.

Sesame sniffed the air. She wriggled nervously. "What's the matter?" Umlaut asked, irritated.

But before she could answer even a few of the nineteen questions, something loomed at the cave entrance. It was huge and ugly, and it snorted.

"What the bleep is that?" Umlaut demanded angrily. He was in a foul mood; the storm was bad enough, without bleeping complications.

A bovine head poked into the cave. Its fur was matted, its eyes were sickly red, and its steamy breath smelled like zombie gas.

Umlaut felt his clothes wrinkling. He felt terrible, and he knew why: The Ptero-bull was returning to his cave. Suddenly he caught the awful pun: Ptero-bull = terri-ble. The creature must have escaped from a comic strip. He wasn't sure whether the bull or the pun made him feel worse.

The bull's gnarly shoulders forged into the cave. Umlaut's

clothing twisted into virtual knots, and he felt, well, terrible. He saw that Sesame and Sammy were no better off; the serpent was tied in a real knot, and the cat's fur was horribly unkempt and even tangled.

"Let's get out of here!" he cried furiously.

But where could they go? The Ptero-bull was still shoving into the cave, snorting putrid steam, and they absolutely could not approach it.

Then Sammy yowled and bounded erratically toward the back of the cave. "Wait for us!" Umlaut gritted, stumbling after. Sesame hissed and writhed like a sidewinder to go there too.

The cave narrowed, winding down to who knew where. Only the faintly glowing moss on the walls allowed Umlaut to see anything, though the cat and serpent seemed to have night vision. In bad temper, they struggled through it, banging against ugly stalactites and homely stalagmites. But as they progressed, their foul moods eased; they were getting away from the Ptero-bull, who couldn't fit into this narrow passage.

They finally came to a deep dark pool. There they paused. "Where do we go from here?" Umlaut demanded.

Sammy pointed at the pool with a paw, but he didn't try to enter the water. It wasn't that he was afraid to get wet; there was an ominous ripple there. Then a long toothy snout appeared.

"An allegation!" Umlaut exclaimed, recognizing the water creature. He had heard of such predators. "It will chew us up and spit us out in a trice."

Sesame eyed the monster. Umlaut understood her thought: She was judging whether she could outchomp it. That might be possible, for she was a big serpent. But then he saw a second allegation, and a third. She couldn't handle all those at once.

Then a dim bulb flashed. "Find us a way," he told Sammy.

The cat ran down along the side of the pool. The allegations paced him hungrily, only their eyes showing above the water. He came to a wider, higher cave section and looked up. There at the ceiling was a cluster of winged things. "But those are crazies," Umlaut protested. "How can they help?"

Then he realized that they were of a related type: bats. Creatures crazy enough to live in deep caves.

Sammy went to a side section of the cave. There was a pile of rocks of all sizes. He nosed a small one.

"What does a stone have to do with getting us across the water?" But Sammy was insistent, so Umlaut picked up the rock indicated. It was rounded and smooth, an easy one to throw.

Another dim bulb flashed. Umlaut turned and hurled the rock at the bats. They dropped off and somersaulted athletically in the air above the lake. They were amazingly adept flyers, real aerial tumblers.

"They're acro-bats," Umlaut said, realizing.

Now that the bats had been started, they felt compelled to put on a show. They dived and looped, barely skirting the water, spinning and recovering, speeding and halting. It was quite impressive as they made fancy patterns in the air. Umlaut was fascinated by their versatility.

Something nudged his elbow. Reluctantly he looked away from the show. It was Sesame. She gestured with her nose, and Umlaut saw that Sammy Cat was quietly walking back the way they had come. He also saw that the allegations were watching the acro-bat show as raptly as he had been. Everyone loved a good show! But perhaps they also hoped that a few of the bats would fall into the water, where they could be snapped up for quick meals.

And this of course was the way to cross the pool: while the predators were distracted. He walked quietly back to where they had first come to it. Sammy was already swimming across, using the cat-paddle stroke. When he reached the far side, he disappeared.

For a moment Umlaut was afraid an allegation had come and pulled the cat under, but then he realized that the way out was below the surface of the water. Sesame was already swimming across, and she disappeared too. So he followed, stroking as quietly as he could, not at all at ease about this, and dived when he reached the place.

There was a hole in the bank not far below the surface. He saw Sesame's tail disappearing in it. He followed, making his way through a narrow passage, and then came up in a new cave. There was fresh air here, suggesting that there was access to the surface.

They followed Sammy upward and outward, and soon they reached the surface. And it was still raining; Fracto had not finished venting his fury. It was not safe to go out there amid the lightning; a hot bolt could land on one of them. What were they to do?

"Sammy?" Umlaut asked.

The cat considered, then followed the cave back to a branch and squeezed through that. Sesame followed, having no trouble, but Umlaut's shoulders did not want to fit. So he emulated a thinner man and managed to scrape by. He still had to crawl, getting his clothing scuffed and dirty, but he had no choice.

This passage emerged in what appeared to be a residential chamber. Two women sat gazing out into the rain, not aware of the arrival of the three.

Umlaut brushed himself off ineffectively and cleared his throat. Both women turned, saw them, and screamed.

"A dirty snake!" one cried.

"A dirty werecat!" the other cried.

"And a filthy spook!" the first concluded.

That bothered Umlaut. "Now wait half a moment," he said.

"Eeeek!" the second woman cried, affrighted anew. "It talks!"

"Of course it talks," Umlaut said hotly. "I mean, *I* talk. I'm a person, and these are my friends Sammy Cat and Sesame Serpent."

"It's an animal invasion," the first woman said. "They want to catch us and gobble us."

"That's what felines and reptiles do," the second agreed.

Umlaut knew better, but this got to him. Probably some of the irritability remained from the Ptero-bull. He went into lecture mode, heedless of the consequences. "You have no right to judge others by mere appearances," he said. "You don't know us. All you see is the dirt we got covered with crawling through the cave, trying to find help to get through the storm. You assume we're bad because we are dirty. If you got to know us you would find that Sammy is a fine feline who can find anything and brought us here because he thought you would be able to help us. Sesame is a superb serpent who can do emulations and means no harm to anyone. I am Umlaut, also an emulator, just trying to deliver a letter to the Isle of Cats. We got caught by a bad storm and driven into a cave, where a Ptero-bull chased us and allegations threatened us. All we want is to get on with our mission, and your prejudice doesn't help."

The two women exchanged a glance that reeked of significance. They remained sitting, twisting around to see back into the chamber. "Do you mean it?" the first asked.

"Of course I mean it!" Umlaut said hotly. "I said it, didn't I?"

"About not judging by appearances?" the second woman asked.

"Yes! Nobody should be judged just by appearance."

"Then we apologize," the first woman said. "I am Cory."

"And I am Tessa," the second woman said.

"Thank you," Umlaut said gruffly.

Then they both stood up.

Umlaut stifled a gape. Cory was so tall that her dark head barely cleared the ceiling. Tessa was so short that her blonde head barely made it halfway there.

Umlaut had been protesting judging by appearances. Had he encountered these two standing, he might have been guilty of that himself. He had almost made himself a hypocrite. "Uh, sorry for my tone. I guess you already know about that sort of thing."

"We do," Cory said. "But you were right: We shouldn't have done it to you."

"And your cat was right," Tessa said. "We can help you."

Umlaut still felt supremely awkward. "I—we have had a rough time recently, and maybe I was taking it out on you. We'll get out of your way now." Though he dreaded going into the storm.

"We will help you clean up," Cory said.

"And we will lead you safely to the road to the isles," Tessa said.

"Oh, you really don't need to do all that." He had just told them off, and they were responding with favors. Why did he always manage to get stuck on the wrong foot?

"We think we do," Cory said.

"The bathroom is that way," Tessa said. "Take a bath."

"But—"

"All three of you go," Cory said. "You can all take baths."

"And toss out your clothing," Tessa said.

What did they have in mind? Umlaut didn't see any un-awkward way out of this awkwardness, so he did what they urged. He went into their bathroom, and Sammy and Sesame joined him there.

They shut the door. There was a big bathtub already full of water that flowed from a crack in the stone behind it. Umlaut put a finger to the water and found it pleasantly warm. The notion of a good bath became tempting.

He looked at the others. "How do you feel about this?"

Sammy shrugged and started licking the dirt off his fur. That was his way of taking a bath. Sesame made a rippling shrug too and slid into the tub. The water rose but did not overflow; there was a drainage channel for it. She ducked her head under, then brought it up while the rest of her body followed in a downward loop. In this manner she slid through the tub, emerging clean. The odd thing was that the water remained clean; all the washed-off dirt went into the drain.

So Umlaut stripped his filthy clothing—he was the dirtiest of the three—and tossed it through the cracked-open door. Then he got into the tub. It was divine; the water had a sooth-ing as well as a cleansing quality, as though there were a trace of healing elixir in it. Maybe there was; it was never possible to be certain where mountain water came from. Soon he felt much better. He ducked his head and rubbed between his toes, cleansing the crevices.

He got out, quite clean. Sesame was holding a towel in her mouth. He took it and dried himself off. When he was through, she had another item: a robe. Where had she gotten them? He decided not to ask. He donned the robe, which fit nicely.

Umlaut opened thc door, and they stepped and slithered out to rejoin the women. And paused, surprised.

The main cave had changed. Now it was a softly lighted chamber with a table in the center, laden with all manner of foods and drinks. The two women had changed too and were elegantly garbed, with their hair done in nice dark and light coifs. Both were seated, so that the disparity in their heights was less apparent.

"It will take a while for your clothing to dry," Cory said.

"So we thought you might like to eat while you waited," Tessa said.

Umlaut wasn't sure about this. "But we were just on our way to the Isle of Cats. We wouldn't have intruded on you if we hadn't run afoul of Fracto."

Cory glanced at the mouth of the cave. "Fracto hasn't yet given up." Indeed, rain continued to drench the forest.

"You must really have irritated him," Tessa said.

Umlaut smiled sheepishly. "I was stupid. I get that way sometimes. I didn't realize he could hear me."

Cory smiled understandingly. "So many things can see and hear, though we don't realize it. It is best to be careful and courteous throughout."

"Now come join us," Tessa said. "We seldom have serious company."

Umlaut realized with a faint shock that they were lonely. They were too tall and too short to associate freely with ordinary folk without awkwardness. They had found each other, but that wasn't enough. They had gone to a lot of trouble to make a nice meal with nice company. And what was his hurry? He had no schedule for delivering the letters. In fact, the answer to the problem of the Red Spot might be found in between letters, at a place like this, if he gave it a fair chance. He glanced quickly at Sammy and Sesame and saw that they were in no hurry to brave the storm either.

"Thank you," he said. "We'll be glad to accept your kind hospitality."

There was a chair for Umlaut to sit on, a high chair for Sammy to perch on, and a cleared region for Sesame to coil on. They took their places and shared the meal. And it was a great meal, with pies and breads and pastries, juices and sodas and boot rear, fruits and vegetables and smashed potatoes, puddings and cakes and eye scream. There was what seemed to be a baked rat in gravy for Sesame, and a pickled mouse for Sammy. They evidently loved it, and Umlaut loved the human food. He had never tasted better. Soon they were all pretty well stuffed.

"Where did you get such wonderful foods?" Umlaut inquired. "Is it your magic talent?"

They laughed. "Indirectly," Cory said. "We found a cornucopia. It will produce anything we want. But we hardly ever get to exploit it fully. It was fun this time."

"Do you mean a horn of plenty?" Umlaut asked. "I should think that would be very rare and not just around for the taking."

"Not in this realm," Tessa agreed. "But in the next realm they are common, so we took one."

"The next realm?" There was something about this that bothered him.

"That's what we call it," Cory said. "We don't know exactly what it is, just that our shared talent is to reach partway into it. That can be quite handy."

"You can fetch things from it?" Umlaut asked, trying to understand what seemed to be a somewhat obscure concept.

"And put things into it," Tessa agreed. "Or just pass through it, as you will see. That can be most convenient."

Umlaut looked at Sammy, but the cat was curled on his high stool, catnapping. He looked at Sesame, but her snout was resting on the edge of the table, her eyes closed; she seemed to be sleeping too. He started to be alarmed but was too sleepy himself to do anything about it. He slumped against the table.

A nasty thought occurred to him: Had he been judging by appearances, assuming that the two women were what they seemed to be? Was that a mistake? Could they be something else? But before that thought could course all the way through his mind and erupt into some kind of action, he fell asleep. His only faint remaining consciousness was of their hands on him, dragging him somewhere.

He woke to find himself lying on a bed. Sammy lay on one side of him, and Sesame was coiled on the floor beyond. He still wore the robe. What had happened?

He sat up. He felt a bit logy but otherwise okay. Was that deceptive?

Sammy stirred. He seemed to be all right too. Then Sesame lifted her head. She was in good order as well. So what was going on?

He got off the bed and went to the door. It opened readily; it wasn't locked. He looked out. There were the two women, working in the main chamber. Cory was cleaning up the room while Tessa was washing dishes. The table and chairs were gone. They must have done a lot of work.

Cory saw him. "Oh, you're up. We were concerned."

Umlaut didn't quite trust this. "About what?"

Tessa glanced across. "When you all fell asleep, we were afraid something was wrong with the food. We moved you to the bedroom so we could clean up, but we were worried."

"It was good food," Umlaut said. "I think I ate too much." And he realized as he spoke that that was surely it. He had not stuffed himself like that in a long time, not even at Castle Roogna, and probably the same had happened with Sammy and Sesame. It had tasted so wonderful they couldn't stop eating. "I think that cornucopia must have really superior food."

"Oh, it does," Cory said. "When we first got it, we stuffed ourselves so much we threatened to put on weight."

"We had to curb our appetites," Tessa said. "Now we eat sparingly. But we didn't think one meal would be bad for you."

"It wasn't," Umlaut said. He was feeling better as he got fully awake and active. "But you shouldn't have gone to so much trouble for us."

"It was nice having good guests," Cory said.

"Very nice," Tessa agreed wistfully. "Your clothes are dry now." She handed them to Umlaut. They were not only dry, they smelled clean and fresh.

He took them and retreated to the bedroom, where he put them on. Everything was in order, and the scattered items in his pockets remained there. Nothing had been taken. He looked at his companions. They were in good order too.

Umlaut felt embarrassed for his suspicious nature. These were truly nice people. "Is there anything we can, uh, do in return?" he asked as the three of them rejoined the women in the main room.

"Oh, no," Cory said, removing her apron. "We have delayed you too long already. We didn't know you would fall asleep."

"But there is still time to get you to the coast today," Tessa said, putting away the last dish. "It is not a long walk, by sidestepping."

"By what?"

"It's our talent," Cory explained. "We call it sidestepping."

"Because we step into the next realm," Tessa said. "It can be quite handy."

"We'll show you now, if you are ready," Cory said.

Umlaut peered out the cave entrance. The storm remained as bad as ever. "We are, but the weather isn't."

"That's the beauty of sidestepping," Tessa said. "It was wonderful when we discovered it."

Umlaut didn't want to admit that he remained confused. "Then I suppose we are ready."

"This way," Cory said, walking to the entrance and standing just beyond the drenchpour.

"Just take our hands," Tessa said. Then she glanced at Sammy and Sesame. "Or touch us. Once we are in the next realm, then you can be on your own, until it is time to return to this one."

"I can carry Sammy," Umlaut said, picking up the cat. "And if one of you lays her hand on Sesame, will that work?"

"Oh, yes," Cory said. She held out one hand, and Umlaut took it.

"No problem," Tessa said, laying one hand on Sesame's lifted neck.

Then the two women took each other's hands and stepped backward into the rain. Umlaut and Sesame followed, trying not to flinch as the water hit them.

No water hit them. The rain was all around, but somehow they remained dry. It was weird.

"We're through," Cory said. "You may release my hand now."

"Oh. Yes." Umlaut let go and saw that Tessa had removed her hand from Sesame. He set Sammy down.

"This way," Tessa said. She walked on through the rain, remaining dry. They all remained dry.

"Keep in single file," Cory said. "The way is not wide."

They walked through the forest but not in any manner Umlaut had seen before. Tessa led, and Cory followed, with Umlaut, Sammy, and Sesame in the middle. Tessa not only walked through the rain, she walked through plants and even trees without pausing—and the rest of their group passed through them too. It was as if the trees were ghosts, with no substance.

"This is the next realm?" Umlaut asked, bemused.

"Correct," Tessa replied. "There isn't much to see except the regular realm, but we are beyond it at the moment."

"How can we walk through trees?"

"We aren't really doing that. We are walking in the next realm, where there aren't any trees, or much of anything else. So what we see is what's in the regular realm; it bleeds over, as it were."

"As it were," Umlaut agreed, not really understanding.

Soon they came to the shore. A huge, seemingly endless sea stretched out before them, similar to the one the snail's river had emptied into. In fact, Umlaut suspected it was the same sea. But they had reached it much too quickly; it should have been days away. "How can we be here so quickly?"

"The next realm is smaller than ours," Cory said, coming to stand beside him. "So traveling is faster."

That too didn't quite make sense to him, but as usual he preferred not to show his dullness. "Where is the Isle of C—" He broke off, because if he named the isle, Sammy would take off for it, and that could be catastrophic in this next realm.

"It is one of the temporary islands," Tessa said. "You will have to wait for its sign to appear."

"I don't under—" But again his reluctance to admit ignorance balked him. He had more than enough of that, without admitting more. "Uh, thank you."

"We have to return now," Cory said. "It takes energy to remain in the next realm, and we get tired, so we need to get home and rest."

It hadn't occurred to him that they were working to make this trip possible. "We didn't mean to put you to any trouble." Yet that seemed inadequate, as his efforts usually did. "If there is any way we can repay the favor." But they had already been through that.

The two women exchanged a glance, which angled at about 45° because of their heights. "There is one thing," Tessa said shyly.

"Anything!" Umlaut said before he thought.

"A kiss," Cory said.

Sherry's kisses had made him drunk, but these women's talent was different. It should be safe. "Okay."

"Thank you," Tessa said. Then Cory leaned down, and Tessa reached up, and they kissed him simultaneously. Cory's was on the top of his head, which was as far down as she could reach, and Tessa's was on the bottom of his chin, as far up as she could reach.

"Now just half a moment," Umlaut said. "I mess up all the time, but there's no need for the two of you to do that. Let's do this right."

The two looked blankly at him.

"Come over here," he said, going to a rock about a foot high. He put his foot on it—and his foot went through it. He had messed up again.

But they had caught on to his intention. "Maybe if we step back to the current realm," Cory suggested.

"Take our hands," Tessa said. "The rain has finally stopped."

So it had; the land looked wet but drying. They got together the way they had before and stepped through to the real realm.

Then Umlaut stepped on the stone, and it was solid. He stood on it and beckoned to Cory. She came close, and he put his arms around her shoulders and brought her gently in to him. "Thank you for everything," he said and kissed her firmly on the mouth.

He let her go, stepped down, and turned to Tessa. She got up on the rock, and he embraced her. "Thank you for everything else." He kissed her similarly.

He stepped back. "And thank you both so much for whatever I forgot to mention," he said.

They stood there, not moving. Was there a problem? Then he realized that they had freaked out. It had probably been years since they had had a serious kiss. He hadn't realized that women could freak out too, since men did not wear panties or have bosoms.

He snapped his fingers, and they resumed animation. "Thank you," they said together. Then they held hands and took a step through a faint shimmer, reentering the next realm. They waved and walked back inland. They passed through a tree and were gone.

Umlaut was satisfied. He had finally done something right.

8

ISLE OF CATS

S ammy settled down to wait. He was expert at waiting; in fact, he was known as the best speed bump in Xanth.

"Now we have to find the Isle of Cats," Umlaut said, bracing himself to chase after Sammy. But Sammy didn't move, of course. The island wasn't there yet.

They saw a sign: CHIDE FOR CHIPMUNKS.

"I don't think that's it," Umlaut said, as if that wasn't obvious. He was decent, for a human being, but not the brightest bulb on a palace chandelier. "We'll have to look for another sign."

But Sammy remained in place, indicating that that was not their proper course. So they waited.

They gazed out over the sea and saw an island appear. "Maybe that's it!" Umlaut exclaimed, evincing further dimness.

But now the sign said CHOOSE FOR CHIMPS. Oh. At least he had learned that they didn't have to search for another sign.

Something came from the island. It was a boat carrying a chimpanzee. It beached at a small dock they hadn't noticed before, and the chimp got out and scampered into the forest.

The boat remained docked. Sammy thought he recognized the boat, but there was no sense in stirring until he was sure.

Curious, Umlaut approached the boat. It was a weird one. It had no oars or paddles, yet it had moved on its own; the chimp had simply ridden. "I wonder what makes it go?"

Sammy decided that it was time to clarify the nature of this unusual craft. He went up and rubbed against its side. The boat rubbed back.

"You mean it's alive?" Umlaut asked, surprised. Duh.

Sammy climbed into the boat. The boat heaved itself out of the water and walked on land. It had ten pairs of webbed feet. It was definitely the one.

Umlaut evidently hadn't thought about how they would reach the Isle of Cats when they found it; thinking ahead wasn't one of his strong points. Slowly he realized that this could solve that problem. "Will you take us to the Isle of Cats, when it appears?" he asked.

The boat nodded, in its fashion, bobbing its prow. Sammy nodded, unsurprised.

Umlaut went into his nineteen-questions mode, questioning the boat, and finally learned what Sammy had known: that it was Para, son of a quack and a dream boat, one of the weirder love spring encounters, and that it liked to take folk places. It wasn't confined to the water so could take them anywhere.

Sesame hissed, attracting their attention. The sign had changed. Now it said COME FOR COWS. Indeed, there was the sound of mooosic across the water. "Not this one," Umlaut said. Double duh. "But keep watching; we don't want to miss the Isle of Cats." For, as Breanna of the Black Wave would have said, sure.

Umlaut continued to talk with Para, who seemed to like the attention. Who didn't? Meanwhile the sign changed to CO-OPT FOR COYOTES. That was not the one. Then it said CROSS FOR CROCODILES. Still not right. CAREER FOR CAMELS. Not yet. CALL FOR CARIBOU. In the course of the next hour several more islands appeared, fading in from wherever they were (perhaps the next realm), their signs changing to match. Sammy snoozed but kept half an eye out for the right sign.

CAPER FOR CATS.

"Not yet," Umlaut said, weary of these endless changes.

What? Sammy nudged him, and Sesame hissed. Then the man did a double take. "That's it!"

Sammy and Sesame exchanged a glance: They had been trying to tell him.

They piled into Para, who duck-footed it to the water and plunged in. There was room in the craft for all of them, though Sesame had to lay herself out in several lines along the bottom. They forged across to the island, which seemed to bear whiskers. They had found it at last.

Meanwhile Umlaut took out the letter to Princess Ivy. Sammy knew he was supposed to read them before delivering them. He watched the human's lips move as he read and picked up the gist of it.

Dear Ivy,

I wish you were here in Mundania. My talent is growing plants, but without the aid of magic, I have to depend on the weather.

Fracto has sent a cohort here who is maniacally controlling our climate's functions. Rather presumptuous of them to expect he'd find a welcome here. At this time of year in our valley, temperatures are usually becoming quite warm and our sun graces us with his presence for several hours daily. Since Fatso's friend has been with us, he lurks about, prowling back and forth, creating ghastly times. We have not seen the sun for many days, wind is constantly howling, and it has been raining continually. For some areas this is typical, but not here! In his lair in the clouds he takes fiendish delight in teasing us. He flicks a wisp of fog, and the rain stops for a few moments. We just dare to hope that the perverse weather patterns have changed, when . . . *blink* . . . it is pouring again, and cold! Our prophets sadly tell me to expect more of the same for quite some time.

Our valley is famous for its fruit production, but the orchards and vineyards are suffering. I have strained my talent to the utmost but am still discovering fatalities. If you were here you could enhance it and we would be fine again.

Ever consider making another visit to Mundania? No, I did not think so, but writing you has made me feel marginally better.

Your friend,
Arjayess

P.S. Tell Fracto to get lost and take his friend Curmudgeon Cloud with him!!

Umlaut looked up. "I don't see anything dangerous about this letter. It just tells the truth about Fracto." He looked at Sammy. "What do you think?"

Sammy thought it was a fine letter. He especially liked the way it called the ornery cloud Fatso. If Fracto heard that, he would blow his top so high it would hit the moon. Theoretically Fracto was now a benign cloud, but he still rained on picnics when he thought he could get away with it.

Umlaut put away the letter, satisfied that it was safe to deliver. Of course Sammy knew it also did not solve the problem of Demon Jupiter's Red Spot, which was even now hurtling toward Earth and Xanth. Sammy had no idea how they were going to handle that. He was afraid the Red Spot was a bigger and worse storm than any Fracto could manage. He didn't see how any stupid letter would deal with that. But the Good Magician was never wrong, in his devious human way, so something was bound to happen.

They landed at another little dock; it seemed there was a pair of them that Para shuttled between, though he was hardly confined to them. "Uh, will you take us back across, when we're done here?" Umlaut asked Para as they disembarked. "We'd really appreciate it."

The boat nodded, glad to be of service.

Sammy stood and looked around. He saw catfish swimming near the shore, and catnip was growing in patches. There was a catsup puddle. Not far distant was the entrance to a catacomb. A river had a cataract, surmounted by a catwalk. There was definitely a feline quality to this island. He liked it.

However, they had come to deliver a letter to Ivy, who was visiting her husband's parents. "Where is—" Umlaut started. But Sammy was already bounding ahead; he knew where they were going. "Wait for us!" the human cried foolishly behind.

What was required, naturally, was not waiting but keeping up.

They passed by a number of prowling cats; this was, after all, their isle. Sammy ignored them; there would be another time. Soon they came to a nice house in a garden. Sammy charged up to the door and scratched on it.

It opened, and the Sorceress Vadne appeared. "Can it be?" she asked, looking down at Sammy.

Of course it was; who else would it be? Sammy brushed by her and went inside. And there was Princess Ivy. "Sammy!" she cried, sweeping him up and enhancing him with a few well-placed strokes. At least she knew what was what.

Sammy settled down in Ivy's nice embrace and endured the dull human introductions. Humans put great store in pointless formalities, usually at the expense of necessary attention to cats. But that was the way they were. Maybe in a few more millennia they would evolve to the point of recognizing what was truly important. But they had a long way to go. Fortunately it was possible to let the dull words roll over him and fade into the woodwork where they belonged.

"I am, uh, Umlaut. My talent is emulation; I can make myself seem like something else, within reason. This is, well, Sesame Serpent, who is helping me, with a similar talent. And I guess you know Sammy Cat, who comes from Jenny Elf. He can find anything except home."

Half right and half outrage. Of course they knew Sammy; they had been at Jenny's wedding to the werewolf prince. But the notion that Sammy belonged to Jenny was preposterous; *Jenny* belonged to *Sammy*. Why did humans and their elf variants think they were the center of the universe? Didn't they pay any attention at all to reality?

"I am Magician Murphy, with the talent of making things go wrong, though I don't practice it anymore. This is my wife the Sorceress Vadne, whose talent is topology; she can change the forms of things without changing their essential natures."

"I am the Princess Ivy," Ivy said, stroking another stroke; at least she wasn't neglecting that. "My talent is to enhance living things." She glanced down. "But of course Sammy doesn't need enhancing."

Now *that* was a worthwhile observation.

"And this is my husband Grey Murphy, whose talent is to nullify magic."

Magician Murphy turned again to Umlaut. "And what is your business with us?"

"I have an, uh, letter to deliver to Princess Ivy." He stepped across to Ivy and handed her the letter. "From Mundania."

"From Mundania!" Ivy said, surprised. "I only really got to know one person there, and I married him." She glanced at Grey.

"All the letters are from Mundania," Umlaut explained. "They seem to be from strangers to different Xanthians. I have delivered letters to Princess Ida, the Zombie Master, Queen Irene—"

"My mother and my twin sister," Ivy said. "You have me bracketed. How did you come across the letters?"

Before Umlaut could go into the dull details of that, Magician Murphy broke in. "All in good time. First we have one other introduction to make: our feline associate, Claire Voyant." He gestured to a cushion set in a nook on the far wall where a cat reposed.

Sammy looked, of course. His gaze met that of the other cat, and he did the feline equivalent of freaking out. She was— just so—feline. He had never encountered a cat like her. Actually he had not encountered many cats at all in the Land of Xanth and fewer he would care to know. This Isle of Cats was a rare discovery and surely had many interesting folk of the feline persuasion. But Claire—what a queen! She was pure glossy black, her fur in perfect order, her whiskers long and fine, her paws delicate, an absolutely lovely creature.

The human dialogue continued, but Sammy tuned it out. His attention was wholly taken by Claire. She stretched languorously and jumped down from her nook, indicating by a significant twitch of her tail that he should follow her.

He wriggled in Ivy's embrace, and she automatically set him down. She was a princess and therefore well trained. Then he moved in a relaxed manner toward Claire and followed her out of the room. She led him through the kitchen and to a cat door in the back, leading to the outdoors. She continued walking along a catwalk, and he continued following.

The isle seemed to be divided into sections, each with its own habitat. They passed through a lion veldt, a tiger jungle, puma country, a jaguar forest, a leopard spot, a Persian carpet, a Siamese temple, and other distinct regions. Claire ignored them all, and Sammy tried to, though they were interesting. He had had no idea that so many varieties of cat existed in Xanth. But of course that was the nature of these special islands: They were only deviously related to mainland Xanth. Sammy thought of the Isle of Women and the Isle of Wolves in the *W* section; they faded in and out as convenient for their inhabitants. Had he realized there was an Isle of Cats he would have sought it long ago.

They almost collided with an unsteady black cat. Claire was annoyed but then picked up on the situation. This was Midnight Cat, recently arrived from Mundania, and lost. Go to the admission center, Claire suggested. They would assign a suitable residence. Midnight nodded appreciatively and headed in the indicated direction.

They came to a massive tree with wonderfully rough bark. Claire shinnied up the trunk, and Sammy followed. They passed branch after branch, some occupied by other cats, some clear. They continued upward until the trunk grew small and swayed in the wind. At last they came to the highest branch, which was actually a triple fork topping the tree, with cords strung between the branches to make a kind of nest. What a penthouse!

Gaze that way, Claire indicated.

Sammy gazed that way and saw a neighboring isle. His ears perked up and his eye slits widened. Birds!

The Isle of Birds, she agreed. Every kind of bird nested there, from humming to roc. Of course the treaty of noninterference they had made with the residents prevented them from raiding it or eating any of the birds, even when they strayed across to the Isle of Cats. But it was always a salivating pleasure just to watch.

Sammy had to agree. Even the little bit of the Isle of Birds he could see was mouthwatering in its collection of feathered flyers, a most pleasant sight. Then he glanced at a giant nest atop a stout tree even taller than this one and saw the head of a roc watching them with similar avidity. Rocs were birds of prey, rather large ones. Perhaps that treaty was just as well; predation was a two-way process.

The small talk was done. Now at last they could relax and converse in depth. They did so by body positions, tail switches, whisker twitches, and spot smells the human folk called pheromones. Taken all together, it was a far more competent language than the limited vocal sounds the humans uttered from their bunghole mouths.

It was time for the formal introduction. He was Sammy Cat, he signaled, actually giving his real name rather than the limited designation humans knew him by. His normal associate was Jenny Elf.

She was Claire Voyant, she replied similarly. Her normal associates were the Magician Murphy and Sorceress Vadne.

His talent was to find anything except home.

Hers was clairvoyance, of course.

Then they went into proper detail. Sammy explained how he had taken Jenny Elf as his associate, because she couldn't see well and constantly needed help finding things. They had resided on the World of Two Moons until Jenny had said she wanted a feather, so naturally Sammy had zeroed in on a good feather. That turned out to be in another realm, a feather from the wing of a flying centaur. Then of course they couldn't get home again so had been stuck here in the foolish Land of Xanth. So they had made themselves useful, keeping company with little Che Centaur and poor lame Gwendolyn Goblin. Eventually, with Sammy's guidance, Che Centaur had become the tutor for Sim Bird, who was destined eventually to know everything in the universe; he was very smart for a bird. Gwenny Goblin, with similar guidance, had become a goblin chiefess. Finally Sammy had guided his associate Jenny to marriage with a werewolf prince. That wouldn't have been his choice, but she had a thing about wolves; she liked to ride them. So now she was happy riding Prince Jeremy in his wolf form, and who knew what she did with his human form, it was disturbing the storks, and Sammy was taking some time off for himself. Since he couldn't find what was now his home, he was associating with Umlaut Human and

Sesame Serpent, both of whom really needed guidance.

Claire had noticed. In fact she found Umlaut distinctly odd, because he wasn't really there.

Not there?

To explain that she had to clarify the nature of her own history and talent. She had dwelt all her life on the Isle of Cats, never feeling the need to wander elsewhere, and now had high status here. But her prior human associates had proved to be unsatisfactory—they had twice forgotten to warm her evening dish of cream—and had to be replaced. The new associates were of magician and sorceress caliber, which qualified them, and had had some experience with cats in Mundania, so Claire had decided to give them a chance and let them occupy her house. That had worked out well enough, so she had kept them. Their son Grey was a magician who married the Sorceress/Princess Ivy, who would someday rule the Land of Xanth. Overall, it was a satisfactory situation, but of course that was not coincidence, because of Claire's talent. Neither had she been surprised by Sammy's arrival, for similar reason: They were going to bat about fine catnip together.

Sammy did not like to confess ignorance—it wasn't feline—but needed a clarification of the nature of clairvoyance. Was it like seeing another place via a magic mirror?

Hardly. It was far broader than that and infinitely more subtle. By expanding her clairvoyance she became very aware of herself, her thoughts, and her beliefs. Most folk, animal, human, and feline, had lives constructed from thoughts that were not even their own. They were actually living other folk's expectations and desires for them. In fact most folk were defined in the past, and the definitions had become irrelevant. They no longer applied to who they were now. But those folk did not realize that and so remained captive of those outdated definitions.

Sammy was amazed. It was true; he had been defined as a routine cat, doing things for his human associates instead of for himself, and had never thought to break out of the pattern. He had guided any number of prominent human folk (Jenny Elf and Jeremy Wolf were human where it counted) to success and satisfaction, but only recently had he tried to guide himself.

And not very successfully, Claire pointed out with justified feline smugness. Instead of guiding Jenny and Jeremy, he was now guiding Umlaut and Sesame. Nice enough folk, surely (some of her best friends were humans or reptiles), but in the end defined by their irredeemable limitations: *They were not felines*. Therefore they could never even hope to achieve ultimate grace.

Sammy had to admit it was true. Their ultimate fault had no remedy. Still, he wished them no ill and wanted to help them achieve their peculiar mission of delivering mundane letters and somehow saving Xanth from the dread Red Spot.

Claire conceded that he was nice to feel that way. Then she resumed her clarification of her talent. As she had expanded her clairvoyance relating to others, she had seen the thoughts, beliefs, and games that were played out in the other folk's realities. As she saw them more clearly, she had also come to see herself more clearly. She had become aware of the aspects of her own existence that held similarly limiting beliefs. She developed tools of understanding that enabled her to surmount these negative patterns within herself that had been holding back her life. She had learned to restructure herself, to fill herself with her own positive energy patterns that could best support her in the present—her *now*. Today she had the full power of her talent available to apply to whatever she chose.

Thus she had known that Sammy was coming, because of his future impact on her own life. His talent of finding complemented her talent of knowing. Together they could perhaps accomplish the salvation of Xanth and, more important, their own uplifting to higher consciousness.

Sammy was impressed. She was correct; she had to be. Her understanding vastly surpassed his, but she was willing to share it with him. But how did this relate to the nonexistence of Umlaut Human?

Well, she hadn't had a chance to study the human carefully, but it was immediately clear that he did *not* relate. He wasn't really there. Oh, she conceded that maybe he thought he was there, but that was a function of his limited perspective. So much of what folk thought about themselves was erroneous, as she had explained. It was possible for them to ascend beyond their illusions, with proper guidance. But not for Umlaut, because there was no there there.

But Sammy had been traveling with the human man, and he not only seemed to be there, he had kissed two women and they had liked it.

Well, she explained, they *thought* he was there. That made the difference.

Sammy remembered what the twin princesses had said to Umlaut, about the state of his existence. Dawn, whose talent was to know anything about anything living, had said he was not living. Eve, whose talent was to know anything about anything that wasn't living, had said that he wasn't dead. He had said that he didn't understand, and they had said that they didn't understand either. That was all there had been to that dialogue. Of course, those princesses were only eleven years old, which was young for their kind. Still, they were both sorceresses and so should have known what Umlaut was.

So their judgment concurred with Claire's, she concluded. That meant it was correct. But there still was no answer. They would have to put it aside for a while, to gather more information and greater understanding.

But they would not be here on the Isle of Cats long, Sammy reminded her. The letter had been delivered, and they would be moving on.

True, and she had known their presence here would be brief. She would have to leave her house in charge of the human tenants and accompany him on the remainder of the mission, in order to fathom what had to be fathomed.

Sammy tried to mask his pleasure at that prospect, but of course she was aware of it. But she had something else to show him before they left this perch. She directed his attention to the other side of the Isle of Cats. There was another island there, overgrown by trees, looking pretty wild.

Sammy wondered whether that would be the Isle of Dogs. No, she clarified, that was beyond. This was the Isle of Dystopia, otherwise known as the Isle of the Damned or the Isle of Dread.

Damned?

Dystopia was the opposite of Utopia, she clarified. A miserable place.

Bad magic?

Worse: no magic at all.

But that was Mundania, Sammy protested.

No, Mundania had some magic. There was gravity, which also helped Xanth, and rainbows, and scattered instances of magical thinking, so it wasn't an entire loss. But the Isle of Dystopia had no magic at all. That was why it shunned contact with Xanth, lest its shame become known.

Sammy could appreciate why.

Of course others avoided it, further isolating its denizens. But there was a legend, she continued. It was that someday an inhabitant of that dread isle would manage to visit Xanth and turn out to have a most awkward magic talent. So it would be shown that the folk there did have magic, but not of any kind they wanted. A supreme irony.

That must be why the original people settled there, Sammy thought. They knew their magic was bad, so they fled to a place without magic and hid from Xanth.

But someday, Claire asserted, that person would escape to Xanth and spoil the effort of centuries.

What was the awkward talent? That she didn't know. But she intended to find out, someday when she had nothing better to do. To have her talent work she would have to set foot on the isle, and no one would help her do that. So that project was on hold for now. There was more immediate business.

They took a last lingering look at the Isle of Birds, then started down the tree. This was harder than climbing up had been, as it always was, but Sammy didn't want to appear incompetent, so he struggled felinefully along. But Claire knew that too and did not bother to mask her amusement.

Finally they reached the bottom. Sammy was afraid his stretched claws would never retract, but they did. He was getting old for this sort of thing.

Claire, still amused, let him in on a secret: She knew where there was some healing elixir—and some youth elixir. It was one of the benefits of her talent. He need have no concern about health or age.

Sammy had been halfway mesmerized by her from the out-

set. This only added to the effect. They had understood that
the delivery of the letters would solve the problem of the Red
Spot. They were coincidentally solving more than that.

Coincidentally, perhaps, Claire indicated. But not accidentally. It all was part of a larger pattern whose meaning even
Claire did not understand. But she intended to, in due course.

The humans were wrapping up their long-winded discussion of inconsequentials, and Umlaut and Sesame were ready
to go. Grey and Ivy would be continuing their visit, however.
That might cushion the despair of Murphy and Vadne when
Claire departed. Sammy didn't envy her the task of conveying
her decision to them.

But meanwhile he had the task of telling Umlaut and Sesame that their party was expanding, and why. They decided
to separate, each cat meeting with the appropriate folk, conveying the news separately but at the same time.

It was a job just getting the parties separate; they seemed
determined not to comprehend. But finally they succeeded,
and Sammy got Umlaut and Sesame outside the house to play
nineteen questions, which was a clumsy but sure way to get
something across.

Soon Umlaut was getting there; he wasn't entirely obtuse.
"You want the other cat to come along with us? Why?"

Sammy tried to explain about clairvoyance, but this concept was beyond the human's intellectual means. So he pretended it was mere romance.

"Oh, she's *the* cat for you, just as Sesame's the serpent for
Soufflé. Now I understand." At least he thought he understood, not having the benefit of clairvoyance. It would have
to do.

"But what about Magician Murphy and Sorceress Vadne?
She's their cat. They may not let her go."

Sammy suppressed his ire at this galloping ignorance. The
man couldn't help it; he was human. Sammy just hoped that
Claire did not pick up on this with her magic perception. He
would have to caution her about this, so she didn't get too
upset. Meanwhile, to Umlaut he simply indicated that Claire
was explaining the matter to her residents now.

"Well, if it's okay with them, I guess it's okay with us,"
Umlaut said, glancing at Sesame for confirmation. She nod-

ded; she had been quicker to understand than he had. That made sense, because she was another animal, even if not a cat.

Soon the Murphys emerged from the house. "It seems Claire wants to accompany you," Magician Murphy said. "If that makes her happy, we would not care to be the ones to deny her. We'll remain here and keep the house in good order. But we'll certainly miss her. She's some cat."

The man was so girt about by his ignorance that it was painful, but he was right about the last of it: She certainly was some cat.

They set out immediately, as they understood that the isle remained in contact with Xanth but would separate in a half hour. If they did not leave it now, they would not be able to depart for several more days.

Para was waiting for them. Claire went up to sniff noses with him, and Sammy saw that he knew her and accepted her. That was probably a good recommendation, not that one was needed at this point.

They got in, and Para duck-footed it into the water. He was orienting to cross to the mainland Xanth when Claire suddenly stood with hair on end, hissing. Para halted immediately.

"What is it?" Umlaut asked, confused. "We need to cross, before—"

Then he broke off, staring ahead, as did the rest of them. There was a stirring in the water, deepening as it moved. The water was moving in a great circle, faster and faster. In fact it was a whirlpool.

"Charybdis!" Umlaut exclaimed. "She would have caught us and swallowed us whole!"

Indeed she would have—and Claire Voyant had known and stopped them before they got too far out to avoid it.

Slowly the whirlpool moved on, pushed by the current. It seemed to want to stay, in the hope that the boat might yet be foolish enough to venture within reach, but Para valued his life as much as anyone did. Only when Charybdis was well beyond their route did Para resume the crossing.

"But how could that whirlpool be here?" Umlaut asked plaintively. "It's on Zombie World."

That was a pretty good question, for a human. Sammy looked at Claire, but she shrugged. She knew only what, not how.

It occurred to Sammy that there had been several problems interfering with the delivery of the letters. Could it be that some power did not want them to be delivered? What power, and why? The question made him unfelinely nervous.

9

SUBMARINE SAND WITCH

U mlaut had not been too keen on adding another member to their little party, but after the way Claire Cat stopped them from going into the whirlpool he was more than satisfied to have her along. He was beginning to wonder whether the problems they had had on the way to delivering letters were not just coincidences. The way the Demoness Metria had tried to distract him from his mission and faded out in annoyance when it didn't work. Or when that girl Caitlin had lured him into the comic strip where there was the panty trap, and then it had seemed that Caitlin wasn't exactly where or what he had thought she was—could there have been a fake Caitlin trying to get him in trouble? And the appearance of the Dire Strait, getting them into trouble again—and the reappearance of the deadly whirlpool. There had also been the way Fracto Cloud had come; had he been looking for them, to mess them up? Umlaut didn't want to be paranoid, but he wondered. Suppose Metria had tried it herself, then emulated Caitlin, then talked Scylla and Charybdis into intercepting the party? She could certainly have talked to Fracto. How she could have gotten the whirlpool to come to Xanth he wasn't sure, but it did seem to have happened.

But there was one big problem with this idea: Why would Metria, or any demon, bother? Delivering letters was dull, harmless business, not worth interrupting. Except that it was supposed to show how to deal with the menace of the Red Spot. If one of those letters led him to that answer, and Metria didn't want him to find it, that might explain it. But why wouldn't she want that problem solved? She was a creature of Xanth too and would suffer if it suffered. So it made no sense after all, and probably his problems were just because he tended to bumble. Metria hadn't been paying any attention, after she learned how dull their business was. He had let his foolish imagination run away with his thoughts.

Claire Cat looked up and made a small hiss that startled Sesame. There was a swirl of smoke before his face. A feminine mouth formed. "Did I hear my gnome?"

"Your what?" he asked before he thought.

"Appellation, designation, classification, denomination, monogram—"

"Cognomen?"

"Whatever," the smoke agreed crossly as it expanded into a voluptuous female form.

"No, Metria, I don't think you did, because I wasn't speaking."

"But you were thinking of me," she said. "I heard the thought."

Oops. "You have me live to wrongs."

"I have you how?" the dusky form asked, reaching for him.

"Dead to rights!" he said, getting it straight before she could lead him into another three-questions routine. That word confusion of hers was contagious.

"Then I'd better give you a nice embrasure." She started to draw him in. It was surprising how solid her front was, considering that her backside still trailed off into curling smoke.

Again his mouth was too fast for his caution. "A nice what?"

"Crenel, battlement, parapet, merlon, turret—"

She was way off on the wrong track. "Hug?"

"Don't mind if I do," she agreed, embracing him. "So nice of you to ask." Her amazingly bouncy front squeezed against him.

He had indeed foolishly asked for it. He managed to avoid her attempt to kiss him by asking another question. "What do you want with me, Metria?"

"Well, now. I—"

He had bungled again. "Don't answer that. I don't want it anyway."

"But you were thinking of me," she reminded him. "What else could it be?"

Umlaut got annoyed. "I was wondering if you are trying to stop me from delivering letters, and if so, why?"

She gazed at him a moment, her mouth forming an O of chagrin. Then she faded out.

Astonished, he gazed at the spot where she had floated. His simple question had truly set her back. That implied guilt. But if she was trying to stop him, why hadn't she simply lied about it? Or tried harder to seduce him? He was becoming rather curious about exactly what seduction entailed.

He looked at Sesame, then at the two cats. It was Claire who had the answer, as about three questions determined; she was remarkably quick to catch on to his method. Yes, the demoness was trying to distract him from delivering the letters. But Claire again knew only what, not why.

Para reached the shore and waddled out on the beach. "Thank you," Umlaut said and got ready to step out of the boat.

But Claire caught his eye. "I shouldn't get out?" he asked. She nodded. "Because there is danger?" She shook her head. Then he caught on. "Para wants to take us!"

For Para was a sociable boat and liked traveling with people who were doing things. Well, why not? Since the boat could go overland as readily as over water, he could be a real help. "Okay."

Para did a little jiggle of joy that threatened to nudge them out of their places.

Umlaut settled back and brought out the bundle of letters. To whom should they deliver next?

The top remaining letter was addressed to Snortimer Bed Monster.

"Who?" he asked.

Sammy had to explain this one. It seemed that every child in Xanth who slept on a bed had a pet bed monster under it. Its job was to grab any convenient ankle and make the child scream, needlessly alarming the parents. The monster could not leave the shelter of the bed because direct daylight destroyed it, and at night it had to stay near enough to grab any unwary ankle. Some bad children teased their monsters by dangling their feet temptingly down and yanking them out of the way just before the monster could grab. But when the child grew up and joined the Adult Conspiracy, at about age eighteen, the bed monster faded sadly away, because it was part of the Adult Conspiracy not to believe in monsters under beds. It was an ongoing tragedy that occurred also in Mundania. Animals believed, but grown humans did not. Surely, Sammy suggested, Umlaut himself had a bed monster back home, so he knew how it was.

Umlaut considered that and drew a blank. He didn't remember any bed monster. Neither did he remember a bed. In fact he couldn't even remember a home. That was weird.

He saw Claire exchange a significant glance with Sammy. "What?" he demanded. "What do you know?"

They were reluctant, but he insisted that they tell him. But what they told him was not to be believed. "I don't exist?" he asked incredulously. "But obviously I do exist, because I'm right here arguing with you, and we're delivering letters." But he remembered what Princesses Dawn and Eve had said about him being neither alive nor dead. They were sorceresses and could tell anything about anything living or unliving. How could they be wrong? But they *had* to be wrong.

Yet Claire was adamant, and Sammy agreed with her. Umlaut had no reality she could fathom. He might not be an illusion, since he seemed to have substance, but he wasn't real.

"Well, I sure don't feel like an illusion," he said hotly. "And I'm not acting like one. I think Claire's voyance just doesn't apply to me. Maybe I'm under a deflective spell so she can't orient on me. Obviously I'm here in all the ways that count."

Claire considered and yielded the point. But that did not fully reassure him. Claire wasn't a sorceress, just a cat with a special talent; she might have limits she didn't know about. But what about the two princesses? And what about the Demoness Metria, who was not only trying to stop him from delivering letters but also had faded immediately out when he accused her of it. Why had she had such a peculiar reaction? It was as if she had truly considered him for the first time and been really set back. And why couldn't he remember his home? Why couldn't he remember anything before he fled Sherry and wound up in the Castle Zombie dungeon? Had Sherry's kisses done more than wipe out his last date with her? Had they destroyed his other memories too? That seemed like too much, for she was no sorceress, just a girl with sweet kisses. He knew she didn't mean him any harm; in fact she wanted to marry him. And surely would have, if he hadn't fled.

Sesame nudged him. She knew he existed, because he had a talent like hers. She didn't care what others thought.

He hugged her neck. "Thank you, snake eyes," he said.

Then he got back to business. "So what happened to Snortimer? Princess Ivy is now grown and adult. Didn't he fade away?"

No, it turned out that he was saved by an unusual development. Princess Ivy also had a pet dragon, Stanley Steamer, who had disappeared, so Grundy Golem went with Snortimer to find Stanley. They succeeded, but Stanley was protecting the fauns & nymphs from predation. So Snortimer took over that job so Stanley could go home with Ivy and later resume his job patrolling the Gap Chasm. That sacrifice of the bed monster had indefinitely extended his existence, because the fauns & nymphs weren't really adult, despite having adult bodies; they believed in Snortimer throughout. So he could receive a letter.

Umlaut realized that there was a lot of Xanth history in obscure bypaths. "So where are the fauns & nymphs?" he asked.

They were in the Faun & Nymph Retreat just south of Lake Ogre Chobee.

"And how do we get there quickly?"

Para, who understood both human and animal languages, made a quiver. He knew a way.

"But we don't want to make you carry us all that way through the jungle," Umlaut protested. "That would wear out your feet."

Para wasn't concerned. He carried them back to the sea and into it. Where was he going?

A human female head popped out of the water. "You called, Para?"

Para nodded, then settled into quiet. Since the swimming woman was human, Umlaut would have to negotiate. "Uh, hello," he said, noticing that her long hair was the color of seaweed.

She eyed him. "Why, you're a young human man."

"I'm Umlaut. And with me are Sesame Serpent, Sammy Cat, and Claire Voyant Cat. Para thought you could help us travel."

"And I am Mela Merwoman," she said.

"A mermaid!" he exclaimed, surprised.

"Merwoman," she clarified. "We are a salt sea subspecies and better endowed." She swished her tail and lifted her foresection out of the water.

Umlaut tried not to stare, but his eyeballs ignored his effort. She was indeed marvelously well endowed. Then she inhaled, and he almost fell out of the boat.

"The seas can get rougher than the rivers or lakes," she explained helpfully, "so we need a bit more padding."

He finally managed to wrench his eyes from the pads. "So can you help us?"

"That depends on where you are going."

"To the Fauns & Nymphs."

Mela considered. "Yes, we can reach that by water, though it's inland. We'll have to use the acqui-fur, which means a sand witch."

"Aquifer? Sandwich?" But her tail was already flipping out of the water as she dived, on her way somewhere.

Then a crack appeared on the surface of the water. It broadened into a crevice. Umlaut watched it nervously. Was the whirlpool coming back? But Para did not seem nervous. What was going on?

Mela reappeared. "I sure found a fish," she said.

"That looks more like a fracture," Umlaut said.

"Or a fish sure."

"Fissure?"

"Fissure Cutbait," she said. "She's the best, for fast work."

The break in the water became still wider and deeper. "What a cleavage!" Umlaut said, alarmed.

"Why, thank you," Mela said, inhaling again.

The boat rode over the brink of the fault and tipped down into it. Umlaut hung on, and the cats dug their claws into the wood, while Sesame braced her coils against the sides. They slid down into the gap. Then the fissure closed, trapping them inside. It was like a giant mouth.

Umlaut held his breath as the water surrounded them, but he knew he couldn't hold it long.

"Oh, don't be foolish," Mela said, swimming into the boat with them. She tickled Umlaut on the ribs, forcing him to burst out laughing, losing his breath. He was afraid he would drown but discovered he could after all breathe. But he was surrounded by water. What was this?

"Cutbait is a water fissure, evolved from a sand witch," Mela explained, flexing her tail. It was certainly a nice tail. "You do get sandwiched between her sides when she submarines, but you can breathe."

So it seemed. "A giant submarine sand witch," Umlaut agreed weakly.

Now the huge fish, if that was what it was, oriented to the south and swam rapidly along the coast. Not only could all of them breathe, they could see the sand, shells, and seaweed of the bottom of the sea. It seemed that Cutbait, being made of water, was completely translucent.

"So what is it you want with the fauns & nymphs?" Mela inquired as she sat beside him. "What do those nymphs have that I don't?"

"Nothing," he said. "I mean, I don't want anything with them."

She frowned. "You spoiled my setup line. You were supposed to say 'legs.' "

He was getting lost again. "Legs?"

"Nymphs have legs. I have a tail. A nice piece of tail."

Oh. "Tail," he agreed numbly.

"Because I'm not that kind of girl."

"Uh, yes." It was still hard to believe that a very full-bodied mermaid—mer*woman*—was sitting hip to hip with him. "You have to swim."

"But then I say, 'I can *become* that kind of girl,' and I change, like this." Her tail shifted and became a fine bare pair of legs.

Umlaut had been preserving his eyeballs by staring ahead instead of sideways, but this caught him by surprise. He had never before seen such legs, that far up.

Then the tail was back. "Are you recovered?" Mela asked.

"From what?"

She laughed, jiggling grandly. "You freaked out, and I'm not even wearing panties. That's a real accomplishment, at my age. So I changed back before your eyeballs fried."

"Your age?" He seemed to be locked into brevity; one or two words were all he could get out at a time in the near presence of this splendid creature.

"I am forty-nine years old."

He turned to stare directly at her. That was another mistake. He blinked, and suddenly she was wearing a piece of cloth over her bosom. He must have freaked out again, and she had taken another step to unfreak him. "I—I'm amazed."

"We water monsters preserve well," she said. "Still, it's nice to know our stuff still works. That way I know Naldo isn't just humoring me."

"Naldo?"

"My husband. Prince Naldo Naga. That makes me a princess. I love it. He's eleven years younger than I am, but princes are ageless. But I also love the sea, so I go out for a swim every so often. So I answered Para's call. Para's a really nice boat. His mother was a dream boat."

"So he told me." There: He had gotten out four words in a row.

"So you're not looking for a nice nymph to play with,"

Mela continued. "Though I understand they play very well. So why are you going to the Faun & Nymph Retreat?"

That he could answer. "To deliver a letter to Snortimer."

"Ivy's bed monster!" she exclaimed. "I didn't know he got letters."

"It's from Mundania. We're delivering a number of them. I have to read them before I deliver them, because the one that went to Demon Jupiter made him hurl his Red Spot at us."

"Those big Demons are touchy when mortals bother them. What does Snortimer's letter say?"

"I haven't read it yet."

"Then let's read it together."

"Uh, all right." Her remarkable assets were covered but still almost nudging him; it was nigh impossible to turn her down. He opened the letter, and they read it.

> Village Kaledon
> Otch Enau Kane Valley

Sir Snortimer:

My residence is with the mundane human adult who has been posting articles of correspondence to Xanth. She is named Arjayess. My correct title is Sir Winslow Cromwell Wentworthy XV. The dratted woman calls me "a dust bunny." Ludicrous expression regarding one of my aristocratic bearing, what? Quite demeaning I say, quite.

I am assuming your position of monster-under-the-bed has more dignity than that of what my life has been reduced to. At the very least your existence has been acknowledged. You are also awarded due respect and allowed to maintain your personal dignity. Here, my human weekly probes under the sleeping platform with a terribly violent machine that inhales everything within reach. Thus disturbing my repose, though "coward" is not in the Wentworthy vocabulary, I prudently retreat to the farthest corner. One must exercise caution about foreign contraptions, must we not? I am then ignored for another seven days.

This day I have become incensed to the point I find

it necessary to advance upon the woman's writing machine. I feel I must state a formal note of grievance. The adults in this world are entirely daft. They deny magic exists. The very young of the species are aware of it; however, the grown-ups refuse to believe. The human here is so involved with growing flowers—I ask you!—that she wouldn't recognize a chimera if it stepped right before her. Likely say, "Oh, do excuse me please, you're treading on my aconites," or some such rot.

Right. What I need is a key—a talisman, an amulet, or a charm of a sort that one could invoke so the woman would comprehend. My situation has now become serious; this foolish human is so blind that my very substance is under threat. Actually she is not altogether a bad sort, if a trifle single-minded. I am certain that if she were aware of my presence, and recognizing my status, we could develop an acceptable relationship.

Please do inform me if there is such an object that would be of assistance to myself in this dire plight. I remain

Your humble servant,
Sir Winslow Cromwell Wentworthy XV

Umlaut looked up from the letter. "What do you think? Is this letter dangerous?"

"That poor bunny!" Mela exclaimed sympathetically. "Stuck in a land where they don't believe in magic. He needs to come here to Xanth."

Umlaut took that to be her agreement that the letter was safe. He folded it and returned it to its envelope.

The ride continued. Sesame, Sammy, and Claire were all gazing out at the colorful sand passing close beneath them, for it contained all manner of shells and plants and fish. The two cats' tails twitched when an especially delicious-looking fish passed, but they did not try to pounce on it. Being sandwiched wasn't so bad; they were traveling quite swiftly.

"How can we get to central Xanth by swimming south?" Umlaut asked Mela.

"We will curve around to the southern tip of the peninsula," she explained. "Then we will use the River of Grass and

finally go into the aqui-fur to reach the lake of the Faun &
Nymph Retreat. It's all by water, you see; otherwise Cutbait
couldn't go there. She's strictly water."

"There's water under the land?"

"Indeed. Where would we merfolk be if there wasn't?" She
twitched her nice tail again. "Not all of us can make legs, so
we need water access to isolated lakes. Those of us who like
fresh water." She grimaced.

Fresh water. For some odd reason that reminded him that
he was getting rather full of it, but there seemed to be nowhere to let it out. He fidgeted uncomfortably.

"There's a water closet," Mela remarked, indicating a section that seemed to be opaque.

"A what?"

"Maybe you should go there and see."

Rather than confess his confusion, he made his way there.
He found a door, opened it, and entered a closet containing
a toilet. Oh. That was just what he needed. What a remarkable
coincidence that the merwoman should mention it just at this
time. He used it, then returned to his place in the boat.

The sea became shallower. Suddenly Cutbait shied away
from something, causing Umlaut to crash into Mela. Fortunately she was quite soft where he landed. "Uh, sorry," he
muttered, extricating himself.

"You mean you weren't overcome by desire?" she inquired.

"Uh, no, I, uh, that is, not, I mean—"

"You have such a clear manner of expressing yourself,"
she said as he blushed. Then she laughed. "Don't be concerned. Cutbait was dodging fly fishing."

"Fly fishing?"

"See, there's another," she said, pointing.

He looked. There was a huge fly standing on the beach,
holding a fishing pole. The submarine swerved to avoid the
bait and hook.

"Why are we going so close to shore?" Umlaut asked. "We
could avoid any such problems by going farther out."

"Cutbait is looking for the river." She leaned forward to
peer ahead. "And there it is."

Umlaut saw a dark torrent of something. It didn't look like

water. The submarine turned into it, and they were surrounded by green flecks. What was it?

Mela reached through the sand witch's substance and snagged a fleck. She showed it to Umlaut. It was a blade of grass. "The River of Grass," she said.

Umlaut decided not to ask for more information on that. He simply watched as they forged through the green current. It seemed endless, extending as far as he could see, though that wasn't far.

"It's part of the Ever Glades," Mela continued, unasked. "They go on forever, especially if you get lost in them. But Cutbait knows the way, so we won't be lost. I think."

"You think?"

"Well, I haven't been this way recently. Maybe the route has changed. We might get stuck together endlessly, with absolutely nothing to do."

Umlaut wasn't reassured. He looked around, and Claire Cat caught his eye. She winked. The merwoman was teasing him. *Now* he was reassured.

"That cat is a spoilsport," Mela muttered.

Cutbait dived. The flowing grass disappeared above, but what was below wasn't an improvement. It was brown and as thick as the grass.

"What—?" Umlaut asked ineffectively.

Mela reached out again. Apparently this didn't bother the sand witch. She fetched in a small clump of fur. "Now we're in the aqui-fur."

"I thought it was water."

"Watery fur." She squeezed the fur between her fingers, and water dripped. "It is under all of Xanth."

It was also all dark now; the fur blocked daylight from reaching down this far. Umlaut hoped Cutbait was competent to navigate in darkness. The only thing he could see was the merwoman's hair: It had a faint phosphorescent glow. At least he knew exactly where she was.

"Don't worry," Mela said. "I can see reasonably well in water, and this is water. We're moving through the subterranean labyrinth."

"Labyrinth?"

"Puzzle."

"I knew that. I mean, what's something like that doing down here?"

"It's just the way the aqui-fur is. It's very devious."

Umlaut realized that the region under Xanth must be as complicated and confusing as the rest of it. Perhaps it didn't have to make sense.

But then progress slowed. Claire Cat came to sit next to them; he could feel her alarm. That made Umlaut suddenly nervous. "What's the matter?"

"The route *has* changed," Mela said. "Cutbait's lost. That's not good in the aqui-fur."

He did not like this at all, but he had to ask. "Why isn't it good?"

"Because there's only so much air in the submarine. If we stay below too long, you'll run out."

"We will? Not you?"

"I can breathe the water, of course. When I have visitors below, I make sure there is enough air to breathe. But this isn't my den."

Suddenly Umlaut felt stifled. "What can we do?"

"We need to find an ox gen tent. That will restore our air."

"An ox tent?" He was baffled again.

"Close enough. But I am not familiar with this region. Cutbait says she followed the sign that pointed the way to the Faun & Nymph Retreat, but this obviously isn't it. She can go back, but not in time to reach the surface for more air."

Sammy Cat became agitated. "You can find one?" Umlaut asked.

"That's right," Mela said. "Sammy can find anything. But he won't be able to run through the aqui-fur."

"Maybe he can show Cutbait the way. Can she see him?"

"I don't think so. Her eyes look out, not in, and it's pretty dark."

Umlaut pondered, then came up with an idea. "Can she feel us? I mean, if we pointed?"

"I doubt it," Mela said. "We really need to signal her from outside."

"I think we can do that. We can have Sammy point the way, while you swim outside and show Cutbait."

Mela nodded. "Now that's half a notion. But I wouldn't be

able to see Sammy point from that distance. He's too small, and there's too much fur in the way."

"Then he can show Sesame, and she can orient her body to point the right way. You should be able to see her, if she straightens out."

"That might work." Mela floated off the seat and swam through the submarine's hull and out into the furry water. Her hair drifted back behind, glowing slightly green, rippling as her tail cleft the water. Then she faded from view, because it was dark out there. He hoped she could see in, even if they couldn't see out.

"Go to it, Sammy," Umlaut said. "Point the way."

Sammy faced to the side. Evidently he was pointing with his nose. Sesame saw that and slithered out from the boat. She floated just above Para; it seemed that they were in water, despite being able to breathe. She oriented so that her body was straight, an arrow pointing the same direction as Sammy's nose.

Mela, outside, must have seen that. She should be swimming ahead of the submarine. Fissure Cutbait followed her; they could feel the motion. They were on their way. Maybe.

Sammy changed his direction. Sesame changed her orientation and wriggled in place to attract Mela's attention. Mela swam at an angle, and the submarine followed. They moved along a rocky passage.

This continued through several more changes, until it seemed that they had entirely turned around. Umlaut began to be concerned that the cat did not really know where to go. Then he realized that they were following a spiral going down. They couldn't go straight, because there was too much rock separating the channels. But he was gasping now; their air was running short.

Then he saw a light ahead. He peered at it, and as they approached it took better shape. It was a big glowing tent. "The ox tent!" he exclaimed.

Cutbait swam right into it. Immediately the air freshened; they were getting it restored so they could breathe.

Mela reappeared. "The ox gen tent really helps, doesn't it," she said.

"It really does," he agreed. All of them were breathing easier.

When the air was fully restored, Cutbait swam back to where she had seen the sign that pointed the way to the Faun & Nymph Retreat. It still pointed the way they had gone: the wrong way.

Claire gazed at the sign. She shook her head. Something was wrong.

In due course they had her information: The sign had been moved. Someone or something had changed it, so that they would get lost. Or worse.

10

FAUNS & NYMPHS

Thereafter their journey was uneventful. Claire had known the way the sign was supposed to point, and it was a good route.

Umlaut took advantage of the time to do something he should have done before. "Sesame, I've been communicating better with the cats because I emulate Feline. But your talent matches mine, so we should be able to communicate even better. If we practice, we should be able to speak really well to each other, so as to be able to handle the next emergency without having to go into nineteen questions."

Sesame nodded, and they worked on it. Soon he was able to interpret her Serpentine body and hiss language almost as if she were speaking. "This is much better," he said.

I agree. She hadn't spoken in Human, of course, but she might as well have; he understood her perfectly.

"I really appreciate your helping me like this," he told her. "I feel much safer with you along."

Thank you. She kissed him on the ear.

They emerged in a warm lake surrounded by a beach, forest, and mountains. Around it ran half a myriad of fauns & nymphs, seemingly aimlessly. The fauns had little hoofs on their hind feet, and the nymphs were quite remarkably bare. "I think this is it," Umlaut said.

"We have to go," Mela said. "Cutbait and I are saltwater creatures; fresh water bothers our skin."

"Thank you for your assistance," Umlaut said as Para walked out of the opening crevice that was Fissure Cutbait's mouth.

She shrugged rather impressively. "Anytime, some other time. I hope you get all your letters delivered." She returned to the crevice just before it closed again. "Farewell." The submarine sank below the surface and soon disappeared.

"Now all we have to do is find Snortimer," Umlaut said.

Sammy faced across the lake. He knew the way.

As they came closer to the beach, they got a better look at the scampering fauns & nymphs. "Oh, my," Umlaut breathed. "What are they doing?"

Sammy and Claire exchanged a feline glance. Then Sammy faced Umlaut for more direct dialogue. The answer, when he achieved it, was not completely satisfactory: "Celebrating."

"They certainly celebrate a lot," Umlaut said, watching as a faun chased after a screaming nymph, caught her, threw her to the beach, and celebrated with her. Then they both washed themselves off in the lake and resumed chasing—with different partners. He couldn't quite see the whole of it, but it seemed to be mainly hugging and kissing, with a good deal of squealing and laughing on the side. Maybe they were tickling each other. He wondered if there was something Sammy had not deigned to tell him. He could appreciate the fun of a hug and kiss, and indeed had done both himself. But why did they roll on the ground while doing it?

They landed near a bed sitting on the beach. Nymphs were piling on it, poking their slender legs over the edge and screaming with delight. "What's going on?"

Claire let him know: This was the bed under which Snortimer Bed Monster resided. The nymphs were playing with him, letting him grab their lovely ankles.

"All day long?" he asked, amazed.

All day long.

"But don't they get bored with such repetition?"

Now Sammy and Claire merged forces in order to provide

him the answer more efficiently: No, the fauns & nymphs would not get bored. They were simple creatures, satisfied with simple entertainments, which never became overfamiliar because they could not be remembered from one day to another, if even that long. Each day was thus a universe unto itself, with everything new.

"They can't remember?" Umlaut asked, finding it hard to believe.

Not only that, they were immortal, as long as they remained at the retreat. They never aged or changed. They spent their time chasing and celebrating. They lived in a perpetual present. It was an ideal existence.

"Ideal!" Umlaut exclaimed, appalled. "That's no life at all, without memories."

The cats shrugged. To each his/her choice.

"And Snortimer, what use to give him a letter he won't remember?"

Snortimer, it turned out, was different. He was not a faun or nymph, not native to the retreat, so he remembered. Of course there wasn't much point in remembering ordinary days, as they were repetitive, but he could remember other things well enough. So he would be able to understand and remember the letter.

They went to the bed. The nymphs retreated, uncertain about these odd visitors. Snortimer couldn't come out from under it, or even show himself, because it was day, but he could hear them.

Umlaut considered and concluded that it was feasible to deliver the letter. But could the bed monster read it?

No, for Snortimer had no eyes. Umlaut would have to read the letter to him.

Very well. Umlaut settled down on the bed and opened the letter. " 'Sir Snortimer,' " he read." 'My residence is with the mundane human adult . . .' " When he reached the mention of the dust bunny, Snortimer had a comment, which he indicated by poking the mattress from below.

Now Umlaut went into nineteen questions with the bed monster, answered by single pokes for yes and double pokes for no. It seemed that some of Snortimer's best friends were dust bunnies. They were little rabbits who constantly sneezed out dust; in fact, they even had sneezing contests to see which one could produce the most dust in the shortest time. Unfortunately they were in bad repute with housewives, who had been known to chase them out with brooms. Most of them had taken to hiding under beds, but they were still pursued relentlessly. Snortimer had a lot of sympathy for them.

"So do you know of a charm that will make this Mundane woman understand about this Mundane version of a dust bunny?" Umlaut asked.

Mundane! Snortimer hadn't picked up on that aspect. No, magic didn't work there. Neither dust bunnies nor bed monsters had any real power in that drear region. So he was sorry, but he couldn't help.

"Too bad," Umlaut said with regret. "Well, I will leave the letter with you. We'll have to be moving on to deliver the next one."

They got into Para and paused. "We can't go back the way we came," Umlaut said. "We can't swim through all that watery fur without Cutbait. We'll have to go overland." He looked at the high mountains that ringed the retreat. "That may be a hard trek."

Claire straightened up, looking across the lake. She was aware of something. But before Umlaut could inquire, there was a scream from that direction, followed by a thunk, as of someone colliding with a blank wall. Then there was a peal of cruel laughter.

"Something's wrong," Umlaut said. He might not be the fastest fish in the creek, but he did get there in due course.

Para paddled rapidly toward the commotion. They could see that the routine celebrations of the fauns & nymphs had ceased in that area, as they stood about two fallen comrades. One was a faun, who lay unconscious, and the other was a nymph sitting on the ground with little stars and planets circling her head. What had happened?

"Maybe they ran into each other," Umlaut suggested.

Claire shook her head. That wasn't it.

As they approached the shore, the unconscious faun was sitting up, and the nymph was comforting him. The other fauns & nymphs were resuming their normal activities, having lost interest.

Para waddled onto the beach, and they got out. "What happened?" Umlaut asked the nymph.

"We ran into a wall," she said. "I glanced off it and fell, but he smacked right up against it and lay down."

"A wall? Where?"

"Right there," she said, gesturing.

"I don't see it."

She walked across, her parts jiggling as she moved. Umlaut succeeded in not staring; because all the nymphs were bare and very similarly formed, this one was less remarkable than she might have been, even nude. She put out a hand. "Here." Then she looked surprised.

"You mean it's invisible?"

"Yes." She felt around in the air. "Well, it *was* here."

Umlaut dutifully felt for it. There was no wall. "Are you sure you didn't imagine it?"

"Could I have done that? We naiads don't have much imagination."

They also didn't leave much to the imagination, but he kept that information to himself. "Naiads? I thought you were nymphs."

She laughed, and that really set off the jiggles. "You're a funny man! Do you want to celebrate?"

"Uh, no," he said quickly, though he felt a strong illicit temptation. "I just don't know what a naiad is."

She seemed delighted. "You mean I know something you don't? Wonderful! We have several species of nymphs & fauns here at the retreat. The dryads and dryfauns live and play in trees, the oreads and orefauns play in the mountains, and we naiads and naifauns play in the water or on the beach."

"Oh. Thank you."

"But sometimes we celebrate with outsiders. They're so quaint, with their clothing."

"No, thank you. I just was concerned that you were hurt."

"We were, but we're all right now." She turned to the faun, who was now standing. "Are you ready?"

"I think so," he said.

She smiled. "Catch me if you can!" She flung her long hair around in a circle, leaped high and kicked her feet higher, screamed pleasantly, and ran away. The faun chased after her. She plunged into the water. He caught her, and they disappeared into a froth of tangled arms, giggles, and legs. They were evidently celebrating.

Sesame nudged him. Umlaut realized that he had temporarily freaked out after seeing the naiad's little dance. There was just something about the way she screamed, flung her hair about, and kicked up her feet. Especially the feet, or maybe the legs, or maybe the—

Sesame nudged him again. He realized that he had relapsed. "Uh, thanks. What were we doing?"

She indicated the nonexistent wall. That was right: If they had imagined it, despite having little imagination, how could it have knocked them both down? Yet there was obviously no wall here. "Well, we might as well be on our way."

The others agreed. They turned to go to Para, who waited at the edge of the water—and walked smack into an invisible wall. "Oof!" Umlaut said. It was all he could think of at the moment, not having much imagination himself. As he clapped his hands to his bruised face, he heard cruel laughter.

After two little planets and a dwarf star cleared away from his head, he saw that the animals were investigating the wall. Sammy was sniffing its base, Claire was standing on its top, and Sesame was circling around its end. In this manner they approximately defined its size and shape. It was about as tall as a man and as wide as a man could reach, and thick enough for a cat to lie on.

He approached it and tested it with his hands. It was smooth and hard, like thick glass; it even clinked when he flicked a fingernail against it. It was solid enough to stop a man in full stride. But it hadn't been there before, because their tracks remained in the sand, going right under it. How had it appeared (so to speak) so suddenly?

Claire dropped to the ground, landing with feline precision. He thought she had jumped off but discovered that the wall had gone, abruptly removing her support. It had been a temporary wall.

"What's going on here?" he asked.

Claire clarified it for him: It had been a magic wall, generated by a mean young man. That was the one who had laughed. He liked to use his magic talent to make walls appear right before moving people and laugh when they smacked into them.

"What kind of person would do that?" Umlaut asked, annoyed.

A juvenile delinquent, she answered. An unsocial brute. In fact a bully. One who had escaped recently from the Brain Coral's Pool. One of six.

"Six bullies escaped?" he asked. "Why did they come here?"

Because it was a water route they had used, that comes out here. They had been able to breathe the water for a while, but as the effect of the pool wore off, they had to come out into air, and this was where they found themselves. So now they were entertaining themselves in their natural manner, by tormenting innocent folk.

Umlaut's slow mind came to a conclusion. "We can't let that happen. We must stop them."

The others agreed. It wasn't right to let the supremely innocent fauns & nymphs be abused by bullies.

"But how can we stop someone who can put a wall in our way?" he asked.

They decided to hold a council of war, or if they couldn't manage that, at least of battle. They returned to Snortimer and had a thirty-eight-question dialogue. It was the bed monster's business to protect the Faun & Nymph Retreat from threats; his bed was athwart the only land entrance. He grabbed the ankles of any monster that tried to pass and tipped it into the adjacent pool, which was infested by loan sharks and allegories. The monsters had quickly learned to stay clear. But no one had invaded by water before, bypassing him. Snortimer wasn't sure how to handle that.

Fortunately Umlaut and his companions were here, so they could help. They formed a battle plan. They would locate and fetch the bullies, and Snortimer would tip them into the pool and prevent them from escaping. Once all of them had been captured and nullified, they would figure out what to do with them so they would never bother the fauns & nymphs again.

Now they got to work. "The wall bully," Umlaut said, and Sammy dashed off around the lake. Claire, Sesame, and Umlaut followed. They passed fauns & nymphs engaging in every kind of fun, playing games of ball, of tag, of hide-and-seek, and frequent celebrations. These innocent creatures paid little or no attention to the various intruders; as long as someone wasn't bothering a faun or nymph personally, that faun or nymph had no concern. That meant that they were vulnerable to any predator that managed to get into the retreat, and would organize no systematic defense. Umlaut became aware that there were consequences of innocence and thought he wouldn't care for it himself.

Claire hissed at Sammy, and he stopped so suddenly that his four paws made skid marks in the sand. Sesame and Umlaut, following close behind, had to brake to avoid colliding with the stopped cats. "What—?!" Umlaut demanded, barely catching his balance.

"Haw haw haw!" someone laughed.

His fingers brushed something glassy solid, but he saw nothing there. Oh, an invisible wall. Claire, with her talent, had known despite being unable to see, hear, or smell it, and had halted them in time. She was turning out to be an excellent addition to their group.

That meant they were close to the bully. It was time to go into combat mode. Umlaut exchanged a glance with Sesame, then they both began their emulations. Sesame slithered off to the side and into the water of the lake, disappearing for the moment; Umlaut jumped up to scale the wall. Meanwhile Sammy and Claire walked around the two sides of the wall and resumed progress, at a slower rate.

A group of fauns & nymphs were playing blindfaun's buff, in the buff of course. Those with their eyes open saw Umlaut. They screamed and fled. Only the nymph with her eyes blindfolded remained. She heard him tramping by and ran to catch him. "I got you!" she exclaimed, feeling all about him with her hands. "And you are—a big hairy ogre!"

"Get she from me," Umlaut said gruffly.

She pulled up the blindfold and looked at him, to verify her guess. "EEEEE!!" she screamed, with five *E*'s and two exclamation points, which was about as piercing a sound as a sweet creature could make. Then she fled so fast that her cute bottom left its twinkle behind.

Umlaut was satisfied. His emulation was working.

He came up on the bully, who was a tousle-haired sneer with an ordinary body attached. "Bash fully mean bully," he said in excellent ogreish.

If there was one thing a bully feared, it was a bigger bully, and ogres were the biggest bullies of all. "You'll never catch me!" he cried and turned to run. And stopped, for there was a ferocious dragon behind him.

"Who you?" Umlaut demanded.

Now the bully's knees began to knock. "I'm Chilk, just passing through, not doing nothing to nobody," he said.

Umlaut made a clumsy ham-fisted grab. "Me squeeze milk from mean Chilk."

Terrified, Chilk dodged past him and fled in the only direction available, toward the exit of the retreat. Umlaut and Sesame followed just fast enough to keep him running, herding him along. When he tried to pass the bed, a hairy hand shot out and grabbed an ankle. He yelled and lost his balance, toppling into the adjacent pond. Immediately the colorful fins of the loan sharks converged, paced by the questing snouts of the allegories.

Chilk yelled again. Suddenly the sharks and gories halted in the water; they had banged into an invisible wall. But when Chilk tried to climb back out of the pond, Para charged him, threatening to ram him back. He was trapped.

"The next closest bully," Umlaut told Sammy, and the cats took off. Soon they came to a region on the slope of the adjacent mountain where the orefauns and oreads were playing chase. Every so often one would screech and clap his or her hands to his or her backside. "Hotseat?" Umlaut asked Claire, and she nodded.

Sesame looped around, still emulating a dragon, and Umlaut tramped straight ahead, still emulating an ogre. They closed on the second bully, who was much like the first, identifiable by his "Har har har!" as he burned the bottoms of innocent folk. He seemed especially to like doing it to the nymphs, who did have nice bottoms.

The fauns & nymphs fled the dragon and ogre. The bully saw the dragon first, turned to flee, and almost bumped into the ogre. "Yaaaaa!" he screamed, which was apparently as close as he could get to a proper *eeeeek*.

"Who you?" Umlaut demanded. He was beginning to enjoy this role.

"Ogre, sir, I'm Numbo," the youth replied. "Please don't hurt me!"

"Me beat he seat," Umlaut said, reaching a ham-hand for him slowly enough so that the boy could escape it.

It worked. Numbo dodged by him and fled toward the retreat exit. They herded him on to the bed and Snortimer reached out to grab his passing ankle and trip him into the pond. They didn't want the bullies to escape, because they might return when the seeming dragon and ogre were gone; they had to be properly dealt with.

This time Umlaut had the wit to do his homework first. "Claire, what's the talent of the third bully we're going after?" It took only about five more questions to ascertain that this one had the talent of manifesting a sword. That was dangerous, because it didn't necessarily appear stationary; it could appear flying toward a person and thus could be lethal against the unwary.

"Can you warn me in time?" he asked Claire. She nodded.

They set off for the third bully. In due course they found him in the dense forest that surrounded the beach, cruelly teasing the dryfauns and dryads who were playing climb-and-peek there. It seemed that the nymphs would climb the trees, and the fauns would run along beneath them and try to catch good peeks. Umlaut could not afford to admit that he might have liked to play that game himself; he had a job to do.

He came up behind the bully. "Who you?" the ogre demanded.

The bully jumped—and so did Claire, leaping to the side. Umlaut did likewise, and the sword that appeared in midair flew harmlessly by and lodged in the trunk of a tree. Then the head of a dragon appeared and caught the bully by the scruff of the neck. The dragon lifted him into the air and shook him. After that he behaved a bit better. "I'm Jama," he confessed.

"One more cut, me pulp nut," the ogre said, raising a ham-fist over the boy's frightened head.

"No more swords," Jama agreed hastily. Like most bullies, he was a coward.

Sesame dropped him, and they herded him out of the forest and to the bed, where he joined the others in the pool. Three down.

The next was Horsejaw, with the talent of projecting booms. He was easy to locate, by the sound. *Boom!* Screams. Laughter. *Boom!* Screams. Laughter. The ogre threatened to lower the boom on him, and he capitulated and joined the others in the pond.

After that came Potipher, with the talent of poison gas. That was dangerous, but of course he didn't care who suffered. Sesame handled this one by emulating a fire-breathing dragon who might set fire to the cloud of gas. Since the gas was part of Potipher's being, the fire would hurt him as it destroyed the gas. He decided to cooperate, and the dragon didn't have to emit any fire. That was just as well, as it would have been beyond Sesame's power of emulation.

Finally there was Zink, with the talent of manifesting mirage holes. They weren't real holes, but they looked real and could really mess up someone who didn't know. The fauns & nymphs were screaming and colliding with each other in their efforts to avoid gaping holes that appeared just before them, while Zink laughed.

Dragon and Ogre cornered him. "Me cajole head in hole," Umlaut threatened. That set the bully back, because of course the hole wasn't really there; the head would be shoved into rock, dirt, or wood. He soon joined the others in the pond.

Then came the next stage. "We've got them; what do we do with them?" Umlaut asked. "We can't let them go." Unspoken was the alternative: to let the sharks and allegories have them. Umlaut didn't have the stomach for any such solution.

But Claire Cat indicated that they should not be concerned; soon there would be an answer. Umlaut hoped she was right.

He tried to relax. The others succeeded, but Umlaut watched the fauns & nymphs and found himself fidgeting. He wished he could have fun like that, only with a real girl, one who remembered and had personality. One whose kisses didn't intoxicate him. Maybe an ordinary girl, with no special magic at all, just a fundamental compatibility. Someone as suitable for him as Sesame was for Soufflé, or Claire for Sammy. Someone he might meet while delivering these letters and instantly know she was the One.

Claire nudged him. He snapped out of his daydream, and the corner of his eye saw a mare galloping away. A day mare! He had been given a nice daydream. He was sorry to lose it. But now he had to return to reality. "Yes?"

It was time. In a few questions he learned that the solution to the problem of the disposition of the bullies was at hand, as she had known it would be. That was important news, of course, yet he couldn't help wishing that the day mare hadn't been scared away just yet. Not before she gave him the identity of his dream girl.

They looked across the lake. There was a large man emerging from the water. No, it was a woman. Or, rather, a female centaur, a heavy one. As she walked along the beach the very ground shook.

Claire bounded along the beach toward the centaur, so Umlaut followed. How could a centaur help them? For that matter, how had she used the water route?

They met the centaur about halfway. "Uh, hello," Umlaut said. "I am Umlaut." It was all he could think of, another attack of inadequacy overcoming him. "My talent is emulation."

"I am Epi Centaur," she replied. "My talent is quaking, as you may have noticed. I am from the Brain Coral's Pool, on a special mission. Have you seen six callow human youths?"

"Yes! They were making trouble for the fauns & nymphs, so we rounded them up, but we don't know what to do with them."

"Splendid!" she said. "You have done much of my job for me. They escaped this morning from the pool, where they have been held in storage for up to six decades. They are not nice boys, which is why they were banished to storage. But someone—we suspect a demoness—lured them to a secret exit from the pool, and they followed it to this site. We feared they would have scattered across Xanth by this time and been irrecoverable before causing much mischief."

"They were causing much mischief *here*," Umlaut said.

"We had to act. What will you do with them?"

"Return them to storage, of course. They are there for the same reason I am: We represent an inconvenience to the Land of Xanth." She lifted one forfoot and set it gently down. A quake radiated out from the contact, as if a meteorite had struck there.

Umlaut was surprised. "I can see why the bullies need to be confined. But you're a decent person, aren't you? And if you aren't, why would the Brain Coral let you out?"

Epi smiled. He could tell by her tone; he wasn't looking directly at her, because her front was outstandingly bare. "I do like to think I'm decent, thank you. But I can't walk anywhere on land without shaking the ground, so folk are not eager for my company, especially near their houses. So I am a voluntary resident of the pool. Sometimes I leave to visit the Region of Earth, where quakes are popular, but there aren't other centaurs there, so soon it palls. But thank you for your concern." She glanced at the pond. "You did a remarkable job rounding up and confining those characters. While I don't wish to seem critical, I wonder how you managed it, since they have some pretty mean talents."

"I didn't do it alone," Umlaut said quickly. "My friends Sesame Serpent, Sammy Cat, and Claire Voyant Cat did most of it. Claire knew what to expect of each one, and Sammy knew where to find him, and Sesame emulated a dragon and drove them here to the bed, so Snortimer could grab their ankles and tip them into the pond. I just helped organize it."

She nodded. Again, he could tell because the ground rumbled slightly. "You're human. I'm surprised you weren't distracted by the nymphs."

"I was," Umlaut confessed bashfully. "I freaked out a couple of times, but Sesame nudged me out of it. When I focused on the job I was all right."

"I don't wish to pry into your private life, but I understand you are looking for a girl."

Umlaut felt himself blushing. "Uh, how—?"

Epi laughed, and the ground shook hard enough to cause ripples in the nearby water. "Imbri told me. We semi-equines sometimes exchange information."

"Who?"

"Mare Imbrium the daymare. She brought you a daydream, then decided that I could handle it better."

"I—I—uh, wasn't looking for a centaur," he said. "Uh, no offense."

This time her laugh shook the whole retreat, causing fauns & nymphs to pause in their games and look their way. "Oh, I agree with her! You're perfect. I understand you are delivering letters?"

"The mare told you that?"

"No. I see the bag of them. Do you have one for Rapunzel?"

"Who?"

"I think that answers my question. Then perhaps Grundy?"

He had seen that name. "Grundy Golem. Yes. But I don't know where he lives."

"As it happens, I do. I believe the pool can help you go there next, if you are amenable."

He forget himself so far as to look at her and saw that she was amused by his evident difficulty doing that. She was not the first who had been amused by his assorted clumsinesses. Maybe he was good at emulation because he was bad at being himself. "Uh, sure, okay, I mean yes, if we can find the way."

"Because you have materially helped us, we feel it is only fair to help you in return." As she breathed, her large breasts jiggled a little, and each jiggle made a ripple radiate out across the ground. "If that is all right with you and your companions," Epi concluded.

Umlaut realized that he had suffered a minifreakout and not heard part of what she said. If only centaurs wore clothing! He didn't want to embarrass himself even further, so he looked around at the others. Serpent and cats nodded, so it must be all right. "Uh, sure, yes, thank you."

"Excellent. I will send them out when we return to the pool." She faced the pond. "Bullies, back to the Brain Coral's Pool. March!" she commanded.

Chilk looked up at her, his eyes rounding as they fixed on her chest; in fact each eyeball reflected one breast. "Make us, booby." The others endorsed his defiance with crude chuckles as they stared at the same site.

"Uh, we can help you herd them," Umlaut offered.

"No need." Epi trod very gently around to the far side of the pond, so that the ground quivered only somewhat. Then she trod firmly. The ground quaked so hard that it cracked open under the pond and the water drained out. The bullies had to scramble to avoid falling into the cracks opening under their feet. In barely two moments they were out of the pond and running ahead of the centaur, who herded them out into the lake. She followed them, and the quakes were muddled by the deepening water. Soon they all disappeared. Evidently the centaur had made it possible for them to breathe the water on the return trip.

So what was next? Umlaut saw that the others were settling down beside Snortimer's bed, composing themselves for a wait. So he settled down similarly, watching the nymphs at their games. Then one came and bounced on the bed, kicking her bare legs high.

11

SURPRISE

U mlaut snapped out of it as Sesame nudged him. How long had he been out this time? He should have known better than to watch that nymph bounce on the bed. But his eyes tended to go where they wished, almost as if wanting to freak out.

A horse and cart were approaching them from beyond the bed. This must be what the centaur had promised. The horse was a magnificent beast, with its head held high and its hooves touching the ground smartly. But the cart it hauled was more remarkable. It seemed to be made of large chunks of flesh. Each chunk had what looked like a fingernail on one side. Taken as a whole, it was one weird vehicle.

Maybe the animals understood this, having paid more attention to Epi's description than he had. He went into a quick dialogue with Sesame, who was glad to clarify the matter for him: It was a high horse drawing a toe truck. They would take the party to Grundy Golem on the trollway.

A toe truck: A truck made out of toes, getting toed, or towed. The toes were fastened to wheels and dug into the ground to get traction. He should have known. "But what's this about a trollway?"

That, it seemed, was a paved road maintained by the trolls. It went the length of Xanth, from the southern tip to the northern marshes, and was excellent for rapid transit.

"The whole way? Then we must have crossed it coming here, unless we went under it."

No, Sesame explained in Serpentine, they probably wouldn't have seen it even if they had stayed on the surface, because it was limited access.

"You mean they let only a few people on it?"

Not exactly.

"Is it limited in some other way?"

The Void.

"What does the Void have to do with a trollway?"

It was that the Void was an extremely potent hole in the Land of Xanth and caused the land near it to wrinkle so that there was more of it, but not all of it was accessible at the same time. The trollway ran along one of the creases.

"Then how can we get to it?"

Here the serpent's powers of explanation via emulation dialogue broke down. It seemed this was a more devious concept.

"Maybe it fades in and out, like the isles," Umlaut concluded. That seemed to cover it. Claire probably could have clarified it but didn't care to bother.

The horse and toe wagon halted by the bed. A ramp let down in back so that Para could waddle up and in. Then the four of them jumped, slithered, and climbed on. "Farewell, Snortimer!" Umlaut called as they started moving. The bed responded with a poke in the center of the mattress.

That reminded Umlaut: "I never actually saw Snortimer. What does he look like?"

Claire responded this time, as she knew the answer. She always knew the answer, but he was too dull to ask her most times, and she did not deign to volunteer information for dullards. Snortimer, like many bed monsters, was all hands. That was because all he had to do was grab ankles. The nymphs loved it; they would arrange to roll off the bed and disappear under it, playing games of kiss-and-grab. If a nymph could kiss the monster in more places than he could grab her, she won. Those outside the bed could keep score: If there were more smacks than screams, she had won. They played the game with enthusiasm, and it didn't seem to matter much who won.

Umlaut thought about playing a game like that with a bare maiden, in a dark place so the sight of her body wouldn't freak him out. He liked the notion. There were only two problems: He wouldn't have the nerve to grab anywhere interesting, and no girl he had encountered would kiss him if he did. So it seemed that only nymphs could play that game. Still, if somehow . . .

Sesame nudged him, and he came out of it. More time had passed, for they were now well out of the retreat and coming up to a wide paved road. A sign said STOP: PAY TROLL, so the high horse had stopped. Indeed, two trolls were standing there, about as ugly as their kind was: somewhere between goblin and ogre.

Umlaut leaned out of the truck. "What are we supposed to pay you?"

One troll said something indecipherable but vaguely menacing. Umlaut was afraid he wouldn't like the answer if he understood it, so he didn't ask for a clarification. Instead he turned to Claire. "What do we need?"

They went Feline dialogue, but again the answer did not quite come clear. There was just something complicated about getting on the trollway. He gathered that he needed to send the trolls somewhere, both of them; then they could get on the paved road. But he wasn't clear where or how.

Finally Claire, in exasperation, turned to Sammy. Sammy gave Umlaut a look, then jumped out of the truck and walked slowly toward the high horse. Umlaut, catching on, followed.

Following the cat's indications, he unhitched the high horse from the toe truck, then climbed on to the animal's back. He was now high off the ground, and felt very superior. "Well, let's go," he said, lifting his nose.

Sammy took off, following a trail that wound away from the paved road. The horse followed, breaking from a standstill into a full gallop in one motion. Umlaut thought he should have fallen off, for he knew nothing about horse riding, but it seemed that part of the magic of this creature was to keep the rider secure on his high perch. And high he was; he felt as if his head was in the clouds, above everything else. Especially above every*one* else. All the rest of Xanth is distinctly inferior.

They passed a young woman standing by the trail. "Hi," she said. "I am Aloe Vera. My talent is soothing burns. May I have a ride?"

"Of course not," Umlaut said snootily, and left her behind. She was obviously one of the lowly commoners who didn't deserve any attention, let alone a ride.

Sammy came to a field of pebbles and stopped. This must be the place. The high horse halted, and Umlaut dismounted. The moment he was off the horse, he felt chagrin: why had he treated that woman, Aloe, so shabbily? At least he could have been courteous.

He saw that the pebbles of the field were labeled. Each one said SENT. Someone must have sent it here. So what did that have to do with the price of beans in a beanie?

Then a dim bulb flashed. He had to send the trolls away so his party could get on the trollway. Once they were away, they would have been sent. These pebbles might be magic, making them get sent.

He picked up a handful and put them in his pockets. Sammy was satisfied, so then he climbed back on the horse. They galloped back toward the troll intersection.

On the way they passed Aloe. "May I have—?" she began.

Umlaut did not deign to answer. He simply flipped her a pebble. She caught it—and vanished. It had worked: She had been sent, probably to the field where the pebbles had come from.

They arrived back at the intersection. "You want to be paid?" Umlaut demanded arrogantly from the high horse. "I'll give you two sents." He flipped one pebble to each troll.

Both trolls vanished. They had been paid two sents, which was probably more than they were worth.

He got off the high horse and hitched up the wagon harness again. Then he and Sammy returned to the wagon. The horse stepped haughtily onto the paved road and increased speed. Soon they were fairly flying along it.

Then something else occurred to Umlaut. The horse—he had been snooty only when on the high horse. That was its talent, to make folk snooty. That was why he had been so mean to Aloe. He was sorry now, as it was not his natural attitude, but it was too late. He resolved not to ride the horse again; he didn't like the memory of himself there.

And now he also understood why the concept of the payment had been so hard to grasp. He had paid the trolls by cheating them. He wasn't proud of that, either.

But one mystery remained: the limited access nature of the road. Sure, the trolls had guarded it, but he didn't think that was what limited it. It seemed more likely that it was limited in the sense of not being there for most folk. Why was it there for their party and not for others? Had Epi Centaur or some other person of the Brain Coral's Pool made a spell that allowed them access? Maybe, but that still didn't explain why it apparently was not even visible to others.

He struggled but could not fathom the mystery. Meanwhile they were moving rapidly north.

Suddenly they came to a monstrous chasm. "What is that?" Umlaut exclaimed, awed by its breadth and depth.

All three of his companions turned their heads to gaze at him, and even Para seemed surprised. He didn't know of the Gap Chasm?

"Oh, that," he said, nettled. He just hadn't realized that it was that big, from ground level. Actually he hadn't known of the Faun & Nymph Retreat before, either, or the Isle of Cats, or the Moons of Ida. Could this be related to the way he couldn't remember his own past life? Yes, he must have forgotten everything he had known before, both personal and general. However, that merely set up the next question: Why? The idea that Sherry's kisses could have done that much damage was wearing thin. The mystery of himself was deeper than his relationship with a former girlfriend.

But he couldn't ponder long; the chasm was fast approaching. "Are we going to plunge into *that*?" he asked, alarmed.

Claire twitched her tail reassuringly. No, they had a safe way to pass it. The trolls used to use a cloud ferry but recently had dug a tunnel.

"A tunnel?"

The Troll Tunnel, otherwise known as the Trunnel. Before Umlaut could inquire further, horse and wagon plunged into a dark aperture he hadn't seen coming. They were going down, down, frighteningly down in darkness. The animals weren't concerned, because they could see better than he could in the gloom. So he got halfway smart and emulated a nocturnal creature and began to see the tunnel.

Why had he bothered? There wasn't much to see. So he settled down to think some more—and fell asleep. It seemed he couldn't do anything quite right.

He woke as light struck his face. They were out the other side. Now they were north of the Gap Chasm and still proceeding north.

"Where is Grundy Golem?" he asked querulously.

It turned out that he lived in Euphoria, just north of Xanth.

"But that would mean it has no magic."

True, Sammy indicated. What was his point?

Umlaut felt awkward yet again. He didn't have a point.

The day was fading, but the high horse didn't stop. Umlaut had had no idea it was so far. "Don't we need to take a break for supper and the night?" he asked.

They shrugged. Apparently not. There turned out to be food in the truck, so they ate. Para didn't seem to need to eat, being magically animated. After that there wasn't much to do, because the surrounding scenery was absolutely dull, so they all slept. The high horse just kept galloping indefatigably, and the toes of the truck did not get sore. The Brain Coral's Pool evidently had good equipment.

When they woke, the dawn was brightening, the horse was slowing, and the scenery was changing. Were they finally arriving?

Yes! The high horse came to a halt at an exit marked EU-PHORIA. This was where they had to get off, Claire clarified; the horse could not go farther because he would lose his magic. Euphoria was a place without magic, she reminded him. That meant that he and Sesame would not be able to emulate others, Sammy would not be able to find things, and Claire herself would lose her voyance. So the sooner he delivered the letter and returned to the magic zone, the better.

"The letter!" he exclaimed. "I haven't read it."

They shrugged. The four of them got off the truck, and the ramp lowered to let Para descend. Then the high horse set off

the way they had come, hauling the toes behind. They were
on their own.

Umlaut brought out the letter and read it.

Dear Grundy,

This is coming to you from Mundania, but I know
you'll have no problem understanding it because of your
talent of interpretation. That was my feeble attempt at
levity because the magic of Xanth converts all words of
foreign places to Xanthian.

There is a famous personage in my world also who
translates all languages as you do. His name is C-3PO.
Mundania seems to have some overlapping qualities of
your home, only it is not magic—we call it science. Perhaps some of the magic of your world is slightly leaking
over to mine. Not enough to diminish yours, just to enhance it here. That would be a wonderful occurrence.

I have been practicing insults in order to write to you.
Being unaccustomed to it, I am nowhere near being in
your league, but I think I may have one you may appreciate: GR*!$&!*~>/*#!∧*!!)##**!!!

Wow! I surprise myself—that nearly scorched the
page! Understand this is not directed at you but at certain
bigoted bureaucrats of my world.

I will end this now without excess information of who
I am. A few letters have gone from my home to some
of your friends. Gossip being what it is—in any world—
you have probably already heard of the strange Mundanian who persists in corresponding with citizens of
Xanth.

Happy cursing, Grundy.

Your friend,
Arjayess

Once again, it did not seem like a letter that was likely to
set anyone off into any fits of rage. But if Grundy's magic
talent was interpretation, would it be working there in Euphoria? If not, that reference might sadden him. Yet it must
have been his choice to move here. Why would he have de-
liberately denied himself and his family their natural magic?

It didn't seem to make sense. In fact, a lot of what Umlaut was learning during this mission didn't seem to make much sense.

Well, it was not his business to decide whether it made sense, but whether it was likely to be harmful to Xanth, and this was another innocuous missive. All of them were, which made Demon Jupiter's reaction odd. Unless there was some hidden message he was missing, these letters were no threat to anyone.

Umlaut's gaze fell on Para. "Um, this is a place of no magic. Can you go there?"

The boat regretfully shook its foresection.

What to do? His brain seemed even slower than usual. It was as if he had never had any practice in thinking and had to learn how to do it for each new situation. "I guess we'll be coming back this way, as soon as I deliver the letter. We could use some transportation, wherever we go in Xanth. So if you care to wait—"

Para nodded. He would be glad to wait. He was a very obliging boat.

There was a path leading into Euphoria. The four of them followed it. Sammy did not lead the way, because his talent was absent here; neither could Claire know their situation. They had been reduced to mere cats, and Sesame was a mere serpent, and Umlaut a mere human youth.

Euphoria was beautiful. The trees might not have magic, but they had solid trunks and foliage. They passed a field of fine flowers. There was a stream that was absolutely unmagical but seemed not to mind; it trickled merrily on its way. There was a garden with many unfamiliar vegetables growing. And finally there was a pleasant little house on a little hill. There was a sign saying GOLEM. That must be the place.

They approached it, expecting it to grow as the magic of perspective reverted it to its real size. But it turned out really to be little. The hill was about knee high on Umlaut, and the house's roof was about waist height. Umlaut realized that he had been thinking magically, allowing for perspective when actually that magic too was gone. So this looked like a dollhouse because it was really that size.

He sat down beside the house, then extended one finger and cautiously tapped on the little door. In a moment it opened and a woman no taller than his spread-fingered hand stood there. "Hello," she said, not seeming surprised by their size.

"Uh, I'm Umlaut. I have a letter for Grundy Golem."

"I'm Rapunzel, Grundy's wife." She touched her hair, which was so long it pretty well surrounded her. "A letter? Who is it from?"

"A woman in Mundania. I, uh, had to read it first. It gets complicated to explain." He held out the envelope.

She looked at it. The envelope was almost as long as she was. "I think we'll have to have our daughter read it to us. She's out on a nature walk at the moment; you can find her if you follow the path on beyond the house."

"Uh, okay, I guess," he said with his usual certainty. "Uh, these are my friends Sesame, Sammy, and Claire. They—"

"Sammy! I didn't notice you. Come give me a kiss. How's Jenny doing these days? Has she signaled the stork yet? And you have a girlfriend now? It's about time, you rogue."

Everybody knew Sammy. Umlaut decided it was okay to leave the others with Rapunzel, since she knew Sammy, and his friends wouldn't hurt her despite being much larger than she was. He walked on along the path.

The country continued beautiful. This was a perfect place, apart from its lack of magic. But there were nice regions within the magic portion of Xanth; why had they chosen Euphoria?

He had no idea where the Golem family's daughter was; she could be anywhere. He didn't want to do something awful, like inadvertently stepping on her, so he kept his eyes on the path and walked carefully. He didn't know how old she was but couldn't envision anyone that small being very old, so thought she might be seven or eight. Why they wanted her to read the letter he wasn't sure; maybe she was learning to read and it would be good practice. They could perhaps prop it up against the house and read it from a suitable distance.

"Hello."

He jumped. The soft voice was close, but he didn't see the child. He froze in place so as to present no danger to her until he saw exactly where she was. But he didn't see her. "Uh, where are you, miss—?"

"Surprise," she said. "I'm up here."

He looked up. There before him was a full-sized human girl. She was pretty in an ordinary way, having some family resemblance to Rapunzel despite the size differential. Maybe it was her hair, which reached to her knees, changing color somewhat as it went. "Uh, I, uh, thought you'd be smaller," he said, then realized how clumsy that sounded. "Uh, younger."

"I'm fourteen," she said pertly. When she twitched her head, the ends of her tresses curled up like little yo-yos. "That's old enough."

He remained taken aback. "Uh, yes, of course. I'm Umlaut. What uh, is your name?"

"Surprise."

"Yes, you surprised me. But what I was asking—"

"You're cute." She stepped into him and kissed him. There was no wine in it, but it made him feel remarkably good. Then, while he stood half stunned by her gesture, she explained: "My name is Surprise Golem. That's because I was a surprise. The storks had a horrible confusion, and by the time I was delivered I was five years old and could already walk and talk. Grundy and Rapunzel accepted me anyway, and we went on from there. My magic was even more surprising."

Everything about her was surprising! "My, uh, talent, is emulation. When there's magic. I can make myself seem like other, uh, people."

She clapped her hands with girlish glee. "That explains it! You're emulating a socially inept boy."

Umlaut blushed. "I, uh, wasn't trying to. I mean—"

"Oh, this is so much fun! Let's walk and talk a bit." She took his hand with her nice fingers and led him on along the path. "Tell me all about yourself."

"But I'm just here to, uh, deliver a, uh, letter."

"And what kind of epistle is an 'uh' letter?"

"It's a, uh—" He stopped. "Are you making fun of me?"

"Am I doing that? I apologize." She kissed him again.

This set him back farther than the first kiss had. "You didn't, uh, need to do that."

"What, didn't you like it?"

He blushed twice as badly. "That's not the, uh, point."

"Yes it is. It's a gourd apology."

"A what?"

"Oh, you don't know about that? This is even more fun."

He tried to get angry, but it was so nice being with her that he couldn't manage it. "All that fun is at my expense."

She put on a contrite mien. "I will explain. In the gourd— you do know what the gourd is?"

"Uh, no," he admitted.

"Then I will explain that too. Come sit by me." She led him to a broad tree stump and made him sit. Then she sat beside him and put one arm around his waist.

"Why are you doing that?"

"First things first, and that's about third. First the gourd: it's known as the hypno-gourd, and it looks like an ordinary garden-variety gourd, but there's a little peephole in the end, and if you look in that, you freeze. All you can do is keep looking, and your mind is inside it, seeing all manner of weird things. That's the realm of dreams, and the night mares go there."

"Night mare," he said. "I met a day mare. They said she was called Imbri."

"Yes, she was a night, but now she's a day. She must have brought you a daydream. What was it about?"

"A girl," he said, blushing yet again.

"How sweet. Was it me?"

He looked at her, not even able to say "uh." She *was* the girl. He was blushing so hard and hot he was afraid the red would start peeling off his face.

"Anyway, that's the gourd," she said. "Now the denizens therein have a quaint custom that is slowly spreading to the outside. They don't apologize by words so much as by gestures. That is, a hug and a kiss. If it isn't accepted—" She broke off, glancing sharply at him. "Did you accept?"

"Accept what?" He was flustered on top of his embarrassment.

"I guess you didn't. So I have to try again. Maybe I can

do it right this time. Let's get you into position." She put her fine hands on his shoulders and turned him half around on the stump, then drew him in for an embrace. Before he could get out another "uh" she kissed him, firmly and lingeringly.

There was still no wine in it, but he did feel as if he were floating. Yet he knew this wasn't right. "You're, uh, only fourteen," he said when she released him.

"That's old enough," she repeated. "Do I take this to mean that you still haven't accepted my apology?"

"I don't even remember what you're apologizing for!" he blurted.

"For teasing you. Since you haven't accepted—"

"I accept!" he cried.

"Awww, spoilsport," she said, making a cute moue.

She was still teasing him, but he decided not to make an issue of it, lest she kiss him again. Besides, he liked it.

"So that's why I'm doing this," she continued after a moment, putting her arm around his waist again. "To be in position for an apology. I trust everything is quite clear now?"

"Nothing is clear!" he exclaimed. "I came here to deliver a letter, and Rapunzel said you would have to read it to them, because it's sort of big for her to handle. So I looked for you, and all you've been doing is—teasing me."

"You really don't know," she said. "That's part of what makes it fun."

"What don't I know?"

"That you are my ideal man."

He stared at her, dumbfounded again.

She glanced modestly down at the ground, then back up to catch his gaze, and smiled. He felt a little thrill when she did that. "I think I had better go back a bit. You see, I have an unusual magic talent."

He started to try to speak, but she laid her finger across his lips. "I'll answer that question in a moment. My talent is to be able to do anything—once. That is, I can make myself fly, but after I'm done, I can't invoke that ability again. It's gone. I can conjure a chocolate pie to eat, and it will be an excellent pie, but thereafter I can never do that again. And so on. I have all the talents in Xanth, but every one I use, I lose. I was brokenhearted when I discovered that, as you might imagine. If I live long enough, I will be entirely out of magic. Unless I never use my talents—in which case, what good are they?" She looked pensive.

"I don't know," Umlaut said. "I'm sorry."

"So am I. The thing is, we use our talents automatically in Xanth; it's part of our natures. I'm sure you do emulations whenever you need them."

"Yes."

"So if I was hungry, I'd use a new way to fetch a pie. If I wanted to go somewhere, I'd use another way to do it. There are many variants of each talent, so I could fly by flapping my arms, or by making myself light enough to float, as the winged centaurs do, or by magnetically repelling the ground so that I pushed off from it. But each time, I lost another talent. I was afraid I'd be out of the best ones before I ever grew up and joined the Adult Conspiracy." She glanced at him. "Do you belong?"

"Uh, not quite. I'm seventeen."

"But you know that a significant part of it is knowing the signal to summon the stork, and not believing in monsters under the bed, and losing your taste for meals consisting entirely of candy, and being able to say bad words—all those supremely dull things that make adults adult?"

"Yes. I dread it."

"So do I. The last thing I want is to lose all my magic talents before I turn adult, because then I'd have none of the joys of childhood left. So I knew I had to protect my talents, even from myself. That's why we moved here, where there is no magic. So I can't waste them inadvertently."

"That does make sense," he agreed. He was feeling more at ease in her presence.

"But the fact is, I *will* turn adult in time, and I figure it will be a lot less worse if I have a good man to love. Of course at my age I have no inkling of what real love is; my parents have assured me of that. But they also say that the right partner can make all the difference, and seeing them together, I believe it. Do you understand?"

"Yes," he said before he thought. "I mean—"

"Oh, don't take it back! So you dreamed of your ideal girl, just as I dreamed of my ideal boy. Then just a few hours ago

I wandered near the edge of the magic region, and a demoness appeared. She tried to be anonymous, but she had trouble with her words—"

"Metria!"

"You got it. She told me that my ideal man was on the way and would arrive any day now. And here you are."

"But I'm not ideal. I'm really not much of anything."

"Metria also told me that you were unreasonably modest. I like that too."

"I've got a lot to be modest about! I mean, because I don't have anything to be proud of."

"And she warned me that you had a double helping of decency. She thought that was a liability. I don't."

He was surprised. "You, uh, don't?"

"She said you kissed two women just because you knew it would make them feel good."

"Well, uh, yes, but—"

"And that you helped the fauns & nymphs just because they needed it."

"Uh, yes, but anyone would have done that."

"Not just anyone, I think."

"But—"

"Oh, shut up." But before he could do that, she did it for him, by covering his mouth with another kiss.

When the little hearts stopped orbiting his head, he tried once more to clarify that he wasn't remarkable. "I'm just delivering letters. It's sheer coincidence."

"Very little in Xanth is coincidence. So I knew who you were the moment I saw you come down the garden path."

"But I'm not anything special, let alone ideal! In fact I'm a klutz."

"I noticed. I like it."

"You can't be serious. A girl as pretty and talented as you, you can do so much better."

"I don't want better. I want appreciation and understanding as my magic diminishes and my age increases. I want a malleable man I can do anything I want with, who will like whatever I do. Who will still love me when all my magic is gone. What do you want?"

"In a girl? I, uh, I guess maybe the same. But—"

"There's always a but," she said. "That's part of the beauty of it."

"You won't like this." He realized that, horrendously against his better judgment, he was falling into the pattern she described. She was exactly the kind of girl he wanted. "I don't seem to have a past. I mean I can't remember anything before I started this mission, and others tell me I don't exist. There's something wrong with me."

"Nothing that love can't fix, I'm sure."

"I don't know. I—"

Then she kissed him again, and all remaining resistance crumbled. It didn't matter that all this was very sudden and completely unexpected on his part. She had overwhelmed him. "Oh, Surprise," he said. "Whatever there is of me, you can have. If you really want it. I'm mal—mal—soft putty in your fingers. But—"

"I know. We have to join the Adult Conspiracy first. I think I can manage that in two years; the age isn't quite fixed. Meanwhile we can have our understanding and feel what we feel."

"And feel what we feel," he agreed, his head spinning. "May I—is it all right if I—that is, uh—"

"Yes, you may kiss me," she agreed. Then they both laughed. And kissed.

12

GROSSCLOUT

They arrived back at the little house. Now Grundy Golem was there too, standing beside his wife. "Surprise!" Rapunzel cried, her size diminishing her annoyance not half a whit. "Your hair is all mussed. What have you been up to?"

"Oops," Surprise murmured, fetching out a comb and straightening her disarrayed tresses. "We'll have to confess." She did not seem overly concerned.

"It's my fault," Umlaut said gallantly.

"Nonsense," Rapunzel said, and he realized that even at this he had messed up. She gave her daughter a stern glare. "Well?"

"Oh, Mother, he's the One," Surprise said.

The woman's endless hair seemed to change color, though of course that couldn't happen without magic. "How can you possibly know that?"

"The Demoness Metria told me my ideal man was coming today, so I knew. And here he is."

"And you believed her? That demoness is full of nothing but mischief."

"Why would she bother? She doesn't care about my life."

Ouch. Umlaut hated the need, but had to speak up. "She may be trying to stop me from delivering the letters. There have been other things."

"Why stop the letters?" Rapunzel asked, fixing him with a stare that left figurative welts on his guilty face.

"I don't know. But the first one went to the Demon Jupiter, and it made him so mad that he threw his Red Spot at us. The Good Magician says I can find a way to stop it, if I deliver the letters. But I'm reading them first, to make sure no one else gets one to make him that mad."

"It may not be the *letter* that makes folk mad," Grundy said significantly.

Rapunzel turned to her daughter. "So you see, it may have been a setup."

Surprise looked in turn at Umlaut. "If it was, do you take it all back?"

"Take *what* back?" Rapunzel demanded.

This was getting more awkward by the moment, and it hadn't been easy to begin with. He was already blushing, but he couldn't deny it. "I, uh, we, uh, that is—"

"We're in love," Surprise said clearly.

Rapunzel's hair darkened another shade. "In one hour? I find that hard to believe."

"Oh, I don't know," Grundy said. "I loved you from the first, Punzel, though I didn't know it."

She dismissed that out of hand. "Well, you're a *man*. Fortunately we can get to the bottom of this." She faced the two cats. "Claire Voyant, is it true?"

The cat nodded.

Rapunzel looked as if she had smelled a stink horn. She looked icily at Umlaut, and her hair seemed to freeze in place. "Don't you have other letters to deliver?"

"Uh, yes," he said miserably. He had been dismissed. He turned to go.

"I'll be in touch," Surprise said.

With no magic? But how could he argue with her. "Okay." He walked away so as not to see Rapunzel's angry stare, but he felt it boring into his back. How had he ever managed to get into so much trouble? He had never sought to set mother against daughter.

And yet it seemed to be true. In only an hour he had found a girl to truly love.

They returned to the magic section. Para was waiting for them. The boat's attitude was a question: How had it gone?

"Mixed," Umlaut said. "I'll try to explain as we travel."

So where were they going next? Umlaut had no idea, so he grabbed the next letter in the pile. "Demon Professor Grossclout."

He had no idea where to find the professor, but evidently Para did. They got into the boat and started heading back south.

As they traveled, Umlaut described somewhat haltingly how he had delivered the letter, then gone to meet Surprise. And, it seemed, fallen in love with her. Sammy and Sesame were interested, as they had not heard the details before.

"She was pretty, she was nice, she was interested in me. She talked with me, she teased me, she kissed me," Umlaut said. "I uh, responded. But it seems it was set up by the Demoness Metria, maybe to distract me from delivering the next letter."

But the day mare's daydream had indicated that this was about to happen, Sesame reminded him.

"That's true," he agreed, brightening.

"You were adhesive in her hands."

Who had said that? "I was what?"

A swirl of smoke was hovering above the gunwale. "Mucilage, cement, glue, gum, paste—"

"Putty?" That had been his term for malleability.

"Whatever," the swirl agreed crossly.

"Metria, what are you doing here?"

"I heard my name. What were you saying about me?"

"That you set me up. You told Surprise that her ideal man was coming, and she thought it was me."

"Exactly. Why didn't you stay with her?"

How he wished he could have done that! "Her mother sent me away."

"Darn!" Sulfurous fumes rose from the bad word.

"So it's true!" he exclaimed. "Why are you trying to stop me from delivering the letters?" He saw the cloud quiver. "And don't fade out this time!"

To his surprise, it worked. Instead of fading, the cloud formed into the voluptuous demoness who came to rest on a seat of the boat. Her legs were toward him, not quite showing anything above the knees. Yet. "It's just something I have to do."

She admitted it! "Why?"

"What's the next letter?"

She was changing the subject, but he wasn't sure he could get a direct answer from her anyway. "To Demon Professor Grossclout."

"Oh, my," she said. "That could be fun."

"Only I don't know how to find him."

"Let me see the letter."

"So you can destroy it undelivered? No way."

She nodded. "You are getting less stupid by the hour. Very well, read it to me."

"You think I won't?"

"I think you're in love."

That seemed like a non sequitur, but he couldn't refute it. He decided to read the letter. He brought it out.

My Dear Professor Grossclout,

This is to bring to your attention a matter of utmost importance. It is to inform you of the impropriety of behavior regarding a past student of yours.

If my information is correct—and it rarely is not—a certain demoness is now in possession of a portion of a soul. This could become a dangerous matter.

It is reported that said demoness has become CAR-ING—a shocking event. While namby-pamby actions suit the fool humans, it is most inappropriate for the demonic race.

This deplorable situation makes us all appear simpering idiots. We demons are meant to create havoc and make as miserable as possible the lives of all with whom we come in contact. You as an instructor must surely be aware of this simple fact. You cannot possibly condone this situation. This dire state of affairs must not be allowed to continue.

This calls for immediate discipline: chastisement, punishment. She must be made to see the error of her ways. The revolting human soul must be removed.

Do something about it, Grossclout! Now! Or else!

A concerned citizen

Metria had been swelling up throughout the letter. Now she exploded, literally. She flew apart, arms, legs, head, and torso scattering across the boat and into the air above. A leg landed in Umlaut's lap. Caught by surprise, he lifted it up, not knowing what to do with it. Then it dissolved into smoke, as did the other parts of her, and the cloudlets drifted together to form a single floating mass, and that mass shaped itself back into the form of the demoness. She came to rest on the seat.

She brushed a stray hank of hair away from her face. "What a missive!"

"That makes you angry?"

"Angry? That was a detonation of laughter. Just the very thought of talking to Grossclout like that—oops, it may set me off again." She wrapped her arms about herself, as if trying to hold things together. But she lost her balance and fell backward off the seat, her legs flying up in the air. Umlaut got one compelling glimpse of her voluptuous panties.

Something was nudging him. It was Sesame, again, bringing him out of his freak-out. The demoness was back upright, her legs decorously covered.

Umlaut realized that the glimpse of her panties had not been accidental on her part. She, as a demoness, formed clothing out of her own substance. She had flashed him on purpose. Having part of a soul did not stop her from being mischievous. But now, satisfied that she could do it at any time, she was covering up and focusing on business.

"So let's go deliver this letter to My Dear Demon Professor," Metria said when she saw that he had resumed consciousness. "I believe he is about to conduct Freshman Nature 101, a class used to wash out any demons who aren't totally serious about improving themselves. I have flunked it many times, of course, and am number one on the Ineligibility List. That's the perfect one to crash."

"But why would you want to?"

"Why else? To annoy His Pomposity, of course."

Umlaut decided to let this pass, like so much else about her. He put the letter in his shirt pocket. "How do we get there?"

"Well, you can't get there from here, of course."

He knew she was setting him up for another put-down, but he had to ask. "Then what—?"

"But I can get there, if I have suitable cover so he won't recognize me. Take off your pants."

Despite his caution, he was caught off guard. "My what?"

"Trousers, nether apparel, slacks, jeans, shorts—"

"I knew that! I mean, why take them off?"

"Whatever," she agreed crossly. "Hey, you didn't follow the form. It's a good thing I'm tolerant, or I'd show you *my* pants." Her dress faded, to reveal full, tight polka-dotted panties, with each dot spinning in place like a little whirlpool.

After a moment he heard her talking again. "Oh, all right. But he should have followed the form. It's expected."

Umlaut realized that all he was seeing was serpent hide. Sesame had interposed her body to block his view of the demoness, and the rotating dots were slowly fading. He blinked and turned his gaze away, and the eyeballs creaked as they cracked off the glaze. He had gotten a dangerous dose that time.

He remembered how Surprise Golem had kissed him but never shown him anything awkward. No declining décolletage, and definitely no panties. That was part of what he liked about her. She was a nice girl, easy to be with. He might never see her again, but he treasured the brief time they had had together.

Sesame lowered her coil and he saw Metria again. She was now wearing slacks, so there was no danger of exposure. Unless she got annoyed again and dissolved them.

"Why do you want me to take off my whatevers?"

"So I can emulate them and hide from Grossclout. He'll zap me if he catches me in the class, but he'll take you for a gawky freshman student. He won't know I'm there because I'll just be dull clothing."

Umlaut thought about her being wrapped around his crotch

and surely tickling him in extremely awkward places. "Wouldn't a shirt do as well?"

"Oh, pooh, he thought of it," she muttered. "If you insist on being dull about it." She fuzzed and formed into a floating long-sleeved shirt.

Umlaut hastily removed his own shirt, so as not to give her time to change her mind. She drifted up to him and held out one armhole for him to put his arm into, then the other. It was actually a silky and comfortable shirt, and it fitted him perfectly. It even had buttonable buttons down the front.

"Tuck me in," the shirt said.

Oh. He loosened his belt, then hesitated. The shirt tail extended a fair way down. She was going to get to stroke his behind anyway. But what choice did he have? So he resigned himself and tucked in the shirt.

"That's better," it said, patting his bottom.

"Let's just go deliver the letter," he gritted. Then he remembered a complication. "Para! How can he go there without giving it away?"

"He can visit ParaDice while he waits."

"Visit what?"

"Heaven, Nirvana, Arcadia, Elysium, Eternal Bliss—"

"Paradise?"

"Close enough," the shirt agreed crossly. "Hang on."

As if he could do anything else, with her surrounding his torso. There was a wrench, and suddenly they were at the verge of what seemed to be two more fading islands. Each was cubical, with black dots decorating the faces, connected by a pair of docks guarded by paratroopers. Para was in the water paddling toward them, but there was something odd about it.

"This is the Celebes Sea," the shirt explained. "Folk here are unable to summon the stork, so their number is dwindling, but they feel great, because ParaDice has that quality. Para will love it here; it's his real home."

So it seemed; the boat was propelling himself eagerly toward the islands.

"Hang on again," the shirt said, and helped by whipping its tail around his posterior from both sides.

There was another wrench, and the four of them were part

of a group of really odd characters following a floating demon in a professorial cape. One vaguely resembled a mundane giraffe with only three legs; another was mostly head with tiny arms and legs; another seemed to be a tangle of black lines. Several were variants of humanoid, ranging from ogre to imp. Most were animalistic in some devious manner.

The demoness was right: Two cats, a large serpent, and a regular man fit right in.

"You come here with heads full of mush," the professor was saying. "But *if* you survive, you may come to deserve the title of demons, instead of remaining like half a passel of zombies with PHSD." He spun on a frog-faced student. "Elucidate the initials."

"The what?" Frogface croaked.

Grossclout frowned, and the frog demon jumped and dissipated into smoke. "You," he said, fixing on a coconut head.

"Pull Her Slip Down?" Coconut asked timorously.

Small sparks radiated from Grossclout's eyes. "Anyone?"

Half a spate of mush faces looked blankly back.

A curl of smoke rose from the professor's left ear. "PHSD: post-hypnotic stress disorder," he said with savage calm. "Occurring after some sad excuse for a creature has spent too much time trapped in the hypno-gourd. That may be on the final exam, if you are fortunate enough to achieve it." He drew up at a garden alcove. "Who can tell me what kind of bug this is?" He gestured, and a buzzing bug flew up.

"Ooo, eeek!" a lady demon cried, her arms windmilling to ineffectively repel the bug that flew at her. In a moment it went on to sit on the head of another female. "Ugh!" she cried, outraged. "It crapped on me!" It moved on to a third demoness, hovering threateningly before her face. "Go away, you nasty fly!"

"None of those answers is correct," the professor said. "The bug will continue until it is correctly identified."

Indeed, the bug flew to another demoness, mussing her hair, and another, making a rude noise in her ear. Then it approached Sesame. She snapped at it, but it dodged clear.

Umlaut was afraid its attention would attract notice and give away the serpent's identity. "A ladybug!" he cried. "Because it bugs only ladies."

Instantly the bug flew back to its alcove. "Correct," the professor said. "There's a head without an undue content of mush." He moved on.

Umlaut was thrilled to have found such faint favor. But he still had to deliver the letter and wasn't sure now was the time. It would be better to catch the professor alone.

The professor came to a niche. A nondescript, somewhat servile-looking man stood there. "Who can identify this man?" he demanded.

No one answered; much was the order of the moment.

"We shall question him," the professor said. He faced the man. "Are you well?"

"Yes," the man answered.

"Excellent. Do you like it here?"

"Yes."

"And do you believe the price of has-beans in Beanovia is fair?"

"Yes."

The professor turned to the class. "You," he said, fixing his inordinate glare on a cowering bug-eyed elf. "Ask him a question."

"But I'm just a lowly mush-minded frosh student," the elf protested.

"Yes," the man agreed.

"You," the professor said, indicating a fainting flower of a demoness.

"Do you wear shorts or briefs?" she asked faintly.

"Yes."

The professor's mush-vanquishing gaze struck Umlaut. "You."

"He's a yes-man," Umlaut said desperately. "He says yes to everything."

The professor's fixed grimace ameliorated almost imperceptibly. "Exactly."

More eyes turned on him, some with awe, others with disdain. He had answered two questions and found faint favor. Did that make him a class pariah?

They moved on to a clothes rack. "Who can identify the nature of this coat?"

They gathered around it. The coat was somewhat drab, with

a dull ruff of fur and old-fashioned fasteners down the front.

"Vintage nineteen hundred Mundania?" a student demon asked, and quailed before the professor's glare of negation.

"Oh, who cares?" a demoness with a troll face asked. "It's wa-a-ay out of fashion."

"Then put it on, D. Base," the professor snapped.

Demoness Base tried to balk but was helpless in the face of the mush-destroying gaze that fixed on her. Gingerly she put the coat on over her shoulders. Then she smiled, and her entire disposition became sunnier. Her face became almost human. "I like it."

"What kind of coat?"

"Who cares? It's very comfortable."

"Pass it on," the professor said.

Reluctantly the demoness did, her expression souring as she parted with it. A frog-faced demon tried it on next. "Extremely nice," he said, brightening.

"What kind?"

"I really can't say, but there is something pleasing about it."

"Pass it on."

Obviously disinclined, he did so. He set it on the shoulders of a ferret-faced demon who was about to squish a butterfly under his foot. But when the coat landed on him, he stooped to pick the insect up and guide it to a nice flower.

"Anyone!" the professor said, exasperated by the sheer volume of mush. When no one answered, he speared Umlaut with another glance.

"Uh, a sugarcoat," Umlaut said. "It makes people sweet."

"Precisely." The professor glared at Umlaut with a tinge of curiosity. "Have you taken this class before?"

"Oh, no sir!" Umlaut exclaimed, terrified.

The professor did not seem quite satisfied, but he let it be. He stopped by a group of stone gargoyles. "Where is the beauty?" he demanded of the class.

They considered the figures. Each gargoyle was uglier than its neighbors. Each had huge glistening eyes set in great long faces, and an open mouth from which driblets of water flowed. They all seemed to be looking at something, but there was nothing but a blank wall in that direction. None of them could by any stretch of fevered imagination be called beautiful.

"Look closely," the professor said. "Find the beauty."

They looked closely, but the ugliness of the gargoyles seemed only to get worse.

"Ceit," Grossclout said, glaring at a halfway pretty demoness. Her top half was pretty; her bottom half was gross.

"I am only auditing this class," D. Ceit said evasively.

"Chickenlips!" the professor rapped.

The demon student with chickenlike lips quailed. "Maybe to another gargoyle they are beautiful," he quavered.

"But you are not a gargoyle."

"I am not," the demon admitted, abashed.

"Hophead!"

A demon with a weird-shaped head tried to answer. "She must be hiding behind the gargoyles—or somewhere," he assayed.

"But you have not found her?"

"No, sir," Hophead said, hunching down as if being beaten over the head.

Meanwhile Umlaut was looking closely at the gargoyles. He saw that their eyes reflected a picture of a lovely young human woman, but when he looked there, there was still only the blank wall.

"Umlaut!" the professor said.

Galvanized, Umlaut responded. "In the eyes! Beauty is in the eye of the beholder."

"To be sure." The professor walked on. The class murmured with mixed awe and envy.

Only after a long moment and a short instant did Umlaut realize that the professor had called him by name. They hadn't fooled Grossclout at all. "Oh, no," he murmured.

There did not seem to be any transition, but suddenly they weren't in the class anymore. They were at the edge of a huge volcanic caldera. Red lava boiled in the base of it, and smoke rose toward them.

"Now before I drop you into this, what is your puny pretext for a lame excuse for disrupting my class?" the professor demanded.

Umlaut was terrified. "I didn't mean to do that. I just came to deliver a—"

"Not you, Umlaut. *Her*."

Umlaut felt his shirt twitch. "Curses, I think he's on to us," it murmured.

"You know you're not supposed to come near my classes."

"Oh, pooh! You can't keep me out."

Umlaut floated off the rim of the caldera and sailed down toward the fiery lava. He tried to take a breath to scream, but the smoke got in his face and choked him.

He dropped down until his feet almost touched the red lava. He felt the heat coming through his shoes.

"Oh, all right," his shirt said. "My quarter conscience won't let you hurt him for his little bit of guilt. Let him go."

Umlaut hoped the demon professor would accede. Maybe the volcano didn't scare Demoness Metria, but it appalled mortal Umlaut.

Then the four of them were in an austere office, facing the demon professor's large desk. "Was your head so full of mush that you thought you could get away with this intrusion, D. Metria?" the professor demanded.

Umlaut's shirt turned to smoke. Metria formed. "Well, it was fun trying."

"What is your mischief this time?"

"Umlaut has a letter for you." A smirk was pushing itself through her mouth, trying to reach her lips. "From Mundania."

"Then let's have it." The letter sailed from Umlaut's pocket to the hand of the professor. Only after half an interval did he remember that it had been in his regular shirt pocket, and then he had removed that shirt. Yet now his shirt was back on him, and the letter had been there to be delivered. They *really* had not fooled Grossclout.

The professor glanced at the letter. Tiny jets of steam issued from his ears, and a faint halo of fire outlined his head, but he did not react overtly. "This seems somewhat misinformed. The acquisition of a soul was intended to bring you under control. It succeeded only partially, unfortunately."

"What do you expect of half a soul?" Metria asked disdainfully. Her skirt shortened until it was at the very verge

of showing a polka dot. Was she actually trying to beguile
the professor? "Even a whole soul would not make *me* be-
have. When I passed a quarter of it on to my son Ted six
years ago, what was left had even less effect." The fringe of
the skirt retreated, showing the edge of a dot.

"True, unfortunately." The professor clapped his hands
with a report like that of a dry tree cracking asunder. "Begone, vamp."

Metria vanished. Only the lone polka dot remained. It spun
to the floor, bounced, and dissipated. Umlaut was impressed
by the way Grossclout had handled her.

The professor looked at him. "What is your impression of
the demoness?"

"Oh, I, uh, wouldn't presume to judge."

A small crackle of glaze appeared on an eyeball, but the
demon's voice remained calm. "Answer the question."

He had to do it. "I, uh, don't quite trust her. She has been
trying to stop me from delivering the letters. I suppose it's
just her natural mischief, but—"

"But what?"

"Well, my opinion is ignorant, of course. But sometimes it
seems as if there is something else, so I can't blame it all on
her."

"Example."

"When I went to Zombie World, a girl tried to distract me,
and I think that was really Metria emulating her, but also there
were the Dire Straits and Scylla and Charybdis, which I don't
think Metria could have managed, and then Charybdis
showed up here in Xanth too. It's as if something wants to
stop me, and maybe Metria is helping it."

"Why would anyone or anything wish to prevent delivery
of ignorant letters?"

"Because somewhere in the course of these deliveries I'm
supposed to find the answer to the problem of the Red Spot
Demon Jupiter hurled at Earth and Xanth. Good Magician
Humfrey suggested that. Something may not want that answer
to be found. Maybe the author of the letter that so angered
Demon Jupiter."

"We shall verify," the professor said. The wall behind his
desk became a great window onto what looked like the night

sky, with myriad stars. Looming in the foreground was a great swirl of reddish light. It expanded visibly as they watched, coming ominously closer.

"That looks bigger than all Xanth!" Umlaut said, impressed and horrified.

"Correct. Its impact will not be kind to our worlds. It will be necessary to halt its progress soon."

"Yes! But how can we do that?"

Grossclout glanced at him. "Are you aware of the nature of the Demons, capitalized?"

"Like the Demon Xanth? They have more power than all the rest of us combined."

"Exactly. Only a Demon can halt the thrust of a Demon, and that can get messy. We need to ascertain why the Demon Jupiter did this and then try to ameliorate his ire. That is the most likely solution hidden in your letters."

"Yes, sir."

"You seem to be a curious choice to handle so important a task."

"Yes, sir. I don't even seem to be a full person. I can't remember my past life, and others tell me I don't exist. I hate that."

"Why?"

"Because I have made some fine friends and maybe fallen in love. Where would any of them be if I don't exist? I mean, maybe I don't deserve anything special, but it's not right to mess up the lives of others."

Grossclout looked at Umlaut without any glare at all; it seemed he was capable of nonglaring when he put his mind to it. "You are indeed innocent." He glanced back over his shoulder, and the window became the wall. "One moment while I investigate." He faded out.

Umlaut shook his head, which was threatening to spin. "Do you make any sense of this?" he asked the others.

Serpent and both cats shook their heads. Claire knew much, but demon business was beyond her.

"I'm glad Professor Grossclout is investigating. I think he's a wonderful person, regardless of what Metria thinks. He knows so much he fairly radiates power of intellect. I wish I could really be in one of his classes."

They nodded; they were impressed too.

Grossclout reappeared; exactly one moment had passed. "The answer to the hazard of the Red Spot is not here. But continue your effort; the mission is important."

"Uh, thank you, sir," Umlaut said.

"You did well in class. Since you may not be graded or promoted for that, not being a registered member, I am minded to do you a favor. What would you like?"

"Oh, I wasn't looking for—"

"I am aware of that. Your head is not entirely filled with mush. Ask."

"I—I want to exist. I mean, if I don't. So I can be with Surprise."

Professor Grossclout considered. "That may be more of a challenge than you understand. I will see what I can do."

"Thank you, sir. I—"

But the professor was gone. Rather, the four of them were gone from Grossclout's domain. They were back at the ParaDice islands, standing at the shore, and Para was paddling across to meet them. He looked happy, though Umlaut wasn't sure how a boat conveyed happiness. It must have been a nice visit.

"Uh, you can remain here, if you want," Umlaut said.

But the boat wanted to help them complete their mission first. That was fine with Umlaut.

13

OGRETS

N ow he had to deliver the next letter. Umlaut decided that trying to make decisions wasn't working very well, so he simply grabbed the next one in the pile. It said TANDY NYMPH.

"Who is Tandy Nymph?" he asked. "One of the folk at the Faun & Nymph Retreat?"

Sammy leaped out of the boat and bounded across the greensward. "Wait for us!" Umlaut called. Naturally the cat ignored that. But he had a new strategy. He turned to Claire, who remained in the boat. "Can you do something? We can't keep up with him through this jungle." For the forest was indeed a jungle in this region.

Claire poked her chin over the gunwale. "Mew," she said faintly.

Sammy screeched to a halt, looking abashed, allowing them to catch up. Then he proceeded at a more sedate pace, and Para followed without difficulty.

It was amazing what impression a lady could make on a man. Or a queen on a tom, or whatever.

That reminded him of Surprise Golem. "Surprise," he breathed, longing for her nearness.

"Oh, there you are," she said, appearing in the seat opposite him. She wore a nice blue dress and looked just utterly completely perfect.

"Surprise!" he exclaimed gladly, grabbing for her hand. But his hand passed right through hers. That brought him to as much of a halt as Sammy had recently made. "What?"

She laughed, and her hair flared. "I'm here in astral projection. You can see me and hear me, but you can't touch me. A girl can't be too careful, you know."

He caught on. "Oh, Surprise, you're using one of your talents! But won't you lose it?"

"Yes, but it's worth it, to be with you a while. After all, one day we will be betrothed."

"Oh, Surprise," he repeated, melting into goo.

"I sneaked out to the edge where there is magic and went astral and looked for you, but I couldn't find you until you said my name. Names are potent."

"I was longing for your company," he confessed. "But I didn't think I could have it. I mean, even if I could return to Euphoria, your folks wouldn't let me be with you."

"We had a real session after you left," she agreed. "Stern as stern could be. But I tolerated it."

"They don't like me."

"They don't dislike you," she said seriously. "It's just that they're parents and I'm a teen. They don't want me dating or even meeting any boy, and when I come of age, they still won't admit that any boy is good enough for me. That's the way parents are; it's in their specifications."

"But then why are you here? I mean, I'm so glad you are, but—"

"That's the way teens are. We never pay much attention to idiotic parental restrictions. Where would they be, if they had listened to *their* parents? I wouldn't even exist."

The very notion appalled him. "You had to exist, so I could meet you!" Then he thought of something else. "But I thought Grundy was a golem. So he never had parents."

"Yes, of course. He was made, not delivered. But later he managed to become real. It's a long story he'll be glad to bore you with some time. And Rapunzel was raised alone in an ivory tower. But when they joined the dread Adult Conspiracy they learned all about parenting; I think it comes in the same manual with summoning the stork. So it's the same. Anyway, here I am, for a while. Let's not argue."

"Oh, Surprise, I couldn't argue with you!"

She frowned. "Oh? Who would you rather argue with?"

"Well, the Demoness Metria, for one."

"While she tries to freak you out by showing her naughty panties? I should think you would think more of me than that." Her expression was severe.

He stared at her, baffled. "I, uh—oh, Surprise, if I said something wrong, I'm sorry! Please forgive me. I don't want you to be mad at me."

She laughed. "I'm teasing, you dope! The same way my parents tease each other. I'm glad you don't want to argue with me. And after we're betrothed, I may even show you my panties."

"You've got panties?" he asked, flustered. And knew he had fouled up yet again. "I mean you're such a nice girl—"

"And nice girls don't have panties?"

"I, uh, don't know." He was blushing.

"They have naked bottoms?"

Umlaut's flush chased his blush across his face. "Uh—"

"You're just an endless bundle of embarrassment, aren't you!" She leaned forward and kissed him, though there was no touch. "You were so polite, never even trying to look, I knew you were decent."

"I just didn't have the wit to think of it," he said, still flustered. His wits were not sharp at the best of times, and in her presence, astral or not, he was hopelessly klutzy.

She began to fade. "Oops, I'm fading," she said. "I can't stay. My astral power is exhausted, and I'll never have it again. Kiss me quickly!"

He tried to, but his face passed right through hers, to his dismay.

"Gotcha again," she said merrily as she disappeared.

"You've got me, all right," he agreed as he settled back. Then he looked around. Sesame and Claire were watching him understandingly. They evidently knew how women handled men, and approved.

Meanwhile Para was running swiftly after Sammy, and the

jungle was passing just about as rapidly behind. Umlaut hoped Tandy Nymph was close; the day was getting late. He brought out the letter and read it.

Dear Tandy,
ARJAYESS ME
TANDY SHE

TO KNOW FRIEND
SO LETTER SEND

WORLDS UNITE
ATTEMPTS TO WRITE

WISH YOU NEAR
SO VERY DEAR.

Hi. I thought I would begin this with a form of communicating you must be familiar with, having ogres as family through marriage.

If you have recently spoken with Breanna, Irene, or Jenny, you will know of me.

I began these letters in the frozen season—winter. Now it is spring, the time of new birth. Many baby animals are being born (as well as human ones, I am sure—it is a very busy time for the storks). Leaves are opening on trees, flowers blooming everywhere, and our sun has returned, bringing with it many species of birds. Two in particular are my favorites. I make flower gardens and need earthworms to enrich the soil. I am always amused when the robber birds with their brilliant red breasts come back to take my worms. Whenever I see one pouncing on a worm, we have a pretend argument with me scolding them for stealing my worms. Truly, though, I do not begrudge them the food for their babies.

The other one I am happy to see returned is the hover bird. They are very small, averaging only about three inches, and build nests around half the size of a human's thumb. Hover birds flap their wings so rapidly that it creates a curious humming sound. I provide their preferred food to attract them, as watching them zip here to there is a great source of joy to me. Compared to the size of your harpies and rocs, our hover birds are like precious flying jewels. Your mother would love them.

It is time to go outdoors and start my morning. I like to see how many hover birds and robbers I can count each day.

Have a sunny day, Tandy. I hope Fracto is elsewhere.

Your friend,
Arjayess

Umlaut considered that. He wasn't sure what the word *born* meant but guessed it was another term for the stork's deliveries. The creatures named were strange, but of course the letter was from Mundania, said to be a very strange place. He did not see anything in the letter to annoy anyone, let alone make the recipient try to destroy Xanth. So this one was safe, it seemed.

Unfortunately, it also gave him no clue how to abate the menace of the Red Spot. He was beginning to wonder whether any of the letters really would do that. So far he had gone to several interesting places and met several interesting folk, and seen Sesame, Sammy, and himself find worthwhile partners. Even Para Boat had found a nice place to return to. So in that sense the mission had done several folk some good. But it hadn't solved the big problem.

He put away the letter. "Do you know Tandy Nymph?" he asked Sesame and Claire. Both shook their heads. Sesame didn't know many humanoid landbound folk, and Claire's voyance did not seem to operate at a distance. Ah, well, he would find out soon enough.

They came to a region of moderate hills. The trees cleared back to give the hills room, and smart little breezes came in to play. It was pleasant, as many areas of Xanth tended to be. Soon they passed a sign that said ZEPHYR HILLS. That explained it; this was where the zephyrs, the cute little winds, lived. Probably when they grew bigger and stronger they would go out and become less cute blowhards.

But now it was really getting dark, and they had not eaten since he remembered not when. "We'd better camp for the night," he said. "Sammy, if you care to find a good place—"

Sammy glanced back at Claire, who nodded agreement. He took off at an angle, and soon they came to a nice little valley. Indeed, a sign said PEARL VALLEY. Umlaut looked around but didn't see any pearls.

They came to a large old house. An old woman emerged. "Have you travelers come to spend the night?" she inquired as Sammy rubbed against her legs.

"Uh, yes," Umlaut said. "I thought there might be a campsite, with pie trees and a spring."

She laughed. "Not here. But I have many rooms, and home-baked pies, and jugs of good well water, and a lava tree. Will those do?"

Umlaut glanced at Claire, who nodded. This was a suitable place. "Uh, yes, sure. We don't want to put you to much trouble. We're sort of a mixed group."

"No trouble at all. I like having company, if only for a night. I am Pearl Valley."

"Uh," Umlaut started, but ran out of words. He found some new ones in half a moment, fortunately. "I thought the sign meant—I was looking for pearls."

Pearl laughed more thoroughly. "That's my sign, so travelers can find my house. And this is my companion, Sheba. She is cautious about cats but will get along if you are polite." She glanced at Sesame. "What is it you eat?"

"Not dogs!" Umlaut said quickly.

"That's good. Sheba came from Mundania the same time I did, so we get along. She's what is called there an Australian shepherd. Some cruel Mundanian cut off her tail, but that did not sour her nature. Come on in." She glanced at Para. "I do have a quack pond out back." Para brightened. His father had been a quack, his mother a dream boat; quack ponds were ideal.

Soon they were in the house, and Pearl was right: There were excellent fresh pies and much else to eat and drink. Sheba was friendly with Umlaut, diffident about the cats, and quite cautious about Sesame. But overall it was a good night. The lava tree was especially nice; it grew toilets that filled with lava after use and became tree stumps, and there were washbasins filled with water. The lava tree's trunk had flat shiny facets that enabled Umlaut to see himself, making sure he was clean.

"I could get used to a place like this," he confided to Sesame.

It did seem nice, for his kind, she agreed in Serpentine. She would rather go swimming with Soufflé.

That reminded him of Surprise. "I think I'm in love."

They all were, she suggested. That much they had gained from the letters, even if they didn't save Xanth.

That was perhaps an odd way to put it, but he had to agree. "I am better off for having come to know you too."

Thank you. She kissed his ear. Umlaut felt guilty for wishing it had been Surprise doing that.

Well fed and rested, they thanked Pearl and Sheba, and set off again next morning. "I hope you are not going too close to the Region of Madness," Pearl said. "We passed through it, but I don't recommend it for travelers."

"We have to deliver a letter to Tandy Nymph."

She shook her head. "I don't know that name. There are some ogres there, though; beware of them."

"Ogres!" Umlaut had emulated one on occasion but wasn't eager to meet one personally. "We'll try to be alert for them."

But Claire was shaking her head. Umlaut dreaded to think what that might mean, so he didn't inquire.

The scenery became somehow different. Umlaut wasn't sure what bothered him about it, as there was nothing obvious. Maybe it was the way the trunks of the trees were turning purple, while the foliage became iridescent. Possibly it was the little animals walking along on their ears while waving their legs in the air.

Then he saw one of the convenient little signs: BEWARE: REGION OF MADNESS. So this was that dread region Pearl had warned them about. And Sammy was leading them right into it.

Well, how bad could it be? They had already been through some pretty odd regions, after all.

They came to a gully traversed by what seemed to be a huge spiderweb. Fortunately Sammy was leading them along the ridge beside it, rather than into it. Umlaut watched as they passed it. He saw that each gust of wind caused the web to ripple, making waves like those of the sea. Then he saw spiders riding little boards on those waves. What was the point of that?

He looked at Claire, and soon he had the answer: Those were web surfers. Well, that wasn't any madder than the rest of this region.

Something charged at them from the side. It was big and fierce, reminding him of a bear, though he had never before seen a bear. Yet there was something odd about it. Para veered away from it—into the big web. Suddenly they were tangled in the endless mesh of the web, to the vast annoyance of the spiders. Then they dropped on through it into the gully, trailing sticky lines.

Meanwhile the bear leaped after them—and also fell into the surfing web, messing up more of it. The spiders, already annoyed, got really mad at this second disruption. They swarmed over the bear, trussing it up with endless web lines. It couldn't escape because, oddly, it wasn't as solid as the boat had been. It seemed to be made of lines rather than firm flesh.

Then a dim bulb flashed, and he understood. "It's a thread bear!" he exclaimed, laughing. Just the kind of creature to be found in a place like this.

Claire looked disdainfully at him. Hadn't that been obvious?

But now they were down in the gully, and the surfing web was above. They couldn't get out without breaking through it, and the spiders would really be enraged if that happened a third time.

The gully ended, but not the web; it stretched rhythmically across the top, sealing it neatly off. The spiders, having repaired the breaks, were surfing again. There were hundreds of them, and every so often several glanced down, almost daring the folk below to mess with the web again. It was clear that web surfers did not like holes in their program.

Para came to a halt. What now?

Umlaut realized that Sammy remained outside. He suffered a rare flash of genius. "Sammy, find help!"

They saw a stir of leaves as the cat took off. Now most of

what they had to do was wait. The rest of what they had to do was worry. Sammy's talent was unerring, but this was the Region of Madness, and that could complicate things.

Soon, however, Sammy returned with two children. "Hi!" the boy called down through the web.

"Hi," Umlaut answered.

"Lo!" the girl called.

"Lo," Umlaut answered.

"I'm Epoxy Ogre," the boy said. "I'm eleven. I make things hard and fast."

An ogre! Umlaut wanted to avoid those awful creatures. But maybe ogre children weren't as bad. "I'm Umlaut. My talent is emulation."

"I'm Benzine Brassie," the girl said. "I'm his identical twin sister. I make things soft and loose."

He was an ogre and she was a brassie, but they were identical twins? Something didn't quite add up here, but Umlaut didn't have time to worry about details. "Can you help us get out of here without annoying the spiders?"

They considered. "I could make the web brittle hard, but the web surfers wouldn't like that."

"I could make it squishy soft, but they wouldn't like that, either."

Together they formed a conclusion: "No."

Then why had Sammy brought them? Umlaut suppressed his burgeoning ire and tried again. "Do you know anyone who might help?"

They considered. "How about our big brother, Brusque?" Epoxy asked.

"What does he do?"

"He makes things hard and heavy or soft and light," Benzine said.

"Isn't that the same as your two talents?"

"No," Epoxy said. "I make things hard but not heavy."

"And I make things soft but not light."

This didn't seem entirely helpful. "Maybe you should fetch him." An older brother might have a better grasp of the situation.

They departed, and Umlaut settled down to wait with the others. So far this did not seem to be going well.

Footsteps approached. "Hello!" a deeper voice called. "I am Brusque Brassy. How can I help you?" A somewhat coppery figure of a young man stood there.

"You can get us out of here," Umlaut replied as evenly as he could manage.

"All right. We'll work together." He bent over to touch the web with one finger.

The fine lines shimmered. Then the center of the web depressed as if a giant hand were pushing it. The spiders, alarmed, retreated. It came down until it almost touched the boat. Umlaut put an arm up to shield himself and found the web like steel wire but much more ponderous; he couldn't budge it. It was indeed hard and heavy.

But by similar token, he could not part it to make a hole for them. The stuff was impervious.

"Benzine," Brusque said.

The girl walked down the web slope to the base just above the boat. Now that Umlaut got a good look at her, he saw that she had fair hair and eyes the same color. She squatted and touched the web.

Suddenly it softened, in that region only. Umlaut was able to stretch a hole in it so that Para could get through. But Para couldn't walk on it because it was too soft; it stretched down to the ground wherever a duck foot pressed.

"Epoxy," Brusque said.

They boy came down the web slope. He had dark hair and eyes. He put his finger to the bottom of the web, and it became iron hard again.

Para walked on up and out. Then Brusque touched the web, and it sprang back the way it had been before, no longer hard and heavy. It rippled and waved. The spiders, relieved, resumed their surfing.

"Uh, thank you," Umlaut said. "I'm Umlaut, and I have a letter to deliver to Tandy Nymph."

"Grandma Tandy!" the twins said together.

Their grandmother? But these were ogres and brassies.

"Take them to Dad and Mom," Brusque told the twins. "They'll decide."

"This way," Epoxy said, starting off. Sammy, not needed for this, jumped back into the boat.

But Benzine lingered behind. "Can we ride in your nice boat?" she asked shyly.

"Welcome," Umlaut agreed.

"And stroke your nice cats?" Benzine asked as they climbed into the boat.

Umlaut looked at the cats. Sammy approved. Claire, after a suitable pause, acquiesced. The boy stroked Sammy and the girl stroked Claire.

"That way," Epoxy said, pointing. Para started moving.

"May I ask some questions?" Umlaut asked cautiously.

"Sure!" Epoxy said.

"We love questions," Benzine agreed.

"How did you come to be—"

"That's easy," Epoxy said. "When the stork brought us, our parents Esk and Bria needed two names in a hurry, so they read the label on the diaper."

"How to clean it," Benzine explained. "And it fits our talents."

That did answer one question. "How can you be—"

"When they signaled the stork—" Epoxy began.

"Twice," Benzine added.

"They specified identical twins."

"But they also specified a boy and a girl."

"I am Mother's boy," Epoxy said proudly.

"And I am Daddy's girl."

"So we were *almost* identical. When we grow up we will be less so. But we're both ogrets."

Ogrets?

"Meanwhile they couldn't tell us apart, so they dyed our hair and eyes to make us different," Benzine concluded. "For now."

That answered another question. "How is it that you—"

"Because Grandpa Smash is half ogre, so his son and grandsons are part ogre," Epoxy said.

"And Grandma Tandy is a nymph," Benzine said. "So I'm part nymph. It makes me cute and empty minded. And when their son Esk Ogre married Bria Brassie, we became part brassie too. So he's Epoxy Ogre and I'm Benzine Brassie. That's with the *ie* to show I'm a girlie; Brusque is *y* to show he's a boy."

"I'm *y* too," Epoxy said. "I've got a *y* chrom—chrom—"

"Chrome O some," Benzine said. "Girls have *x*'s, so we can kiss." She kissed the air, and sure enough, little *x*'s flew out. "Ask a boy for a kiss, and he asks, '*Y?*'" She giggled while her brother glared.

"But you seem to be mostly human," Umlaut said.

"Well, it's a common element," Epoxy said. "But we don't brag about it. Would you?"

"Maybe not," Umlaut agreed, laughing.

"So we just prefer to be ogrets."

There was that word again. "What—?"

"Ogrets," Epoxy repeated. "Little ogres. The same way a young nymph is a nymphet, and a young brassy is—" He broke off. "What is it, Benzine?"

"A brassiere? No, that's not it."

"Brazier? No, still not it. Anyway, there's a word."

"I'm sure there is," Umlaut said.

"We had a real scary dream about our origin, I mean where the stork got us," Benzine confided. "Something to do with Mundania. But we don't believe it."

"I don't think anybody knows where the storks get the babies they deliver," Umlaut said diplomatically. But it made him wonder whether any stork had brought him. If not, where had he come from?

They arrived at a den in the jungle. An ordinary-looking man was working in the backyard. If he was part ogre, it didn't show. "This is ours," Epoxy said.

As they approached, a woman came out. She seemed to be made entirely of brass but was rather pretty for all that. "Mommee, companee!" Benzine called.

There were more introductions, while Umlaut remained bemused. How could a living woman be all metal? How could a living man ever relate to her, especially when it came to romance?

Bria Brassie seemed to catch his thought. "We can be quite soft when we want to be," she said.

He felt himself blushing. Again. He tried to cover by repeating his mission. "I have a letter for Tandy Nymph."

Bria nodded. "She'll like that. She doesn't get much mail." She focused on the children. "Very well, you may ride in the duck boat to show them where your grandmother lives. But stay clear of the madness."

"We will, over hill!" the twins chorused.

Bria smiled tolerantly. "They take such pride in being ogrets," she explained. "When they think of it."

Para moved on. Suddenly he stopped. There was a brutish looking creature. "Oopsy," Epoxy said. "A peccadillo."

"What's that?" Umlaut asked.

"A crossbreed between a pig and an armadillo," Benzine explained. "They can be mean."

"They're always at fault," Epoxy said.

"We heard they are popular with lady pigs," Benzine said. "And lady armadillos. But we can't think why."

Because that came under the heading of Adult Conspiracy, Umlaut suspected. "I think we can handle that." He glanced at Sesame. She nodded and slithered out of the boat, forming her emulation as she went.

The peccadillo pawed the ground, getting ready to charge them. But then Sesame got there. She was impressive; she seemed to snort smoke, and her teeth glinted hugely. She looked a lot like a hungry dragon.

"Wow!" Epoxy said. "I didn't know she was a weredragon."

"She's not," Umlaut said, satisfied.

The peccadillo was taken aback. He had thought he had a defenseless duck-footed boat to gore, and suddenly he was confronted with a dragon. But he wasn't ready to quit. He tried to sneak around the dragon. Sesame cut him off, lunging for him. He retreated so fast he skidded. He crashed into a pie tree, and pies were jarred loose. But there was something funny about them; they were small and seemed to be in the shape of letters of the alphabet, all jumbled. "That's not a regular pie tree."

"It's a pi tree," Benzine said. "See, it's printing on the pig."

Sure enough, the irate tree was stabbing hot letters at the peccadillo's hide, leaving tiny brand marks. The creature had had enough; he scooted out from under and fled the scene.

Sesame let her dragon emulation fade and returned to the boat. "That's great!" Epoxy said as she slithered back onto the bottom of the craft. "May I pet you?"

The serpent was taken aback; evidently no one had wanted to pet her before. But she agreed, and the ogret petted her head.

"He's a dragon fan," Benzine explained.

They moved on. Evidently news of the seeming dragon spread, because no other creatures threatened the boat. Soon they came to a section of the forest where a number of medium-sized trees had their trunks twisted into pretzels, and stones were lying on the ground in rather squashed condition. "What's this?"

"Oh, they're just from Grandpa Smash when he's in ogre mode," Epoxy said. "He twists up trees and squeezes juice from stones one-handed."

"And teaches young dragons the meaning of fear," Benzine added. "It's what ogres do."

So it seemed.

They heard a crashing in the forest. This turned out to be an ogre chopping wood. He was huge and hairy, and he didn't use an ax: he simply sliced his ham-hands through the trunks of trees, sundering them, then put the fragments to his mouth and chewed them into small billets, spitting out splinters.

"Grandpa!" Epoxy called, and the ogre paused, turning to face them.

"Go human!" Benzine called.

The ogre pondered two moments, evidently not being smart enough to manage a full thought in one moment. Ogres were justifiably proud of their stupidity. "What hash? Me bash!" He made a ham-fist.

"Give him the peace pipe," Benzine said.

Epoxy produced a pipe. "Smoke this, Grandpa," he said, giving it to the ogre. But when the ham-hand closed on it, the pipe shattered.

"Oopsy," Benzine said. "It fell to pieces."

"It's a piece pipe," Epoxy agreed. "He held it wrong."

But then the ogre managed to catch on. He shrank into mere human size and form. "Hi, grandkids!"

The two ogrets ran into his embrace. Then they introduced the travelers. "Grandpa Smash, this is a nice boat," Epoxy said.

"With a big snake and two cats," Benzine added.

Umlaut cleared his throat. "And a man," Epoxy added be-latedly.

"They use him to talk for them," Benzine explained.

"I, uh, have a letter for Tandy Nymph."

"This way," Smash-human said cheerfully.

Tandy turned out to be an old nymph, something Umlaut hadn't realized existed. She accepted the letter graciously. She looked at it. "Hover birds!" she exclaimed.

Several flying creatures came to hover near her. Their wings extended upward from their small bodies and rotated in a circle above. They did make humming sounds.

They had a nice meal of mashed wood pulp and freshly squeezed rock juice, then were ready to deliver the next letter. Umlaut thanked Smash and Tandy and the ogrets, and they got back into the boat. The delivery hadn't been nearly as bad as he had feared.

14

COM PEWTER

Umlaut took the next letter from the pile. It was addressed to Com Pewter. "Who is that?" he asked.

Sammy, Claire, and Sesame all looked at him. He didn't know that?

"There's something funny about my memory," he reminded them. "There's a lot I don't know."

Sammy set off, leading Para, while Claire and Sesame clarified this basic education. Com Pewter, it turned out, was an ornery machine that had supposedly been turned to good but, like Fracto Cloud, still could be pretty difficult about it. He could change reality in his immediate vicinity by printing a correction on his screen, making it very hard for a person to get away from him if he didn't want it to happen. He had a lady machine friend called Com Passion who resided near a love spring and was far more friendly. Almost too friendly. The two of them liked to play card games on their screens. Each had a mouse that could change into human or other form to help out.

Umlaut shrugged. "It doesn't seem too complicated. I'll deliver the letter and depart before Pewter thinks to have me stay."

Sammy Cat changed course. Umlaut was about to ask why, since the way straight ahead was relatively open. But then Para almost collided with a nondescript girl standing in the path. His twenty duck feet skidded as he halted.

"Hey, what are you doing there?" Umlaut called, annoyed.

"Ifmmp," the girl said.

"I don't understand."

"J dbo'u tqfbl Ybouijbo."

This did not help. Umlaut looked at Claire and soon had the answer: The girl did not speak Xanthian. That seemed to be her magic talent: Somehow her words came out hopelessly mundane. That in turn was odd, because she was not from Mundania. Her name was Tacy. She had said hello, then explained, but of course he hadn't understood. It was her curse, and she wished she could be rid of it.

"Maybe if you went to the Good Magician," he suggested. But she shook her head in incomprehension. She couldn't understand him any better than he understood her.

Para was traveling again, and Tacy was riding with them in the boat. Umlaut wasn't sure when she had gotten in; that had been lost somewhere in the session of feline clarifications. He wanted to translate his suggestion for her, but the animals couldn't voice any words, and Tacy didn't know how to play nineteen questions. So they were stuck.

"Maybe we should just take you to Com Pewter and see if he can change your reality so you can talk," he said. She looked at him blankly, but he still thought it was a moderately good idea.

Then Tacy's expression changed. "What are you doing with another woman?" she demanded.

"What other woman?" Umlaut asked. Then he did two-thirds of a triple-take. "You spoke intelligibly!"

"Well, I should hope so. What did you expect?"

"More Mundanian. How did you manage to change so suddenly?"

She smiled, then tried to stifle a giggle.

A dim bulb glowed. "Surprise?" he asked.

"Who else? I said I'd look in on you, but I can't use astral projection again. This time I used spirit overlapping. That is, it's my spirit borrowing her body. I'll have to use something else next time."

"Surprise," he repeated gratefully. "I wish I could have stayed with you."

She shrugged. "Maybe you can, sometime. So what have you been up to, aside from riding with strange women?"

"I was just trying to help her—"

"Oh, you were, were you?"

"It was innocent!" he exclaimed. Then he saw her laughing and realized that she had been teasing him again. She was a great tease.

He caught her up on the ogre visit and explained that they were now heading to Com Pewter. But she had little interest. "Let's kiss," she said.

"But you're not in your own body."

"I'm still me." She pursed her lips.

Still he hesitated. "I'm not sure this is proper."

"What's miscalculated about it?"

"What's what?"

"Error, mistake, inaccurate, blunder, boner—"

"Wrong?"

"Whatever," she agreed crossly. "A kiss is a kiss." She put her arms around him and drew him close.

"What's wrong," he said carefully, "is that not only is it the wrong body, it's the wrong spirit, Metria."

"Oh, you guessed," she said, dismayed. "Bleep!"

"Don't you have a little boy to take care of?"

"Oh, Ted's with DeMonica. They get along great."

"So what do you want with me?"

"Only to pass a little time."

"Why are you trying to distract me from delivering the letters?"

She gazed at him. Her face was placid but there were little flames in her eyes. "I love my son."

"Of course you do! What does that have to do with—"

But she had faded out.

"Something is weird here," Umlaut muttered. "Claire, do you know what's going on?"

But this time the cat had no answer. Which was another oddity. Why should the motive of a demoness turn off her voyance? It was all part of the strangeness of his situation. For it seemed to be Umlaut himself who had some mysterious wrongness. If only he could figure it out!

Para slowed, seeming uncertain. That was because Sammy had stopped leading the way. "What's the matter?" Umlaut asked. And, by dint of a few questions, he had the answer: Sammy was lost.

"Lost?" Umlaut repeated blankly. "But you were on the way to find Com Pewter. How could you be lost?"

Claire clarified that. Something had changed, causing Sammy to go the wrong direction, and now they were in the Realm of Lost Objects. In fact they had become several of those objects.

"But that isn't where we were going," Umlaut protested. "What happened?"

Claire didn't know. Her talent operated at close range, so she knew where they were but not what distant thing had caused Sammy to lose track. It seemed that first Com Pewter's cave had changed its location, then that location turned out to be here. Which of course didn't make sense, as this was definitely not Pewter's cave.

Umlaut made a vague connection. "I wonder whether Metria's interference is related to our getting lost? I saw Sammy change course and was about to inquire, but then Metria came, pretending to be Tacy, and then Surprise. That held my attention until we were here."

Claire nodded. That did seem to be the case.

But the mystery of why remained. He had asked the demoness why she was trying to stop him from delivering the letters, and she had said she loved her son, then faded out. She had, he thought, been troubled. There had to be a reason, if only he could figure it out.

But first he had to focus on how to get to Com Pewter's cave when Sammmy Cat couldn't find it. "Can you find a way out of here?" he asked Para.

The boat tried but soon ran afoul of a labyrinth of piled socks. This much Claire understood: Each sock was different, no longer one of a pair, making them all useless. They had been lost in the course of time and space and finally landed here, and formed into a maze. It just went on and on. However, there was a way out of this much: Para merely plowed across the maze walls until he was clear of the labyrinth.

"Hey, what are you doing?" someone demanded.

Umlaut looked and saw twin imps. "We're trying to get unlost. Who are you?"

"I am Finders," the left imp said. "We collect things from all over everywhere."

"And I am Keepers," the right one said. "And we save them all here."

Claire shot Umlaut a glance. He understood. "You're stealing them!"

"We're kleptomaniacs," Finders agreed smugly.

"And all the people, all over everywhere, think they're just carelessly losing them. You're getting away with a monstrous crime."

"We sure are," Keepers agreed just as smugly.

Disgusted, Umlaut urged Para to head on out, anywhere. Then he had another notion. "Maybe Metria told Com Pewter to reverse his magic, to make it seem he's not there. So Sammy went in the opposite direction. If he goes opposite to what his talent tells him, maybe we'll get there after all."

Claire and Sesame nodded. That made sense to them.

Sammy set off again, looking doubtful. But at least they had a direction. If it didn't work, Umlaut would try to think of something else.

And there in the path was Tacy, the girl who couldn't speak Xanthian. "Get out of the way, Metria!" Umlaut shouted.

She looked blankly at him. "Xibu?"

Umlaut opened his mouth, but Claire caught his eye. "You mean she's real this time?" The cat nodded.

Acting on a ludicrous hope, he gestured the girl into the canoe. She joined him there.

"Maybe Com Pewter can help you," he said. "At least temporarily. And maybe someone else can. See if you can say the word *Surprise.* Can you say that?"

He drilled her in that one word, and finally she managed to say it, though obviously she did not understand it. "Surprize."

Then a puzzled expression crossed her face. "It's all right?" she asked and nodded as if hearing an answer.

"Who are you?" Umlaut demanded.

She looked at him. "This is Tacy. She can't speak Xanthian."

"Can't speak what?"

"Xanthian. It's her negative talent. She hates it but can't seem to do anything about it. She said it was all right for me to borrow her body for a little while. I'm Surprise."

She hadn't gone into the confused-word routine, so it wasn't Metria this time. Still, he wanted to make sure. Metria, being all magical, had not been able to go into the unmagical region where he had met Surprise. That meant she was unlikely to know the details of what had happened there. "How did we meet?"

She smiled. "You were walking along staring at the ground. I think you were looking for someone my parents' size. You didn't see me at all. I said 'Hello,' and you jumped. Then you didn't believe my name."

"It really is you!" he exclaimed, gratified.

"Who else would it be?"

"The Demoness Metria. She pretended to be you. She wanted to kiss me."

"So do I."

"But she was trying to distract me from delivering the letters. And when I asked her why, she said she loved her son and faded away. I'm trying to figure that out."

"I have an ugly idea why."

"What is that?"

"Maybe someone threatened Ted if she didn't stop the letters."

And that suddenly made sense. It explained the demoness's curious reaction and fading out: She couldn't tell about the threat, lest her child suffer. But who or what could successfully threaten a demoness?

"Are you going to kiss me?" Surprise asked. "I can't stay much longer."

"I can do that? I mean, it's all right with Tacy?"

"We made a deal. You kiss each of us once."

"But you're the only one I want to kiss."

"There is a price on it. She says there is something about you." She winked. "As if I didn't know that. So kiss me, then kiss her. I promise not to be insanely jealous."

He didn't argue further. He embraced her and kissed her, and she kissed him back. "Just crazily jealous," she said. But she smiled; it was another tease. Then her body changed subtly, and he released her.

"Nz Uvso?"

He wasn't sure of her words but understood her query. He kissed Tacy similarly and knew that she was indeed a different person. The kiss was quite unlike the first. That, oddly, confirmed the authenticity of the first one. And that first one had been far superior.

They rode on. Umlaut brought out the letter and read it.

Dear Com Pewter,

As the source of knowledge in Xanth, this is a short note of inquiry to you requesting some information. For some time now we in Mundania have pondered the problem of how to*********. It is my understanding that in Xanth, with the help of magic, you are able to ^^^^^^^^^^^.

Please excuse the appearance of this letter #########. Here on Earth, and specifically in Mundania, I battle with an affliction of killer headaches. We call them migraines.

Thousand of tiny imps have taken up residence in my brain and let loose a swarm of nickelped . . . . . . who seem bent on destroying it by inflicting as much pain as poss————. White-hot lights perform a macabre dance behind the eyeballs, and stomach contents refuse to stay where they belong. I have often considered the option of screaming my head off—if it was detached the pain level would be more tolerable.

Please send the requested information ASAP. Thank)()()(><><><><>.

En route to oblivion now . . .

Sincer=====,
Arjayess

"My grain!" Umlaut exclaimed. "We have that in Xanth. How can they have it in Mundania, without magic?"

Nevertheless, it appeared to be so. Meanwhile the letter seemed safe enough. He was beginning to wonder whether any of them were actually dangerous. Yet that one to Demon Jupiter obviously had been.

Meanwhile, it seemed that Sammy's reverse-seeking tactic was working. They were moving right along, presumably in the correct direction now. The trip was beginning to consider becoming slightly dull. Sesame and the cats were taking a snakenap and two catnaps. He wished he could do the same.

He discovered himself slumped against Tacy, who was holding him upright. He must have fallen asleep. He straightened up in a hurry, embarrassed. "I—uh, I'm sorry."

"Uibu't bmm sjhiu."

He had forgotten about her language problem, but her tone indicated that she wasn't offended. She must have caught him when he nodded off, and it must have been a while, because now they were approaching the Gap Chasm.

Para headed right up to the brink. "What are you doing? We'll fall in!" But then the boat ran out over the edge and didn't fall. Umlaut stared, wondering what was happening.

"Jowjtjcmf csjehf," Tacy said. She gestured, forming the outline of a bridge.

"A bridge!" he exclaimed. "That we can't see."

She surely did not understand his words but got his meaning. "Zft."

"That's a relief."

Sesame and the cats found the chasm as intriguing as Umlaut did, and they all stared down at its immense emptiness. The walls were almost sheer, and the bottom was flat with trees growing. Overall it seemed to be another world, a nice one. A few small harmless clouds hung partway down, enjoying it also. This was perhaps the only place in Xanth where a cloud could sink below ground level yet still be safely in the air. He was glad Para had known about the invisible bridge. And Tacy.

That sent him on another thought, as they reached the north side and visible land. He had nodded off, and instead of complaining, Tacy had held him up. He had kissed her; did she have the wrong idea? No, she had accepted Surprise as a visitor, so she knew how he felt. So she was just being companionable. Probably because she was not a fouled-up person, just a fouled-up speaker.

In due course they came to a valley with a number of crushed trees. This was not the work of an ogre; they weren't twisted into pretzel shapes but were pressed into the ground as if stepped on. But what could squish a full-grown tree flat?

Then he heard a distant stomping that rapidly approached. The others heard it too. "Uif jowjtjcmf hjbou!" Tacy exclaimed.

"Whatever it is, I don't like it," Umlaut said. "I don't want to be squished flat."

Para scooted into the entrance of a dark cave. Then they came to a lighted chamber, where a rather junky contraption sat, with a vertical flat screen. Words printed on it: **GREETINGS**.

"Com Pewter!" Umlaut exclaimed, getting out of the boat. "I have a letter for you."

A troll approached. "I am Com Pewter's mouse, Tristan Troll. I will handle the letter."

"You don't look like a mouse," Umlaut said.

"It is a term for a special service," Tristan explained. "Pewter does not move about himself, so I perform physical tasks." He opened the letter and held it before the screen.

SEND ARJAYESS AN EEEE-MAIL the screen printed.

"Now, sir, that would not be nice," Tristan told the screen. "The Eeee is such an ugly creature, and its Eeee-mail makes recipients scream in rage or agony."

PRECISELY.

"Surely we can do better for her than that. She is evidently a nice person, for a Mundane. We can't in conscience allow her to suffer longer."

YOU HAVE TOO MUCH #### CONSCIENCE, TROLL.

"Of course," Tristan agreed complacently. "Shall I summon a search engine from the Electri-City to range the Information Highway for a suitable answer for her?"

$$$$.

That was a bad word. Pewter was being mean.

"Thank you, sir. I will get right on it." The troll went into a backroom cave to attend to it.

It occurred to Umlaut that this was a rather noble troll. He wondered how he had come to serve the evidently disreputable machine.

WHY ARE YOU HANGING AROUND, BOATLOAD OF BAGGAGE?

It would be possible to dislike the machine, if one put one's mind to it. Of course Umlaut had delivered the letter, despite Demoness Metria's distraction. Still, there were a couple of things. "We had some trouble locating you, though Sammy Cat can find anything except home. I wondered whether there was some contrary magic involved."

THE DEMONESS METRIA DARED ME TO REVERSE MY LOCATION MARKER.

That explained that. So Metria had tried more than one way to interfere with the delivery of this letter. First by messing up Sammy's search, then by distracting Umlaut when he was about to notice. In the process, it had involved another person, Tacy. So he had to try to do something about that.

"We have in our number a person who can't speak Xanthian. I wondered whether with your power to change reality in your vicinity, you could enable her to communicate more effectively."

WHY SHOULD I BOTHER?

"Well, it would be a nice thing to do for one in need."

PRECISELY.

Umlaut realized that this was a negation. Without the benign influence of the troll, Pewter was his normal ornery self. "Maybe she could be useful to you in some way, as a return favor."

HOW?

"Well, uh—" Umlaut glanced at Tacy, realizing that he didn't have a good answer. "Maybe if you asked her, she might know something."

BRING HER FORWARD.

Umlaut turned back to the boat and put his hand on Tacy's elbow, urging her out. She was hesitant but obeyed. She came to stand before the screen.

WHAT CAN YOU DO FOR ME?

"Well, I might be able to sweep your cave, or—" She broke off, surprised. "I understood you!"

OF COURSE. I CHANGED YOUR REALITY TO MAKE YOU IN-TELLIGIBLE.

She looked at Umlaut. "Do you understand me also?"

"Yes I do. But probably you can speak and understand Xanthian only in this vicinity, where Com Pewter governs."

"Oh, that's just so wonderful!" She flung her arms about him and kissed him.

Before Umlaut could properly (or even improperly) react, the screen printed **GIRL LOSES INTEREST IN MAN.**

Tacy immediately turned Umlaut loose and faced the screen, having no further interest in him. Maybe that was just as well—but he knew better than to say so.

WHAT ELSE MIGHT YOU DO?

Tacy glanced around. "I see that this cave is rather spare of furnishings. Ugly, in fact. That's what comes of having a troll take care of it. I could fix it up to look better. Maybe some curtains here, and a rug there, and some chairs for guests to sit."

DO YOU PLAY CARDS?

"I love card games! But I haven't found anyone to play them with, so I'm not very good at them."

YOU WILL DO. A deck of playing cards appeared.

Tacy glanced at them. "You play cards? But who moves them for you?"

MY MOUSE. NOW I WON'T HAVE TO PLAY COM PASSION ALL THE TIME. I HAVE TO LET HER WIN TOO MUCH. I LIKE WINNING.

"Well, then, we will get along, because I don't mind losing. I like games just for the fun of playing them." A table appeared, and she began to deal the cards. Umlaut wasn't clear how she knew what card game to play.

Tristan Troll returned. "What is this?" he asked.

YOU HAVE A GIRLFRIEND.

Tacy looked startled, but it was Tristan who answered. "But I already have Mouse Terian, Com Passion's mouse. She's the only woman I desire."

Umlaut knew this was none of his business, except in the sense that he had precipitated it. "Uh, I didn't mean to complicate your life, Tristan."

UMLAUT CHANGES SUBJECT.

Umlaut discovered he could no longer argue the case. "But I'm sure you know best, Com Pewter. May I bring up another matter?"

DO SO.

Umlaut had not meant to raise this subject, but it was the only other one on his mind. "I have a, uh, romantic problem."

"Romance!" Tacy said, interested. "Surprise?"

"Yes. I, uh, want to be with her. But her folks won't let me. What should I do?"

"You should find another girlfriend," Tacy said immediately.

"I can't do that. Surprise is the only one I want."

She sighed. "Then I suppose you will just have to persevere. Maybe in four years they will relent."

"Four years!"

"When she is eighteen and they can't stop her. Meanwhile—"

"How old are you?" Tristan asked her.

"Eighteen. I'm not limited in that particular manner."

THEREFORE YOU ARE ELIGIBLE FOR TRISTAN.

Tristan shook his head. "But I already said—"

TROLL CHANGES MIND.

"Ouch. I may be stuck for it. I can't overrule my mentor."

Tacy was not so limited, however. "I'm very glad finally to be able to speak and understand the local dialect. But I was not looking for a troll for a boyfriend."

TACY CHANGES MIND.

She looked speculatively at Tristan. "On the other hand, it is clear that you are a very nice person."

Tristan shuddered. "I fear it is my curse."

"Curse? I haven't been called that before. At least, not in any language I understood at the time."

"It requires some explanation. But that would be tedious to detail."

DETAIL IT, the screen printed. Umlaut realized that the irate machine was getting back at the troll for being so decent.

Tristan, of course, was unable to argue. He launched into his explanation. "It relates to my name. I was not a perfect troll, because I did not like to perform brutal deeds, so my kind punished me by naming me after a fantasy hero who was cursed. Now it seems his curse is mine."

His namesake Tristan, it turned out, was a fantasy hero in early Mundania, back in the days when there was some magic there. His father was king of Lioness, and he crossed the sea to come to the aid of Mark, the king of Corn-wall, saving him from his enemies. Mark was grateful and gave the king his sister White-Flower to wed. From that union came Tristan, but alas, his father died in battle before he was delivered, and his mother died of sorrow even as he arrived. Thus his name meant sorrow, and he was raised by a loyal servant. He grew up to be a talented and handsome warrior and went to serve his uncle Mark. He fought very well and saved the kingdom from a ruinous annual levy of copper, silver, gold, and youths and maidens. When Mark decided to marry a very pretty princess of Angry-land named Iseult the Fair, Tristan went to fetch her for the king. She was indeed beautiful and had fair hair that reached to her knees and was as bright as gold thread. She didn't like Tristan, for he had slain her brutish brother in battle. But by mistake a servant gave them a magic love potion to drink, and they fell deeply in love with each other. Of course Iseult married the king, but that drink cursed them, for she could not stay away from Tristan, nor he from her.

They had many trysts and somehow always managed to escape detection, though there were several nasty members of the king's court who suspected and tried to trap them. Finally King Mark caught on and banished Tristan and made ready to burn up Iseult in a fire. But Tristan charged in and rescued her, and they hid in the forest together for several months. There was little to eat, and Iseult got very thin. Rather than let her suffer further, Tristan arranged to return her to the king, then he moved to Brit-any across the sea and married the king's daughter there, who was named Iseult of the White Hands. But he did not love her, though she was a good and lovely princess. Not only was he cursed to endure sadness himself, he brought it to those he associated with, so that Iseult the Fair was sad because she could not be with him, and King Mark was sad because his wife did not love him, and Iseult of the White Hands was sad because Tristan would not touch her.

When Iseult the Fair learned that Tristan had married another woman, she was sorely grieved. But Tristan crossed the sea and visited her and convinced her that she was the only Iseult he loved, and that was true. Then he returned to his wife, but she was angry when she found out that he loved a different woman. When he was foully ambushed and wounded by a poisoned spear, and lay dying, he sent his ring to Iseult the Fair, begging her to come to him before he died. The ship that went for her was to spread a white sail if she was aboard, and a black one if she was not. As it came into view, Tristan asked his wife what color the sail was, and she told him it was black though it was white. "Iseult," he said, grief-stricken, and died. Then Iseult of the White Hands lamented at the evil she had done; she had not meant to kill him, only to punish him. Then Iseult the Fair arrived and said, "Lady, move over," and she lay down beside the dead man, hugged him and kissed him, and died of grief.

The ill-fated lovers were buried beside each other in two tombs, and from Tristan's tomb grew a leafy green brier that came to root again by Iseult's tomb. The peasants cut it back three times, but always it grew again, until King Mark told them to leave it alone. So the lovers were together at last in death, leaving all around them saddened.

"And that," Tristan Troll concluded, "is the curse of my name. I must love one I can't have, and marry another I don't want, and make both of us unhappy and those who associate with us miserable. I had thought to escape it by loving Mouse Terian, but she is bound to Com Passion and I to Com Pewter, and we are separated by the Gap Chasm. Now here is Tacy, a similar name to Terian, and I am required to be with her instead. Thus is the curse fulfilled."

"But I don't want to be the cause of such sadness," Tacy said.

TACY CHANGES MIND.

"Let's get married," she said. "And if I catch you with Terian, I'll blacken your sail." She hugged Tristan, who was unable to resist.

A wall became transparent. Beyond it was a device similar

to Com Pewter, only somewhat more feminine, and a truly lovely woman. Umlaut realized that this was Com Passion and her mouse. *CARDS, ANYONE?* Passion's screen scripted.

"Tristan!" Terian cried, appalled. "You're with another woman!"

"But I love only you," he cried back, trying to disengage.

"A likely story! It seems I can't let you out of my sight half a moment without you being untrue to me."

MALES ARE LIKE THAT, Passion agreed.

"Terian! Please!" But Passion and Terian were already fading out.

"Maybe we can explain," Umlaut said.

UMLAUT CHANGES MIND.

"But I guess it's none of our business."

VISITORS DEPART.

Umlaut got back into the boat, and Para waddled out of the cave. They were, it seemed, finished here. Somehow, without meaning to, he had succeeded in making mischief for innocent people. How did he always manage to be such a klutz?

Sesame nudged him. It was Tristan's curse, not Umlaut's, she suggested, and Claire agreed. Somehow that did not make him feel much better.

15

SIX EAGER GIRLS

They were on their way again, heading back south toward the Gap Chasm. Umlaut brought out the next letter, addressed to BUBBLES DOG.

Greetings and salutations to Bubbles,

As one member of the most superior species to another, I send barks from Mundania.

To get it off my chest, I think Bubbles is a sissy name for a canine. I won't hold it against you, however; humans choose the oddest names to saddle us with. It's not your fault. Having said that, at point of poisoned raw meat, I'll never divulge the name my human has seen fit to burden me with. I call myself Alaric, meaning "Ruler of all." It fits with my breed, which is rottweiler. Most folk around here are plain scared of me, which suits my lifestyle just fine. I'm usually given a wide berth and left alone to contemplate life. Of course I often have to perform bouts of snarling and jumping around just to keep up appearances.

It was good of your friend Kim to release you from that confining bubble. Floating around indefinitely is no

life for a dog. My friend Arjayess is another decent human type like Kim. She's the only one who understands
me. She feeds me well when there's a shortage of cats,
mice, moles, and the sick to gnaw on. She'll romp with
me when I feel like getting some exercise and keeps me
in huge bones as special treats. She even knows enough
to leave me alone when I give a bit of a growl because
I'm feeling solitary.

Yup, that makes two special humans in our worlds.
Out of . . . how many are there now? Could that be an
exaggeration? Naw, didn't think so. Too bad they
couldn't coach the rest of the canine-ignorant ones, huh?

So stick around, little buddy. Just thought I'd say hello
and farewell.

                                      Alaric
                               Friend of Arjayess

Umlaut considered that. If there was anything to generate
mayhem here, he couldn't see it. So far, most of the letters
he had delivered had been downright innocuous, and the rest
had not been bad. Was there really a point to this? Of course
they needed to be delivered, because their recipients deserved
to see them, but just how did any of them relate to solving
the problem of Demon Jupiter's hurtling Red Spot? Neither
the letters nor the folk receiving them seemed to have any
relevance to that.

Yet the Demoness Metria was trying to prevent him from
delivering them, sometimes quite deviously. That meant there
was a reason. Maybe not her own reason, but one sufficient
for whoever or whatever was threatening her son, Demon
Ted. Could it be Demon Jupiter himself? Could he know that
there was something to balk the Red Spot, and he didn't want
that to be found, lest it ruin his strike? But this was the Land
of Xanth. How could there be anything in it to interfere with
another big-*D* Demon?

And Umlaut himself: He seemed pretty dull normal, until
he tried to remember his past life. It was as if he had just
come into existence for this purpose, to try to deliver—

The huge Gap Chasm loomed again, distracting him, and
his thought evaporated. That was the trouble with thoughts,

they were easily lost when any distraction came. Well, he would surely return to it in due course.

This wasn't the same place where they had used the invisible bridge, yet Para was swiftly waddling right up to the verge. "Uh—" he began uncertainly.

Then the boat went over the brink and into a sidelong gully leading down into the chasm. That wasn't necessarily better. What about the dread Gap Dragon, the one that snorted steam and could cook his meals at yea many paces? Para would never be able to run fast enough to escape that monster. "Uh, are you sure—?"

The boat did seem sure. Sammy was riding, and Claire was napping. Sesame was viewing the steep scenery with interest. They weren't worried, so why should he be? Still, he was.

The slanting ledge-path managed to reach the base safely. Para set out across the bottom of the chasm, which was much like any other scenery, with patches of grass, copses of trees, and even a stream meandering its way as if looking for even lower ground.

Then he heard an odd sort of thumping or pounding. Whomping, that was it. He knew that it had to be the Gap Dragon. Oh, no, it had spied them! Worse, Para was waddling right toward the sound.

The dragon came into sight. It was green, with stubby wings and three sets of legs. It lifted one set at a time, moving it forward in semi-inchworm style and slamming it down on the ground while another lifted. This might have seemed like a clumsy mode of locomotion, but in practice it was efficient enough. And while steam might seem less formidable than fire or even hot smoke, the puffing clouds of it surrounding the dragon seemed sufficient to bring down any fleeing prey quickly enough.

Para and the dragon rushed together—and stopped. They sniffed noses, or rather, snout sniffed prow. And that was it. The dragon did not gape his jaws, and the boat did not try either to ram or flee. It looked as if they were friends.

"Friends?" Umlaut asked Claire. She nodded.

So that was why there had been no concern. Para and the Gap Dragon knew each other. He had been worrying about nothing. As usual, it was the things he didn't worry about that made the most trouble.

"Hello, Stanley Steamer," Umlaut said. "I am Umlaut, and these are Sesame Serpent, Sammy Cat, and Claire Voyant Cat." He realized as he spoke that this was largely unnecessary; Sammy obviously knew the dragon, and Sesame probably could communicate in Serpentine. "We're on our way to deliver a letter to Bubbles Dog."

The dragon nodded; he understood human speech. But he did not get out of their way, and Para did not try to move forward. Something else was expected.

Then he had it. The Gap Dragon was friends with one of the human folk they had encountered. "We delivered another letter to Princess Ivy. She's fine. So are her children."

Stanley nodded. Then he moved out of the way, and Para resumed motion. Umlaut breathed a silent sigh of relief. It wasn't that he distrusted the judgment of the animals, just that errors or confusions sometimes occurred, and a confusion here in the bottom of the chasm could be extremely awkward.

They came to the far side. There was another slight ledge-path scraping its way upward. It looked precarious, but it turned out to be just wide enough for Para to fit on. The slope above and below it was almost sheer, so Umlaut made sure to sit in the center of the boat and not rock it. It would be so easy to overbalance and tumble out and awfully down.

At last they crested and were back on safe land. Now all they had to be concerned about was regular dangers.

"This should be fairly easy now," Umlaut said.

A cloud formed. "That's what yooouuu think!"

"Get out of here, Metria!"

"I prefer to timepiece."

He knew better but couldn't help it. "To what?"

"Chronometer, lookout, measure, clock, alarm—"

"Watch?"

"Whatever," she agreed crossly. "You will have to choose."

"Choose?"

"You'll see." The cloud dissipated, but he knew she was still watching.

He turned to Sesame. "Do you know what she means?"

Maybe she was bluffing, she said in Serpentine.

That hadn't occurred to him. If Metria could stop him with a bluff, she surely would do it.

They came to a slight vale with a small red river meandering from one side to the other. It looked innocuous, but Claire suddenly took note. "Meow!"

Para skidded to a halt. "What is it?" Umlaut asked the cat. In a moment he had it: fire ants.

"Those are bad?"

Sammy, Sesame, and Para all nodded. They did not want to pass through that column of ants.

"Well, let me see," Umlaut said, suspecting that they were making too much of it. "I've got shoes on; I'll check." He got out of the boat and walked to the column.

It did indeed consist of red ants. There were hundreds of them marching the length of the vale. They did not look fierce. "If I had a broom, I could sweep a channel clear so Para could cross," he said. He looked about for something he could fashion into a suitable sweeper.

He spied a pine tree with one low branch. That should do, if he could break it off. He put his hands on it and pushed.

"I wouldn't do that if I were you," the tree said. "Of course that's just my opinion."

"What?" Umlaut still tended to be stupid when caught by surprise. And at other times.

"In my opinion, it won't work."

"You're a talking tree?" he asked dumbly.

"I am an O-Pinion pine tree," the tree said proudly. "I have opinions on everything."

Umlaut belatedly caught on to the pun. "Well, thanks for your opinion." He broke off the branch.

"Ouch! That's just my opinion."

"I'm sure it is." Umlaut carried the branch to the narrowest part of the ant column and used the tufts of pine needles to brush the ants out of the way.

Something stung his forearm. "Ouch!" he screamed, for it burned like fire. An ant had stung him. He slapped it off, but the pain did not abate. In fact he saw that a little tongue of flame was flickering over it. No wonder it burned!

He grabbed a handful of dirt and rubbed it on the burn, but it did no good. The pain continued just as fiercely. He ran back to the boat. "Fire ant!" he cried, showing his burning arm.

Sesame dived for the end of the boat. She dug out a little wad of balm Umlaut hadn't known was there. She used her teeth to hold it while she rubbed it across the burn. In two and a quarter moments the pain faded. The balm had done the job.

"Thanks," Umlaut gasped. "An ant must have gotten on my broom. I didn't see it."

Para suddenly backed up, startling him. Then he saw why: The ants, now alerted to the presence of potential prey, were swarming toward them. They could not move very fast, but it would not do to stand and wait for them.

Sammy was agitated. The way to Bubbles Dog was across that column of fire ants. What were they going to do?

Umlaut sighed. Where was there a zombie roc bird, or a toe truck, or a tunnel, or a demoness, or something when they needed it? He was pretty sure that if they ran along beside the ant column they would find it reached all the way from the sea to the Gap Chasm, and they would not be able to cross it. So what could they do?

He came to a momentous conclusion: "I think we need help."

The others looked at him as if awed by his profundity, or whatever. He felt the heat rising to his face. He had such a genius for being if not outright stupid, at least somewhat dull. "I mean, maybe we should seek help."

They still gazed at him. Para sidled away from an extending pseudopod of the ant column. It was up to him to seek that help.

So he tried it the dull direct way. "Help!" he called.

Something flew in from the horizon. It was a bird, no, a harpy, no, a lovely butterfly-winged woman. Her dress was almost as brightly colored as her wings, and her hair matched. She came to land beside the boat. "Hello. I am Phanessa. Can I help you?"

Umlaut got out and stood before her. "I'm, uh, Umlaut, and these are my friends Para Boat, Sesame Serpent, and Sammy and Claire Cats. We need to cross the fire ant column to deliver a letter. Do you have a way we can do that?"

She glanced at the column, which showed pale flames close above it. "Why, yes, I do happen to know of a way. What will you give me for that information?"

"Give you?" Umlaut asked blankly.

"Well, you don't expect me to do it for nothing, do you?"

It was another signal of his dullness that he *had* rather expected it for nothing. "Uh, what do you wish?"

She looked at the boat. "I'd really like to have an interesting craft like that."

"I can't give you that! Para doesn't belong to me."

"Or a pet cat."

"Those cats don't belong to me—any—anybody, really. They're my friends."

"Or maybe a nice serpent."

"Sesame? She's her own person too."

Phanessa sighed. "Then I suppose I'll have to take you."

"Me?"

"As my boyfriend. I had hoped for one who could fly, but there aren't many winged boys in Xanth. They don't want to look like fairies."

A vision of the plight of poor Tristan Troll flitted across his mind. "I can't do that. I'm committed elsewhere."

"Oh, that's too bad," she said sympathetically. "I hope you do make it safely past that horrible ant column." She spread her wings and flew away.

But now someone else was approaching. This was another girl, with violet hair and eyes. "Hello," she said. "I am Violet. And no, I'm not an African flower."

Somehow that didn't surprise him. He introduced himself and his friends. "We need to get across that fire ant column. Can you help with that?"

"Why, yes, I believe I can," she said. "My talent is to make living things friendly. I'm sure I could befriend the ants so they would let you pass."

"Great!" But then he got cautious. "What would you expect in return?"

"You seem like a decent boy. I would like—"

"I'm committed elsewhere," Umlaut said quickly.

Violet frowned. "I am so disappointed. Won't you reconsider?"

"Uh, no," he said, feeling somehow guilty.

"Then I suppose there is nothing for me to do but look elsewhere." Violet departed.

Umlaut shook his head. "Why is it that now that I have found the girl of my dreams, others are offering? I'm sure either of these two would have been nice, if it weren't for Surprise."

The others shrugged. It was, it seemed, just the way a fellow was fondled by the fickle finger of fortune.

Another girl approached. She looked fairly ordinary, which was to say that her hair was hair brown and her eyes were eye blue, and her figure was not the kind to madden a man's mind with half a glance. "Hello. My name is Sage. Were you calling for help?"

"Yes," Umlaut answered guardedly. "We need to cross that fire ant column?"

"I could enable you to do that," Sage said. "At least, my dragon could."

"Dragon?" He looked around a bit nervously. "Is it close?"

She laughed. "He doesn't just walk behind me, silly. He has better things to do. But if I'm in danger, he comes immediately to protect me."

Umlaut saw the ant column extending toward her. "You had better step back. Those ants—"

"Eeeek! Fire ants!" she screamed.

Suddenly there was a motion in the ground around her. Four mounds developed, and from each burst a dreadful head. "Dragons!" Umlaut cried, more than alarmed. "Run!"

"Don't be concerned," Sage said. "That's just Guardian, my four-headed dragon."

The four heads rose up on four necks. Then the ground between them humped, right under Sage, lifting her up. It was indeed a single dragon, and as the dirt fell away, she was nestled comfortably between the four extended necks. The four heads cast about and soon spotted the encroaching fire ants.

The first head oriented and blasted out a jet of fire. It bathed the ants but did not bother them at all. So that head swung aside and the second one oriented. It blew out a blast of smoke. That didn't stop the ants either; smoke was a natural concomitant of fire. So the third head oriented and issued a shaft of steam. The ants didn't like that, but the heat didn't bother them. Finally the fourth head oriented and gushed pure water. That washed away the ants, and the column retreated. The dragon, satisfied, sank back into the ground, leaving only disturbed earth.

"That will do it," Umlaut said, pleased. "If Guardian cares to wash out a path for us."

"He will if I ask him to," Sage said. "But why should I do that?"

Uh-oh. "You want something."

She nodded. "At is happens, I have a crush on a handsome young magician, but I haven't told him. So I need someone else until—"

"I'm not available," Umlaut said quickly.

"Oh, well. In that case, good-bye." Sage walked away.

Umlaut looked at his friends. They looked back. They weren't blaming him, but somehow he felt blameworthy.

Soon another girl approached. She too seemed ordinary, but Umlaut knew that that was no sign she was. "Hello. I'm Janel. I heard your call. You need help?"

"I'm Umlaut. Yes, we need to get past those fire ants."

"Why, I could help you do that. My talent is persuading people. I could persuade them to let you through."

"That would be wonderful. But what would you want in return?"

She looked at him appraisingly. "You seem like a nice boy."

"I'm spoken for!"

"Oh. Still, perhaps I should persuade you to give her up in favor of—"

"Please don't do that!" Umlaut said desperately. "I love her!"

Janel considered. "I suppose it wouldn't be nice to take you, then." She walked away.

What was going on here? Every person who came was a girl, and every one of them wanted him as a boyfriend. There might have been a time when he would have loved that, but that was BS: Before Surprise.

Another girl showed up. Umlaut didn't even notice her details, though all of them were in place. "I am Annie Mation. I can make pictures come to life."

"That's surely a fine talent," Umlaut said warily, "but will it help us get beyond the fire ants, and what will it cost me?"

"All you have to do is draw a picture of something that will help you, and I can bring it to life so you can use it."

That seemed promising. Umlaut was not the best at drawing things, but if he drew a package of ant repellent and she made it real, maybe that would help. But she hadn't named her price. Somehow he knew what that would be. "I am already committed to another girl," he said.

"Oh, pooh!" Annie stalked away.

Yet another girl appeared. That was almost literal; he hadn't seen her approach, but there she was. "Hi! I'm Cindi with an Eye and See."

Umlaut spelled it out in his mind. "An *I* at the end and a *C* at the beginning?"

"That too. I can see whatever I name."

"I'm Umlaut, so I guess you can see me."

"Oh, I do. But what I mean is that if I want to see something, like maybe a huge eye scream cone, I can do so. Like this." She paused, then spoke again. "I see."

There, hanging in the air before her, was a huge eye scream cone, looking every bit good enough to eat.

Umlaut was impressed and abruptly hungry. He reached for the cone, but his hand passed through it. "Oh—illusion."

"Well, yes, in that case. But some things don't need to be physical. Like the way to get past those fire ants."

Something bothered Umlaut, and this time he was lucky enough to catch it. He hadn't told her about their problem yet. "Who are you?" he demanded.

"Are you intimidating I'm not me?"

"Am I what?"

"Citing, referring to, specifying, suggesting, proposing—"

"Intimating?"

"Whatever," she agreed crossly.

"Hello, Demoness Metria."

"Oh, bleep! What gave me away?"

"There have been too many girls wanting to make me their boyfriend. They were all you?"

"More or less. They all exist on Ptero, but I borrowed their descriptions for this purpose."

"The purpose of distracting me from my mission."

"It could have been a very good distraction. You have no idea what any of those girls could have offered you, but soon you would have found out and thus joined the Adult Conspiracy."

"I'm not ready to do that, but at such time as I am ready, Surprise Golem is the only girl I want to do it with."

"But she's only fourteen."

"I'll wait."

"You're incorrigible."

"I'm what?"

"Oh, never mind." She disappeared into a roiling cloud of smoke. But after three instants it reversed the roiling and reformed her face. "Anyway, I had it right that time." She roiled on out of sight.

So he had fathomed that little mystery. The idea of having a number of girls interested in him was appealing, even if he didn't want their company, but he knew he was too ordinary for such attention, so it had been suspicious from the outset. He would have caught on sooner if he hadn't been so eager to find a way past the fire ants. But not for the price they— or, rather, Metria—were demanding.

"Oh, Surprise," he murmured, longing for her company.

"Here I am," she said.

He looked around. "Where?"

"Here in your head. Telepathy. It's another talent."

"You shouldn't waste your talents on me!"

"I can't think of anyone I'd rather waste them on. You were great."

"I was just trying to find a way across the fire ant column, but I couldn't, uh—"

"You couldn't forget me. I heard. You were so sweet."

"I suppose. If only you were older."

"I happen to know where some aging elixir is. I could add two or three years to my age just like that. Then I'd be right for you."

That was wickedly tempting. "But your parents—"

"They couldn't stop me if I was over sixteen."

"It's not that, exactly. They love you and want what's best for you."

"Except true love. I told you, it's the way parents are."

"Let's wait, anyway. I want them to approve."

He heard her sigh. "I suppose you're right, though your determined decency can get annoying. Well, let's get you across that ant column before I lose my concentration."

"You know a way?"

"Yes. When I was casting about for your mind I had a brush with the demoness's mind. She really would have helped you cross, you know, if you had accepted any of her forms. Then she would have—well, I don't know the details, of course, but I gather she had several storks in mind."

"I don't know why adults are so eager to signal storks. It must be a chore."

"Well, adults live for chores. That's why they eat wholesome food and make themselves unhappy in so many pointless little ways." He felt a tear in his eye and realized it was hers. "Oh, Umlaut, I want us to be together before we get abducted into that awful Conspiracy, so we can have some fun."

"It does seem like irony," he said. "The moment you get the chance to do whatever you want, you start doing chores instead. But your folks are happy, aren't they?"

"Oh, sure, they love each other. So I guess it's not so bad. Still, I hate waiting several years. I want you *now*."

And he wanted her now. But he knew it wasn't practical. "We need to deliver that letter."

"Of course," she agreed sadly. "Just walk over the hill to the north and you'll find a colony of water ants. Make a deal with them, and they'll open a path through the fire ants."

"Thank you!"

"Anything," she said. "I don't know what it is, but I want to give it to you."

"I'll settle for your kisses."

"You're so sweet," she repeated and faded from his mind, leaving the suggestion of a kiss on the inside of his cranium.

He faced the boat. "Surprise was here. She told me there is a water ant colony over the hill."

The others perked up. They knew that would do it.

Umlaut got back into the boat, and they went over the hill and found the water ant nest. It resembled a hillock of water. Para and the others waited a reasonable distance away while Umlaut sat down beside the mound and emulated an ant as well as he could. First he had to satisfy them that he was not an enemy, lest they sting him and turn parts of his flesh into water.

It took more than nineteen questions, but he finally learned what they wanted: There was a distant watermelon they dearly desired, but it was too heavy for them to carry whole, and it would spoil if they tried to cut it into carryable pieces.

He returned to the boat. "Sammy, find the watermelon. Para, follow him."

Sammy took off, and Para followed, and soon they found it. Umlaut heaved it into the boat, and they brought it back to the ant mound. He heaved it out and rolled it to the mound. Then the ants formed a column and marched for the fire ant formation.

The moment the fire ants saw the water ants, they backed off, and Para passed across their line with no trouble. They were through, just like that. "Thanks," Umlaut called to the water ants. He saw a squirt of acknowledgment.

The rest of their trip was uneventful, and soon they reached the ugly little house that Sammy indicated was where Bubbles Dog lived. Umlaut knocked on the door.

It opened to reveal the ugliest woman he had seen. "Yes?" she grated.

"I'm, uh, Umlaut, and I have a letter for Bubbles Dog."

"A letter for a dog?" she graveled. Her voice was as ugly as her face.

"I know it seems odd, but—"

"Wonderful! Bubbles will love it. I'm Anathe Ma. Come in, you dear boy, and have some gruel."

Now the dog came to the door, wagging her tail. She seemed to be healthy and happy. She spied Sammy and went to sniff noses; evidently they knew each other. Regardless of the way Anathe looked and sounded, it seemed she was a kind person. They entered her house and shared her gruel, and it was surprisingly good.

It had been a long day, and they wound up spending the

night there. This gave Sammy and Bubbles more time to renew their acquaintanceship and catch up on news about their associates. Bubbles had arrived in Xanth in a floating bubble from Mundania. She had been rescued by Kim, a visiting Mundanian, but in time Kim left her with Anathe Ma, because Bubbles could live far longer and better in Xanth. So she was here, and her only regret was that she wasn't able to see Kim more often. Kim had married and settled down in Mundania.

In the evening when cats and dog were conversing and Anathe Ma was putting the house in order, Umlaut and Sesame went outside. The house was in a jungle, but Umlaut had no particular concern when in Sesame's company; she could handle just about anything.

"I keep being surprised by things," he said. "Today I learned that pretty girls are not necessarily worthwhile for me and that an ugly woman can be an ideal person."

The girls looked delicious, Sesame agreed in Serpentine. And the old woman would hardly do to clean one's teeth. But it was true: The girls weren't real, and Anathe Ma was. Sesame had the impression nevertheless that they all liked him, or would have, had they had the chance. There was something about him. He was klutzy but appealing.

"I'm appealing? I don't see why."

There was no why to it. He just was. If she were of his species, she would have trouble being his friend.

He didn't understand that so ignored it. "I'm glad I was loyal to Surprise. I didn't know she was listening."

She must have been very pleased with him.

"She was. She said she wanted to give me everything, once she found out what it was."

Sesame glanced sidelong at him. She happened to be of age, for a serpent. She could assure him that not all the secrets of the human Adult Conspiracy were unpleasant.

"She said she could take aging elixir and become of age now, but I thought she should wait."

That was sensible of him, Sesame felt. Some of the responsibilities of adults took time to appreciate, though children didn't understand this. They needed to achieve an emotional balance before they acquired significant power to influence events.

"I just want to be with her! But I'm not quite sure I even exist. Sometimes I think I'm just a—a little golem made to do something, that can be abolished when it is done. So what good would I ever be to her?"

The night around them assumed an eerie quality, as if some momentous decision was about to be made.

He surely existed, Sesame indicated. He had done so much good for Sammy, and for Sesame herself, and for Surprise, and she thought for others along the way. Maybe he lacked a memory of his past life, but that did not negate his present life.

"Oh, I hope you're right! I must just be imagining things. You're such a wonderful friend."

They had befriended each other. She was glad it happened. In his company she had had all the adventure she craved and had met Soufflé.

"Let's stay friends after the letters are delivered. I know you will be going to the sea with Soufflé after you figure out how to lift his curse, but we can meet on occasion, can't we?"

Surely they could.

Something bothered him, and again he was lucky enough to figure out what it was before it escaped. "I said you would figure out how to lift the curse, but I should have said *we*. You're helping me; I want to help you."

Thank you, she indicated. They could do that next, after the letters were done.

"Yes." Umlaut looked around. "Was there something funny about the night? I had the oddest feeling for a moment."

So had she. But it must have been a passing thing, because it was gone now.

The two friends turned around and went back to the house.

16

GOBLIN MOUNTAIN

The next letter turned out to be addressed to PRINCESS NADA NAGA. Umlaut read it before they left Anathe Ma's house, so as to know where they were going next.

To the Snake Broad:

What kinda snake are ya, anyway? Snakes are s'posed ta be evil, dangerous, and way cool. You and your brother give reptiles a bad name. Hangin' 'round with sissy princesses is bad enough, but the thought of marrying a wimpy princey-boy makes me wanna puke. It's just gross!

Naga, now that's cool. Think Cobra, think Asp, think Viper. And Python, Copperhead, and Rattler. Now those dudes are mean! Slither around and jump on things to chomp 'em. Poison till you're dead. There's no question who's in charge. That's the way ta be. Power unto yourself, y'know?

Shape up, lady, you're doing a lousy job of bein' a snake.

KING COBRA
Mundania

Umlaut shook his head. This was no polite effort. It might not be the one that would set off a war, but he wasn't sure whether he should deliver it. "What do you think, Sesame? You're better versed in serpent matters than I am."

Princess Nada was not a snake, she was a naga, Sesame said in Serpentine. A cross between serpent and human.

"A naga," he repeated, not quite getting it, as was his wont.

She saw that he didn't quite understand about crossbreeds. Suppose the two of them had met at a love spring instead of in a dungeon and drunk its elixir without knowing. They would have signaled the stork together, and the stork would have brought a naga baby.

"A naga baby," he said, blushing so hard that he was afraid his hair would curl. He had never thought of Sesame as a girlfriend, just as a friend.

She ignored his embarrassment. She understood his limitations and was fond of him. A naga could assume the form of either of its species of origin, she explained, but its normal mode was in between: a serpent with a human head. Because it chose its form when it changed, it could become any size serpent. That made it fairly formidable. Since Nada was a princess of her kind, she was more formidable, and because she was married to a demon prince, more formidable yet. He certainly wouldn't want to annoy her.

"So I shouldn't deliver this letter?"

But the word among serpents was that Nada was a very nice person. She was betrothed to Prince Dolph Human when young and pretended to be even younger so that he would not feel out of place. Then when he married Princess Electra, Nada graciously let him go and later found a different prince to marry. Now they had a cute little girl, DeMonica, who played with the demoness Metria's son, Demon Ted.

"So I should deliver the letter after all?"

She wouldn't know. She was not a naga princess.

He gazed at her. "Are you teasing me?"

No, merely providing some background.

"Can naga hurl spots?"

Not that she knew of.

"Then I'll deliver it."

Sesame would have smiled if her face had that expression in its repertoire. It would be nice to meet her.

But Umlaut retained some caution. Before he told Sammy, he checked for location. "Where does Nada Naga live?"

She wouldn't know, Sesame repeated.

So much for that. They would have to try to follow Sammy pell-mell, trying to keep up, unless Claire restrained him. But then he thought of another way. It was a virtual act of genius for him.

"Sammy, I want to deliver the next letter, but I'd rather find a comfortable way to travel. Can you find a nice route, rather than a direct one?"

Sammy nodded and took off.

"Wait! You don't even know which person yet!"

Claire gave him a stare of disgust, then glanced at his hand. He looked at it and saw that he was still holding the letter. Sammy had seen the address. He felt foolish yet again, but Claire gave him an *I know you can't help it you innocent creature* look that made him feel better. She looked down on him, of course, but seemed halfway fond of him too. That reminded him irrelevantly of what Sesame had said about his mysterious appeal. Why couldn't she have been his friend if she were of his species?

They bid hasty adieu to Anathe Ma, who seemed genuinely sorry to see them go, and piled into the boat. Para followed Sammy eastward through the jungle. Eventually it opened out onto the east coast of Xanth, and Para splashed happily into the sea. They moved north, following the coastline.

A sea monster spied them and came over to investigate. Sesame slid into the water and swam out to intercept it. Soon the monster nodded and departed; one sea monster did not intrude on the territory of another. Then a flying dragon oriented on them and came down for a strafing run. Umlaut stood and emulated an ogre and made as if to hurl a rock at the creature's snoot; it veered off and went elsewhere. Ogres might be justly proud of their stupidity, but they could hit a flying target at inordinate range and knock the stuffing out of it. Any flying creature who tested that would fall below the ogre range of stupidity, which was impossible.

"If we had realized how well we work as a team," Umlaut

remarked, "we could have saved ourselves some trouble earlier." Sesame nodded.

The shoreline receded, forming a giant U valley. "What's that?" Umlaut asked.

Claire gave him another idiot stare. Sesame answered in Serpentine: That is the Gap Chasm.

Oh. "We're going around it! We've been under it, over it, and across it, so this is the next way." He didn't think to mention that he hadn't realized that their destination was north of the big cleft.

Water travel was easy for them, but Para was doing the work and needed to rest at night so went ashore at a convenient beach. It was evening, but the tons of sand glowed so brightly that the area remained as bright as day. Then he saw the sign: DAY TON A BEACH. That explained it.

But there was nothing to eat. They looked and looked, but there was only the day-bright beach sand. Umlaut hesitated to ask Sammy to find food, not knowing where he would go.

A young woman approached, walking along the beach. Umlaut was wary, having encountered so many of her kind recently, but he was the one who spoke Human, so he nerved himself and greeted her. "Hello. I am Umlaut, and these are my friends. We're traveling north."

She glanced at him as if measuring him for a bed. That made him more nervous. "I am Andrea. My talent is becoming a carrot."

Umlaut reacted with his customary acumen. "Uh, what?"

"Hold out your hand."

Now she wanted to hold hands? "Uh, why?"

She laughed. "Do you think I'm going to kiss it?"

His slow thoughts hadn't gotten that far yet, but it did seem to be a reasonable threat. "Uh—"

"Just hold it out."

He did so, and she took it. Then she flickered and was gone. He was holding a nice yellow carrot.

Then the carrot was gone and the girl was back. His hand was on her blouse. Blushing, he snatched it away. "Uh—" Oh, he was being so intelligent! "What do you want?"

"Gee, I would really like to have a ride in your weird boat."

"Well, I'm sure Para would be glad to give you one."

"That would be wonderful, especially with you beside me."

"Uh, sure." Then he caught Claire's stare. He was evidently being stupid again. It seemed to be his natural state. After not much more than half a moment he figured it out. "Maybe we can make a deal. Do you know of any food near here?"

"There isn't any close by. The perpetual daylight dries up the plants. But if you'd like some carrot, I can provide plenty of that."

He was appalled. "Eat you? We wouldn't do that!"

She laughed. "I can't think of anyone I'd rather be eaten by. But don't be concerned. I can become a very big carrot. I'll be all right as long as you don't eat all of me. You can cut off twenty-four pieces and make golden soup."

"Golden soup?"

"Twenty-four carrots," she clarified with half a smile.

Umlaut didn't get it. Maybe if she had expended a whole smile he would have. "If you're sure it's all right."

"I'm sure. I have fed our village before, when things got tight. But first I'd like my ride."

Para gave Andrea an excellent ride across the bright sand and over the water. She oooed and ahhhed obligingly and flung her arms around Umlaut when they crested a wave.

Then, back at the beach, she turned herself into a giant carrot. Umlaut carefully carved pieces from it, fearful that there would be a protest, but there was none. It seemed it didn't hurt her. When he had enough, she became a girl again. "Fair exchange, no loss," she said.

"Uh, yes, thank you."

"Would you like to stay with me? You would never go hungry."

"I'm, uh, promised to another girl."

"Lucky girl," Andrea said regretfully and went her way.

So she had not been another manifestation of D. Metria. That was a relief, but he wasn't too relieved, because he wasn't sure where the demoness was or what other mischief she was cooking up.

It was excellent carrot. There was a self-heating pot under one of Para's seats, and they found a spring and dipped it full of water. They cooked twenty-four pieces, and it did make beautifully golden soup. Even the cats and Sesame liked it, though they normally did not eat straight vegetables.

They curled up on the bright beach and slept as well as they could in the perpetual day.

Umlaut dreamed of Surprise. She was standing before him in a bright dress, looking ethereally pretty. "Do you like me this way?"

"I like you any way," he said. "But how can you be here on the beach?"

"I'm not on the beach. I'm in your dream."

"My dream girl!" he agreed blissfully.

She smiled, looking even prettier. "It's another talent. I just can't stay away from you, but I have to find a new way to reach you each time. We can't keep meeting like this."

"I would come to you, if your folks let me."

"I know. I'm working on them. They have this thing about age. Are you sure I shouldn't fetch that aging elixir?"

"I'm not sure, but I think it best to wait. There are things to learn before reaching adult status, so it's best to take proper time."

"Who says so?"

"Sesame Serpent. She's adult, for a serpent, so she knows."

"But she's not human."

"She's my friend, and she wants what's best for me."

Surprise sighed. "I suppose she's right," she grudged. "But I already know I love you, Umlaut. I would do anything for you."

"Surprise, please, just be yourself for me! That's all I want. I don't want to spoil it. I love you too."

"If you weren't so decent, you wouldn't hesitate to take advantage of a smitten girl."

He wanted to laugh but realized she was serious. "I'm sorry. I guess that's the way it is."

"I forgive you."

"Uh, thank you. Uh, Surprise, Sesame told me something. I don't know if I understand it."

"Tell me, maybe I will."

"She said that there's something about me that makes females like me."

"That is so true."

"But if—if it's like magic, I mean, uh, not being because of any merit of mine, maybe you, uh—"

"Umlaut, are you trying to tell me I'm a victim of some sort of spell?"

"Uh, I guess maybe so. So if you, uh—"

She frowned. "Do you want me to leave you?"

"No!" he cried in anguish. "I mean, I don't want to be unfair to you. If the only reason you like me is this, well, I know I'm really not much, and—"

"You're so sweet, Umlaut. I don't care if it is magic, I do like you and don't want to let you go. I don't think you understand just how fervently I mean that."

He was enormously relieved, but naturally his words remained clumsy. "I, uh, thank you."

"Was there anything else?"

"Well, Sesame said that if she were of my species, she couldn't be my friend. I don't understand that."

She nodded. "I do, Umlaut. She means that she'd be romantically attracted to you too. That can be hard on friendship."

"But she's a serpent!"

"Exactly. So she can be your friend, not liking you in that way. I'm not your friend."

That tossed him for another loop. "Uh?"

"I'm your beloved."

Oh. "I guess maybe that's it. Those girls I've met—when they find they can't be my, uh, beloved, they don't want to be my friend."

"Which is exactly as it should be. Oops, I have to go. Kiss me."

He embraced her, expecting her to be illusion, but she felt real. This was a dream, and the things of it seemed real. He kissed her, and it was delightful. "Oh, Surprise, thank you for coming to me! You make it all worthwhile."

"I should hope so." She smiled and faded, leaving him with an empty dream.

He woke and found it day. But of course it was always day here on the beach. He looked more carefully and saw that it was day out over the sea also, so it was real. He got up, had a bit more golden soup, and washed. By then the others were stirring too.

They continued north, then returned to land where Sammy indicated. Here the beach was normal, except that there was yet another young human woman standing there. It was as if they saw him coming. Was Metria back at her tricks, or was this a real person?

"Hello. I'm Umlaut, and these are my friends. We're going to see Princess Nada Naga."

She seemed to hesitate, then spoke. "That's nice. I'm Gail Marie, just out for a walk on the beach."

Her words were innocuous, but there was something more than strange here. Umlaut was almost knocked off his feet, as if he had been riding standing in the boat and it had come to an abrupt stop. But he was standing on the beach, and nothing had changed. In fact things seemed to have returned to normal. What had happened?

"I, uh, did something just occur?" He suspected that he was being dull again, but he had just been literally shaken.

Again she seemed to hesitate before speaking. "I'm sorry." And as she spoke, there was that same weird halting, almost immediately resuming, if that was the correct concept.

"I don't understand."

"It is my talent. The world listens to me."

Again, the lurching-seeming motion, though he could only feel it, not see it. The others felt it too; Para was halfway sprawling, and the cats and serpent were looking anxiously around. "I mean that motion."

"When I speak, the world pauses to listen. Normally it is turning, so you feel it when it stops. That's why I prefer to walk alone. It utterly ruins my social life. But I didn't want to be impolite when you addressed me."

He was beginning to get it. "The world itself stops to listen?"

This time she merely nodded, and the effect did not manifest. It seemed to be true: Everything stopped when she spoke, just as if the world were a boat that abruptly halted, spilling its occupants. He couldn't see it because everything stopped together.

This was awkward. "Then maybe you shouldn't speak anymore. I mean, we shouldn't require you to."

She nodded again, sadly. He realized that her life was bound to be lonely, because so few would care to tolerate her dialogue. She looked as though she were attracted to him, but he knew better than to broach any subject like that. That made him feel guilty, though he wasn't sure he had sufficient reason.

They moved on, leaving the woman behind. Umlaut felt somehow guilty. But what else could he do? Her talent made her almost impossible to deal with.

They moved inland. They saw a range of mountains ahead, and it seemed they would have to wend their way through it. There was a dragon circling around the peak of one mountain, then it dived down and disappeared. Its nest must be there. Unfortunately their path seemed to pass right by that mountain.

They climbed a winding path that finally managed to slip between two peaks and descend beyond. But beyond it was another mountain, and they were heading for that. Nada Naga lived on a mountain?

Then they passed a sign: GOBLIN MOUNTAIN. "But we want the naga territory," Umlaut protested.

Sammy shook his head. He knew where Princess Nada was.

"Among goblins?" Umlaut asked incredulously.

A cloud of smoke formed before them. "That's what the tomcat witnesses."

"He whats?"

"Testifies, asseverates, indicates, pronounces, affirms—"

"Says?"

"Whatever," the cloud agreed crossly.

"You're too late, Metria. We've already located Nada Naga."

"Of course, and I wish you all the best with her. But it's really Sesame Serpent I came to see."

Sesame's head jerked up. What?

The demoness seemed to understand Serpentine. "I know where to find the end to Soufflé's curse. So if you really want to abate it, now's the time."

Sesame looked at Umlaut. He looked at Claire. "Is this true?"

Claire nodded, though she seemed ill at ease. Apparently it was true, but there was a kicker somewhere. Still, it was a chance that needed to be taken. "Better go for it, then," Umlaut said.

Sesame wriggled uncertainly. She didn't want to leave him alone among the goblins.

"You aren't the one to go," Metria said. "The cats can handle it. You can stay with Umlaut."

Sesame wasn't entirely easy with that, either, but did not protest.

The cats departed, Claire with some reluctance. Was there some price to be paid for the abatement of the curse? "What's the catch?" Umlaut demanded of the demoness. But he was too late; she had dissipated.

They proceeded on to the mountain. It was rounded, with tiers and apertures galore. Goblins were running in and out of the multiple entrances, doing obscure things. The scene reminded Umlaut of a huge busy anthill. Each goblin was about half the height of a human man, dark skinned, with a big ugly head and big hands and feet. Every goblin was scowling, sneering, or looking angry.

They were challenged at the main entrance by a goblin guard. "What do you jerks want?"

"I am Umlaut, and this is Sesame, and this is Para Boat. We have come to deliver a letter to Princess Nada Naga, who we understand is here."

The guard checked a listing. "Who do you claim to be, knothead?"

"Umlaut," Umlaut repeated, annoyed.

The guard pointed at a particular entrance. "Take that one, joker."

Sesame and Para started to follow. "Not you, snake eyes. Or you, quack foot."

Sesame raised her head and gaped her mouth impressively, emulating an annoyed dragon. The goblin hastily rechecked his list. "Okay, you're on," he conceded grudgingly.

They entered the indicated hole. Beyond it was a long, dusky tunnel. They followed it down, down into the very depths of the mountain. Umlaut began to feel claustrophobic; if there were a collapse of the tunnel, they would be trapped and perhaps suffocated. But Sesame was handling it well, so he tried to emulate her attitude.

The passage ended at a stout closed door. Uncertain what was expected, Umlaut knocked on it.

It opened to show a lovely goblin woman in a sleek black gown. She was dark in the goblin manner, with long black hair, small hands and feet, and attractive face and figure. She stood less than half Umlaut's height but was aesthetic in all the ways the goblin guard had been ugly. "You would be Umlaut and Sesame," she said, her voice dulcet. "And Para Boat! I am so glad to meet you at last. I am Gwendolyn Goblin, chiefess of Goblin Mountain, but please call me Gwenny. Do come in."

"Uh, thank you," Umlaut said. "I think we came to the wrong door. We were looking for Nada Naga."

"She is here, but I decided to interview you first. A princess can't be too careful."

"Oh, I don't mean her any harm! I just have a letter for her."

"Similar to the letter that caused Demon Jupiter to hurl his Red Spot at us?"

"I hope not! The Good Magician told me to deliver the letters, and we'd find the answer to that, uh, problem. So I'm doing it." But she had made her point: Folk had to be careful about letters.

"Do sit down. I have prepared a repast for you."

"A, uh, what?"

"I thought you would be hungry after your arduous journey here."

The last good meal he had eaten had been carrot. He settled down on the plush low couch she indicated, and Sesame coiled beside it. Para relaxed his feet and rested on the carpeted floor.

Gwenny brought an ornate tray set with two crystal goblets, a plateful of cookies, a parchment, and a freshly stunned rat. She gave the rat to Sesame, who appreciated it and set about swallowing it whole, and the parchment to Para. "My scouts were scouting around a distant lake," she explained. "They found this and brought it back for burning in a fire, but I rescued it. Male goblins don't have much sense. I believe it is a picture of your mother." She unrolled it, and sure enough, there was a painting of the loveliest boat anyone could have imagined. Para didn't seem to have eyes but evidently was able to see the picture. He gazed at it and faded out, leaving the picture on the floor.

"I didn't know he could do that," Umlaut said, surprised.

"It's not magic," Gwenny explained. "He is so taken with it that he is entirely tuned out, not aware of anything else."

Umlaut realized that he had been slow again. Of course when a person tuned out he became invisible to the world. He had somehow thought it was the other way around.

"And that leaves us," Gwenny said, sitting down beside Umlaut, halfway facing him, and crossing her legs. They were very nice legs. "Have some boot rear and a cookie." She held the tray toward him.

"Uh, thank you." He took one goblet—naturally that would be the kind of drinking vessel goblins had—and a cookie. He was prepared for the drink, which gave the drinker a pleasant kick in the rear when sipped and a harder one when gulped. But the cookie was odd; it looked like a mass of lines and wires. "I haven't seen one like this."

"It records your identity and tastes," she explained. "So that every cookie thereafter will be perfect for you. Com Pewter discovered this kind and likes it very well."

"Oh." Further protest seemed pointless, so he ate it, and it actually tasted very good.

Gwenny sipped from her own goblet and nipped from her own cookie. The thought of her being gently kicked in the rear, or spanked, and her private tastes checked out made Umlaut almost lose his concentration. "I think we have much in common," she said, recrossing her legs. Umlaut almost choked on his mouthful; they were extremely nice legs.

He realized belatedly that she was expecting a response, but he had no idea what to say. "Uh, maybe if you read the letter, you could decide whether Nada Naga should see it." He leaned down to get the letter from the bundle and inadvertently saw even more of her legs under her short black skirt. He barely got the letter and straightened up without freaking out. "Uh, here." He held it toward her.

She leaned forward to take it. She was well below him in height, and her gown was not tight in front, so that he saw down inside it. This time he did freak out. He knew it because the next thing he was conscious of was her standing beside him, wiping his face with a cool cloth. "Are you all right, Umlaut? I'll never forgive myself if my food made you ill."

"I uh, I'm all right," he said. "I, that is—" What was he to say? He decided on the truth. "I am a bit, uh, naive about things. I, uh, saw something I shouldn't and freaked out."

"Why, how utterly charming," she said and kissed him on the cheek. There was a faint scent of roses about her. "You are just the way Metria said you would be."

"Metria!" Here was more mischief. "What did she, uh, tell you?"

"Oh, must I give that away already? Very well. She said that you are actually a distant prince who is looking for an economic or defensive liaison with a goblin tribe. That you are traveling incognito in the company of two natives to conceal your identity, so that others won't judge you by your rank instead of yourself. She said you are rather young and shy, but very good-hearted."

"But I'm just here to deliver a letter!"

"Yes, that is your pretext, so that you can travel around the country looking for a suitable princess or, in this case, chiefess."

"Looking for a princess? Why?"

"Why, to marry, of course. To make the liaison."

"To marry!" he said, shocked.

"Perhaps you are concerned because you are human and I am goblin. I assure you that there is no problem an accommodation spell can't handle."

His mind was going numb, and it wasn't unduly sharp at the best of times. "A what spell?"

"Since you ask, I will invoke it." She did something. Then she was his size. Or rather, he was her size, because the couch seemed twice as big and so did the rest of the chamber.

"I, uh, see," he said, amazed.

"So if you would like to make that liaison with me, I am available. I must confess that since my closest friend Jenny

Elf got married, I have felt somewhat out of sorts."

"But, uh—" He ran out of words before getting fairly started.

"You are evidently not accustomed to this sort of interaction, being just barely below induction into the Adult Conspiracy. But you surely understand political expediency. I think a liaison with Goblin Mountain will be mutually beneficial, and I assure you that I can be as accommodating as the spell."

How had he gotten into this? Oh, yes, Metria had set another trap for him. Now he understood why she had found a different errand for the cats: Claire would have fathomed the situation immediately and protected him from it. Now how was he going to get out of it? "I, uh—"

"But before we take it farther, I have a confession to make." Gwenny made a pretty frown. "I have two physical imperfections."

"You look perfect to me!" he blurted, blushing. Indeed, she was overwhelmingly perfect. It was hard to believe that a goblin female could be so different from a goblin male.

"First, my vision: I don't see well naturally. Fortunately the centaurs located a lens bush, and contact with the lenses corrects my vision. So that need be of no further concern, unless I should lose a lens. Second, I am slightly lame. I have grown out of it to a considerable extent, but I can't walk any significant distance without limping. It is something to do with my knee, I think." She sat back down on the couch and lifted her knees, putting her feet on the seat.

"They are perfect knees," Umlaut said sincerely.

"Thank you. But I was not referring to appearance but to function. One just doesn't flex quite right." She demonstrated, lifting one foot. Umlaut suddenly saw well beyond her knees. Blackness blotted his vision.

He found himself lying on the couch. She was mopping his face again. "I'm so sorry," she said. "I forgot how susceptible you are. It's much worse with humans than with goblin men, who are insatiably crude. I fear I inadvertently showed you my panties. I apologize profusely."

So that was the blackness. It was the stiffest jolt he could remember. But he had to correct her misunderstanding. "I, uh—"

"But once you join the Conspiracy, you will gradually learn to handle panties, at least when they are familiar. Illicit glimpses will always retain their potency, of course. Meanwhile I hope a gourd apology will do."

"No, I—" But he was too late. She kissed him on the mouth. It was not wine sweet so much as mind-blowingly pleasant, as was everything about her.

He must have faded out, because the scene shifted again. "So if you will forgive me for my eyes and knee," she was saying, "I will do my best to satisfy you in every other way."

He finally got it out. "It's a mistake. I'm not a prince. And I'm taken."

She gazed quizzically at him. "But Metria said—"

"Metria's trying to stop me from delivering the letters. She's doing anything she can to mess me up. You can't believe her."

"But in that case—"

"I'm not a prince. I'm just a dull, ordinary guy."

"Are you sure?"

Umlaut discovered that he wasn't sure. "Actually I can't remember anything from before I started this mission, really. I don't know what I did before."

"So you could be an anonymous prince."

"I suppose. But I don't believe it. I really am ordinary. And I really am taken. I love Surprise Golem."

"Rapunzel's daughter? I didn't realize that she was of age."

"She's not. She's only fourteen. But I'll wait for her."

"Of course," Gwenny said faintly. "Youth must be served."

"I sure didn't mean to mislead you."

"You didn't, Umlaut. I think I misled myself. I should have questioned the demoness's words; she's an endless fount of mischief. Oh, this is so embarrassing!" Now she was blushing, her dark face turning bright red.

"I'm sorry," he said, newly ashamed.

"I suggest we make a private agreement: to separate and never speak of this matter after."

"Agreed!" he said. He looked at Sesame, who had swallowed her rat, and Para, who was no longer tuned out. Both of them nodded.

"Princess Nada Naga is in the next chamber with her daughter DeMonica. Be wary of the child; she is half demon."

"I will," Umlaut promised.

"Now I will disband the accommodation spell." And abruptly she was half his size again, still very pretty but in miniature.

He wasn't quite satisfied to leave it at that. "I uh, just want to say that if I had been a prince, and not, uh, committed, I would surely want to marry you. You're so pretty and nice and thoughtful. But I know I'm not worthy of you and never will be."

"You're sweet," she said, much as Surprise had in the dream. "And I think you overrate your unworthiness. Were I not required to marry a prince for political reason, I think I would be jealous of Surprise."

Then she conducted them to the next chamber, where her friend Nada Naga was staying. Nada turned out to be a beautiful cross between serpent and human, intriguing both Umlaut and Sesame, and her daughter was a bundle of mischief who was soon riding Para around the mountain passages.

"This letter is, uh, not polite," Umlaut said. "I'm sorry."

"I have had nasty letters before," the princess said. "It comes with the territory." She accepted it and did not look at it while they remained. Umlaut was glad of that.

DREAM REALM

C laire appreciated Sammy Cat's magic talent, as it nicely complemented her own. He knew where to find anything except home; she understood the situation when they got there. He did have a certain impulsivity that he should have outgrown a decade and a half ago, but this too complemented her own rather more set nature. They were a good team and would make beautiful music together in due course. Naturally she had no use for ignoramuses who called it yowling. There were several ignoramuses in the bogs near Cat Isle; they were big ungainly beasts with bovine opinions.

However, Claire had never been one to accept a pig in a poke; such pigs were seldom pleasant company, especially when they kept poking others. She did not quite trust the demoness Metria, whose agenda did not seem to mesh well with their own. So she soon brought Sammy to a halt. Unfortunately it happened in midair, and he dropped abruptly to the ground.

"Exactly where are we going?" she inquired in Feline.

"To where Soufflé Serpent's curse can be abated," he replied.

"And where geographically is that?"

"I'm not sure, but I know I can find it."

"I prefer to know where I am going before I get there."

"Well, you're female," he said, thinking that explained it.

The cloud that portended the arrival of the demoness formed just before them. "What is the substantiality?" it inquired in the human idiom.

"The what?" Sammy asked in Feline.

"Element, medium, substance, constituents, body—"

"Matter?"

"Whatever," she agreed crossly. "Why aren't you running recklessly on your way?"

"Because I dislike accepting an oink in an outhouse," Claire said. "Where precisely is this solution to the curse, and what is its nature?"

The cloud shifted evasively. "That would take some exegesis."

"Some what?" Sammy asked.

"Explaining," Claire said shortly, preferring to avoid the thing's game. "So explain it, Demoness."

The cloud hovered a good moment and a half, but when it was apparent even to an airheaded creature that the cats were not going anywhere without it, the demoness relented. She formed into a big lion-striped cat who spoke Feline. "It seems there is a magician, actually a lesser demon, whose job is to assign magic talents to humanoid babies and some related species when they are about to be delivered to their families."

"I thought the storks did that," Sammy said.

"The storks merely receive and deliver orders; they don't make the babies or infuse their souls or talents. The talents are crafted and applied by the Magician Tallyho. Regular Xanth folk don't know about him; it's a classified position, the most restricted aspect of the Adult Conspiracy."

"What does that have to do with the curse?" Sammy asked. He did not inherently understand things the way Claire did so needed to ask.

"Only the one who assigns the talent of cursing can nullify that talent," Metria explained. "So if you go to him and persuade him to nullify the curse fiends' curse on Soufflé Serpent, that will solve his problem so he can slither soulfully with Sesame."

Claire still did not quite trust this. She was aware that the demoness was speaking truth but not whole truth. Because the source of the problem was elsewhere, Claire could not fathom its full nature. "What is missing from your summation?"

"My what?"

"What are you hiding?"

Metria sighed, the air of it emerging from either end. "There may be a complication reaching the magician."

"And that is?"

"He works in the gourd."

The realm of dreams. "We can't go there."

"Yes, you can. You just can't take your bodies along."

That was a formidable catch, but it appeared to be the extent of it. They would have to do it. "Thank you," Claire said, absolutely not meaning it.

"You're welcome," the demoness replied with muted malice. She dissolved into smoke and floated away.

"Resume motion," Claire told Sammy.

He bounded on, and she followed. Soon they came to a patch of greenish gourds under a spreading tree. They settled down by two whose peepholes were adjacent, touched tails, and peeped. That way they were assured of arriving in the same region of the extensive dream realm.

The scene that opened out was surprisingly dull. It consisted of two blank doors before which were two statues of sphinxes. Possibly they were real sphinxes in repose; the distinction could become academic, and it wasn't worth the effort to make it. There were two pedestals labeled TRUTH and LIE. Evidently the sphinxes normally rested on them but had left them in favor of the ground. A sign said ONE QUESTION.

Sammy's sense of direction left him. He did not know which door would lead to the Magician of Talents. But Claire divined the situation: One door was correct, the other spurious. They could take only one. They had to ask a sphinx. Unfortunately they did not know which sphinx was the truth teller and which was the liar. Had they been able to ask multiple questions of both sphinxes, they could have determined which one spoke truth and ask it about the doors. But they were limited to one question. Sammy was baffled.

Fortunately Claire wasn't. Her talent enabled her to know a question that would give them the correct answer, regardless of the nature of the sphinx asked. There were several such questions to choose from, but one was all she needed. She approached the sphinx on the left and said, "If I asked the other sphinx which door is correct for us, what would it say?"

"It would say the door on the right," the sphinx replied promptly.

"Thank you." She turned to Sammy. "We shall take the door on the left."

Sammy looked uncertainly at her. "But it said the other door."

"Here is the logic," she told him patiently. "If I asked the truth teller, it would report what the liar would say, which would be the wrong door. If I asked the liar, it would lie about what the truth teller would say and tell us the wrong door. So the answer has to be wrong."

He nodded somewhat blankly. Reasoning wasn't his strong point, but he trusted her judgment. Still, she preferred to reassure him, in the interest of future trust. "I could have asked it, 'If I asked you which door is correct, what would you say?' The truth teller would give the correct door. The liar would lie about what it would say, and since what it would say would be a lie, it cancels out and it would tell the correct door. So I could have accepted the answer of either one. The key is the fact that the truth teller always tells the truth, and the liar always lies; we can use their own consistency to get the right answer."

He still looked somewhat blank, so she twitched whiskers with him and let it be. He would digest it in time. "Go through the left door," she told him firmly.

They went through the left door. It opened on a rocky vista that descended precipitously to a violent river. A number of birds perched on boulders, and on occasion one would launch into the sky and swoop down on some helpless little creature trying to pass by. Claire assessed the situation immediately: "This is the setting for a bad dream intended for small furry creatures who misbehave. They have to run the gantlet of raptors."

"Of what?" Sammy asked.

"Predatory birds. See, there's a hawk on the near stone and a roc on the huge distant rock. In between is—" She paused, not recognizing the white-headed bird on the intervening boulder. So she approached it in order to get it into her voyancy range.

The bird rotated its head without moving its body and looked at her. "Ha, a furry creature!" it squawked in Avian.

Claire lifted a forepaw and sprang out four claws. "Try it and I will show you how it feels to be prey instead of predator," she said in Feline. Then she smiled, showing efficient carnivore teeth.

The bird pondered three quarters of a moment and relaxed. "I was merely making small talk."

Uh-huh. "What kind of bird are you?"

"I am an eagle from Mundania."

"My associate Sammy is from an alien region too: the World of Two Moons."

"Fascinating," the eagle said in a bored squawk.

"What is the best way out of this scene?"

"I don't have to tell you that, pussy. I am obliged to help only lost Eagle Scouts. That's why I'm here."

There were limits to Claire's tolerance. She had tried to be polite. Now she pounced, but the eagle took off before she got hold of it. She landed neatly on the boulder. Well, she had made her point: She did not accept insolence from birds.

"Find a safe way through," she told Sammy, "in the direction of Magician Tallyho."

He walked to the side, picking his way between stones and birds, and she followed. They came to a fort fashioned of stacked stones. There was no way around it, so they cautiously went toward it.

A human man sat therein, laboring on a long arrow. He looked up as they approached. "Hello, cats," he said in Human. "You're not part of this setting."

"Can you understand Feline?" Claire asked and knew immediately that he did.

"Of course. All denizens of the dream realm understand each other."

"I am Claire, and this is Sammy," she said. "We are look-ing for Magician Tallyho."

"And I am Thorin, master archer and magic arrow maker. I don't know the way to reach Tallyho; I'm confined to my station here, making powerful barbs."

Claire was aware that something remarkable was here that might be worth knowing. "What kind of arrows are they?"

"I shall happily demonstrate, if you wish. I seldom get the chance to show off my wares. The birds are definitely not interested."

Claire could appreciate why. Normally nothing on the ground was a threat to a flying bird, but an archer with arrows was. "Please demonstrate."

"This is an arrow of betrayal," Thorin said, holding up a thin, dark one. It didn't look very formidable. "I need a vol-unteer to walk in my line of fire. This will not be lethal, I promise. It is just that showing is better than telling." He picked up a bow.

Sammy glanced at the arrow, which looked too weak to penetrate cat hide. He walked before the archer.

Thorin nocked the arrow on his bowstring and fired it. It missed the cat and struck Sammy's shadow. Immediately the shadow detached itself from the cat and rose up and grabbed Sammy's tail.

"Yowl!" Sammy cried, surprised. He whirled and bashed the shadow with a paw. The shadow fell apart and dissipated.

"You see, it causes a creature's shadow to attack its former master. A shadow normally can't do much damage, as we saw, but it comes as a surprise, and if the creature is in a precarious situation, this could make it do something foolish, such as falling off a high branch. I also make arrows of fire, light, darkness, and love."

"That last does not seem dangerous," Sammy said.

"That depends on whom it strikes. A creature who stays well clear of a love spring could nevertheless be caught by such an arrow and thereafter be bound in love to one he might otherwise hate. It can be extremely awkward if she does not return his passion."

Claire nodded appreciatively. The arrow of love could be

deadlier than any of the others. "Thank you," she said. "We must move on now."

"I appreciate your brief company," Thorin said. "Much better than those birdbrains."

"Find someone who can and will help us through this labyrinth," Claire told Sammy.

They proceeded to the edge of the set and found a yellow horse grazing on a patch of grass. Claire knew that he was no night mare but wasn't sure what he was. She would have to get closer to him, so that her talent could take hold.

The horse saw them coming. "Hello, cats," he said.

"Hello, horse," Claire replied, then paused, surprised. "Did you speak in Human?"

"I did. I am Xanthus, from Greece, Mundania, circa three thousand years ago. I have an illustrious heritage, being the offspring of the West Wind and a harpy. I have been looking for a home and seem to have found it here in the dream realm. I do on occasion get lonely for company, however; my natural taste does not run to human bad dreams."

"I am Claire Voyant, and this is Sammy Cat. We are looking for Magician Tallyho, but the route seems devious."

"All routes are devious here," Xanthus said. "That's the nature of dreams. They are seldom straightforward. In addition, Tallyho is reclusive, hidden beyond a number of unpleasant settings. However, I will be happy to carry you there, for the pleasure of your brief company."

That was why Sammy had located this horse. It seemed that company was a valuable commodity here in the dream realm.

They jumped up onto a pad set on Xanthus's back and rode through the ensuing sets in style. They saw communities of centaurs, pools of merfolk, clumps of ogres, and all manner of monsters. "They are all players in bad dreams," Xanthus explained, happy to be their tour guide. "Every day the dreams are carefully crafted for the night mares to carry to deserving sleepers. It's a tremendous industry and constantly growing. It seems that people don't learn well from experience and so deserve worse dreams."

"Are there no good dreams?" Sammy asked.

"Oh, not here! The day mares carry day dreams, and I

suppose some carry good dreams at night. But there's really not much point in good dreams, because they don't cause errant folk to change their ways."

"Doesn't anybody do what is right simply because it is right?" Sammy asked.

Xanthus turned his head back to look at him. "You're new here. You haven't seen into the minds of ordinary folk."

"I have," Claire said. "In my fashion. Few are concerned with what is right or honorable in the larger sense. Most want simply to secure their own safety and pleasure. If there were not some mechanism to keep them in line, they would soon be very bad neighbors."

"But Jenny Elf is good." Sammy paused, considering, then added grudgingly, "And so is Jeremy Werewolf."

"There are exceptions, of course," Xanthus said. "But from what I have seen, the bad dreams are more than necessary."

Claire saw that Sammy didn't really believe that. He was delightfully naive in some respects.

At last they reached a rather pleasant cottage set in a mountain glade. "Here is where Tallyho retired," Xanthus announced.

"Thank you for bringing us here," Claire said as they jumped off the horse's back.

"It was a brief pleasure. I will return to take you back." Xanthus trotted off.

They approached the cottage and scratched at its door. "What's your talent?" a voice came from inside.

"Finding anything except home," Sammy answered.

"I didn't assign that talent! Who are you?"

"Sammy Cat."

The door opened. A somewhat bedraggled bearded human man stood there. "Oh, from the World of Two Moons. That explains it. You weren't one of mine." He glanced at Claire. "But you were. Voyance."

"True," Claire said. "We came because we understand you can undo a curse for us."

"Come in." He led them into his house. A fire crackled in the middle of the main chamber. There was no fireplace; the fire was contained in midair, burning without logs. This was after all the dream realm; physical things were beside the point.

They settled on a plush rug and watched the fire. The flames formed different shapes as they rose: a thorny berry vine, a winged dragon, a twisting castle, and half a slew of dancing maidens. All were fleeting, disappearing as they reached the ceiling. The figures did not seem to repeat; new ones formed as the old ones faded.

"Unfortunately, I can't void a curse," Tallyho said. "Who suggested to you that I could?"

"The Demoness Metria," Sammy said.

"That bundle of mischief? Why should you believe her?"

"Because in this case she was telling the truth," Claire said. "But there was something missing that I couldn't fathom."

"There certainly was! Let me explain: I assign talents, but I don't use them. Once a baby departs with its talent, that remains pretty well fixed for life. Only forces like the Demon Xanth or the Random Factor can affect it, and they seldom bother. So if you have been cursed, you will have to deal with it on your own."

"It is Soufflé Serpent who was cursed," Claire explained. "By the curse fiends, whose play rehearsal he messed up. Now he has a chance for happiness with Sesame Serpent, but the curse prevents it."

"That is the way of curses," Tallyho agreed. "They are seldom convenient for the recipients."

"But there must be a way," Sammy said, "or there would not have been any truth to what the demoness said."

"That would be that I could assign a talent of abolishing or ameliorating curses, and that person might then be prevailed on to help your friend. But since the talents are assigned to babies, it would be several years before the child was old enough to use it effectively."

Claire nodded. "So it can be done but not swiftly. We had hoped for better."

"Things often work out that way," Tallyho said.

"You assigned the same talent to all the curse fiends," Claire said. "Why was that?"

"I didn't."

"But all the curse fiends have the same talent of cursing," Sammy said.

"My predecessor did that. There were a lot of them, and he lacked imagination, so he simply put in a standing order for the curse for all of their babies. There were no complaints, so that has remained."

"Your predecessor," Sammy said. "There are different magicians who do this work?"

"Yes, and none of us are listed in the official tallies of Magicians, so we won't be corrupted by attention. After all, mortals are very jealous of their talents; each one wants to be a Magician or Sorceress. Only the descendants of Magician Bink have been granted that, because of a whim of Demon Xanth. I have held the position for several centuries and think I have earned my retirement. So as of now I am passing the chore on to Magician Teillo."

"Why right now?" Sammy asked.

"It's your fault."

"Mine!"

Claire was amused. "Tallyho was destined to fill the position until asked a non-self-serving question about his job. You just asked that question, Sammy. I wondered if you would."

Sammy bristled just slightly. "Why didn't you ask it?"

"Because it had to be asked honestly. I had already fathomed his situation so kept my muzzle muzzled."

"But to turn it over, just like that—randomly, really—this makes little sense."

"It makes perfect sense," Tallyho said. "It is the way demons do things. I hope Teillo doesn't make too many errors."

"Errors?"

"Talents ideally should be appropriate to the babies and their situations. Such as the power of lightening things, granted to most winged centaurs, so they can make themselves light enough to fly. It wouldn't do to give it to a mermaid, for example, unless she planned to fly. Actually there are a few winged merfolk, but I trust that makes the point."

"It does," Claire agreed. "We had not thought about the matter." She glanced at Sammy. "I think we must return to report that there is not a feasible avenue for Soufflé here."

"The Demoness Metria surely knew that," Tallyho said. "I

wonder why she sent you on this wild-duck chase."

"She must have had an interior motive," Sammy said.

"What kind of motive?"

"She gets words wrong. She would mean ulterior."

"And we had better get back to Goblin Mountain and find out what that motive was," Claire said urgently.

"I am inclined to agree," Tallyho said. "But I thank you for bringing me to my retirement. I plan to relax for several decades; the job has been wearing."

"That's nice," Sammy said.

But Claire was uncertain. She sensed formidable mischief here, though the situation extended far beyond her immediate range. There could also be trouble for Umlaut and Sesame. She feared that it would have been better if they had never come on this spot mission. "We must go," she repeated.

They left the house. Xanthus trotted up just at that time; somehow he had known when they were ready. But this was the dream realm; he was probably in tune.

"We need to return as fast as we can," Claire told the horse. "We fear mischief for our friends."

"I regret I must detour, at least briefly," Xanthus said. "The Night Stallion wishes to see you."

"What interest does he have in us?" Sammy asked.

"I don't know. But his will is paramount in the dream realm." The horse galloped in a new direction, passing settings so rapidly they were a dreamy blur.

Then they were in an indistinct hall, facing a large, formidable, dark horse. It was the dread Night Stallion. They did not dismount; they were frozen in place.

"Why did you come here?" The horse did not actually speak, but they heard his words as though he had.

"Demoness Metria told us that we could find a way to end a curse here," Claire replied. "But while technically true, it was flawed and not feasible."

"Like Mundane software," the stallion agreed. "The demoness knew that?"

"We believe so. We suspect her motive."

"What motive?"

"I was not able to fathom it," Claire replied. "But it may be that she wanted us separate from Umlaut, so that she could try again to stop him from delivering his letters."

"Why does she wish to stop him?"

"Again, I have not fathomed her motive. When we inquired, she simply said she loved her son. It seems she is under some kind of duress. Yet the deliveries have beneficial purpose, because the Good Magician told Umlaut that this chore would enable him to find the way to stop Demon Jupiter's Red Spot from destroying Xanth."

"I must investigate this." The Night Stallion turned his head. "Day Stallion!"

A golden horse appeared. "You wish dialogue?"

"I must investigate why a demoness opposes the salvation of Xanth. It became my business when she sent folk here who might have prevented mischief elsewhere. You must take over here until my return."

"Gladly."

Then the Night Stallion was gone. The Day Stallion looked around. "This is my chance to reform this pesthole," he said. "The bad dreams will end immediately."

"But without them, folk will have no incentive to—" Xanthus began.

"Begone," the Day Stallion said.

They were on their way back. "This makes me nervous," Xanthus said. "The Day Stallion lacks experience with evil. He should not be doing this."

"I wonder whether Metria knew that these complications would occur when we came here," Sammy said. "The change of talent Magicians, and now the change of Stallions?"

"The mischief being with us!" Claire agreed. "That could be it."

Xanthus halted. "Uh-oh. The sets are changing. I no longer know the fastest way through."

"Changing?" Claire asked nervously.

"They are all set up by the directive of the Night Stallion. Now the authority is the Day Stallion. He's dismantling the horror sets."

Before them was a haunted house. Three ghosts were floating aimlessly around, and several walking skeletons were taking up hammers and nails to repair sagging porticoes. A mummy was planting a rose garden.

"What are you doing?" Xanthus asked.

"We're making this into a nice dream setting," a skeleton said, "so as not to scare the recipient."

"Disaster," Xanthus muttered as he picked his way around the house. Claire was inclined to agree. Even if the change was warranted, it was generating disruption.

The next set was a wet one, with huge water monsters engaged in painting a lovely sunset backdrop. "What is the dream realm coming to?" a monster muttered, disgusted.

Claire feared that the demoness had accomplished her purpose, whatever it was. There was certainly mischief to spare here in the dream realm.

They finally returned to their starting point and exited. There was a moment of disorientation as they lifted their eyes from the gourd peepholes. Ordinarily that could not be done, but this was a special case; the gourd was letting them go.

They bounded back toward Goblin Mountain. When they got there, Para was just emerging with Umlaut. They jumped into the boat. "Did you abate the curse?" Umlaut asked.

It was a bad lead, Sammy said in Feline. They were back in the real world now and couldn't speak freely with everyone. Not that it made much difference with Umlaut and Sesame. The curse could be undone but would take years. And they might have sowed a lot of mischief there.

"In the dream realm? How is that possible?"

It was possible, Claire assured him. They had inadvertently brought about a change in the way magic talents were assigned and saw the Day Stallion take over the dream realm. There would be no more bad dreams for a while.

"No more bad dreams! Isn't that good?"

No, because it means bad deeds will no longer be punished. What of his time in the mountain?

"Metria had set me up to marry Chiefess Gwendolyn. She's very nice, but I'm not the prince she thought I was, and of course I wouldn't want to leave Surprise."

So it had been mischief at both ends. Claire was not sure they had seen the end of it.

What was in the next letter? Sammy asked.

Umlaut drew it out. "It is to Jenny Elf."

But he couldn't find Jenny! Sammy protested.

It was time to clarify something for them all. Couldn't he? Claire asked.

"I can find anything but home," he reminded her, speaking directly to her.

"See if you can find Jenny."

"But I can't!" he protested.

"Try anyway."

He shrugged and focused—and was amazed. "I can find her! But that can't be."

"It can be if you know that your home is now with me."

He stared at her, realizing. "I do want to be with you. To share your house."

"I know." She had of course known it long before he did.

"That means that your house is now my home—and I can't find it."

"Fortunately I know where it is. Now you orient on Jenny. You will not be neglecting her; you will merely be visiting her from another home."

"Another home," he agreed in wonder. Then he reoriented on Jenny and told Para where to go.

"I'd better read that letter," Umlaut said. He opened it and read it aloud.

Dear Jenny Elf,

This is a letter of congratulations to you and Prince Jeremy Werewolf, on your royal wedding at Castle Roogna. You have been so good for him and I know you will be a fine wife. I was very happy that you were the one, Jeremy's ideal wife to break the curse. I like wolves too, except I have seen only one in his natural homeland, when I was visiting the far North. They do not live around here where I do.

Maybe before I go any further I should tell you who I am and how I know of you. My name is Arjayess and I live in Mundania. Our village is a pretty place in a valley surrounded by lakes and tree-covered hills. It is called Pen-Tak, which means "Stay forever" in the ancient languages. The village is in Otch Enau Kane, which means "Near the Waterfall at the End of the River." Pen-

Tak is in the middle or central part of Otch Enau Kane Valley.

For many years I have been having daily visions of a land far away from my home. At first they were vague and blurry like a very weak illusion. It was like seeing pictures through a heavy mist or cloud. I could see a people and a country, but the people and creatures were unknown to me and the land was like none I have ever seen before. After many months of viewing frozen picture visions, the scenes began to slowly move about. It was as if I were watching the tapestry in the castle but through a dense vapor. When a year had passed and the motion got to normal speed, I started hearing heavy, muffled conversation. How I would have liked to have Grundy with me then to translate, but I did not know about him yet. What was that man's name? Bimp! Who would name her child Bimp? Oh, no, he was facing a court of some sort, he was being made to leave his home. But why? Altogether puzzled by what I saw and did not understand because I could not hear clearly, I became very frustrated. I did not understand what was happening to me, either—where these visions were coming from, why, and who these people were. I never did discover the where or the why, but I am content with it now. I feel it is a special gift and I am thankful. I am also grateful that I now see it clear and sharp and hear all of it with ease. It seemed the poor young man in my vision was being exiled from his home because he had no magic talent. Well, of course, I thought at the time, if he has no mag—wait a minute here. No magic? But no one has magic, does he? At least not where I come from. But it seems in Xanth they do. You do. For of course, as I realized later, it was Xanth I was seeing. As the sounds finally came clear I discovered it was Bink I was seeing, not Bimp, and that he had a powerful, magician-caliber talent. My first year of mind pictures after that was of Bink meeting Chameleon and the adventures they shared.

That was quite some years ago now, and I feel as though I have known Xanth forever. All your friends feel like close friends of mine too. I particularly like Sammy because I have a special place in my heart for cats. I do not mean that their bodies go right into my physical heart, just that I love cats best out of all mundane animals. I have two cats, Fellini and Misha. Misha is ten, which is getting pretty old for a cat here. She has soft, pure white fur and likes to cuddle and purr. Fellini is like a baby tiger lily without the flower part. He's orange striped, what we call a tabby. He likes to growl and run, and pounce on poor old Misha who just wants to be left alone to sleep. Fellini really is just a baby—he's not yet a year old, so he is only playing, even when he is being naughty. The really funny thing about him is his tail. Most cats here have a long, straight tail, probably like Sammy's. Some have just a little stump of tail, and some have none at all. But Fellini's tail has two bends in it toward the tip. It looks something like this:

The cat doctor said he was probably born with it like that, and he did not get it hurt badly when he was very young as I had thought. I was very happy to learn that because I did not like to think about an innocent little baby cat being in so much pain. Neither Misha nor Fellini has any magic, but Misha is affectionate and Fellini is entertaining, so that is talent enough for me. I love them both very much.

Our friend Meatron came to our house today for a visit with my husband Jehial and me. We ate scones and drank juice of apple fruit, much like you had tea and crumples with Millie, only I made the scones with ground wheat, sugarcane, and other things we grow. That is, of course, when the weather is good for growing. Here we call that summer, and the temperature is what some people claim is too hot but what I find quite comfortable. Right now we are having winter, when our part of the world is turned away from our sun. It is freezing outside right now so I stay in the house cozy and protected for most of the time until it warms up again when winter is finished. I saw on our talking box called television or TV that today in Xanth the temperature was eighty degrees. That is the way I like it and how it will be here again in a few months' time. I am really looking forward to it. I do not like winter at all.

I have really enjoyed writing to you, Jenny. I hope to do so again, only I do not know if it is allowed. I am not sure of the laws and rules of Xanth. If it does not show in my visions, then I just do not know. I hope this letter does not get you into trouble, because I really do not want that. You are too nice an elf person, and I like you.

Your friend,
Arjayess

Claire Voyant observed how Sammy reacted to the mention of his name. He thought himself the center of the universe, which was of course correct; any cat was. He had surely had a good effect on Jenny Elf. But now he did have a new home.

18

CONSEQUENCES

U mlaut saw that there were only two letters remaining after the one to Jenny Elf. That was a relief in one sense, because it meant that their job was nearly done. But they still had not found the way to abate the hurtling Red Spot. Suppose they delivered the last letter and didn't find the solution?

A ball of smoke formed. "So how was your fig?" it inquired.

"My what?"

"Bother," the cloud muttered. "I think I got the wrong fruit. Assignation, appointment, rendezvous, clandestine meeting, tryst—"

"Date?"

"Whatever," it agreed crossly. "How did you make out with Gwenny Goblin?"

"I had no appointment with her. The letter was for Nada Naga, and I gave it to her."

"Don't give me that," the cloud said, forming into the Demoness Metria. Somehow Umlaut was not surprised. "I told Gwenny that was just your pretext to come to her. She was waiting for you."

Confirmation! But he kept his tone level. "And why did you do that?"

"Oh, bleep! I let the pussy out of the pot." She started to fade. Both cats glared, not appreciating the figure of speech.

But Umlaut had a different concern. "Metria, you can't fade out of all your problems. Why are you trying to stop us from delivering the letters?"

The fading became a sigh. The demoness re-formed and sat down opposite him in the boat. This time her clothing was completely decorous. She wasn't trying to vamp him. That made him uneasy. "I suppose you'll wedge it out of me anyway. Maybe the truth will change your mind."

"About what?"

"About delivering those letters. I can't let you do that, and it's already pretty far gone."

"But we need to deliver the letters in order to find out how to stop Demon Jupiter's Red Spot from destroying Xanth. How can you be opposed to that?"

"I'm not opposed, exactly. But I have to stop you."

"This must make some kind of sense only you could appreciate."

"Exactly. Demoness Fornax told me to stop those deliveries, or she'd take my son Ted's soul. He has only a quarter soul, but she'll take it, making him a soulless crossbreed. I wouldn't care, except that I have a quarter soul myself, so I *do* care. I couldn't stand to have that happen to him."

Umlaut found that her answer merely brought forth a larger question. "Who is Fornax? What's her role in this?"

"She is the Demon who governs the distant galaxy of Fornax. She had quite a contest with the local demons last year. The locals finally won, but it seems she hasn't given up. I don't know what their wager is this time, but it's usually something obscure, such as whether some mortal will say certain words before or after he catches on to their significance. I guess this time it is whether all those letters will be delivered. So she wants to stop them, so she can win. And I have to help her, because I love my son. I just have to." She lifted the hem of her dress and dabbed at her face.

Umlaut was surprised to see real tears there. Of course she could surely conjure tears as readily as clothing, but he had the distinct impression that she was not doing so. He glanced at Claire, who nodded: The tears were genuine. So probably her story was true. "So you have been causing all this mischief in order to save Demon Ted?"

She nodded. "He's a little crazy, but he gets along well with DeMonica, and some distant day they'll grow up and marry. It would be a shame to ruin all that."

"But what you are doing may ruin all Xanth."

"I can't help that. I'm just a demoness. She's a Demoness. I have to do her bidding to save Ted's soul."

"Maybe we could find some other way to save it."

"Against a Demoness? It is to laugh, if I could evoke a laugh at the moment."

Umlaut shook his head. "If Xanth is destroyed, I'll lose Surprise. I can't let that happen."

"Maybe I miscalculated on that. I thought if I set you up with her, you'd stay there and stop delivering letters."

"I suppose I do owe you that. Without you, I might not have met her. Now I just want to be with her, when this is over."

"And that ruined my other diversions, like Gwenny Goblin. I definitely outsmarted myself that time."

"Maybe you did. I just want to get this job done, save Xanth, and return to Surprise."

"Too bad. But I've still got to stop you."

"I suppose you do. But you haven't been able to so far."

"The game is not over." She faded.

"What do you make of it?" Umlaut asked Claire.

She meant it, but she was limited, the cat responded in Feline. She couldn't snatch his letters and destroy them, and she couldn't do him any physical harm. In fact she couldn't directly touch any of their party. She could only try to distract him directly, or interfere with him indirectly. The rules of the game were specific. He had to be alert for further tricks.

"I'm glad you're along, Claire. Your information really helps." He glanced at the others. "So does your talent of finding, Sammy. And yours of emulation and threat, Sesame. And you have really helped us travel, Para."

Sesame was slightly embarrassed, so she changed the subject. It was getting late. They should find a safe campsite.

This way, Sammy indicated, pointing with a paw.

They headed that way, and Sammy and Claire caught up the others on their activities searching for the cure for Sesame's curse: It had been a fair adventure, with fair mischief resulting.

Dusk intensified, trying to catch them out, but they beat it to a nice campsite by a protected path. There was a small pond so Para could soak his feet and a comfortable tree house for the others. They harvested pillows and meat pies and settled for the night.

There came a loud crashing in the forest. Startled, they piled out of the house to investigate. It was a great brightly winged creature with impressive antlers, fleeing half a passel of goblin hunters. Umlaut knew the word *passel* because he had heard Demon Professor Grossclout use it once.

Claire was annoyed. That was a rare and protected species, she said. It was not supposed to be hunted anymore, despite the appeal of its horns and elaborate wings.

"Then let's see if we can stop this," Umlaut said. He went into ogre emulation, while Sesame went into dragon mode.

This way for safety, Sammy told the desperate mothalope. It looked uncertainly at him but didn't have much choice; it was worn out from the cruel chase.

Meanwhile Umlaut intercepted the goblins while Sesame quietly circled behind them. "Goblins flee, or deal with mee," he said, beating his chest with his ham-fists to make a wonderful booming sound.

But goblins were not noticeably timid, and there were a number here, armed with spears and clubs. "Oh, yeah, bonehead?" their leader demanded.

Umlaut reacted as an ogre would, pleased by the recognition of his dullness. Ogres were of course justly proud of their stupidity. But he also saw fit to remind them of what normally happened when goblins tangled with an ogre: Some got their heads rammed through knotholes in trees, others wound up in orbit around the moon, and the rest were less fortunate.

The goblin subchief considered this truth. "But some also get away," he pointed out. "And those can get that mothalope."

"But it's not supposed to be hunted," Umlaut protested.

The subchief stared at him. "Say, you're no ogre! You're a fake. Now we'll ram *your* head through a knothole." And the whole half passel advanced on him.

There was a hissing roar behind them. They turned to see a dragon closing in.

Goblins weren't cowards, but neither were they fools. They scattered and fled. But Sesame pounced, catching one by the britches and lifting him into the air. He screamed, but for some obscure reason his companions did not come to his rescue.

Umlaut reverted to human, as his ruse had been penetrated anyway. He questioned the goblin. "What made you think you should hunt a protected creature?" he demanded.

"Why should I tell you, faker?" the goblin demanded.

Sesame shook him. "Because you don't want the dragon to eat you," Umlaut said.

"Oh, that," the goblin agreed, seeing the logic. "It's okay to hunt helpless innocent rare beautiful creatures now, because the word's out: No more bad dreams. We can't be punished by night for what we do by day."

Suddenly Umlaut appreciated the mischief being done by the Day Stallion. The goblins were held in check only by fear of nocturnal reprisal, and now that was gone. The lady goblins seemed to be lovely and nice, but the male goblins were typically brutes. It gave him some sympathy with Gwenny Goblin's quest to find a decent prince to marry; why should she want a goblin chief? He was sorry to have messed up her wish, but of course he had never qualified for that. Still, if he had qualified, and not been committed to Surprise, it could have been nice with a creature like Gwenny. Those legs . . .

But there was an immediate job to do here. "Well, you're not getting this mothalope, regardless. Now you have a choice: Go home and tell your henchmen that, or stay and get eaten by the dragon."

The goblin considered, and after giving it due thought, concluded that he would prefer to go home. Sesame tossed him into the brush, and he scrambled away.

"I think the demoness Metria has indeed worked some extra mischief," Umlaut said. "Not only did she separate me from Claire so I couldn't be warned about what Gwenny Goblin had in mind, she got the two cats into the dream realm where more things are going wrong. She is working overtime."

Sesame supposed that if she had a little serpent to protect, she would work hard too.

"I suppose," Umlaut agreed. "But I am not at ease with this. Xanth seems to be getting into some real trouble. All because of some stupid Demon bet."

All they could do was try to deliver the remaining letters, she responded. And hope that saved Xanth.

"And hope," he agreed.

They returned to the camp. The cats rejoined them. There was no more nearby mischief that night, but Umlaut did not rest easy. He was delivering the letters, but how much trouble was he generating in the process?

In the morning they resumed travel and in due course reached the coast. They followed it past the various alphabetical signs. When the WORK FOR WO sign appeared they settled down to wait for the one they wanted: the Isle of Wolves. It was several hours before it appeared, but Sammy knew it when it did. It was evening again.

Para forged across. Then they headed inland to reach the palace. Somehow Jenny Elf knew when they got there. She dashed out to hug Sammy. "Sammy! You're back!" She was about three quarters Umlaut's height—small for human, large for elf—and she wore spectacles. She also, Umlaut noticed with surprise, had pointed ears and only four fingers on each hand. She had evidently not originated in Xanth.

There followed introductions and explanations. Jenny's husband Prince Jeremy was affable in human form. Jenny was happy to meet Claire Voyant but sad to learn that Sammy was moving to the Isle of Cats.

Umlaut gave Jenny the letter. She was thrilled to receive it. It was evident that she did not think of herself as a princess so much as a person who loved animals, especially wolves and cats.

They spent a nice night but had to resume their mission in the morning. The next letter was addressed to GOOD MAGICIAN HUMFREY. Had he realized that that one was in the pile, he could have delivered it when he was at the Good

Magician's Castle before. But of course then he hadn't known that he would be delivering the letters. Umlaut hesitated, then decided not to make an exception; after all, the key letter had to be one of the final two, and Humfrey certainly had much power to make mischief if sufficiently annoyed. He read it as Para carried them across land and water back to Xanth proper.

Dear Humfrey,

I daresay you have never had a question via snail mail before. You may choose to ignore this altogether due to the fact that I have not had the three challenges to face and simply see no way of performing a year's service in payment.

However, I have a serious problem there seems to be no solution for here in Mundania. I have in my home a magnificent ancient clock that was bequeathed to me. No one seems to know its history and even the so-called antique experts can tell me nothing about its origin. There has never been a problem with the timepiece in all the time I have had it. Last night, though, something strange occurred. At midnight the clock struck the hour and chimed the usual melodious twelve notes. Yet five minutes later, it marked the hour again, this time with a deep, resonant *Bong*. It then continued and sounded 1...2...3...4...5...6...7...8...9...10... 11...12, and after a tiny flicker of a pause, 13. Thirteen? Could I have dozed off and miscounted? No, I was still up, alert and working. Besides, what of the change in tone? I became uneasy in the certainty that this happening would gravely, perhaps dangerously, affect me—I could feel it in my bones. The stillness became expectant, with the entire building holding its breath. The air in the room pressed against me like a straitjacket, forming a question. "All right, Arjayess, what are you going to do about it?"

"Me? Nothing why should I probably just wound it too tight or something it just needs repairing that is all," I mindlessly babbled. But my feeble attempt to reassure myself fell flat. Deep within me I knew it was not simply a matter of malfunction.

Now every quarter hour when it strikes—always with the chilling basso pitch—I feel it drawing me forward, compelling me to enter within. I cannot even remove it from the house. When I try to touch it, tiny jolts of electricity spark out from the case.

Humfrey, I am pleading with you to understand my dilemma and help in any way you can. Please help me, I am so frightened and becoming desperate!

Arjayees

Umlaut considered. "She has a problem, but not one that will destroy Xanth," he concluded. "Maybe the Good Magician can help her."

In Mundania? Sesame asked.

"There's something funny about that stopwatch."

"About that what?" Umlaut asked before he thought. He was forever doing that.

"Timepiece, alarm, chronometer, pendulum—"

"Clock?"

"Whatever," a wisp of smoke agreed crossly.

"Hello, Metria. How is Ted?"

"I brought him along." A second wisp of smoke formed and developed into a six-year-old boy.

"Hi, folk," he said, looking tousle-headedly mischievous. "Wow! Who's the big snake?"

"That's Sesame Serpent, honey. I'm sure she'll be glad to play with you. She does emulations."

Sesame seemed less sure but cooperated by emulating a dragon. That thrilled the boy.

"What's that other wisp?" Umlaut asked, not completely trusting this.

"DeMonica. D. Vore and Nada Naga's girl. They like to play together. It's my turn to baby-sit. Form, Monica."

The second wisp formed into a cutely rebellious six-year-old girl. "Sammy Cat!" she exclaimed, spying him immediately.

Metria faded quietly out. Umlaut realized that their boatful had been co-opted as assistant baby-sitters. Still, it was a diversion while Para moved on toward the Good Magician's Castle.

"Where are we going?" Demon Ted asked.

"To the Good Magician's Castle."

"But there are ogres and trolls on the way there," De-Monica protested.

"We'll try to avoid them."

"But they're fun," Ted said.

Maybe to a little demon. "We have enough challenges with rivers and forests," Umlaut said firmly.

The two children burst into song. "Ogre the river and troll the woods, to the Magician's Castle we go!"

Umlaut sighed. This might be a long trip.

Then there was a heavy flapping sound. Umlaut looked and saw a harpy flying toward them. Oh, no!

"Don't wince, Umlaut," the harpy called. "It's me."

That was a familiar voice. "Surprise!" he said gladly. Indeed, now he saw that it was her face on the bird. Most harpies were dirty of body and fowl of mouth, or maybe it was the other way around, but she was clean.

She came to perch on the gunwale. "I can't visit you the same way twice," she reminded him. "And I can't stay long. It took a while to fly here, and I don't want Mom to miss me."

"I'm glad you came," he said. Then his gaze dropped from her face to her bare breasts, and he felt himself blushing.

"This is the way harpies are," Surprise reminded him. "They don't wear clothing, just feathers."

"Uh, yes." But his blush continued. He wondered whether that part of her looked the same when she was in human form and suspected it did. He was getting a considerable peek at her. He hoped the children wouldn't notice.

"Wow! Look at those boobs!" Ted exclaimed, staring.

"Go wash your eyeballs off with soap," Surprise snapped at him.

"Awwww." But the boy heeded the voice of authority and looked away.

"It's wonderful to see you," Umlaut said. "Uh, that is, that you're here."

"Shut up and kiss me."

He leaned across and kissed her on the mouth. "Oh, Surprise, I wish we could be together all the time!"

"Is that a proposal?"

His blush got twice as bad. "Uh—"

"In that case, I accept. We'll get married."

He was thrilled and appalled. "Uh—"

"You proposed and I accepted. We have witnesses."

He had to try to protest, though he didn't want to. "Your age—"

"A betrothal isn't a marriage, it's a promise. We can be betrothed until I'm of age, the way Justin and Breanna were." She looked around the boat. "Isn't that right?"

"Right!" the children chorused, and the cats and serpent nodded.

How could he resist? "I guess that's, uh, right."

"I'm glad that's settled. Come see me when you're done with the letters; I'll have my folks browbeaten into submission by then."

"Don't you need a 'gagement ring?" DeMonica asked.

"That's right," Surprise agreed. "Umlaut, give me a ring."

"A ring," he said, bemused.

A cloud formed. "What's going on here?"

"Oh, Metria, Umlaut and I just got plighted."

"Got what?"

"Promised, affianced, pledged, betrothed, engaged—"

"Stuck?"

"Whatever," Surprise agreed, trying to look cross. But in half an instant her joy burst out. "Isn't it wonderful?"

For once the demoness was serious. "Yes it is, girl. I'm glad for you. I will shed a tear at your wedding."

"But I need a ring."

"I'll look." The demoness disappeared with a pop. In half a moment she was back with an extremely ornate ring. "This is the best I could find on short notice. It's from an old lost treasure chest. I think it's called the Ring of the Nibble Lung."

"It's beautiful," Surprise said. She glanced at Umlaut. "Put it on my toe. I'll transfer it when I revert."

"But how do we know this ring is okay?" he asked. "Maybe it's magic."

"Of course it's magic!" Metria said. "All these old lost treasures are. Maybe it summons demons." She paused, startled. "Bite my tongue!" She chomped down on her tongue, and the tip of it dropped into the boat.

"But if it's dangerous—"

Metria grew a new tongue tip. "I wouldn't do that to you. Not for a betrothal. In fact I don't really want to do to you what I've been doing, but—" Her eyes flicked to Ted and away before the child could notice. Evidently she hadn't told him about that aspect. "I love weddings. I had my own, you know; that's where I got my half soul, which I then shared with Ted. Have you any idea how many times we had to signal the stork before we got its attention? A few more years of that could become wearing. Ted's one of a kind." Then, reminded of the threat to him, she clouded up. Her body became a vertical column of fog and her head a thunderhead.

Umlaut concluded that the ring was probably safe; the demoness did seem sincere. He took the ring and slipped it on Surprise's bird claw. "With this ring I thee betroth."

"That's so sweet! My folks will have two and a half fits when they see me wearing this! Well, I have to kiss and fly. I love you."

"I love you," he echoed gladly. This had been sudden but welcome.

She spread her wings and lurched toward him for a kiss. He met her halfway, but she was flying too high and his face collided with her breasts. They were remarkably soft. "Not there, dummy," she chided him. "Yet. Wait for the wedding." She slid down and managed to kiss him on the face. Then she was gone, flying for home, leaving him dazed. Had she been in fully human form, he would have freaked utterly out, but harpies weren't as freakable in that manner, any more than centaur fillies or nymphs.

"Bet she did that on purpose," Ted said zestfully. "She smacked his face."

But DeMonica was cannier. "On purpose, yes. Smack, no. She was making sure he wouldn't forget to marry her."

"Of course," Metria agreed, re-forming. "She's young, but a woman."

She certainly was. He was engaged to marry her, eventually. Umlaut's day did not let go of him for some time. He recovered awareness when day became night and it was time to camp. The children were gone; Metria must have taken them home.

He heard snoring, but it wasn't any of the others. So where was it coming from? He tried to stand up in the boat to look around better but discovered that his feet were asleep. *They* were doing the snoring. He should have known.

But with night came more mischief. There was the beat of hoofs on the ground, and two horses charged in, pursued by several human villagers with spears. Claire read the situation immediately: Those were Khan and Smuggler, new from Mundania. They came through the Region of Madness, and the men started hunting them. They didn't know what to do.

That snapped Umlaut the rest of the way back to reality. "The good dreams!" he exclaimed. "I mean, the loss of bad dreams. People are doing more bad things without fear of consequences. We have to stop them."

He went into ogre emulation and Sesame into dragon mode. They intercepted the men and drove them off. Then Sesame emulated an equine and reassured the horses that they were safe for the night. But stay clear of humans, she warned them. They might have been the horses' friends in Mundania, but they weren't here.

They had alleviated this problem, but what of the rest of Xanth? Umlaut knew that people must be getting worse all over. All because his news had caused the Night Stallion to depart for a time. He hoped the stallion returned soon, lest everything be ruined even before the Red Spot struck.

Next day they reached the Good Magician's Castle. This time there were no challenges; they were, after all, already performing a task for the Good Magician. Para swam across the moat and waddled into the castle.

Wira met them at the gate. "Why, Para," she said, "how nice to meet you again. And Claire Voyant." She turned to Umlaut. "You have delivered the letters already?" She could not see them, but surely she recognized the sound of Para's duck feet on the ground. How she had known who was in the boat Umlaut could only guess. Probably a sighted person had seen them coming and told her.

"Almost," Umlaut said. "I have one for the Good Magician himself."

"Oh, that's nice. I'll see if he's available. Here is the Gorgon." She disappeared into the gloom as they joined the Gorgon.

"It has been very busy here recently," the tall veiled woman confided. "Things are going wrong all over."

"I know," Umlaut said. "The bad dreams have stopped, and people are doing bad things."

"That is only part of it. Entirely inappropriate talents are being assigned to new babies." The little snakes that served in lieu of her hair wriggled, intriguing Sesame.

"How can any talent be inappropriate?"

She laughed. "How about the talent of breaking things, for the child of a family of egg and crystal polishers? Of making big balls of gas for the child of a mining family that must avoid gas? Of making things heavy for a flying centaur? Of projecting videos for a blind baby?"

Umlaut saw her point. "I guess it takes time to break in a Magician of Talents."

"But what about those children as they grow up with useless or dangerous talents? Can we afford to wait out that break-in process?"

"I don't, uh, know," Umlaut said unhappily.

Wira reappeared. "Magician Humfrey will see you now."

They followed her up the winding stairway to the gloomy, cramped den where the Good Magician sat hunched over his monstrous tome.

"Magician, Umlaut has a letter to deliver to you," Wira said. Then, privately to Umlaut: "He's very grumpy today. Don't say anything to annoy him."

The old gnomelike man glanced at her, and his sour features sweetened somewhat. "Give it here."

"Yes, Magician." Wira took the letter from Umlaut and handed it to the magician.

He paused to read it. "That woman has a problem." He turned pages of the Book of Answers. He found the place and read the Answer. "The clock is correct; it is Arjayess who is wrong."

Umlaut considered that Answer and wasn't satisfied. "Is a clock supposed to bong thirteen times in Mundania?"

"Of course not," Humfrey said. "There's no magic there, and Mundanes lack imagination. In Xanth there can be any number, but twelve is the limit there."

"But then what does the Answer mean?"

"It means she miscounted," Humfrey said, on the verge of a grump.

Umlaut remained uncertain. "Claire, is that right?"

Claire shrugged. She could not fathom the reality of a situation that wasn't close to her.

"Please, don't annoy him," Wira pleaded.

"But the letter," Umlaut said. "You can verify that. If she's wrong, then her letter must be wrong too."

Claire nodded and walked across the chamber. She jumped up onto the desk and sniffed the letter resting there.

"What is this?" Humfrey grouched.

But Claire had her answer: She did not miscount.

"She did not miscount," Umlaut repeated. "But that suggests that the Book of Answers is wrong!"

Claire sniffed the book and nodded: It was wrong. Wira, picking up the emanations, winced. How would it be possible to head off a calamitous grump if this continued?

"Ridiculous, Cat!" Humfrey snapped, his annoyance threatening to pass beyond mere grumps. "The Book of Answers is the final authority on everything."

But Umlaut trusted Claire's voyancy. "Ask it a Question to which you absolutely know the answer," he suggested. "Such as who is the Magician of Information?"

Humfrey was plainly on the verge of a volcanic grump but perhaps realized that the fastest way to get rid of this nuisance was to oblige him. He turned the pages and read: " 'Sorceress Iris.' "

There it was. "Not Magician Humfrey?"

Humfrey cogitated. He was very old, and his thoughts were slow and somewhat ossified, like his grumps, but in time they got there. "That Answer is wrong."

"So what you have there is a Book of Wrong Answers," Umlaut said. "How did that happen?"

"It couldn't happen," Humfrey grumped.

Yet obviously it had.

Claire had the answer: There was reverse wood under the book. "Reverse wood," Umlaut said, translating for her.

Humfrey pondered for a long moment, or perhaps two short moments, then slowly closed the book. There, where the cover had covered it, was a sliver of wood. "Take this away."

Wira came and picked up the sliver. Then she turned and walked into the wall. Oops, the wood had reversed her sense of direction, or her mental layout of the castle, and she had gone the wrong way. Of course.

"I can't find my way out," Wira said.

"Maybe you can put it where it will reverse something that needs reversing," Umlaut said. He looked at the shelves behind the Good Magician and saw a bottle labeled CONCENTRATED STINK HORN EXTRACT. That would surely be Xanth's worst smell. He fetched it down and took it to Wira. "In here." He turned the cork in the bottle.

"Don't open that!" Wira cried.

She was too late. Concentrated utter stench oozed from the bottle and began to spread in an ugly little cloud. Umlaut quickly took the sliver of reverse wood and slid it into the bottle, then jammed the cork back in.

The label changed: DIFFUSE SWEET ROSE INTRACT. The wood had reversed the contents of the bottle. Umlaut set it back on the shelf.

But meanwhile the cloud of stench was diffusing and expanding. It smirched Umlaut's arm, making it look ogreish. Then it touched Wira's hair, making it look as if she had just worked two years in dragon manure without even thinking of washing. Then it reached their noses.

Umlaut couldn't remember when he had smelled a worse stink. The fetor was so rank it transcended mere malodor and reeked to low hell. It gave the very concept of foul a puny name. Could saving Xanth possibly be worth this putrid odor? The others were quietly choking. He had forgotten that actions had consequences, and this was one such.

Then Umlaut got another notion. He grabbed the bottle again and twisted out the cork. The divine diffuse rose smell wafted out and spread, nullifying the corruption. Soon they were able to breathe free again.

"Thank you," Humfrey said.

Wira wobbled. Umlaut caught her before she fainted from the shock. He understood her problem: It was the first time she had heard the Good Magician say those words to a visitor. She hadn't known it was possible.

"You're welcome," Umlaut said, pleased. He had accomplished something worthwhile. That was rare.

19

RORRIM

The Gorgon met them downstairs. "You must be just about done with your deliveries," she remarked.

"I have just one more letter," Umlaut agreed. He brought it out. "To Rorrim. I have no idea who that is."

"Then how can you deliver it?"

"Sammy can find—"

Immediately the cat took off. But Claire's warning mew caught him again in midleap, and he dropped to the floor.

The Gorgon nodded. "You manage him very well," she remarked.

Claire shrugged. It was a matter of course.

"Why did you stop him?" Umlaut asked.

Because the situation was devious, she replied.

"I love devious situations," the Gorgon said. "I remember when Humfrey tackled the Demon Xanth to get his former wife Rose of Roogna back and wound up with five and a half wives. We are still enduring the complications of that."

"What's devious about this?" Umlaut asked.

Read the letter, Claire suggested.

"Oh, uh, yes." He opened it and read:

GLASSCO IMAGERY

RORRIM:

Your actions are outrageous! Magic mirror, indeed! You have been successful in keeping yourself hidden from us for many a long year and have deceived multitudes of innocent creatures.

No longer will we watch worlds in vain. Your presence in the land called Xanth has been discovered by a young Mundane woman. During the time she—but no, this information is not, I think, for your knowledge. Just could not resist the publicity, could you? Vain, strutting peacock!

From this day forth it will be impossible to stay concealed. The item you stole from us to enhance your image shall be removed. This substance is extremely powerful, and once stripped of it you will revert to your ordinary appearance for eternity.

Your time of concealment is through. We want what is rightfully ours, and rest assured, we *will* retrieve it. We will arrive soon and bring you back to await trial. Know too that your accomplices will be apprehended in due course.

Appointed Elders and Council of
GLASSCO IMAGERY

Umlaut looked up. "That's no friendly missive."

"It certainly isn't," the Gorgon agreed. "And it looks as though Rorrim is a magic mirror, or at least associates with one. That narrows the options somewhat. There are only so many of those in Xanth."

"But if Sammy can find the right one, we shouldn't have a problem," Umlaut said.

No, Claire clarified. The moment he tried to deliver the letter, Rorrim would flee instantly to another mirror.

"But how can I catch him, then?"

Claire sniffed the letter. The Glassco folk were from a far region. They could track magic when it was used. That was how they discovered that Rorrim had come to Xanth. But they couldn't zero in specifically as long as he stayed put. So they sent the letter to rout him out. If Umlaut found him and delivered it, they would know his location. If he forced Rorrim to flee, they would know his location within five mirrors. If he traveled a second time, they would nail him right there. So he could flee Umlaut only once; then he must remain put, because he feared Glassco more than anything else.

"Why is he limited to mirrors?"

Claire gave him a *stupid human* stare and answered: He was an aspect of a magic mirror. He changed it to broaden its power. An ordinary magic mirror reflected reality, one place or another. In Mundania a mirror's magic was limited to reflecting here and now. In Xanth it reflected other places too so could be used to communicate or discover hidden reality. Rorrim refracted, showing many possible realities and times, so could be used to see futures. But he had no substance aside from that magic; he had to reside in a magic mirror or perish.

"That's amazing," Umlaut said.

It was all part of the situation of the letter, Claire clarified. But that should have been obvious regardless, since Rorrim was mirror spelled backward.

Umlaut's jaw dropped. "I never thought of that!"

She switched her tail. Well, he was human.

So he was. "So Rorrim will flee before I can deliver the letter, and go to another magic mirror. How can we know which one?"

"We can narrow it down," the Gorgon said. "There are only five we know of in Xanth, and those must be all, because Humfrey would know if there were more. The one here at the Good Magician's Castle, the one at Castle Roogna, at Castle Zombie, the Nameless Castle, and Castle Maidragon."

"We're here, and we've been to Castle Roogna and Castle Zombie," Umlaut said. "But I never heard of the other two."

"The Nameless Castle is where Nimby and Chlorine live now. It floats on a cloud over Xanth, constantly changing its location. That's obviously where Rorrim will go. So go ahead and try to deliver your letter here, then we'll help you reach the Nameless Castle."

"Uh, okay, I guess," Umlaut said with his usual certainty. "Where—"

Sammy resumed motion. They followed him to another chamber where a mirror hung on the wall. It looked ordinary, but of course that was deceptive.

"Rorrim," Umlaut said. "I have a letter to—"

There was a flicker in the glass. He was gone, Claire indicated with a flick of her tail.

Umlaut didn't question that; it had been expected. "Now how do we get to the Nameless Castle?"

"You don't," the Gorgon said.

"But—"

"I spoke loud enough for Rorrim to hear. Since he figures you'll look at the Nameless Castle, naturally he's gone to Castle Maidragon."

Umlaut felt even duller than usual, which was an effort. "Why?"

"So you won't find him, of course. Not without considerable loss of time, which could make all the difference. After all, you could lose the letter, or change your mind."

"I won't—"

"I hope not. Now, do you know where Castle Maidragon is?"

"I guess Sammy can find it."

"To be sure. Let me give you something to eat along the way as you travel."

Umlaut finally figured out the rest of his objection. "What about Castle Roogna and Castle Zombie? Why couldn't he be there?"

"Because the three little princesses are at the first, and they would quickly catch on to his nature and ruin his anonymity. The zombies are at the second, and he won't like the way they clean him off with liquid putrefaction. Castle Maidragon, in contrast, is clean and private. It's his only satisfactory choice."

"That must be right," Umlaut agreed. "Thank you for your logic. It's so much better than mine."

Her little snakes writhed with pleasure. "Let me get those goodies." She left.

Soon they were on their way, the boat stocked with Gorgonzola cheese and assorted breads and pastries. Umlaut concluded that he liked the Gorgon.

It was some distance south, and they had to spend a night on the trail. They stopped at a camping site, ate, washed, and settled in a giant nest to sleep. Sesame curled around it, her body forming a pillow for Umlaut. Para preferred to float on the surface of a passing stream, and the two cats disappeared into the night on feline business.

"Umlaut."

He woke with a start. That was Surprise's voice. He quickly climbed out of the nest, not disturbing Sesame, and looked around in the darkness. "Surprise."

"Oh, Umlaut, I'm so glad I found you!" she said, hugging him. Her body was surprisingly bouncy.

"How did you come here? I thought you couldn't repeat talents."

"This time I took the form of a nymph," she said. "That's not the same as a harpy. Here, feel me." She took his hand and passed it along her body, and he almost freaked out. It was definitely nymphly.

"I, uh, thought the talent was of assuming another form. Any other form."

"No, each different form counts as another talent," she said. "Now come with me; I have made a wonderful bower."

"Bower?" he asked dully. "What for?"

"To summon the stork in, of course. Come on." She tugged on his hand.

"But I thought you didn't know how to do that."

"Nymphs know how. When I assumed this form, suddenly I knew. I am eager to celebrate with you."

"Celebrate," he repeated, remembering the way the fauns and nymphs of the Faun & Nymph Retreat had hugged and kissed. It had certainly looked like fun.

"Yes, we'll do it again and again," she said eagerly. "We'll have such fun."

Something bothered him about this, but when he tried to hold back, she kissed him again and set his hand on her bare bottom. This time he did freak out, for when he came to, they were well away from the camp and coming to her bower.

But the botheration remained. "Surprise, I don't think we ought to do this yet. We agreed to wait until you were of age."

"Oh, pooh! I decided not to wait. No one will know." She tugged him onward through the darkness.

Then she collided with something. "Eeeek!" she screamed in perfect nymphly manner, flinging her hair about. "What is this?"

There was a hiss. Umlaut recognized it. "Sesame!"

"What are you doing here?" Surprise demanded. "This is private. Get out of the way."

But Sesame continued to block their way. She hissed again, and Umlaut recognized what she was saying: How had Surprise gotten across the Gap Chasm?

That made Umlaut pause. As a harpy, she had been able to fly across it, if she had to cross it. But as a nymph she couldn't do that. So he repeated the question. "Sesame wants to know how you crossed the Gap Chasm."

"I used the invisible bridge, of course. Now get out of here, you constrictor."

"You what?" Umlaut asked.

"Snake, python, viper, reptile—"

"Serpent?"

"Whatever," she agreed crossly.

A dim bulb glowed, brushing back the darkness for a moment. "Hello, Metria."

"Oh, bleep! What gave me away?"

Now that he had confirmed his sudden suspicion, Umlaut found a number of prior indications. "I think different forms don't count as different talents, so you couldn't be Surprise. And it would have taken you all night to get here from there, with no time left over to make a bower. And Surprise would never try to entrap me like that."

"Try to what you?"

"Entice, allure, beguile, debauch, tempt—"

"Seduce?"

"Whatever," he agreed crossly.

"So you might as well let me do it, since she won't. You have no idea how much fun it can be." She tried to tug him onward again.

"But I wouldn't do it with you," he protested.

"Let's find out." She embraced him again, trying to kiss

him while she wriggled her remarkably plush body against him.

Such was the evocative power of that body, he found himself tempted. He didn't know exactly how such celebration occurred but was extremely curious.

Sesame hissed again, distracting him. Beware the bower, she said.

"But that's where we can do it most comfortably," the demoness protested. "Come on, it's right here. If you don't like it, you can go back to your camp."

That seemed fair. He started to walk forward.

Sesame flung herself at him, pushing him back. Do not go there!

"But she says she'll let me go if I don't like it."

It is beside a thyme plant.

"A thyme plant?"

It changed time in its vicinity, she explained. A year might seem like an hour.

Suddenly it clicked into place. "If I go there, I'll never deliver the last letter!"

"Oh, fudge," Metria swore and dissipated into a very cross cloud of smoke.

Umlaut realized that he had had a really close call. "Thank you, Sesame," he said, hugging her.

It is what a friend is for, she said, wriggling.

Then they made their way back to the camp. Sesame led, being able to see better in the darkness than he could.

They retired to the nest and settled again for sleep. But then he heard something else. It was a faint call. "Umlaut!"

"Go away, Metria," he said. "I'm on to you."

"Metria! Has she been annoying you again?"

"You know you have. Trying to lead me into that thyme plant. Go away."

"Umlaut, this is Surprise! How can I convince you?"

He began to doubt. "Tell me exactly how we met." Because that had been in Euphoria, with no magic, so Metria couldn't have been there or seen it.

"You were walking along the path, eyes downcast. I was standing there, but you didn't see me. You were looking for someone small. I said, 'Hello, I'm up here,' and then you saw me and were embarrassed, so I kissed you."

But then he remembered that he had challenged her that way before and gotten the same answer. That time she had been genuine, but Metria might have overheard that and used it this time. He needed another way.

"Okay, Surprise. You're you. Let's summon the stork together."

"Umlaut!" she cried. "We can't do that!"

He was satisfied. "It *is* you. I knew the real you wouldn't do it."

"Actually, that's not quite it."

"What?"

"I couldn't do that now. But if I could, I'd be tempted."

"You mean if you were of age?"

"I mean if I were in a real nymphly body."

"But I was only trying to be sure you weren't Demoness Metria. She'd have agreed instantly."

"I know. And I don't want her to fool you. But you need a better test."

Umlaut was uneasy. "How did you get here this time? I thought you had run out of options."

"Not quite. I'm here in ectoplasm."

"In what?"

"It's a magical substance a person can send out, thicker than a soul, that can float and shape itself into different things. It looks weird, so it's better in the dark. I'm using it to talk to you, but I'd rather you didn't see me."

"But if you're really you—"

"I'm really me, but at the moment I would look like hanging intestines. So I don't want you to see me or touch me, just talk with me. I love you."

"And I love you," he said. "But—"

"Are you sure I shouldn't take some aging elixir? So we can marry now?"

"I'm not sure," he admitted. "But I think it's better to wait. If we can manage it."

"I suppose so," she agreed reluctantly. "But I'll be very disappointed if something prevents it, after all that waiting."

"Yes. But we can stay in touch, if we find a way."

"I really am about out of ways to get to you."

"How about a magic mirror? So we could talk to each other?"

"That would take two mirrors, and ordinary folk like us can't get even one."

He sighed. "I guess it was one of my usual stupid ideas. Maybe your folks will let me visit you in Euphoria."

"I like your stupid ideas; they're always nice. Now I have to go, before my ectoplasm dissipates. Lie still and I'll kiss you slightly. Don't move."

He lay still and felt a faint, light, soft touch on his lips. She had touched him with her ectoplasm. Then she was gone; he could feel her absence.

He just *had* to find a way to be with her more often and longer. But he couldn't think of it.

In the morning they resumed travel. Their journey was uneventful, and that made Umlaut uneasy. This was the last letter delivery, and Demoness Metria would be determined to stop it. What would she try next? Would she manifest as a horrendous monster, or try to plant a detour sign to lead them astray, or make another attempt to seduce him away from his mission? He was sure there would be something, and he wanted to see it, identify it, and nullify it, rather than be uncertain about it. But there was nothing.

Sammy showed them to Castle Maidragon. It was hidden in deep jungle, with the path to it barely showing; obviously few folk visited it. Umlaut seemed not to be the only person who hadn't heard of it. It was thoroughly obscure, which of course made it an excellent place for an errant magic mirror, or aspect of one, to hide.

In the afternoon they reached it. The castle was beautiful, with towers and turrets galore, and multiple levels with stairways and walls. It would be possible to get lost in such a castle. In fact it looked like fun. There was a faint aroma of chocolate in its vicinity.

Then they saw the dragon. It was racing around the castle on a well-worn track. There was no moat, but that hardly seemed to be necessary, considering the dragon. It had bright green scales tinged purple at the tips and folded wings. So it seemed to be a flying dragon that preferred to run on land to guard the castle, somewhat the way a moat monster confined itself to the limited water of a moat.

Para halted, and Sesame slithered forward to meet the dragon, who paused for the encounter. They sniffed noses and wriggled.

Then Sesame returned to explain: The dragon was Becka, daughter of Draco Dragon and a nymph. The castle belonged to the three little princesses, and Becka was caretaking it for them. She normally did not let strangers into the castle, but she knew Sammy Cat so would admit them on his authority.

Para approached the dragon, and it changed into a girl of his own age. She was cute, with blonde hair and brown eyes, and her dress was of green scales with purple tinges. "Why, hello," she said, spying Umlaut.

He got out of the boat. "I, uh, am Umlaut. I have to deliver a letter to Rorrim."

"No one by that name lives here," Becka said.

"He's a, uh, magic mirror, or an aspect of one. We think he came here to avoid receiving this letter."

"Why would anyone want to avoid a letter?"

"It's not a nice letter. Someone is looking for him and will find him when the letter is delivered. He doesn't want to be found."

"Then why deliver it?"

"Because that's my job. Uh, the Good Magician told me to deliver all the letters and I would find out how to save Xanth from the Red Spot, and this is the last one."

Becka blinked. "I'm not sure I understand all of that. But maybe I don't need to. It does sound important. Come in; the magic mirror's on the wall of the office chamber."

"Uh, thank you." They followed her inside the castle.

Becka turned to Umlaut. "I like you. Are you taken?"

"Uh, yes," he said, disconcerted. There was that odd appeal of his again. Klutzy as he was, girls still liked him.

"Too bad. Who is the lucky girl?"

"Surprise Golem."

"Her? I didn't know she was old enough."

"Uh, she's not, uh, yet. But we'll wait. I love her."

"Para, let me show you where our pool is," Becka said to the boat. "Your feet must be tired." She glanced at the others.

"I'll be back in a moment to show you to the communications room."

She was embarrassed, Claire indicated. So she had to get away from Umlaut to compose herself.

They waited in the main receiving chamber. This castle seemed to be very well appointed, considering that it was hidden in the middle of nowhere. The cats found a couch to lie down on, concluding that Umlaut would rather let Becka show him to the mirror. Actually if it wasn't for Surprise, he would have been quite interested. But of course she was a dragon girl, which complicated things. He wasn't sure he would want to keep company with a girl who could change forms and chomp him at any time. But of course that could be one of Surprise's talents too; it didn't matter that she could not repeat, once would be more than enough. So he took a chair and waited.

Sesame had serpentine curiosity, so she slithered around the room, then explored the adjacent chamber. In almost a moment she hissed: Come here.

Umlaut went to her. There on the wall was the mirror. He had had no idea it was so close; it had sounded as if it was more complicated to find.

"Hello, Rorrim," he said, bringing out the letter.

HELLO UMLAUT the mirror printed, much in the manner of Com Pewter.

"I think you can't flee anymore, so now I'll deliver the letter to you. Sorry about that."

YOU HAVE CAUGHT ME FOUL AND CUBED. GIVE ME THE MISSILE.

"The what?"

NOTE, MESSAGE, STATEMENT, COMMUNICATION, EPISTLE—

"Missive?"

WHATEVER, the mirror printed crossly.

"Hello, Metria. I wondered when you would show up again."

CURSES! FOILED AGAIN. The mirror dissolved into smoke.

"It almost worked this time. If I had given you the letter, I guess you would have taken it away, never to be seen again, and so the final delivery would not have been made."

The smoke formed into the shapely demoness. "Something like that," she agreed. "And I would have saved my little boy."

That made him feel guilty. She had been little but trouble for him, but he understood her devotion to her son. And really, Demon Ted was not all that bad. "I've got to try to save Xanth," he said somewhat lamely.

"You're a decent guy. That's your problem."

Becka appeared in the doorway. "Oh, there you are, Umlaut. And D. Metria, what are you doing here?"

"It's a complicated story," Metria said, fading sadly out.

Becka led them through devious winding passages to the real mirror. "I hardly ever use this," she said. "Mainly when Princess Ivy buzzes me to let me know the three little princesses are coming. It's their castle, and they like to play here. It's amazing what they can do with their magic."

"They made this in play?"

"They did make this castle, but when they were older."

That didn't make much sense to Umlaut, but he didn't want to admit that he had missed something, so he didn't. "That's nice."

"First they made it in chocolate. Then they made it in stone, larger."

This hardly made more sense. "I smelled the chocolate."

"And here's the mirror." She indicated it on the wall.

Umlaut, Sesame, and the two cats drew up before the mirror. "Hello, Rorrim," Umlaut said.

The glass flickered, but no print appeared.

Claire stepped forward. This was the real mirror, she indicated. She understood his situation. Rorrim wanted to bargain with him.

"I just want to deliver the letter and be done with it."

Rorrim says that he is prepared to offer you his services, if you do not deliver the letter to him.

"Why should I want his services?"

"This is an interesting dialogue," Becka said.

Rorrim says he can show you your future of one year hence. That is what he is tuned to. Only his former master, Glassco, can tune him to any other range of time. But a year is good enough to enable you to have the best possible life.

"I don't understand. What's going to happen is going to happen. What good would it be to see a year ahead?"

The future is not fixed, it is mutable. What you do now can change it significantly. Rorrim can show you the result of your present actions, so that you can select the very best future for yourself. Because it continues to be mutable, he can continue to guide you in this manner, so that you will never need to make a bad mistake.

Umlaut had not anticipated such a dialogue, but it was becoming interesting, as Becka said. He made mistakes all the time and felt stupid about it. It would be nice to be able to avoid that. Still, he had a job to do. "No thanks."

He wants to show you a sample, Claire continued.

Umlaut shrugged. He did want to be fair. "All right."

You can do one of two things right now. You can give him the letter, and he will soon be captured and reduced to servile status. Or you can decline to give him the letter, and he will enable you to have your best futures. Here is your scene a year hence, if you accept his offer.

A scene appeared in the mirror. It showed Umlaut walking with Surprise. They were holding hands, and a little cloud of floating hearts surrounded them.

"I like that," Umlaut admitted.

Here is your scene if you decline his offer.

The image shrank to fill one third of the mirror. The rest of it was blank.

"I don't understand," Umlaut said, disturbed.

Neither does Rorrim, exactly, Claire indicated. Usually his images are clear. It seems that if you decline, you will soon face another choice, and that leads to three futures, two of which are blank. It may be that you will cease to exist.

That gave Umlaut a pang. He had faced that specter before. "I will likely be killed?"

That is not clear. If you die, your grave should show, and it doesn't. Maybe you are transported far away, beyond Xanth, where you cannot be tracked. It is odd; Rorrim has not seen this kind of ambiguity before. As far as he can tell, you will make some kind of decision that will lead to one of the two blanks, but someone else will try to act to give you the third. It will not be under your control. He needs to be closer to the "now" to tune properly to "then"—a year thereafter. But all that risk can be avoided if you accept his deal now.

Umlaut thought about being certain to have Surprise with him a year down the path. He certainly wanted that! But what, then, of Xanth? The other choice must be the one that showed how to save Xanth. Maybe it was only a third of a chance, but still, Xanth needed to be saved. How could not delivering the letter save Xanth? So he suspected that Rorrim was faking that.

"What about the others?" he demanded. "Sesame, Para, Sammy, Claire? Where are they a year from now?"

The mirror clouded, then showed another split screen. In half was swirling chaos; in the other half were two views of Sesame. In one she was frolicking in a moat with Soufflé; in the other she was still confined to the Castle Zombie dungeon.

This is beyond my fathoming, Claire indicated. Apparently your present decision can throw Sesame into chaos or into another choice between good and bad. She cannot affect this herself; it depends on you.

This was confusing, and not comfortable. "Try Sammy."

Again the split screen, with chaos on one side, two views of Sammy on the other. In one he was twining tails with Claire; in the other, he was alone, looking bored and unhappy.

This too is outside my range, Claire indicated. I think he meets me in only one future. That is, he has met me in one and never met me in the other. Which is odd, since he has already met me. How can the future change the past?

"I don't know," Umlaut said.

Rorrim says you don't need to gamble. Make the agreement with him, and he will enable you to track the futures of your friends also, so that they will go neither to chaos nor loneliness.

That really tempted Umlaut. But it didn't answer how Xanth could be saved if he did not deliver the letter. "I am here because Xanth is threatened by Jupiter's giant hurled Red Spot, and delivering these letters will somehow show how to solve that problem. You show no problem if I deal with you. How can that be?"

Rorrim says he does not know. He just sees the future, and there is no problem unless you don't make the deal. So you should make it.

Umlaut's head was spinning. He turned to Becka. "What do you think? Can I believe this mirror?"

"I don't think so," Becka answered. "Rorrim wants to save his own hide, or glass, or whatever, so he's bound to tell you that his way is best."

Rorrim says he is telling the truth, Claire indicated. He can't fake images of the future; he must show only what is there. He doesn't think there *is* a threat to Xanth, at least not by the Red Spot.

"But he could be lying about his inability to fake images."

Claire shook her head. He is not lying, nor is he misinformed. The truth is merely too complicated for him to grasp, and for us too. There is something here that is larger than we are.

That set Umlaut back in another way. "There's been something funny about me all along. I can't remember my past life, and Dawn and Eve said I wasn't alive or dead. Sometimes I wonder whether I really exist."

There was a soundless, sightless looming. Something horrendous was on the verge of happening.

"Maybe you had just better do the right thing," Becka suggested. "Whatever it is."

Umlaut nodded. "If there is something wrong about me, at least I can do what I set out to do. And that is to deliver the letter." He held it out. "Rorrim, here is your letter. Take it." He touched the envelope to the surface of the mirror.

Then everything changed.

20

DECISIONS

Umlaut stood in the center of a large stage. Before him were three scintillating entities and a beautiful woman. Offstage was a huge and empty auditorium with space for hundreds of people. He had no idea how he had come here or what this was all about.

"It has been decided," the lovely woman said. "The icon delivered all the letters before confirming his nonexistence. Demoness Fornax does not acquire the Land of Xanth, and her contraterrene equivalent is transferred to our possession. Demon Jupiter's motivating mock threat of the Red Spot is withdrawn. We have only details to conclude at this point."

This was utterly weird. "Who are you?" Umlaut asked. "What's going on here?"

Demoness Fornax formed into the aspect of D. Metria. "How cute, it talks."

"Abolish it," Demon Jupiter said. "Its usefulness is done."

"Spoken like a Demon without a conscience," the woman said. She turned to Umlaut. "I am Chlorine, speaking for Nimby, otherwise known as the Demon Xanth." A second scintillation formed into a donkey-headed dragon. "Demon Jupiter made a wager with Demoness Fornax, and you were crafted to decide it. Had you failed to deliver all the letters, or had you verified your own nonexistence before completing that chore, Demoness Fornax would have won, and the Land of Xanth would have been turned over to her for vivisection. I believe that answers your two questions. Have you anything else to say before being dissolved?"

"Dissolved?" he asked numbly.

"You do not exist. You are merely a construct with certain characteristics put into play for the purpose of deciding the issue. Your name signals that: It means a mark used to show that a vowel has a different sound. You look like a person, but you have a different reality. You are more apparent than real."

Suddenly his worst fear had been confirmed. He had no memory of his past because he *had* no past. The two princesses had not been able to classify him because he had no classification. He did not truly exist.

Yet he was here, for the moment. "What about the others?"

"You are the only one."

"I mean my friends, and the people I, uh, interacted with. What happens to them now?"

"Why, they go about their business as usual. Unlike you, they exist."

Umlaut was having trouble organizing his case, but he was used to that. He plowed on. "But I affected them. I changed their lives, maybe only in little ways, but they have those experiences and memories. What happens if I disappear?"

Chlorine turned to Nimby. "He has a point. How can his associates deal with his nonexistence?"

The dragon wiggled a donkey ear. "Very well," Chlorine said. She turned back to Umlaut. "You may decide. Either those experiences can be subtracted, so that the others never interacted with you, and you will have retroactive nonexistence. Or they can be confirmed, so that the others do remember and their lives remain changed, only without your presence. Which do you prefer?"

Either way, he was gone. He remained too numbed to be completely surprised or dismayed. But he did care about his friends and wanted them to have a fair say in the matter. "*They* should decide. It's their lives."

Chlorine glanced at Nimby again. He wiggled the other ear. "Very well," she said. "They shall decide."

Suddenly the auditorium was filled with folk. Many of them were familiar to Umlaut, but most were not. Most of them looked somewhat surprised; they must have been minding their own businesses and suddenly found themselves here. "I didn't, uh, interact with all these."

"Chain reaction," Chlorine explained. "The ones you knew personally then affected others in an expanding ripple effect. By the time it runs its course, a significant portion of the population of the Land of Xanth is affected."

"I, uh, see." Now he spied Sesame Serpent in the front row, and Sammy Cat next to Claire Voyant, and Para Boat. They gazed at him encouragingly, now understanding his nature.

Chlorine faced the audience. "This person, Umlaut, was crafted to represent the Demon Jupiter in a contest with Demoness Fornax. That contest has now been concluded in Jupiter's favor. Umlaut exists only for the moment, having no past and no future. You are here to decide the extent of your interactions with him. How do all of you feel? Do you prefer to retain your direct or indirect experience with this nonexistent man, or to have it deleted so that you are unchanged from your former state, in this respect? You will indicate your preferences by turning green for keeping it, or red for deleting it."

The people considered. Umlaut recognized tall Cory and short Tessa, whom he had kissed, and Breanna of the Black Wave, and Princesses Dawn and Eve. There were the little half demons Ted and Monica, with their parents, and Tristan Troll, seated uncomfortably between Terian and Tacy. There were six brutish bullies and six eager girls. There were the three little princesses beside Becka the dragon girl. There were Wira, and Caitlin, and Anathe Ma. Everybody with whom he had interacted, and many more. They all consulted among themselves, and soon a consensus developed: They wanted to retain their experiences. First a few turned green, then more, and finally a green wave spread across the audience. Only his four friends in the front row remained uncolored, but they would have to go with the majority.

"That can't be right," Umlaut said, troubled. "There were significant changes made because of me. What about the loss of bad dreams?"

"You mean you were responsible for that?" a voice cried from the audience. It was Mela Merwoman, wearing legs. "All those mean goblins jumping in the water and trying to grab my tail, because they know they won't be punished in their sleep?"

"Well, uh—"

"So it's your fault my wife has been so irritable recently," a man who must have been Prince Naldo Naga said. "You should be abolished!"

"But I was just trying to do my job."

"What job?"

"The one that Good Magician Humfrey—"

"So is he here too?" Naldo demanded.

"Yes," Magician Humfrey answered from another section of the audience.

"So there you are!" another man exclaimed, forging toward the Good Magician. "I hereby arrest you for obstructing justice."

Umlaut stared and so did half the audience. "You are Detective Patrick," Humfrey said, as he tended to know such things. "You did not get your Answer because you refused to give a year's service."

"I didn't owe you any year!" the detective protested. "I was investigating a crime. You made me go through three stupid challenges, and then you wanted to charge me for the Answer." He closed on Humfrey.

"You can't arrest the Good Magician," a veiled woman cried.

"Who the bleep are you?" the detective demanded.

"I am his wife, the Gorgon." She touched her veil. "Take one step more and I will remove my veil and look at you."

Now there was riotous chaos in the auditorium. Most folk knew that the Gorgon's direct stare stoned whatever she looked at. "Don't do it!" Umlaut cried. "There are too many others here to make it safe."

Several rabbits appeared, jumping in every direction. "What's this?" the Gorgon asked.

"The thought of you lifting your veil is a hare-raising event," Humfrey explained.

Another man stepped forward. He was young, with blond-tipped brown hair and hazel eyes. "Let me handle it," he said, unlimbering a thin club.

"And who the bleep are *you*?" the detective demanded as before.

"I am Beau. I don't think you should be such a bad loser. The Good Magician doesn't have to do your job for you."

"You can't intimidate me," the detective said. "I represent the law!" He reached for Humfrey.

Beau touched the detective with the club. Suddenly the man tore off his own clothing.

"What are you doing?" a woman demanded, shrinking away from the detective. Umlaut recognized her as Mouse Terian, Com Passion's beautiful mouse in human form, whom he had noticed before. "This is indecent exposure."

But in the process of retreating, she brushed against Beau's club. Then she tore off her own clothing. This drew considerable additional attention. Terian changed into her mouse form and scurried away under the chairs. Dozens of girls and women screamed vigorously, projecting healthy *eeeeek*s. There was more jostling as others tried both to move away and to get a better view. Then more of them were removing their clothing.

"The club!" someone cried. "What's the club?"

"It is a strip club," Beau said. "It makes people strip. That's why it is so effective as a way to break up aggression."

"This is all up in a, uh, heaval," Umlaut said, turning to Chlorine. "Can you—?"

Chlorine glanced at Nimby, who wiggled an ear.

Then the audience was as it had been a few minutes before, with every person in place. The detective was wearing a gag.

"This all started with the loss of bad dreams," Umlaut said. "Maybe, uh—"

Nimby wiggled an ear. "The bad dreams have been restored," Chlorine said.

"Then there's the mixed-up talents—"

Chlorine's eyes almost (but not quite) rolled. "There has hardly been time for such a problem to appear. Talents don't manifest until children are old enough to use them."

"But we have ways of knowing," a woman cried from the audience. "There are seers who can tell."

"Is anyone complaining?"

"Me mad! Me had," an ogress exclaimed. It turned out that her just-delivered ogret had been given the talent of accommodation, so that he would be able to find peaceful ways to help himself, such as using a stink horn as a defense. The problem was that ogres were supposed to be very strong and stupid, so they preferred to solve problems with ham-fists. A talent of accommodation would be an embarrassment to an ogre. It was definitely awkward.

Then a demoness gave her objection: Her half-mortal child had been given the talent of exorcising demons. How would she ever be able to take care of him when he reached brat age? How would he ever get along with his demon relatives?

A goblin was furious: His son had the talent of unknowingly helping those in need. What kind of a disgustingly nice pantywaist would he grow up to be?

A mermaid called out from her tank of water. "All my family have the talent of lovely, seductive singing," she said. "But yesterday the stork delivered my daughter with the talent of summoning any kind of cheese."

"So your fishy brat got the talent my cub should have had," a mouse/woman crossbreed cried. "What's mine going to do with lovely singing?"

"And what about mine?" a lovely creature said. She was a voluptuous woman from the front but hollow from behind. "She'll be a woodwife, like me, destined to seduce unwary men. She got the talent of making herself and others sneeze. I have had to name her Gazun Tite. She'll never make it!"

Umlaut tried to picture a seductive forest creature tempting a man who sneezed violently every time he tried to approach her. He tried not to laugh, knowing it was a serious matter to the woodwife.

Soon the audience was back up in a heaval. Nimby had to wiggle his ear again, and revert it, and see to the reassignment of talents. But he looked as though he were becoming impatient. Umlaut felt even more guilty than usual; all this had happened because of events he had set in motion.

"So are we satisfied now?" Chlorine inquired of the audience.

The people did not seem completely satisfied, but they decided that things were now tolerable. Greenness spread.

Then a new spot of redness showed. "I have a question," Tessa said.

"Stand up," Chlorine said.

"I *am* standing."

There was a murmur of mirth. That bothered Umlaut. "How short or tall a person is shouldn't be cause for humor," he said. "She has something to say."

The murmur subsided. "What is your concern?" Chlorine asked.

"You said something about a contraterrene equivalent to Xanth. I just wondered whether that could be where we sidestep."

The faces of the audience were generally blank, but Umlaut remembered how Cory and Tessa had led them through an alternate realm. Could their magic be addressing the land Fornax had had?

Chlorine glanced at Fornax.

"Yes," the Demoness said. "Two of your creatures possess magic to provide access without instant destruction. You will want to employ them in that capacity now that it is yours to colonize."

Umlaut looked at Tessa. "I think the two of you will have a very important job soon."

Nimby wiggled an ear. "That is true," Chlorine said.

Both Cory and Tessa flushed, looking forward to it.

"Very well," Chlorine said. She turned back to Umlaut. "Have you any concluding statement to make before the decision is implemented?"

"I, uh—" But he found himself at a loss for words, as was usual when there was anything significant to say.

"Now just half a moment!" It was an exclamation from the audience. One person stood apart, flaring red. Umlaut saw with a flare of joy that it was Surprise. Of course she was here too!

"Surprise Golem, you have an exception to note," Chlorine said.

"Yes! I'm in love with Umlaut. How can you just—just *dissolve* him? You will make me a widow, and we haven't even been married yet. Where does that leave me?" She dabbed at her face with a hank of her hair.

"You do have the individual option of deleting your experience with him," Chlorine pointed out. "That way you will not suffer."

"While everyone else remembers?" Surprise demanded tearfully. "They'll tell me, and then I'll know what I never had. How can you do that to me?"

Now Sesame turned red, and so did Claire. They agreed with Surprise. Several other members of the audience went from green to normal, changing their minds.

Chlorine looked at Nimby. "We shouldn't balk love," she told him. "Remember how it was with us?"

"This is getting complicated," Demoness Fornax protested. "Secondary characters can't make decisions for the primary one."

"Then let the primary one decide," Demon Jupiter said, focusing his Red Spot on Umlaut. Umlaut realized belatedly that this explained another mystery: Rorrim had shown no threat to Xanth if Umlaut agreed to withhold the letter. That was because the threat, like Umlaut himself, had never been real. It had been there merely to motivate him to do his best. And delivery of the letters, or failure to deliver, would have settled the issue. That was how the letters related. So that assignment solved the problem. But if he hadn't delivered the letters, that would have given the victory to Fornax, and all Xanth would have suffered. There would have been chaos, or maybe that blank future. Unless Rorrim had a way to nullify that. Yet—

"Umlaut, the decision is yours," Chlorine said. "Should Surprise Golem remember you or forget you?"

"But I can't, uh, decide that," he said. "I don't want her to forget me, but I don't want her to suffer either. I don't want anyone to suffer on account of me."

"Of whom else are you thinking?" Chlorine asked.

"Well, uh, Sesame Serpent. She can't be with Soufflé Serpent because of his curse. They met because of me and will hurt if I go without enabling them to be together."

Soufflé, in the audience, turned red.

"Anyone else?" Chlorine asked, on the verge of impatience.

"Demoness Metria, her son's soul will be lost because of me. And Rorrim Mirror is losing his freedom. That's not right."

Two more red spots appeared in the audience: the real Metria, and Rorrim, propped in a chair. They were plainly amazed but appreciative.

"But they were opposing you," Chlorine pointed out.

"They were just doing what they had to do, and I messed them up. They should be set right too."

Chlorine's toe tapped the floor significantly. "Any others?"

He plowed stupidly ahead. "Well, yes, actually. What about Tristan Troll, cursed to be torn between two decent women? Gwenny Goblin, who can't find a suitable prince to marry. Gail Marie, who can't speak without the world pausing to listen. So many people have unfair problems, and I haven't helped them at all."

Chlorine looked at Nimby again. He wiggled an ear.

"The Demon Xanth, to get this settled, proffers you this choice: you to have continued existence so that Surprise is not bereaved, or all the others to have their problems resolved—abatement of curses, Demon Ted's soul saved, Rorrim's freedom retained, marriageable prince found, world no longer pausing to listen, and so on. Choose: your happiness or theirs."

Umlaut struggled, knowing that the attention of many was on him, especially of the four most concerned: Surprise, Sesame, Metria, and Rorrim. He could have existence and happiness with Surprise, or the others could have their problems solved. It was painful, but he knew what he had to do. "Help the others and give Surprise another man so that she can be happy without me."

"You just *had* to do the most decent thing!" Surprise said accusingly.

"I'm, uh, sorry," he said, feeling guilty.

"And I love you for it. But I can't let you go."

"The choice is not yours," Chlorine said, "except to accept or reject the decision with respect to yourself only." She looked at Sesame. "Do you accept?"

The serpent wriggled uncomfortably, looking at Umlaut. "Do it," he said. "It's the only way."

She nodded and slowly turned green. Then Soufflé slithered across to join her, and they twined tails, no longer cursed.

Chlorine turned to Metria. "Do you accept?"

The demoness held her son Ted to her bosom. "I have to." She turned green.

"It was a bluff, anyway," Fornax said. "A soul can't be taken; it must be given. I am inordinately curious about its nature, because it leads to such nonsensical situations."

"Even Umlaut's mere emulation of a soul leads to remarkable things," Jupiter said. "I am becoming curious about souls too."

"We should find a free one and split it for vivisection," Fornax said.

"True."

Chlorine turned to Rorrim. "Do you accept?"

The mirror turned green. Glassco would not have him.

"And you others," Chlorine said. "Do you accept?"

There was a flicker, then more green. All of them, however reluctantly, accepted. How could they do otherwise?

Now Chlorine turned to Surprise. "Do you accept?"

"No!"

"But you'll get another man," Umlaut said. "A real one you can keep and love, who maybe will be smart and not klutzy. It won't make any difference to me because I'll be gone. It's the most reasonable thing. I want you to be happy, with or without me."

"I know you do," she retorted. "You're so decent it gets sickening, but I'd rather be miserable with the memory of you than happy with someone else."

Umlaut spoke to Chlorine. "I can't stand to have her miserable. Maybe if you present the other man, she'll change her mind."

"I won't!"

Chlorine gazed at the audience. "Brusque Brassie, come forth."

The coppery figure stood and walked to the stage. Umlaut remembered him; he had worked with his younger siblings the ogret twins to free them from the spiderweb-covered valley when they had to deliver the letter to Tandy Nymph. He had helped, then departed, a good young part-ogre man. He was eighteen, and his talent was to make things hard and heavy, or soft and light. He was indeed an ideal young man.

"Would you like to have Surprise Golem as your girl-friend?"

"I don't know. What does she look like?"

"Surprise, come to the stage."

Reluctantly, Surprise came, her hair swirling lustrously about her. "This won't work," she muttered. "I don't care how handsome or talented he is. I love only Umlaut."

"Will she do?" Chlorine asked.

"Sure. She looks great."

He was right: Surprise, in her adamant bright red color, looked beautiful from her pert face to the end of her flowing hair. She was every inch a wonderful young woman.

"Well he do?" Chlorine asked Surprise.

"No!"

"Please, Surprise," Umlaut said, "give him a chance. He's a good man. He helped us out of a gully."

"Kiss him," Chlorine said.

"No!"

Nimby wiggled an ear. Surprise, abruptly compelled, stepped into Brusque, embraced him, and lifted her face to kiss him. They seemed like the perfect couple. Umlaut's heart ached, but he knew it was right. He could leave happiness behind him.

Then they separated. "She's not the one," Brusque said, turning away.

Jaws dropped across the audience. Chlorine waggled a forefinger at Surprise. "You used magic to turn him off."

"Darn. I hoped you wouldn't notice."

Umlaut had to admire her pluck. She had used up one more talent so as to preserve herself for him. But that would merely lead her into heartbreak. He was trying to give her up so she could be happy, and she was refusing to accept it.

"We can negate it." Chlorine glanced at Brusque, who remained standing, apparently not able to return to the audience until given Demon leave.

"Then it wouldn't be my decision."

Chlorine glanced again at Nimby. "There are things to be admired about this young woman. Can we give her more of a choice?"

Nimby wiggled an ear. Chlorine turned back to Surprise. "Serious choices have consequences. Particularly when they relate to Demons. You may accept everything Umlaut has done, and achieve his existence, if you enter into a Demon contest. If you win, you get it all. If you lose, his choice prevails, and he will be abolished and you will be with Brusque. But you will remember."

"You are offering me heaven or hell."

"Actually, the Demon Xanth is offering you heaven *and* hell. Life with Umlaut would not be perfect, because he isn't perfect, and life with Brusque would be no torture. But yes, you would always remember and regret what you lost and never be quite satisfied with what you had. You would always know that you could have had satisfaction, but threw it away, and would condemn yourself for that. You might well consider walking into the Void and kicking the bucket there, just to get rid of your horrible doubting. No one else would understand. So it would be a hell of your own making, but implacable. Demons don't deal for nothing; that would be your forfeit for contesting and losing. I think you would be better off to accept the offer now. There is nothing wrong with it that doses of love elixir can't cure, and it is far less risky."

"Yet if I don't try, I would know that I could have tried for more and lacked the gumption."

"For that there is lethe water. You can forget."

Surprise pondered further. "I don't want to forget. Not if it means Umlaut is lost. I'll take the Demon contest."

"No!" Umlaut cried. But he was too late, as he tended to be.

Demons Jupiter and Fornax came forward. "You must convince these two antagonists to allow Umlaut to exist," Chlorine said. "You will have three tries."

Surprise looked daunted, which was quite reasonable in the circumstance. "I suppose simple logic won't do it?"

"Only if it is persuasive in a purely rational, unfeeling manner."

"I can't do that. Feeling is what motivates me. What about an appeal to decency?"

"Demons are soulless; they have no concept of decency. That was why Demon Xanth needed my help in crafting Umlaut."

"Then what can I do?"

"You must make them an offer for trade. If they accept, you win. If they do not, you lose."

"But what do I have that a Demon could possibly want?"

"It is your challenge to find something—or withdraw. There may be nothing; that's the risk you take. I recommend that you withdraw."

Surprise looked at Umlaut. "I love you," she said.

"And I, uh—"

"Of course." She faced the two Demons. "I will play the game."

"Granted," the two Demons said together. There was a sigh of apprehension through the audience; they knew the risk she was taking.

Surprise visibly nerved herself and spoke. "I offer my talent. It is the talent of talents. I can do any magic talent once, but then I lose it. You might find it interesting to study."

Demon Jupiter responded. "That does interest me. I have not had experience with limited mortal magic. My animation of Umlaut showed me that it can be intriguing in its quirks and consequences."

"It does not interest me," Demoness Fornax said. "The form I assumed for this venture can do many kinds of magic and is immortal. I see no mystery worth fathoming."

"The first offer fails," Chlorine said.

Surprise looked depleted but tried again. "I offer my life. You both are immortal; mortality might amuse you."

"No!" Umlaut cried. "What good would it be to save me, if you die?"

She faced him sadly. "You would exist, and you might be happy with another girl, just as you wanted me to be happy with another boy."

"I don't want another girl!"

"I understand perfectly." Many in the audience nodded; she had already demonstrated that.

"Perhaps we could verify that," Fornax said, evidently enjoying the conjecture. "Becka Dragon-Nymph, come forth."

The girl of Castle Maidragon walked out of the audience. "Yes, I would like him," she said. "And I think I could make him like me too, in time, even without love elixir."

"Don't do this!" Umlaut pleaded.

"If you feel that way," she agreed. "I want only someone who truly wants me, knowing my nature."

"There's nothing wrong with you!" Umlaut said. "You're cute and talented and your dragon form is great. It's just that, uh—"

"That I'm not Surprise. I understand. I admire your loyalty to her and hers to you. So I will not do this." She turned around and started walking away.

"If Surprise yields her life, you will do it," Fornax said. There was a faint shimmer of magic, and Becka turned about again.

Umlaut remembered the way Tacy had reversed herself, when Com Pewter changed her reality. Human conscience had little relevance in the overpowering realm of Demons.

"If they accept my life, take her," Surprise told Umlaut. "I want you not only to exist but also to be happy. I can see that she's a good match for you."

"Surprise is as self-sacrificing as Umlaut is," Fornax said. "I believe I will accept her life. It should be a fascinating vivisection."

Umlaut froze in horror, unable to get out even an "uh."

"I won't," Jupiter said. "Mortals die all the time and are easy to observe. I don't need to trade any commitment for that."

"The second offer fails," Chlorine said.

Surprise's red was fading to greenish around the gills. But she renerved herself and made her final try. "I offer my soul. That's the one thing you Demons lack, so it should be interesting."

"A soul," Jupiter said. "The thing that makes mortals act in weird ways, evincing conscience, love, and decency."

"I have been looking for a soul to dissect," Fornax said. "This one I could take, since it is offered."

"No!" Umlaut cried despairingly. "Take mine instead!"

"You have no soul," Jupiter reminded him, "only an emulation of one."

"With your related talent of emulation," Fornax agreed. "Now we have a chance to possess a real one."

Umlaut turned to Surprise. "But if you save me and you, but lose your soul, you won't be anyone I could live with."

"Not so," Jupiter said. "We'll give her a soul emulation like yours. You won't know the difference."

"But it won't really be *her*!"

"In any event, this is not your decision to make," Fornax said. "It is ours." She glanced at Jupiter. "Are we agreed?"

"Yes. We accept the mortal's offer of her soul. We shall each take half."

"The third offer succeeds," Chlorine announced.

"Nooo!" Umlaut cried again. But he was helpless.

Surprise spread her arms and lifted her chin. "Take it." There were tears leaking from her eyes, but she held her pose.

There was a mass wince in the audience.

Both Demons swooped, with their arms passing through Surprise's body without apparent resistance. Something seemed to tear. Surprise seemed to deflate. Then each Demon clapped hand to chest, taking in the half soul. It was done.

There was a pause. Then Jupiter spoke, horrified. "What's this? Suddenly I *care*."

"Suddenly I feel conscience," Fornax said, appalled.

"This will cripple my operations," Jupiter said. "I can't wear this soul myself. I must park it somewhere."

"Umlaut now exists and lacks a soul," Chlorine reminded him.

Jupiter swept his hand through Umlaut's body. Simultaneously, Umlaut felt his emulation soul replaced by the real thing, and it was a qualitative difference that was awesome. He had been doing what he did because he judged it to be the right thing to do; now he no longer needed to judge, he *knew*. It was immensely comforting.

"I will park mine also," Fornax said. "It is simply too inconvenient to keep with me." She swept her hand back through Surprise's body. Surprise seemed to recover animation but swayed and seemed on the verge of fainting. Both Umlaut and Brusque ran to catch her before she fell.

"This contest is done," Chlorine said.

Then the Nameless Castle vanished. They were standing where they had been, in Castle Maidragon, before the magic mirror. Except that Surprise was there with them, and so was Brusque, apparently because Umlaut had been touching them when the contest ended. Soufflé Serpent was also there; he had been twining tails with Sesame so got carried along too. It was fairly crowded in the chamber.

"I'm all right now, I think," Surprise said. "Losing my soul, then getting it back—it was a shock."

"I think I know the feeling," Umlaut said. "I have half your soul now."

"Keep it. I would have shared it with you anyway, had I known you needed it." She looked around. "Where are we?"

"Castle Maidragon. This is where Becka stays. We were here delivering the last letter when the Demon contest ended."

"And so I got to visit you again, this time personally," she said. "I'm so glad. I love you."

As if that had not been abundantly obvious. "And I love you," he said. "Now I don't *think* I do, I *know* I do."

She laughed faintly. "You forgot to say 'uh.' "

"I fouled up again," he agreed. "But I guess you're used to that."

"And I love it." She stepped into him and kissed him.

After the little hearts ceased swirling around his head, he made an effort to get practical. "I guess we can take you home now. Your folks will wonder where you went." He glanced at the others. "And I guess drop you off at your sites." He glanced at the mirror. "I'm glad you're free now."

Rorrim says you gave him his freedom without obligation, but he will serve you anyway, Claire indicated. It seems a bit of the soul fractured off and struck him.

"He's welcome to stay here," Becka said. "I can turn dragon and fly to deliver his news if an awkward future threatens."

"I should get back to the jungle," Brusque said.

"Must you go so soon?" Becka asked. "You and I seem to be loose ends. I mean, I won't be with Umlaut and you won't be with Surprise. I don't get a lot of company here."

Brusque looked at her. "You don't mind that I'm part ogre and part brassy?"

"Do you mind that I'm half dragon?"

"Are you as pretty as a dragon as you are as a girl?"

Becka blushed. "She is," Umlaut said.

Brusque nodded. "I'd like to stay awhile, in that case. We have had a certain remarkable common experience."

"We have indeed."

They did seem to be a nicely matched pair, of similar age and isolation. Maybe it had not been total coincidence that Brusque had been transported here.

Becka addressed the others. "The rest of you can stay the night, at least. I'd love to show off the castle. Everything except the forbidden chamber."

Umlaut looked around, receiving nods. "Surprise and I will need, uh, separate rooms."

"Oh, he remembered," Surprise said, pouting.

"Of course," Becka agreed. "So will Brusque and I." She glanced at the cats and serpents. They were all thoroughly adult. Then everyone broke out laughing. There was even a cartoon smile on the mirror.

Author's Note

The big story of my personal life as I wrote this novel was a nonstory. I had decided to change from the Windows computer operating system to Linux, and from the MS Word word processor to Word Perfect, because that's what's available for Linux. I planned to get the new system in AwGhost 2000, then write this novel on it SapTimber, OctOgre, and NoRemember, learning as I went. By the time I've done a novel on a system, I know the system. Why did I want to change? Because I'm an independent cuss, and I like to do things my own way. Microsoft prefers to make me do things its way. So I watched the "open source" Linux, and when it seemed viable I made my move. It would be the fourth operating system and seventh word processor. I started in 1984 with CP/M, went to two variants of DOS, Windows 3.1, and Windows 95, which was a considerable change. The word processors were Select 86, PTP, Edward, Final Word, Sprint, and MS Word. In general, each was more powerful than the preceding ones, as technology and software advanced. The first word processor was klunky and balky, handling just one file at a time, and you had to close the file to save it. Operating system commands were in obscure codes.

Backing up with CPM was really user unfriendly: The first time I did it intuitively, using its PIP mechanism to select my file, then its destination. But when I invoked it, it trashed my file. It seemed that I was supposed to select destination first, *then* the file, and when I did it backward it tried to send nothing to the file, destroying it. This is called learning the hard way. The first hard disk was 10 megabytes, and we had several crashes, destroying everything. The 5¼-inch floppy disks frequently went bad, losing their content. The speed of the system was, I think, 6 MHz. But it was better than the pencil first draft and manual typewriter second and submission drafts I had been doing for seventeen years. Much has changed in the subsequent sixteen years.

But advancing to Linux turned out not to be all that easy. First I couldn't find a local dealer. I wanted local service, you see, because I knew that the system would never work for me if I had to assemble mail order components myself. The local Linux organization—SLUG, for Suncoast Linux Users Group—was friendly but suggested no dealer closer than Tampa. I got on the phone and started querying every local computer dealer and finally found one that didn't blanch at the word Linux. In mid-AwGhost I ordered my system. But there kept being delays, and rather than wait on *Heaval*—I had a deadline to meet, after all—I started it on my old system, hoping to transfer it to the new system soon. That was not to be. Things were all up in a heaval. The Linux system would not address the printer and was hung up for weeks there. By the time everything was working, and I brought it home, I had written the first 100,000 words of the 120,000-word novel. So I had to finish it on the old system. Just as well; Linux proved to be just as difficult, obscure, and balky as Windows, taking five minutes to load on the 600-MHz system and locking up with the first touch of a key. We're working on it. Ah, well, my *next* novel should show the flair and novelty of Linux.

Of course that's not all that got all up in a heaval during the writing of this novel. You might think that current Mundane events would have little effect on fantasy writing, and fantasy would have less effect on reality. Well, the Mundane state of Florida, USA, bears a suspicious resemblance to the

Land of Xanth. I get fan letters from Florida residents who may refer to the portion of Xanth they live in, such as Kiss Mee, or the Gold Coast, Lake Ogre Chobee, the With A Cookee River, or Lake Tsoda Popka region. Some suggest notions for their areas, such as Cross City with all the crosses, or Crystal River, where there is a river of crystals. The comparison of Florida and Xanth geography can be a fine study. The magic does seem to leak through. This was especially true on this occasion, because as I wrote the novel there was a campaign for president and a number of other offices of USA, Mundania, and the day after I completed the first draft there was the election. Of course the leaking magic, which gets especially strong when I'm actually writing a novel—the channel is open, as it were—pied the Florida portion. The main presidential candidates were called Bore and Gush—oops, let's untangle the savage political parodies that abounded at this time. They were Al Gore and George W. Bush. At 8 P.M. on Election Day, Florida was declared a win for Gore. Since as Florida goes, so goes the nation, that meant he would be the next president. But a couple of hours later they undeclared it, then later still gave it to Bush, so that he was the next president. Then they undeclared it again. Then it went into a recount, invoking magical terms like "hanging chad," and at this writing two weeks after, the election is undecided while Florida figures out exactly for whom it voted. In short, it is all up in a heaval. And you were so naive as not to know that Florida is the center of the Mundane universe, or that leaking magic pies elections? Let this be a lesson.

I get suggestions galore from readers, and I use as many as I can. For one thing, it keeps a certain trickle of originality flowing into my writing, to the annoyance of critics: These are notions I didn't think of. The following credits will show how many there were this time. But I found that there were a number I just couldn't use. Just about every Xanth character has his, her, or its fans, who want to see more of that one. But the total list of Xanth characters is over six thousand and growing at the rate of a hundred or more with each novel; I can't have every character in every novel. As a general rule, the main character for an individual novel is someone new, or was a minor character in a prior novel, so that the wonders of Xanth can unfold for that character and the reader. Thus Umlaut this time, with his friend Sesame Serpent, both new, with Sammy Cat and Para Boat, both minor before, and Claire Voyant, new. Surprise Golem was a significant character in *Geis of the Gargoyle*, but she was only six years old then. When she took a shine to Umlaut, I couldn't tell her no. The demoness Metria did have her own novel with *Roc and a Hard Place* but is so much naughty fun in her mischief that I can't keep her clear of the action. So that was most of the cast, and there simply was not room for Grey Murphy as a major character, as suggested by Steve Stewart; his status in *Man from Mundania* has to do. Stephanie Leonard suggested that I have a merfolk story, and I tried, but again it just didn't fit here. Jessica Grider suggested that I cover the history of centaurs, but again the novel didn't cooperate. Novels and characters tend to go their own ways, regardless of the wishes of readers or writers; this is a phenomenon most writers encounter. Greg Vaughan suggested sacrificial Dungeon Masters; that wound up in a novel of a different series, *Key to Havoc*. Often I can't do justice to the suggestions I do use, because they are suitable for major treatment while all I have available is a passing mention. I regret that and sometimes make a mental note to return to them in greater depth in a later novel. For example, the talent of exorcising demons could be the centerpiece of a story about someone who gets fed up with Demoness Metria, but it was squeezed into a mere mention. There is not world enough and time to do justice to the imagination of all my readers.

Sometimes I get gratifying responses from readers. Let me quote from the E-mail Rebecca Bragg sent: "I would also like to tell you that for an assignment in Philosophy class at UCA we had to read a thought-provoking piece of literature to the class, and hold a class discussion about it. I chose the section of *Ogre, Ogre* about reality in the Void. Our class discussion continued for an hour and a half after the class period ended, and dominated the class for the next three weeks. I got an A. The professor made the book a reading requirement for all of her future classes. My friend and I respect your literary insight more than the great classical authors—we find them boring.

I thought you would like to know." Indeed, I am glad to know; this is not the normal reaction of philosophy professors to Xanth fantasy. Thank you, Rebecca.

But some elements have a more downbeat reality. Two readers suggested that Sammy Cat have his own adventure (see the credits section) and that I managed to arrange. I wrote him into the novel SapTimber 15, 2000, and told Jenny Mundane about it in the following week's Jenny letter. SapTimber 26 Jenny's folks called me: Sammy Mundane died the 18th, three days after entering Xanth. He was seventeen years old, and youth elixir is scarce in drear Mundania; it was time for him to go. They were in grief for him, but at least he did make it safely to Xanth to stay. He'll be happy with Claire Voyant, I'm sure, even if she does know what he's up to before he does.

There's a story behind the story of the twins Epoxy Ogre and Benzine Brassie too. In 1992 I was solicited for a story for a rather special anthology edited by Norman Spinrad, *Down in Flames*, wherein the authors of popular series torpedoed their own creations. I understand there were some remarkable examples by other writers. So I wrote the naughty 4,000-word story "Adult Conspiracy" wherein the awful secret of the stork works was revealed: exactly how babies are made, for the storks to deliver. That of course must never be told in Xanth; it would be the end of the Conspiracy as we know it. So this was formidable stuff. I'll tell you this much, trusting that Mundane parents will not hang me by the, I mean, in effigy for revealing it: Esk Ogre and Bria Brassie put in an order for identical twins, male and female, and took delivery in due course. So they became part of Xanth. But the anthology was never published, so they languished in limbo for eight years until finally I put them into Xanth proper in this novel. Now at last we get to meet them in person. Too bad about the anthology.

The horse Xanthus is historical, that is, really did originate in Greek mythos, and first appeared in *Swell Foop*. He was suggested again by another reader, and I had room for him again. This time, verifying his origin, I discovered that he has an unusual place in my dictionaries: He stumps them all except my big old 1913 secondhand Funk & Wagnalls that I received on my tenth birthday in 1944. Today I also have a big Webster's, and a big Random House, and the encyclopedia-sized Oxford English Dictionary, the compact edition that requires a magnifying glass to read. Generally the others skunk the Funk on rare terms, but in this one case it skunks the rest. Good for it. It has been with me fifty-six years and I'm glad it hasn't let those other whippersnappers get it down. I like dictionaries, and you should see my collection of atlases.

And now the credits. Some are incomplete because E-mails did not provide full names. If you note an occasional correspondence of character names and those who suggest them, this is not necessarily because readers asked to be named. Sometimes when I needed a name I borrowed that of the one who suggested a talent. I do this whimsically and seldom when asked to, and most suggestors will be surprised and possibly not entirely pleased to find themselves so named. To borrow a phrase from the novel (I'm smarter in fiction than in real life): It is not always convenient to be fondled by the fickle finger of fortune.

Rock hound—Eric Jacobs; Wetti shirt contest, Void wrinkling land near it—Scott Patri; Miss Guide, Miss In Form, Miss Chief—Timothy Saxton; letters from Mundania, snail mail—Rhonda Singer; Fay Tall—Adam Veats; Sammy Cat adventure—Amy Silverman, Olivia Stevens; sweetie pie, lava tree—Arlen Phillips; speed demon—Cheryl McCurley; Path of Least Resistance, search engine on Information Highway—Christine Read; Intellig Ant—Todd David Johnson; Reason and a porpoise—HMM; Demon Jupiter hurls Red Spot—Jessica Grider; talent: make any drawn thing real—Aaron Nassiflents of creating and molding—Molly Suver; talent of adaptation—Kiel Hynek; cross word puzzle—Terry Adcock; spell checker, N fruits—Chris Pettway; shoe horn, Depressant—Travis Wardell; coma toast, cellulight—Dale Carothers; cakewalk, fly fishing, toe truck, thread bear—Kacy Monahan; Caitlin—Caitlin Dawkins; My Grain—Dylan Williams; X-rated vision—Ron Fitch; panty trap—Jeff Bodkin; cantilever bridge—Mary-K Hering; creek that creaks—Kiel Hynek; chain reaction—Molly Suver; story of Matt A Door, Roc of Ages, Arme Dillo—Joel L. Collins; zom-bee, fate of

early bullies—Jorge De La Cruze, Dylan Byrne; Preston
Black—Preston Black; Emergen Sea, sugarcoat—Anna Bry-
ant; Dire Straits—Eric; Soufflé Serpent's story—Danfor; Dor
makes tapestry figures talk—Kevin S. Brockman; liverworst,
best, okay—Arlen Phillips and Lars Neufeld; Ptero-bull—
Rich Dahl; clothes wrinkle on depressed folk, ladybug, yes-
man—Rebecca Bragg; acro-bats—Dylan Byrne; Cory—Cory
Roessler; Tessa—Tessa Lehne; Claire Voyant—Amy Silver-
man; Midnight Cat—Mimi G.; story of the Isle of Dread—
Heather Babcock; dust bunnies—Lorraine Tarryu; Epi Centaur—Diana Litsch; high horse—Dylan Williams; Aloe
Vera—Ed-X; Euphoria—Lisa Browning; ParaDice island—
Warren Jameson; PHSD—Jannice Shroeder; beauty in the
eye of the beholder—Greg Laabs; twins with talents of mak-
ing things hard and soft—David Abolafia; Zephyr Hills—Lisa
Browning; Pearl Valley—Cindy Taysin; web surfer—Jacob
Berryman; peccadillo, hare-raising event, abasement—
Barbara Hay Hummel; peace pipe that falls to pieces—Mi-
chael Boyd; printer's pi tree—Mary K. Hering; Tacy, who
doesn't speak Xanthian—Monica Meyerhardt; the Realm of
Lost Objects, sock maze, Finders and Keepers—Paul Lafleche;
Eeee-mail—Bill Purcell; Electri-City—April Nell; O-Pinion
pine tree—John Hugens and Coach Bill; Phanessa, Thorin
makes magic arrows, arrows of betrayal, fire, light, darkness,
love—Phil Gates; Violet—Sara Gee; Sage, with guardian
dragon, right and wrong doors, Book of Wrong Answers—
Nik Mateer; Janel, talent of persuading people—Chris Allen;
Annie Mation—Nathaniel Sheidenen; Cindi with an Eye and
See—Cindilou; aging elixir—Alexandra Ghaly; talent of becoming a carrot—Andrea Crumpler; talent: the world stops
and listens when she speaks—Gail Marie Menius; magician
who assigns talents—Emily Marie Howlett; eagle helps lost
Eagle Scouts—Robert Wilson; Xanthus horse as a character—
Rachel Clair; Day Stallion takes over dream realm—Clayton
Overstreet; mothalope—Lynn Conover; ogre the river, troll
the woods—Dave Morgan; feet fall asleep and snore—H. B.
Shawshail; Khan and Smuggler—Alexis; talent of breaking
things, of making big balls of gas, of making things heavy,
of projecting videos—Bryan Bergstrom; magic mirror refract-
ing possible realities—Brenda Roberts; detective arrests Ma-

gician Humfrey for obstruction of justice—Patrick Lindsay; Beau—Beau Chapman; strip club—Melinda Wolfe; talent of accommodation—Mary Aigler; talent of exorcising demons— Donovan E. Dion; talent of unknowingly helping those in need—Cathy Denning; talent of singing—Elizabeth Koerber; talent of summoning any kind of cheese, Gazun Tite, D. Base, D. Ceit—Nehemiah Green-Will.

Readers who wish to reach me on the Mundane Web can visit http://www.hipiers.com, where I am even more talkative than I am in Author's Notes.

Turn the page
for a preview of the latest
from Piers Anthony

CUBE ROUTE

(0-765-30406-6)

Now available at
your local bookstore!

I

REAR VIEW

L ooking back, as was natural in the circumstance, Cube concluded that it all started with the rear-view mirror. What a complicated route, from such a minor trigger.

She was out picking bubble gum from the bubble gum tree beyond the hay field when there was a swirl of smoke beside her. "What are you doing?" the smoke inquired.

Startled, Cube gazed at it. "Talking smoke?"

"That doesn't exactly answer my incertitude," the smoke said, forming a set of eyes.

"Your what?"

"Dubiousness, skepticism, suspicion, mistrust, uncertainty—"

"Question?"

"Whatever," the smoke agreed crossly.

"I don't see why I should answer you if I can't see you," Cube said. "Are you a refugee from the smoking section?"

The smoke formed a mouth. "Ha. Ha. Ha," it said. "Very funny. Not. Don't you recognize a lovely demoness when you see one?"

"A demon!" Cube sidled nervously away from the smoke. "I never did anything to you. Why are you harassing me?"

"Because that's what demons do." A head formed around

the eyes and mouth, framed by smoky hair. "Demoness Metria, not at your ritual."

"Not at my what?"

"Observance, rite, liturgy, ceremony—"

"Service?"

"Whatever! So who are you?"

"I'm called Cube."

"Cube! What kind of a stupid name is that?"

"It's not my name."

The hair spread out and formed a question mark. "You just said it was."

"I said I was called that. I didn't say it was my name."

The smoky features swirled a moment, then coalesced back into the face, which was now pretty in a dusky way. "Score one for you, drab mortal. So what is your name?"

"Cue. But when other kids saw me, they nicknamed me Cube, because I'm just not with it. I tried to pry it off, but that nickname stuck fast."

"They do," Metria agreed. "That's part of the curse of being human. Now answer my first question and I'll give you something."

Cube decided that she should do that, before the demoness got angry and did her some harm. "I was just picking bubble gum for the boys."

"What use have you for boys?" the demoness asked.

"I like them. But they don't like me."

The smoke formed a vaguely human female body below the head. "Of course they don't! Look at you."

"No thanks. I know I'm not pretty."

"That's the understatement of the hour. You give plain a bad name. Whatever made you suppose that any boy anywhere would ever be interested in you?"

"Well, I do have a certain quality of character."

"Like what?"

"Gumption."

"What?"

"Initiative, courage, aggressiveness, resourcefulness, common sense—"

"Guts?"

"Whatever," Cube agreed, frowning. "I've got gumption

galore, but that doesn't seem to be what boys want."

"Naturally not. Boys can see, not think. They don't much notice character."

"So I have learned. But I thought that maybe if I got them something nice, like fresh bubble gum, they might let me hang around, and maybe get to know me."

"Not without a better appearance. Look at this." A dusky hand extended toward her, holding something. "Use the mirror. It is my promised gift."

Cube took the mirror and held it up before her. But it did not show her homely face. It showed an unsightly posterior in a dull skirt. "It's not working."

"Yes it is. It's a rear-view mirror."

"Rear-view mirror?"

"It shows your rear, idiot."

"Ugh! That's worse than my face. Take it back." She pushed the mirror toward the demoness.

"Nuh-uh! That gift can only be given, not taken back."

"I don't regard it as a gift. I don't want it."

But the smoke was fading, and in half a moment it was gone. She was stuck with the mirror.

She set it on the ground and turned away. And found it back in her hand. She threw it at the trunk of the gum tree, but it returned to her hand before striking the tree. She tried to smash it against a stone, but it shied away.

"!!!!" she swore, absolutely disgusted. At age twenty she was old enough to use an ugly word if so motivated. The demoness had succeeded in making a dull day into a bad one. That must have been why D. Metria had bugged her in the first place: to get her to accept the mirror.

She looked at the next tree, which bore pretty colored gum drops. She was half tempted to eat some of those, but they would just make her teeth drop out of her gums. That would make it difficult to chew.

She jammed the mirror into a pocket and headed for home, disgruntled. Maybe she could find someone else to give it to, someone with a prettier rear than her own.

That reminded her of her condition. "I wish I were beautiful!" she exclaimed. "Then I could nab a good man and settle down and have a nice family. Or something."

The demoness reappeared. It seemed she hadn't gone far when she faded out. "Ha. Ha. Ha!" she laughed in a carefully measured cadence.

"What's so funny?"

"You think pulchritude would solve your dreary life?"

"What?"

"Beauty," the demoness said crossly. "Whatever."

"Do you have a problem with vocabulary?"

"However did you guess?"

"Sometimes I get lucky, if the subject isn't men."

"Answer the question."

"Yes, beauty would transform my existence. Pretty girls have great lives, even if they have no perceptible minds. Everybody knows that."

Metria's form firmed into sheer loveliness. "Like this?"

"Yes!"

"You're wrong."

"How would you know? You're a demoness. You can assume any form you wish. You can stun any village lout with your beauty."

At that point a village lout appeared, walking down the path toward the gum trees. Metria turned toward him, opened her blouse, and inhaled. The lout felled stunned, blindly smirking at the sky. "True. But who wants a lout?"

"You could do it to a good man too."

"Yes. I did. I'm married."

"So you see. That's what I want to do. Then I'd be happy."

"Maybe. Lovely women traditionally make poor choices in men."

"I wouldn't. I'd choose a good one to stun. Because I have as much character as I don't have body." Then reality crashed in on her. "But what's the use? I'll never be beautiful, so I'll never nab a man."

"If that's what you want, why don't you do something about it?"

"What can I do about it?" Cube demanded. "I am the way I am."

"You can go see the Good Magician Humfrey, dummy, and ask him how to get beautiful."

Cube stood still for a good three quarters of a moment. "I never thought of that!"

"That's why you're a dummy."

Cube realized that in time, without a whole lot of effort, she could get annoyed at the demoness. But it was a good idea. "I'll do it."

"Of course he'll charge you a year's service, or the equivalent."

"I know that," Cube said, annoyed.

"And his Answer will be confusing, so you won't properly understand it until it's too late."

"I know that too. But his answers are always true."

"Also obvious in retrospect, making you feel even more like a dummy." The demoness faded out again.

It was true. But what other choice did she have? If there was any barely possible, remotely conceivable, faintest shadow of an obscure hint of half a chance that she could become even marginally pretty if you liked that type, she had to try for it. What was gumption for, if not to do something brave and foolish? Thus was her decision made.

"Ha. Ha. Ha," the voice of the demoness came, with just a wisp of swirling smoke.

Cube frowned. She hadn't even voiced her decision, but the infernal demoness knew. Still, she felt buoyed, because now at last she was setting out to do something about her plight. Even if the Good Magician couldn't tell her how to become beautiful, she would know she had done her best.

And if, just maybe, somehow, there was a way—what a change that would make in her life!

"That's what yooo think," the singsong voice of the demoness came.

"Oh, go soak your face."

"If you insist." There was a sound of sloshing water. "Glub. Glub. Glub."

Cube had to smile. Metria was some character.

"Thank you."

Cube ignored her. The demoness had to be guessing at her thoughts.

"No, your smile gave you away."

Oh.

The demoness reappeared, evidently about to speak some other incidental mischief. Her feet touched the ground.

"Hay!"

Metria jumped and puffed into smoke. "Who called?"

Cube laughed. "You touched the hay field. It always gets your attention, the first time."

"Bother!" the demoness said crossly, and faded. Cube was glad to have seen her get fouled up, for once, instead of doing the fouling.

"At least you didn't land on the romants hill," Cube said to the space Metria had faded from.

Sure enough, there was a response. "What kind of hill?"

"Romants. When the ants bite you, you fall in love. I think there's a small love spring under the hill."

"That's novel."

"A romants novel?" Cube could take or leave puns, but this did seem to be a good occasion for one.

"I'm gone." And maybe this time she was.

So when should she make the trek to the Good Magician's castle? Well, there was no time like the present. It wasn't as if she had anything worth returning home for. She lived alone, without even hope of male company.

She headed for the nearest enchanted path. Those paths were always best for traveling, because dragons and other noxious beasts couldn't get on them, and they had regular rest stops with pie trees and shelter. In fact she had always wanted to travel, but never had a reason to do it. Now she had the best one: her future happiness.

Cube walked swiftly. She was a good walker, having muscles in her legs and stamina in her torso. Of course that was part of the problem; she had muscles instead of feminine curves. So she could out-walk any girl she knew, but of course they didn't need to walk. Men came walking to them.

Soon she was out of familiar territory, but she wasn't concerned. She could defend herself if she needed to. Which was another part of the problem: her talent was an ugly aggressive one, befitting her character, when she would have preferred an appealing feminine one.

She approached a huge mound. It looked like an ant hill, except that water was flowing down its slopes. She didn't trust this, but the trail led right by it on the way to the enchanted path.

A huge insect came out to challenge her. It was larger than she was, and had about thirty heads, each of which had a snout looking rather like the nozzle of a hose. What in Xanth could it be?

Then she saw the sign: BEWARE THE HYDRA ANT. Oh, no—this was one of those water-spouting bugs.

She reversed course, backing away. She didn't want trouble. But the hydra ant followed. Then it squirted water from one of its nozzles. The jet missed, but soon it would get the range, and Cube would get soaked. It was looking for trouble.

There was no help for it. She had to defend herself, because this was the only access in this area to the enchanted path, and she had to reach that path. It wasn't as if she lacked gumption to do it, just that she preferred to try to seem halfway feminine if that was manageable. But this was the time for boldness.

She invoked her talent. In a moment a swarm of little silvery bugs appeared. They were nickelpedes, the scourge of caves and crevices. "Sic 'em," she said, pointing to the ant.

The nickelpedes charged the big ant. In a moment they were chomping its feet, gouging out nickel-sized chunks of flesh. The hydra danced away, but they pursued. It aimed jets of water at them, but though it was able to wash any one nickelpede away, or any thirty, there were over a hundred of them. Soon it gave up the fight and retreated into its hill.

"Enough," Cube called. "Thank you."

The nickelpedes left off the chase, and faded into the woods. Cube walked on by the ant hill and reached the enchanted path.

Now she was safe, but unsatisfied. She didn't like having to use her talent, because every time she did it reminded her how unladylike she was. Summoning and controlling nickelpedes—what delicate flower of a feminine girl would ever be caught with a talent like that? There were probably plenty of male roughnecks who would love it. But they hadn't gotten it; she had. She hated it.

Well, she shouldn't have to use it any more, because the enchanted path had no threats. She wasn't even sure she would be able to use it here, since nickelpedes were monsters. Little ones, but no less deadly for all that. So they probably were barred.

The enchanted path was nice. No brambles overlapped it, no tangle trees lurked beside it, and of course there were no dragons, griffins, or other dangerous creatures. It occurred to her that life should be like this, with a clear path and no dangers. It would be nice to travel forever on such a path. Except that she didn't want to do it alone. She wanted to travel with a man—a man she loved, who loved her too. And that was impossible as long as she was not beautiful.

It kept coming back to that. What would she do if the Good Magician couldn't help her? Now that she had gotten up the gumption to try to do something about it, she just had to succeed. Somehow.

The path wound into valleys, around hills, through forests, and wherever else it thought of, being in no hurry to get where it was going. It finally came to a camp just as evening was approaching. That was part of the enchantment, of course; it was as if the path knew who would be walking on it, and arranged things to be convenient. Yet again, Cube wished that her life could be like that.

She entered the camp, and found a nice little stream cutting across a corner, with assorted pie plants growing by its bank. There was a curtained shelter made of soft cottonwood beside a pillow bush. She was about to pick a nice apple pie when she heard something. She paused, listening.

It was footsteps. Someone else was coming to the camp, from the other direction. Cube wasn't sure whether to be nervous; would it be a nice person, or not?

It turned out to be a handsome young man with blue hair. He spied her as he entered the camp, and waved. "Hi! I'm Ryver."

That was straightforward. "I'm Cue—Cube."

"I didn't know anyone would be here. Is it okay to share?"

What could she say? She was nervous about strangers, yet he seemed nice enough. If he was as nice as he looked, he was exactly the kind of company she wanted. "Of course."

Then he paused, glancing at her more closely. "You're a girl!"

He had been in doubt? "And you're a boy."

Ryver evidently realized that he had been clumsy. "Uh, I mean—"

"Never mind. Make yourself at home." But they had gotten off to an awkward start. Which was the way it usually was, with her, with men.

He looked at the shelter. "Share that too?"

"Of course." Staying the night with a young man—how nice it could have been, if only she were the kind of girl to make a boy get ideas.

Nevertheless, after they had eaten, they harvested pillows and settled in the cottonwood shelter. Each plank was full of soft cotton, and the pillows made it that much more comfortable. It was dark outside, but there was a faint glow from the walls so that they could see well enough. "Wanta talk or sleep?" Ryver asked. Then, realizing that sounded wrong, he tried to backtrack. "I mean—"

"Talk," she said quickly. "Tell me about yourself." Because then she could listen and pretend she was part of his life.

"Sure. I'm twenty-three years old and on my own. My name's Ryver because of my talent. I can work with water. You know—make water balls and things. What's your talent?"

She had to tell him. "Nickelpedes. I can summon and direct them."

"Say, that's great! Can you make them go away, if you have to go through a cave or something?"

"Yes."

"That must be fun. Everybody's afraid of nickelpedes."

"Yes." Which was the problem. So she changed the subject. "Where are you from? Where are you going?"

"I'm going nowhere in particular. I just like to travel. So I'm coming from home and going back there. Nothing much else to do. Last night I met a pretty girl with the talent of negativity; that was a frustration."

"She had a bad attitude?"

"Not at all. She was nice. She said she expected to have a hot night with me, and I liked that idea. But then we slept in separate cabins and had nothing to do with each other."

Cube wished he had a similar idea about her, but of course he didn't. "Why?"

"Her talent reversed her expectation. What she thinks of won't happen, and it didn't. I was just as annoyed as she was, but I couldn't get close to her."

If only he wanted to get close to Cube! "Why didn't she announce that the two of you would never get together?"

Ryver stared at her. "She never thought of that. Neither did I. What a waste!" He shook his head. "How about you?"

It kept coming back to her, and not in any way she liked, which was exactly where she didn't want it. But she had to answer. "I'm just a dull village girl. I'm going to see the Good Magician."

"That so? What's your Question?"

Ryver was a bit too open for her taste, being short on sensitivity in the masculine manner. Now she was stuck with the answer. "How can I be beautiful."

"That makes sense," he agreed. Then, yet again, he caught up to the awkwardness too late. "I mean—"

"I know."

There was another ungainly silence. Finally he broke it. "That's my problem. I keep saying the wrong thing."

"I'm used to it."

"I guess so. But you know, sometimes things work out anyway. They did for my folks."

"Oh?"

"My mother, Lacuna—she liked this man, but he didn't notice her, so nothing came of it. Then his life didn't work out, and hers didn't, and she wished it had happened differently, but it was too late. They had both ruined their lives by not getting together."

"But then she found your father," Cube said.

"Not exactly. He was the one she liked, who married someone else and made a mess of it."

"A mess? But in Xanth marriages always work out."

"Marriages last, yes. But she was a mean woman, so he was stuck, and probably wished he hadn't done it. Certainly my mother wished he hadn't. So she made it a Question to the Good Magician. He wasn't there, then, but Magician Grey was substituting, and he told he she should have proposed to Vernon."

"That wasn't much help! How long had it been?"

"Twelve years. And of course she couldn't go back. But then she got a wish, and she wished she had proposed to him, and then she discovered her change of life."

"Change of life?"

"Yes. When she got home, she was married to him, and I was her first male child. She calls it her retroactive marriage. I mean, she changed the past, with her wish, and then just sort of stepped into how her life would have been, and now really was. I get confused when I think about it too much."

"That's not surprising."

"But anyway, it all worked out well, for my folks and for me. I had a good childhood, after having been alone for ten years. I mean, that change of life affected me too, so I had no longer lived alone, and that was great, but I remembered some of how it had been, so I was really grateful. Except for Lacky, my big sister who never existed; I still miss her. Does that make sense?"

Cube pondered it. Vernon must have had a daughter in the bad marriage, who was undone by the change, and Ryver retained some memory of her. Changes of life did have consequences. "I think so. If I could somehow change my past, and make myself be delivered beautiful, I'm sure I'd be grateful, if I remembered my present life."

"Right. That's how it is with me. I hope the Good Magician comes through for you."

He seemed sincere, and she realized that she liked him. He was sometimes socially clumsy, but he had a good heart. "I hope so too." Then she got bold, which often as not got her into trouble. That was the liability of gumption. "If—if he has an Answer for me, and I get beautiful, maybe after I work my year off—where will you be?"

He looked at her in the dim light. "I'm afraid I'll say something stupid. I do that often enough. Maybe I don't understand your question."

"I'm twenty years old and have always been, well, plain. I'd like to—to have a relationship with a good man. Just as your mother did. She changed her reality and got it after she thought she'd lost it. If I got beautiful—would you care to be the man?"

He considered for a full moment, which was the time required for the average man to make such a decision. "Sure."

"I mean, I'd have the same personality. The same talent. I'd be the same person. Only lovely."

"That's what makes the difference."

How unfortunately true. He didn't care about her character, just about her appearance. He really was a typical man. "So if it works out for me, as it did for your mother, maybe I'll come to your house."

"Sure. Just ask for Ryver. Everybody in my area knows the water boy."

This seemed too easy. Did it mean he thought she was joking, or that he didn't believe she'd ever be beautiful? Was he humoring her so as to get rid of her without making a scene? Had she just made a worse fool of herself than she thought? Maybe she should cancel it now. "Of course, if—"

"Let me give you something, so you can find me better. When you come, I mean."

He was taking it seriously! "Oh, you don't need to—"

"I'll fetch it from the river." He got up and stepped out of the shelter.

Bemused, she followed. Now she saw that the rest of the camp was outlined with glow, including its internal paths, for the convenience of travelers. What could he give her, that was from the water?

At the river, he leaned down and swooped one hand through the water. He shaped something with his other hand. Then he offered it to her. "Here."

She couldn't quite make it out in this light. It seemed to shimmer. "What is it?"

"A water ball." He put it into her hands.

She held it. It was indeed a ball, cool and soft, but it couldn't be water because it held its shape. Yet she had seen him swoop it from the river. "How—?"

"I told you: my talent is water. I can shape it into things, and it will keep. Show that to anyone in my neighborhood, and they'll know I gave it to you. If you get caught without water, you can drink some of it, but don't drink it all. If you get tired of it, return it to any river or pond. It deserves to be with its own substance."

"I won't get tired of it," she said, amazed. "This is—amazing."

He paused. "Maybe I'd better show you the rest."

"The rest?"

He faced away from her, then quickly got out of his clothing. She saw just the shadow of his lean bare backside. What was he up to? Then he jumped into the river and disappeared.

"Ryver!" she cried, bobbling the water ball. "Where are you?"

His head appeared, rising from the surface. "Here's my head."

She laughed nervously. "And the rest of you, I trust."

"Not at the moment, exactly. Feel."

"What?"

"Put your hand down in the water. Feel where I should be."

"I can't do that! You're naked!"

"Not exactly. Feel."

Bemused, she held the ball in one hand and put the other down to feel his neck under the surface.

There was no neck.

She felt further. There was no body. Just the head.

"What is this?" she asked, growing alarmed.

"It's me. I'm made of water."

"Made of water!" Realizing that this must be a trick or illusion, she put her hand under the head and lifted it up. It came out of the water, like a shaggy ball.

"At least, when I enter water," the head said.

"Oh!" She was so startled she dropped the head. It splashed into the river and dissolved.

Then she saw it form again, downstream. This time it came out of the river by itself. His body was under it. She turned her eyes away, lest she see something she shouldn't, even in the darkness. Actually she was old enough, and was a member of the Adult Conspiracy, not that it did her any good. But she lacked experience, because of her appearance.

In one or two moments—certainly no more than two and a half moments—Ryver had recovered his clothing. "So you see, I'm not a regular man. That is, not when I'm in the water. Originally I was all water, and I longed to become flesh. When I became Lacuna's son, I became flesh—except when I get too close to my origin. I thought maybe you should know that, when you're beautiful, before you come to—to—"

"To have a relationship," she finished for him.

"Yes. This—this has turned off other girls. So if you don't want to do it, I'll understand."

Cube looked at the water ball in her hand. He was indeed not a regular man. But was it worse than the way demons were? He just had a more serious relationship with water than she had realized. "I think I can handle it."

"That's great!"

They returned to the shelter. On the way, she thought of something else. "You gave me something. I should give you something. But all I have is—is something you might not want."

"What is it?"

"A rear-view mirror. But I have to tell you, it's not quite what you think, and you can't get rid of it unless you give it away to someone else."

"That's okay. Let's see it."

She fished the mirror from her pocket and gave it to him. "It's what it shows."

"Seems like a regular mirror to me." He held it up before his face. "Say—what's that?"

"Your derriere," she said delicately.

"Isn't that something!" He changed the position of the mirror, getting a better view in the dim light. "I like it. It reminds me of my early life."

"How does it do that?" she asked surprised.

"When I look back, to see how it was and how it became, it's a rear view. Not quite the same as the front view other folk see. The mirror's like that, maybe."

She was relieved. "It's yours, as long as you want it." She glanced at her ball. "Is it safe to set this down?"

"No, not exactly. Keep it with you, or with something that's yours, like your clothing. If it leaves you, it will revert. That's why folk will know I gave it to you; no one else can touch it."

"That's sweet."

"So are you. I hope you get beautiful."

On that nice note, they went to sleep. Maybe if she got beautiful she would get to sleep in his arms. As it was, she was satisfied to have their agreement for the future. Maybe it wouldn't work out, but at least she'd be in the game. That would be far more than she had ever had before.

In the morning they took turns using the sanitary facilities, then had a breakfast of milk and honey pies. Then Ryver went his way, and Cube went her way. Her determination to get beautiful had been reinforced; now she knew exactly what to do with that beauty. Until then, she could dream.

Outside the camp was a warning sign: DO NOT LAUGH. Cube looked at it and shrugged; she hadn't been planning to laugh anyway.

As she set forth, a shape looked up beside the path. "Come here and I will really send you," it called.

Cube realized it was a male demon. She knew better than to leave the path. "Where will you send me?"

"To Mundania," he said, chortling. "I am Demon Port."

Demons generally had a simple translation code, except for Metria, who evidently hadn't gotten her word quite right. Demon reduced to D, and the name. That would abbreviate to D. Port, or deport. "No thanks." And suppose she had laughed? Would she have fallen into the demon's power despite the protection of the path? Now she appreciated the sign's warning.

Another figure appeared. "Come to me," he called. "I reduce things to simpler forms. I am Demon Volve."

Which would be D. Volve—devolve. Cube did not want him either, so she kept walking, with a straight face.

A third demon appeared. "I am Louse. I hate bugs."

That would be D. Louse—delouse. Cube did not find that funny at all, because of her talent. Bugs could be very beneficial on occasion.

A demoness appeared. She was absolutely lovely as she preened; she looked like a goddess. She sang a brief melody, and her voice was divine. Then she paused. "Well, aren't you going to applaud?"

That surprised Cube. "Applaud?"

"I am Demoness Va. I expect my due."

D. Va—Diva. A prima donna. Probably the only way to get rid of her was to give her the applause she craved. Cube clapped her hands together several times.

D. Va made a bow and faded out. Cube smiled, but refrained from laughing.

Another demoness appeared. It seemed there was a whole troupe of them. "Tell me your secrets, and I will spoil them," she said enticingly.

Cube couldn't figure that one out. "Who are you?"

"Demoness Mystify."

Demystify. "No thanks."

The next demon was different. It was a fat male in a big washtub. He was scrubbing his own back with a long-handled brush. "Rub-a-tub-tub!" he sang, well off-key. He sounded intoxicated. "Rub my tub, summon me. Rub my back, I'll grant you three." Sparkling water sloshed as he moved.

"Really? Three wishes?"

He looked at her. "Of course not. This stuff is alcoholic. I can't focus well enough to get myself out, let alone grant wishes. But it's a fine-sounding promise." He belched.

What was the pun? "Who are you?"

"I'm a bathtub jinn."

Cube, surprised by the change in the code, laughed before she caught herself. And a bucket of dirty water that smelled of gin drenched her. The demon laughed so hard he and the tub exploded into smoke and dissipated.

Well, she had been warned. Apparently the magic of the path couldn't protect her entirely from her own folly. She paused at the next stream, rinsed out her clothing and herself, put it back on wet, and let it dry on her. At least the demons hadn't stayed to laugh at her unsightly body as she rinsed.

Her hand brushed something on her damp clothing. It turned out to be several stick-hers. She must have overlooked the stick-her bush when she took off her clothes. There were also a few stick-hims, as though the bushes hadn't been sure of her gender. Even plants rubbed in the fact that she was no lovely creature.

Later, a small boy was standing at the edge of the path. He

was staring at her midsection. "What are you looking at?" she asked sharply.

"I see your pan-tees!" he said in a singsong voice.

Cube refused to be fooled; she knew they were completely covered by her skirt. "No you don't."

"Yes I do. They're ugly. And they're wet."

That got to her. Her outer clothing had dried, but her underwear remained damp. "How do you know?"

"It's my talent. I can see panties, covered or not."

It seemed he could. "But that's a violation of the Adult Conspiracy."

"Yeah," he agreed zestfully.

Cube was annoyed. Then she realized that when this obnoxious boy grew to manhood, his talent would cause him to be perpetually freaked out. So that situation would take care of itself. She walked on by him.

She walked well that day, and knew she was getting close to the Good Magician's Castle. That was because there were signs along the way, saying GOOD MAGICIAN'S CASTLE TWO AND A HALF DAYS' WALK, and ONE AND A HALF DAYS' WALK. So her third day's walk should be half a day, and she'd be there.

She felt something in her pocket. She brought it out. It was the rear-view mirror. How had that gotten there? She had given it to Ryver yesterday, and not taken it back. Had he returned it to her in the night? That seemed unlikely; she didn't think he would have done such a thing without telling her, and in any event she would have been aware if he had come close enough to do it.

She had not been able to get rid of it before; could this be another aspect of that? She could give it to a person, but then it quietly returned to her? Magic objects could have odd properties. She'd have to try again, and stay alert. Meanwhile, she put it from her mind. At least she still had the water ball Ryver had given her.

She passed another sign: HEADLINE. At this point she was taking signs seriously. But what did it mean?

Then she saw a line of balls along the side of the path. Only they turned out to be heads. A head line.

"Step over me so I can see the color of your panties and

freak blissfully out," the first head said. Then it blinked, getting a better look at her. "Cancel that." The eyes squeezed closed.

Cube almost ground her teeth. Even her panties were not good enough!

Just at the right place there was another campsite. She entered it, and discovered someone else there: a winged centaur filly, with the large human breasts and handsome brown equine flanks and tail of her kind. She also wore a quiver and bow, the harness nicely framing her front. "Hello," Cube said, surprised.

"Hello. I am Karia Centaur. Please don't repeat my name."

"I am Cube Human. I'm on my way to see the Good Magician."

"I just came from there. It's less than an hour's flight from here."

"Half a day's walk," Cube agreed. "But why are you here, since you're not land-bound?"

"I am a winged monster," the filly agreed, though she hardly resembled a monster. "But I can't fly indefinitely, so I need a safe place to spend the night."

"I'm happy to share the night with you, if you're satisfied to share it with me."

"Of course. I don't have human company very often."

They handled the routine of harvesting supper and pillows for the night, then settled down in the shelter and talked. "You said you just came from the Good Magician's Castle," Cube said. "May I ask—"

"I'm a flying centaur, so my talent is flying. That is, flicking myself light enough to float. But I have an associated side effect that I would like to be rid of. So I went to ask the Good Magician."

"As I am doing. Did he help you?"

"No." Then before Cube could look surprised, she explained. "I didn't get to ask my Question. I did not make it through the three challenges. In fact I didn't pass the first challenge. So now I am returning to the herd with my tail between my legs, as it were."

"But I thought centaurs were smart." Then Cube realized that she was being just as awkward as Ryver had been. "I mean, it must have been a formidable challenge."

"It was a stupid challenge, but it stymied me. It was a path that forked. One side passed close by a sticker bush that stuck me when I got close, so I had to avoid it."

"A stick-her bush," Cube said. "It probably stuck only females. I encountered one of those today."

"Oh, a stupid pun. I hate puns!"

"But there are puns all over Xanth; you can't avoid them."

"Yes I can; I fly over them. I make sure to land on pun-free terrain. It's just too awful when I accidentally step in one and get it stuck to my hoof." The filly shuddered. "There is nothing more revolting than having to scrape squashed pun off your foot."

"So maybe the Good Magician was forcing you to face what you hated. That was the real nature of the challenge."

Karia frowned. "I suppose so. I think it was unkind of him."

It was apparent that the centaur had lacked the gumption to tackle something she found objectionable. That would never stop Cube, of course, but there was no point in pointing that out. "Where did the other side of the forked path go?"

"I couldn't make head or tail of that. It terminated at a door. I opened the door, but it became a jug in my hand, and there was just a blank wall beyond it. When I moved the jug forward it became the door again, closed. It was no help at all. I was most frustrated."

Cube laughed. "You opened the door and made it a jar!"

"I fail to see the humor."

"A jar. Ajar—open. Another pun."

"Oh," the centaur said somewhat sourly. "No wonder I didn't appreciate it. In any event, it was of no use to me. So I turned around and flew for home."

"I wonder," Cube said. "Couldn't you have used the jar to catch the stickers, so they couldn't stick you?"

"I suppose I could have, had I thought of it. But I was already pretty upset, and it seemed pointless to continue."

"I'm sorry," Cube said. "It must be a big disappointment."

"It is. I so much wanted to have a rousing good adventure, but I can't risk it as long as I have the complication."

"Complication?"

"The side effect. You see, I get carried away when anyone else speaks my name. That can be extremely awkward."

"Another pun!" Cube exclaimed. "Karia. Carry-a! You must really hate that!"

There was no answer. Then she saw that the centaur was floating out of the shelter. She wasn't flying; she wasn't even walking. Her four legs were folded under her as they had been in the shelter, only now she was drifting in the breeze. Her eyes were glazed, as if she were distracted and not paying attention to her surroundings.

In fact, she was being carried away. "Oh, I'm sorry!" Cube said. "I said your name!"

Karia continued to drift. Cube ran after her, catching at a leg. "Please, I'm sorry! Please come back!"

The centaur opened her eyes. "Oh, did it happen again?"

"Yes! I said your name, and you got carried away. I didn't mean to. I didn't realize—"

"That's all right. But now you appreciate my problem."

"Yes I do. I won't speak your name again."

Karia straightened her legs and touched the ground. She walked back to the shelter. "I would like to go where nobody knows my name. Then I'd be safe. But there's always the chance I would meet someone unexpectedly, who would say my name, and then I could be in trouble. So I suppose I'll just have to stay home, where folk know to call me 'hey, you.' Not that I like that much either."

"That side effect—it's another pun," Cube said. "No wonder you hate puns!"

"No wonder," Karia agreed wryly. "Why are you going to see the Good Magician?"

"I want to be beautiful."

Karia looked at her more closely. "I suppose you aren't. I hadn't noticed."

"If you were a man, you wouldn't notice me at all. I want to marry and have a loving husband and a nice family and live happily ever after, but it will never happen as long as I'm homely."

"Oh, I'm not sure of that."

"You're not homely. You have a pretty face and a bosom

that would make men stare even it weren't bare."

"Point taken. I have not suffered that particular problem of being unnoticed. Yet I would exchange a portion of my assets with you, if I could abate my side effect."

"And I would gladly have that portion! If I had your breasts, no one would notice my face."

"Oh, I don't know. Others do notice my face, and of course my rear."

"Your rear?"

"Like most centaurs, I have a handsomer posterior than face, and of course I am duly haughty about it." Karia reached back and gave her haunch a resounding slap. "I just wish I could see it better."

"I have just the thing for you," Cube said, fishing out the mirror. "Try this."

"I'm not certain how this relates," Karia said, accepting it.

"Try it and see."

The centaur held the mirror up before her face. "Oh, my! Can that be my rump?"

"Yes. It's a rear-view mirror."

"Delightful! It's even handsomer than I thought."

"Keep the mirror," Cube said.

"Oh, I couldn't! I like it, despite the pun, but I have no return gift for you."

"I will be glad if you can keep it. A demoness with a speech impediment gave it to me, and I didn't want it, but I can't be free of it unless I give it way. I gave it away yesterday, but today I had it again. So it may not stay with you anyway, though I hope it does."

Karia considered. "In that case, I will keep it, and hope that it remains with me. If not, I will understand." She paused. "The demoness—would that by any chance have been Metria?"

"Yes. How did you know?"

"She's just about the only one who interacts with humans more than briefly, usually mischievously. And she has trouble getting the right word. She doesn't hurt people, merely annoys them. This is the kind of trick one might expect of her."

"That's interesting." Actually Cube had encountered several other mischievous demons, but they had departed once they tricked her into laughing and getting drenched. "But I still hope you keep the mirror."

"We shall see." They composed themselves for sleep.